W9-BLU-899

PURGATORY RIDGE

Also by William Kent Krueger

Iron Lake
Boundary Waters

Available from POCKET BOOKS

PURGATORY RIDGE

A CORK O'CONNOR MYSTERY

WILLIAM KENT KRUEGER

POCKET BOOKS
New York   London   Toronto   Sydney   Singapore

POCKET BOOKS, a division of Simon & Schuster, Inc.
1230 Avenue of the Americas, New York, NY 10020

Copyright © 2001 by William Kent Krueger

Library of Congress Cataloging-in-Publication Data

Krueger, William Kent.
    Purgatory Ridge : a Cork O'Connor mystery / William Kent Krueger.
        p. cm.
    ISBN: 0-671-04753-1
    1. O'Connor, Cork (Fictitious character)—Fiction. 2. Private
    investigators—Minnesota—Fiction. 3. Minnesota—Fiction. I. Title.

    PS3561.R766 P87 2001
    813'.54—dc21   00-060648

First Pocket Books hardcover printing March 2001

10   9   8   7   6   5   4   3   2   1

POCKET and colophon are registered trademarks of
Simon & Schuster, Inc.

Printed in the U.S.A.

For Diane,
who is the first blessing each morning
and the final beauty each night,
and
for June and Lloyd Peterson,
who welcomed me as a son

AUTHOR'S NOTE

This book is fiction. At its heart, however, is a true story.

On November 29, 1966, while northbound on Lake Huron and making its final passage of the season, the ore freighter *Daniel J. Morrell* encountered a horrific gale. Battling winds of sixty-five miles per hour and seas with twenty-five-foot waves, the old carrier suddenly broke apart and sank. Of her crew of twenty-nine men, only three managed to make it aboard a small pontoon life raft. Within twelve hours, two of the men were dead, victims of injury and of exposure to both the frigid water of the great lake and air temperatures that hovered around freezing. One man endured. Dressed only in his peacoat and underwear, watchman Dennis Hale drifted for nearly thirty-six hours before he was spotted by a Coast Guard heli-copter and airlifted to a nearby hospital.

In 1996, Hale published *Sole Survivor,* his account of the sinking, of his remarkable experiences adrift on that tiny raft in angry water, and of the effect the incident has had on his life since then. It is a book worth reading.

Of the myriad stories spawned by the infamous November storms that rail over the Great Lakes, the sinking of the *Daniel J. Morrell* is, in terms of loss of human life, the most tragic. In what it says about human courage and endurance, Dennis Hale's story must surely be the most inspiring.

ACKNOWLEDGMENTS

I discovered the heart of this book because of Catherine O'Geay. She shared with me the story her father, Albert Whoeme, who was among the crew lost in the sinking of the *Daniel J. Morrell*. Kaye, I owe you much.

Several good men generously offered me their expertise and advice regarding issues of law enforcement. Thanks to Agent Raymond DiPrima of the Minnesota Bureau of Criminal Apprehension; to Supervisory Special Agent Fred Tremper of the Minneapolis Field Office of the Federal Bureau of Investigation; and to Ken Trunnell, who has many years of experience across many levels of law enforcement.

I am indebted to Dave Loomis, who described to me in such evocative detail his dives to the wrecks in Lake Superior that I was able to accompany him to the lake bottom several times without ever leaving my armchair.

My friends and colleagues of Crème de la Crime, who help me enormously in unraveling the mysteries of mystery writing, always deserve special mention. They are Julie Fasciana, Scott Haartman, Betty James, Michael Kac, Jean Miriam Paul, Susan Runholt, Anne B. Webb, and, especially, Carl Brookins, who is our heart and our fire.

I am blessed with an agent—Jane Jordan Browne—wise in the ways of this complex business. And I am incredibly fortunate to have had in the past year the editorial guidance of Jane Cavolina and George Lucas. Not only are they savvy, but they are charming as well.

I would be remiss without thanking Megan "Doc" Gunnar for her support and encouragement over the course of many years.

To the Ojibwe Anishinaabe people, upon whose territory I

timorously trespass: I thank you for your generosity of spirit; I envy your rich heritage and traditions; and I admire your perseverance in the face of so much ignorance and intolerance.

For their generous financial support as I developed as a writer, I would like to thank the McKnight Foundation, the Bush Foundation, and the Minnesota State Arts Board.

Finally, I am ever so grateful to the St. Clair Broiler, whose neon flame has found a place on the historical registry. From the bottom of my heart, I give thanks to Jim Theros and Elena Vakos, to all the staff who tolerate my long presence every morning and who keep my coffee cup filled, and to the regulars who tell me their stories and tell me I am free to use them.

PURGATORY
RIDGE

PROLOGUE

NOVEMBER 1986

ABOVE ALL THINGS in heaven or on earth, John LePere loved his brother. It was a love born the moment he watched Billy slide from between their mother's legs in the tiny house built in the shadow of Purgatory Ridge.

His father was dead by then, killed several months earlier while pulling in his fishing nets off Shovel Point. The rudder of his small vessel snapped during a sudden squall and the boat foundered on a shoal two hundred yards from shore. His father didn't drown—a life vest kept him afloat in the high waves. It was hypothermia that killed him, the icy water of Lake Superior. Eight-year-old John LePere didn't understand death exactly. Nor did he have time to grieve much, for his mother's deep grief drove her nearly mad. She retreated into solitude and refused to leave the house at all. After that, it fell to young John LePere to hold things together.

He was alone with his mother when she went into labor. He begged her to let him get someone to help. She screamed at him, ordering him to stay. For weeks afterward, his arm carried the bruises where she gripped him during her contractions. He was scared, more scared even than when the sheriff's men had showed up bringing the news about his father. But his fear melted when he saw the purple body that was Billy squeezed from his mother's womb.

He laid the baby on his mother's sweaty bosom, covered them both with a clean sheet, and walked to Beaver Bay two miles north to get help.

1

His story appeared in the *Duluth News-Tribune*. They called him a hero. An Indian hero. People who didn't know them figured his mother must have been drunk.

He raised Billy. He taught his brother how to fish, how to throw a baseball and a football, how to fight when he was taunted about his crazy mother or his Indian heritage. As much as he could, he took the blows of life and protected Billy. Even as he suffered, he thanked God for allowing him to be the shield.

After high school, John LePere was hired as a hand on a Great Lakes ore carrier. His job took him away from Purgatory Cove for long periods, and he was concerned. His mother earned a meager living as a cook in a diner on the north shore highway, but she was a distracted woman who required the care of both boys to keep her together. John hated the thought of this burden falling to Billy alone. But the money LePere earned—most of which he sent home—was good, and as it turned out, Billy did just fine. Whenever LePere returned from a passage, he found the house on the shore of Lake Superior well kept. Billy made repairs when necessary, made sure the refrigerator was stocked, got his mother to work every day on time and home safely. He seemed to grow up quickly, different in many ways from his older brother. He was like their mother, slender and tall, with dark straight hair and dark eyes. He had an easy smile. LePere, on the other hand, was stocky and strong and given to an earnest silence, more like the voyageurs who were his father's ancestors.

For five years, LePere worked the ore boat plying the waters of the Great Lakes, and for five years, things seemed fine. Then one morning Billy found their mother floating in the cold water of Purgatory Cove. Whether she'd got there by accident or by choice was never determined, but Billy took it hard. Although her death released her youngest son in one way, it bound him in others—to grief and guilt and remorse. When LePere saw Billy sliding toward the darkness that had swallowed their mother, he invited him aboard the *Alfred M. Teasdale* for the last passage of the season, a run from Buffalo to Duluth. He hoped the open water and the slow crawl under a late fall sky would bring Billy around.

*　　*　　*

The *Teasdale* entered Lake Superior via the locks at Sault Ste. Marie under clear skies. Since leaving Buffalo, the great ore boat had encountered only good weather. This was rare for November on the Great Lakes, and John LePere, as he went about his duties as a mate, watched the horizon carefully. The *Teasdale,* oldest of the boats in the Fitzgerald Shipping Company's ore fleet, was carrying her final cargo. Once she'd been unloaded in Duluth, the crew would sail her back to Detroit to be cut into scrap. LePere, whose responsibility it was to monitor the holds for leakage, knew the end was long overdue.

On the afternoon of November 16, the *Teasdale* rounded the Keweenaw Peninsula, that iron-rich finger of the Upper Peninsula of Michigan. She was making twelve knots against a mild headwind. Within an hour, the barometer began to plunge and the wind to rise. Dark came early, hastened by a bank of charcoal-colored clouds that seemed to materialize out of the lake itself and that quickly ate the sky. The temperature dropped twenty degrees. Bow spray began to freeze on the railings, and the decks were awash in icy slush. Captain Gus Hawley came to the pilothouse to confer with Art Bowdecker, the wheelsman. In her long service, the *Teasdale* had weathered many Great Lakes gales, and Hawley, captain during the last fifteen years of that service, was not greatly concerned. They were less than ten hours out of Duluth, and Bowdecker was the best wheelsman in the fleet. Captain Hawley gave the order to proceed on course, and he returned to his cabin.

At eight bells, John LePere completed his watch in the pilothouse with Bowdecker and first mate Orin Grange. Billy was there, too, taking in the talk of the men, getting a lesson from Bowdecker on guiding the huge boat through rough seas. The bow leaped and plummeted, disappearing for long moments under twelve-foot waves. Along with the bow spray, snow spattered the windows of the pilothouse, making it difficult to see anything. LePere could tell his brother was scared. He himself had never been through a storm as bad as this, but the other two men were old hands. They'd seen plenty of rough seas. If they were concerned at all, they didn't show it. As he left his watch, LePere offered to go down to the galley and bring back coffee for them all.

The cold November wind tore at LePere as soon as he

3

stepped outside. He shielded his eyes with his hand and looked aft. The *Teasdale* was 603 feet from bow to stern. She was carrying a full cargo, 221 tons of bituminous coal. On a calm day, she was a sight moving across the water, a mammoth creature of ungainly grace, ruler of her domain. As he watched the huge waves slam against her sides and flood her deck, LePere knew her greatness was an illusion. After he'd made coffee in the galley, he timed his return up the ladder to the pilothouse so that he wouldn't be soaked by the spray of the breaking waves. Even so, water hit him in the face—but it was not the cold spray of the lake. He realized with alarm that the wind was so strong it created a vacuum as it passed over the spout of the pot and was sucking the hot coffee out.

In the pilothouse, the men were laughing.

"I'm going below," John LePere told his brother. "You coming?"

"Ah, let 'im stay," Bowdecker said. "A few more hours and we're in Duluth. He's good company, John."

LePere could see his brother was flattered. He nodded to Bowdecker. "Just don't tell him about the Erie whorehouse, okay?"

Bowdecker smiled, and a gold tooth glinted in the light. "Too late. Already have. You go on and get some sleep. We'll take good care of Billy."

LePere went to the cabin he shared that voyage with his brother and crawled into bed. He read from a book, *The Old Man and the Sea*. He liked it because it was about a regular guy, a guy who knew big water and was trying to stay true to a few things. The pitching of the boat made it difficult to follow the lines of print, so he didn't read long. After only a few minutes, he closed his eyes and fell asleep, knowing that when he woke, they would be anchored outside Duluth harbor waiting for permission to enter.

He had no idea how much time had passed when he was awakened by a great *boom* that ran through the ship. After that came a scream of metal, long, like an animal in pain. The ship jolted, and he was thrown from his bunk. Sparks flew from the striker of the bell as the general alarm sounded. In darkness, he flipped the light switch in his cabin, but the light would not come on.

"Billy!" he called.

His brother didn't answer.

LePere stumbled across the tiny cabin and grabbed frantically for the life jacket in the rack over his bunk and then for Billy's. He snatched his pea coat from its hook and headed up top. He remembered Bowdecker's promise—*We'll take good care of Billy*—and he held to that as he stumbled into the companionway and toward the ladder. When he reached the spar deck, he saw that although the rest of the ship was completely dark, the stern was still brightly lit. That gave him hope—until he realized what was actually happening. The center of the *Teasdale* had begun to lift, like a playing card being folded in the middle. As he watched, the inch-thick steel decking started to rip from starboard to port, and the sound of its rending drowned out even the howl of the wind. Sparks shot into the night like fireworks and great clouds of gray steam erupted. LePere gaped in horror as the *Teasdale* broke in half.

"Billy!" he cried and rushed up the ladder to the darkened pilothouse.

Orin Grange was at the radio, speaking frantically, trying vainly to send a message on a dead set. LePere grabbed his shoulder.

"Where's Billy?"

Grange shrugged off his hand. LePere grabbed him and spun him around. "Where's Billy, damn it?"

"He went aft with Bowdecker," Grange hollered, then turned back to the radio.

LePere headed toward the lighted stern. He passed a group of men gathered at the pontoon raft between hatches two and three. The captain was among them.

"Where are you going, LePere?" Captain Hawley cried out to him.

"My brother. He's somewhere aft."

"You can't get there now." Hawley grasped his arm. "Get into the raft, man."

LePere pulled free and ran on.

As he approached the place where the deck had split, he stopped abruptly in terror. The severed stern of the *Teasdale* was rising up, driven forward by the propeller that was still turning. For a moment, LePere was sure the whole aft end would ride up onto the deck where he stood and crush him. He could see the open sections of the severed cargo hold lit by lights, full of fire and swirling clouds of steam. It was like looking through the doorway to hell. He had a moment of perfect calm, sure he was about to die, and he saw, or thought he saw, silhouetted in one of the lighted windows aft, the shape of Billy standing all alone.

Then the stern veered to starboard. As LePere watched, it passed him slowly and headed off into the night and the storm like an animal crawling off to die.

"Billy!" he cried out in vain. "Billy! God, Billy!"

He teetered at the brink of a section of ship that was tipping, preparing to slide into the deep. Hands pulled him back, and he found himself with half a dozen other men struggling to climb aboard the life raft. He moved in a daze, his feet slipping on the sharp angle of the tilting deck. Like all rafts on the older carriers, the pontoon raft on the *Teasdale* was too heavy to be manually launched. It was designed to float free of the deck as the ship sank beneath it. However, as the bow rose, pointing ever skyward, the raft suddenly broke loose, tumbled down the deck, and hit the water. A moment later, so did John LePere.

The icy water took his breath away, squeezed him mercilessly so that his whole body cramped at once. A wave lifted him and slammed him against the tilted hull. He managed to push off the metal and he sliced into the next wave, swimming hard away from the sinking bow section. When he lifted his head, he found that he was only a few yards from the raft. Skip Jurgenson, another of the *Teasdale*'s wheelsman, leaned over the side and extended his hand. LePere fought against the waves. His fingers touched the raft. Jurgenson grasped the collar of his peacoat and helped him aboard. LePere fell against the prone form of another shipmate, Pete Swanson, a coal passer, who lay nearly motionless in the center of the raft. Swanson's duties were in the engine room and his quarters were aft where Billy had gone. LePere grabbed him and screamed over the wind and the crash of water.

"Where's my brother? Did you see my brother?"

Swanson was shaking violently, his face ghostly white.

6

Although his lips formed words, no sound seemed to come forth. LePere bent close to his lips.

"I blew it," Swanson said hoarsely. "I blew it."

"What about Billy?" LePere shouted into his ear.

Swanson stared blankly, as if he didn't see LePere at all, and repeated only those three words—"I blew it"—over and over again.

Jurgenson, who'd been hollering into the dark for other shipmates, quit and dropped in a dejected heap next to LePere. "I didn't see noboby else," he said. "Not one blessed soul."

The storm pushed the raft far from the bow of the *Teasdale*. LePere and Jurgenson watched the last of the ore boat sink in a huge bloom of dark water. Then John LePere lay down and wept, crying *"Billy"* over and over again as he held to that tiny raft in the middle of the big lake his ancestors called Kitchigami.

1

CORCORAN O'CONNOR WAS PULLED instantly from his sleep by the sound of a sniffle near his head. He opened his eyes and the face of his six-year-old son filled his vision.

"I'm thcared," Stevie said.

Cork propped himself on one arm. "Of what, buddy?"

"I heard thomething."

"Where? In your room?"

Stevie nodded.

"Let's go see."

Jo rolled over. "What is it?"

"Stevie heard something," Cork told his wife. "I'll take care of it. Go back to sleep."

"What time is it?"

Cork glanced at the radio alarm on the stand beside the bed. "Five o'clock."

"I can take him," she offered.

"Go back to sleep."

"Mmmm." She smiled faintly and rolled back to her dreaming.

Cork took his son by the hand, and together they walked down the hallway to where the night-light in Stevie's room cast a soft glow over everything.

"Where was the noise?"

Stevie pointed toward the window.

"Let's see."

Cork knelt and peered through the screen. Aurora,

Minnesota, was defined by the barest hint of morning light. The air was quite still, not even the slightest rustle among the leaves of the elm in Cork's backyard. Far down the street, the Burnett's dog Bogart barked a few times, then fell silent. The only thing Cork found disturbing was the smell of wood smoke heavy on the breeze. The smoke came from forest fires burning all over the north country. Summer had come early that year. With it had come a dry heat and drought that wilted the undergrowth and turned fields of wild grass into something to be feared. Lake levels dropped to the lowest recorded in nearly a century. Rivers shrank to ragged threads. Creeks ceased to run. In shallow pools of trapped water, fish darted about wildly as what sustained them rapidly disappeared. The fires had begun in mid-June. Now it was nearly the end of July, and still the forests were burning. One blaze would be controlled and two others somewhere else would ignite. Day and night, the sky was full of smoke and the smell of burned wood.

"Do you still hear it?" Cork asked.

Stevie, who'd knelt beside him, shook his head.

"Probably an early bird," Cork said.

"After a worm." Stevie smiled.

"Yeah. And he must've got that worm. Think you can go back to sleep?"

"Yeth."

"Good man. Come on."

Cork got him settled in bed, then sat in a chair near the window. Stevie watched his father a while. His eyes were dark brown, the eyes of his Anishinaabe ancestors. Slowly, they drifted closed.

Cork's son had always been a light sleeper, awakened easily by noises in the night, disturbances in the routine of the household. He was the only one of the O'Connor children who'd needed the comfort of a night-light. Cork blamed himself. In Stevie's early years, when the dark of his closet or under his bed first became vast and menacing, Cork wasn't always there to stand between his son and the monsters of his imagination. There were times, he knew, when the monster was real and was Cork. He thought often these days of the words that ended the traditional marriage ceremony of the Anishinaabeg.

10

You will share the same fire.
You will hang your garments together.
You will help one another.
You will walk the same trail.
You will look after one another.
Be kind to one another.
Be kind to your children.

He hadn't always been careful to abide by these simple instructions. But a man could change, and watching his son crawl back into his dreaming, Cork vowed—as he did almost every morning—to work at being a better man.

By the time Cork finally left Stevie to his dreaming, morning sunlight fired the curtains over the window at the end of the hallway. Cork thought of returning to bed for a little while, but chose instead to head to the bathroom, where he showered, shaved, splashed on aftershave, then looked himself over carefully in the bathroom mirror.

Corcoran Liam O'Connor was forty-seven years old. Part Irish, part Ojibwe Anishinaabe, he stood five feet eleven inches tall, weighed one hundred seventy-five pounds, and had brown eyes, thinning red-brown hair, and slightly crooked teeth. He suffered from mild rosacea that he treated with prescription ointment. In wet weather, his left shoulder—twice dislocated—was prone to an arthritic aching. He did not consider himself a handsome man, but there were those, apparently, who found him so. All in all, what stared back at him from the bathroom mirror was the face of a man who'd struggled to be happy and believed himself to be almost there.

He returned to his bedroom, a towel about his waist. The radio alarm had gone off and WIRR out of Buhl was playing Vivaldi's *Four Seasons*. Cork went to the dresser, pulled open a drawer, and took out a pair of black silk boxers.

Jo stirred. She took a deep breath but kept her eyes closed. When she spoke to him, the words seemed to come reluctantly and from a distant place.

"Stevie all right?"

"He's fine."

11

"Another fire's started. Up in the Boundary Waters near Saganaga Lake." She yawned. "I just heard it on the news."

"Oh?"

"Get this. The guy who started it is a lobbyist for the tobacco industry. He was shooting off fireworks. In the Boundary Waters—can you believe it?"

"I hope they fine his ass big time," Cork said.

"He's a tobacco lawyer. He can pay from his pocket money." The room was quiet. Bogart started barking again down the block. "I can feel you watching me."

"What else?"

"I smell Old Spice."

"Anything else?"

"If I had to guess, I'd say you've put on your black silk boxers."

"What a detective you would have made." He sat on the bed, leaned down, and kissed her shoulder.

"I was dreaming before the radio came on." She rolled toward him and opened her eyes.

"What?"

"We were trying to fly, you and I. A plane we had to pedal. But somehow we couldn't quite get it off the ground."

Cork reached out and brushed a white-blond strand of hair from her cheek.

She reached up and drifted her hand down his chest. "You smell good."

"Only Old Spice. You have pedestrian tastes."

"And, my, aren't you lucky."

He bent to her lips. She let him kiss her but kept her mouth closed. "I'm all stale. Give me five minutes." She slid from the bed. She wore a gray tank top and white cotton underwear, her usual sleep attire. "Don't start anything without me." She smiled coyly as she went out the door.

Cork drew back the covers, straightened the bottom sheet, fluffed the pillows, and lay down to wait. The bedroom window was open. Bogart had ceased his barking and the only sound now was the call of a mourning dove perched in the big maple in the front yard. Aurora, Minnesota, deep in the great North Woods, riding the jagged edge of the Iron Range, had not yet wakened. This was Cork's favorite time of day.

Although he couldn't actually see it, he could picture the whole town perfectly. Sunlight dripping down the houses on Gooseberry Lane like butter melting down pancakes. The streets empty and clean. The surface of Iron Lake on such a still morning looking solid as polished steel.

God, he loved this place.

And he'd begun to love again, too, the woman who now stood in the doorway with a gold towel wrapped about her and tucked at her breasts. Her hair was wet. Her pale blue eyes were wide awake and interested. She locked the door behind her.

"We don't have much time," she said in a whisper. "I think I heard Stevie stirring."

"We're the experts at putting a lot into a little time."

He smiled wide, and widely he opened his arms.

An explosion kept them from beginning anything. The house shook; the windows rattled; the mourning dove fell silent, frightened to stillness or frightened away.

"My God," Cork said. "What was that?"

Jo looked at him, her eyes blue and shiny. "I think the earth moved. Without us." She glanced at the window. "Sonic boom?"

"When was the last time you heard a sonic boom around here?"

From the hallway beyond the bedroom door came the sound of voices, then a knock.

"Jo? Cork?"

"Just a minute, Rose." She blew Cork a kiss. "Rain check." She headed to the closet and grabbed a robe from the door hook.

Cork quickly exchanged his silk boxers for a pair of jogging shorts and went to the window. He stared north over the roofs of Aurora where a column of smoke rose thick and black somewhere beyond the town limits. Just above the ground, the air was calm and the smoke climbed straight up four or five hundred feet until it hit a high current that spread it east over Iron Lake. The sky was a milky blue from the haze of the distant forest fires. Against it, the smoke from the nearer burn was dark as crude oil.

At his back, Cork heard the door unlock. Rose stepped in, Stevie at her heels.

"Whatever that was, it didn't sound good." Rose tugged her beige chenille robe tight about her broad waist and stuffed her plump, freckled hands into the pockets. She was Jo's sister and for more than fifteen years had been part of the O'Connor household.

Stevie ran to his father. "Thomething blew up."

"I think something did, buddy." Cork put his arm around his son and motioned the others to the window, where they huddled and stared at the huge smoke cloud fanning out above the lake.

The siren on Aurora's only fire station began to wail, calling the volunteers to duty.

"See the direction that smoke's coming from?" He glanced at Jo. "Are you thinking what I'm thinking?"

From the concern on her face, it was clear to him that she was. She straightened and turned from the window. "I'd better go."

"I'll come with you." Cork started toward the dresser to get his clothes.

"Cork." Jo put a hand on his arm to restrain him gently. "I have clients to protect. I need to be out there. But there's no reason for you to go. You're not the sheriff anymore." She seemed reluctant to add that last bit of a reminder, as if she were afraid that even after all this time, it still might hurt him.

He smiled gamely and said, "Then let's just chalk it up to morbid curiosity."

2

THE LINDSTROM LUMBER AND PLYWOOD MILL stood within a stone's throw of the Superior National Forest, on three dozen cleared acres, hard up against the shoreline of a small oval of water called Grindstone Lake. Normally, the only smoke coming from the mill was generated by the kilns and smokestacks. However, as his old red Bronco broke from the pines along County Road 8, Cork could see clearly that the billow of smoke rising above the clearing came from the trailer of a logging rig parked in the mill yard and from the burning remains of a building just beyond.

At the mill gate, Deputy Ed McDermott stopped Cork and leaned against the driver's-side door.

"Ed," Cork said to the deputy in greeting.

"Morning, Cork."

"What's up?"

"Big propane tank blew, set things on fire. Murray's men have it pretty well under control now. In this drought, lucky it didn't spread to the woods."

"Mind if I go in?"

"Be my guest. Sheriff's over by that stack of logs there." He looked past Cork and gave his head a slight nod. "Morning, Ms. O'Connor."

Cork parked the Bronco next to a Land Cruiser with the Tamarack County Sheriff's Department insignia on the door. Jo got out with him.

Sheriff Wally Schanno stood beside a huge stack of pine logs that was awaiting milling. He was a tall man who, in his prime, had been every bit as strong and rigid as those sections of cut timber. But he was over sixty years old now. There was a slight bend to his tall frame, and time had rubbed its hand deeply into his long face, giving him a gaunt and haunted look. When he glanced at Cork and Jo, his gray eyes seemed tired.

"Heard the explosion," Cork said.

"They heard the explosion in Brazil," Schanno said. "Morning, Jo." The sheriff gave her a grim purse of his lips, as near to a smile as he could apparently muster.

"What happened?"

"Ask Murray."

Alfred Murray, the fire chief for Aurora, and only one of three paid firefighters who manned the station in town, walked toward them from one of the yellow pumpers that was dousing the last of the flames among the logs on the trailer. He wore a black rubberized firefighter's coat, black boots, and a yellow hat that said CHIEF.

"Looks like we'll have it all extinguished in a few minutes," he told Schanno.

"What happened, Alf?" Cork asked.

"Well . . ." He seemed reluctant to commit. "To tell you the truth, at first I figured the LP tank went up, demolished part of that old equipment shed, and set the rest of it on fire. I figured burning fragments must have jumped to the logs on the trailer, and they went up, too, along with the cab."

"At first?" Cork said.

"Yeah."

"Then?"

Instead of answering Cork, Murray watched a dark blue Explorer swing through the mill gate and head toward them. The Explorer moved quickly across the mill yard that was becoming muddy where the water from the fire hoses ran. It stopped next to Cork's Bronco, and Karl Lindstrom stepped out.

He was technically Karl Magnus Lindstrom III. The mill was his. Had been his father's, and his father's father's, and another generation yet again. At one time, there'd been nearly a dozen mills just like it in the Lindstrom empire that had stretched across the Upper Peninsula of Michigan, northern Wisconsin, and Minnesota. But declining resources, cheap foreign lumber, and the profligate lifestyle of Karl Magnus Lindstrom II had brought the holdings down to this one.

In his late thirties, Lindstrom was a tall, slender man with thinning blond hair kept short in a sharp military cut. His bearing was stiff and military as well, the legacy of Annapolis and eight years in an officer's uniform. In the few times he and Cork had exchanged words, Lindstrom had spoken crisply and to the point. The only thing about him that had any look of softness were his eyebrows, so blond and fine they looked like a couple of delicate feathers stuck to his forehead. What kind of man he really was at heart Cork could only guess, for Cork didn't know Lindstrom well at all. As far as he could gather, no one did. He wasn't from Aurora. The Lindstroms had always been like absentee landlords, directing the business of the mill from their headquarters in Chicago. Karl Lindstrom had moved his family to a home on Iron Lake only a few months before. All anybody really knew about him was that he'd kept the mill open and kept a lot of people in Tamarack County working.

"Was anybody hurt?" Lindstrom asked.

"Fortunately, no," Schanno replied. "Only person here was your night watchman, Harold Loomis. He was way over to the other side of the mill when it happened. He called in right away."

"Did he see anything?"

"Harold?" Schanno asked it seriously. "He's seventy-two, Mr. Lindstrom. Even when he stays awake, he probably doesn't see much."

Lindstrom stepped away from the others and went to a fragment of blackened metal a few feet away. He stooped and reached for it. "Any idea what happened?"

"Don't touch anything," Schanno warned him.

Lindstrom shot a look his way. "Still hot?"

"Evidence," Schanno said.

"Evidence?" Lindstrom stood up quickly. "You never answered me, Sheriff. What happened here?"

"We're not sure yet." Schanno looked to Cork. "You ever work a bomb scene? In Chicago maybe?"

"Only crowd control, Wally. You think this was a bomb?"

"Alf sure does. And I'm figuring it probably wasn't too far

from your own way of thinking, else why would you and Jo be here? With all this ballyhoo over logging those old white pines, I've been worrying it was only a matter of time before something like this happened."

Lindstrom turned to the fire chief. "Was it a bomb?"

Alf Murray looked toward the flame and smoke. "Well, like I said before you came, I thought at first the fire must've started with the explosion of the LP tank. That was the big bang we all heard. Blew down the equipment shed like the big bad wolf blowing down a straw house. Seemed possible anyway, the tank going first and everything else following from that. Except those tanks are plenty safe. Never heard of one going up by itself. So I did some more looking around. There's a small crater in the ground under the cab of the logging rig. Now, when the gas tank on the cab caught fire, it made for some pretty good fireworks, but it wouldn't account for that little crater. Only thing I can think of would've left that kind of scar in the earth'd be an explosive device of some kind, probably attached to the undercarriage of the cab. So if it was a bomb, and I ain't for a moment saying it necessarily was, then I'd say the cab went up first, and everything else happened because of that."

It was only a moment before all eyes had turned to Jo. She didn't say anything, but Cork could feel her harden, prepared to defend.

" 'Course, I ain't an expert," the fire chief hastened to add. "Mostly I deal with house fires, grass fires. We won't know for sure until Wally gets someone up here who knows what the hell they're doing."

Schanno rubbed his jaw with his long fingers. "I've already got a call in to the BCA," he said, speaking of the Bureau of Criminal Apprehension, Minnesota's version of the FBI.

Cork saw Hell Hanover on the other side of the demolished shed. Helmuth Hanover was publisher and editor of the weekly *Aurora Sentinel*. He had lost the lower part of his right leg to a claymore mine in Vietnam, and he dragged that history with him in a gait that was becoming, with time, a dire limp. He'd balded young and had chosen to shave clean what little hair remained to him, so that in the morning sunlight, his bare white skull reminded Cork of something on the desert even the buzzards would ignore. Although his byline read Helm Hanover, to those who liked him not at all—Cork among them—he was known as Hell.

Hanover had been taking photos of the men hosing down the smoking debris, but now he got into his car, a maroon Taurus wagon parked near the far fence, and came around to where the other vehicles sat.

Lindstrom didn't seem to notice Hanover's approach. He was intent on Jo.

"We've been on opposite sides of this issue, Ms. O'Connor." Hard eyes looked at her from under those feathery eyebrows. "And I always believed we could reach a peaceful resolution—"

"Karl," Jo said, interrupting, "before you say anything more, I just want to point out a couple of things. As the fire chief has said, the cause of all this hasn't been confirmed. He's only guessing. And if he's right, there's currently no evidence that would implicate my clients, or anyone, for that matter, who might be opposed to you on the logging issue."

Lindstrom held off speaking for a moment. Hell Hanover stood quietly off to the side, a small notebook in his hand, taking notes. Nobody except Cork seemed to be aware of his presence.

"It's easy for you, isn't it," Lindstrom finally said. "Your business hasn't been threatened. Your livelihood isn't at stake. In fact, you're probably the only one who is benefiting from all this."

"Easy, Karl," Cork said.

Lindstrom turned on him. "I'm at a loss to understand why, exactly, you're here. You're not the sheriff anymore. You've got no business here."

Before Cork or anyone else could reply, the insistent chirp of a cell phone cut among them. Hanover pulled a cellular from his pocket and stepped away. He listened, tried to speak, then terminated the call. He spent a moment scribbling furiously in his little notebook.

Lindstrom went on, addressing himself to Jo again. "If this is the kind of fight your people want, then this is the kind of fight we'll give them."

"Mr. Lindstrom," Schanno said, "I don't think you want to make that kind of statement."

"Just whose side are you on, Sheriff?"

Hell Hanover came back, a look of mild satisfaction on his face. "Wally, that was a phone call from someone claiming responsibility for all this mess."

"Who?" Schanno snapped.

"Calls himself—or herself—the voice was disguised so it was impossible to tell—calls himself Eco-Warrior. Claims to be part of a movement called the Army of the Earth. The statement read"—he glanced down at the notes he'd written—" 'The desecration of Grandmother Earth must end. Violence toward anything sacred will not be tolerated. I am the arrow of justice.' "

"That's it? All of it? You're sure?" Schanno asked.

"Grandmother Earth." Lindstrom cast a cold eye on Jo. "That's how your clients refer to it, Ms. O'Connor."

"Words are free, Mr. Lindstrom," Jo replied. "Anyone may use them in any way they wish. Or misuse them."

"Chief!" One of the men near the burned shed waved furiously. "Bring the sheriff, too!"

They all followed Murray to the shed.

"What is it, Bob?"

"Smell that? Made me think I'd better check the debris here carefully."

With the head of his ax, he reached into the charred wreckage of the equipment shed, hooked a burned panel, and lifted.

"Jesus," Schanno said.

Jo turned away.

An upper body had been exposed, most of the skin burned to char, the muscle tissue underneath visible in visceral red and purple. The heat had caused the eyes to bubble away and the brain to explode out the back of the skull. The lips were burned off completely, leaving a skeletal grin that made the corpse look grimly delighted.

"Welp," Hanover said as he lifted his camera for a shot. "It ain't just arson anymore."

3

History, in Cork's opinion, was a useless discipline, an assemblage of accounts and memories, often flawed, that in the end did the world no service. Math and science could be applied in concrete ways. Literature, if it didn't enlighten, at least entertained. But history? History was simply a study in futility. Because people never learned. Century after century, they committed the same atrocities against one another or against the earth, and the only thing that changed was the magnitude of the slaughter.

Except for the particulars dictated by its geography, the history of Tamarack County was little different. The streams, clear and clean since the days of the great glaciers, ran red with the blood of the Dakota as the Anishinaabeg invaded from the east and forced out of the forests along Kitchigami all the people not their own. Although less bloody, the confinement of the Ojibwe Anishinaabeg to a very few reservations was accomplished through threat and deceit and with the complicity of educated people who considered themselves enlightened. The devastation of the land—the clearing of the magnificent white pine forests, the deep gouging of the mine pits on the Iron Range, the dumping of toxins into the crystal water of Lake Superior—was justified as the fulfillment of God's plan, the "manifest destiny" of America.

Conscience was a devil that plagued the individual. Collectively, a people squashed it as easily as stepping on a daisy.

Or so it appeared to Corcoran O'Connor on that summer morning when smoke hazed the sky and Tamarack County seemed poised for war over the destruction of one of the last good stands of old-growth white pine left in the North Woods.

The Anishinaabe people called them Ninishoomisag, Our Grandfathers. There were more than two hundred acres of them, all over a hundred feet tall, their trunks better than four feet in diameter, some said to be at least three hundred years old. To the Anishinaabeg, they were sacred. For generations, the young men of the Iron Lake Ojibwe had sought out the shelter of Our Grandfathers, and under their watchful eyes had undergone *giigwishimowin*, the fasting ritual that brought to an adolescent the dream vision that would guide him into manhood. How the great trees had been spared from the rapacious saws of the crews who'd leveled the forests—most of them on a Lindstrom wage—was a bit of a mystery. Henry Meloux, an old Ojibwe medicine man, claimed the trees had been protected by *manidoonsag*, little spirits of the woods. Although Cork was ever respectful of Meloux's vast wisdom, he'd heard another, less fantastic, explanation for the trees' survival. In the days of the early logging boom, timber companies hired estimators to survey the forests and report probable lumber footage before a company bid on the right to log a particular section. For years, the man who'd worked in that capacity for the Lindstrom mill in Minnesota was Edward Olaf. He was mixed blood, half Swede, half Ojibwe. He knew how important Our Grandfathers were to the Anishinaabeg, and he simply lied in his reports about the area, ensuring the great white pines would be bypassed.

By the time extensive forest service surveys made the Lindstrom executives aware of Our Grandfathers, the trees had been included in an area of national forest no longer open to logging. The ban was in place for many decades until 1995 when President Clinton signed into law a bill creating the Energy Salvage Timber Sales Program. The law opened the door to public forest lands full of old-growth timber, among them Our Grandfathers. Karl Lindstrom's company bid immediately for the right to cut the great white pines, and that bid had been accepted.

The plight of Our Grandfathers brought together an alliance

of disparate groups bent on saving the trees. The Sierra Club, the Nature Conservancy, Earth First, the Iron Lake Ojibwe, and a handful of other organizations and unaffiliated individuals had descended on Aurora to protest the proposed logging. Court battles had thus far prevented any cutting from taking place. In the legal maneuvering, Jo O'Connor had been the major voice for the Anishinaabeg. Now, arguments had ended. A federal judge in St. Paul had promised a ruling soon. In the tense quiet, some of the environmentalists had issued statements indicating that a ruling in favor of the logging interests would not deter them from doing what had to be done to preserve Our Grandfathers. Aurora, Minnesota had seemed on the eve of war. Now it looked like the body count had already begun.

"You didn't do much talking back there," Cork noted as he drove the road toward Aurora.

Jo stared out the window, lost in the familiar landscape of red pines and underbrush. "There wasn't much to say. Because the Ojibwe are my clients, I thought restraint was best at this point."

"You don't think your clients did it?"

"Of course not. Do you?"

"No."

Jo gave a disgusted little grunt and said, "Helm Hanover."

"What about him?"

"Did you see the look on his face when he saw the body? Like a vulture."

"Yeah, well, you know how I feel about old Hell."

Although they'd never been friends, never come near to anything like friendship, Cork had known Helmuth Hanover his whole life. Hanover's father had been publisher and editor of the *Aurora Sentinel,* and Helm took over after his father's death. The elder Hanover had been a cantankerous freethinker, a man of independent politics and social philosophy. He'd hated FDR, had revered Truman, made sport of Eisenhower, and was fond of saying—though never in print— that *JFK* stood for *Just a Fucking Kid.* Locally, his political endorsements meant little. He often threw his support to a candidate for reasons wholly unrelated to issues, such as a man's ability as a deer hunter, and he withheld his approval for reasons equally ridiculous—a candidate's noisy dog. Helm, his only child, had been a quiet, bright, thoughtful kid. In '68, he'd been drafted and sent to Vietnam. Like many veterans, he returned altered, darkly and forever. Physically, he came back with a right leg that was mostly a plastic prosthesis. Emotionally, he carried a bitterness that showed on his face and, ultimately, in his editorials. He deeply distrusted government in any form and harbored a particular animosity toward the federal government for the sacrifice of his own flesh and bone in a war he believed was utterly useless and the fault entirely of cowardly, stupid, and self-serving politicians. On the Iron Range, he wasn't alone in his assessment of that conflict or of politicians in general. A wise publisher, he used the *Sentinel* well in reporting on the people and activities of Tamarack County, never misspelling a name and making every attempt to include even the smallest of events, from church socials to league softball games. The editorial page, however, he used like a howitzer. Hanover had blasted Cork many times during his tenure as sheriff, and Cork had long ago joined the legion of those who referred to the bitter newspaperman as Hell.

Nearly a year and a half earlier, Cork had uncovered a direct connection between Hanover and a militia group called the Minnesota Civilian Brigade. Although Cork was absolutely certain the group had been involved in the illegal procurement of arms, none of the brigade was ever charged. Partly this was because evidence had been lacking. The weapons were never found. But it was also partly because the political sentiment on the Iron Range was not entirely unsympathetic to the antigovernment ideology of the brigade. Nothing had been heard from the group for a long time. The official position of those law enforcement agencies concerned—mostly Tamarack County authorities at this point—was that such close legal scrutiny had forced the brigade to disband. Cork believed differently. He'd read about strains of plague that became active when archeologists dug too unwarily. That's how he thought of the brigade. It was simply underground, waiting to surface, as deadly in its purpose as ever.

Cork's stomach growled. "I don't suppose you're hungry?"

"Hungry?" She looked at him, appalled. "After what we just saw? How could anyone be hungry after that?"

"I don't know. I just know I am." He felt her edge away, as if repulsed. "Look, Jo, when I was a rookie cop in Chicago, my first partner—Duke Ranham, you remember him?—Duke told me that after I'd seen death, I'd have one of two reactions. I'd be hungry or I'd be horny. His theory was that it was a subconscious assertion of life. All I know is that he was right, and at the moment I'm hungry."

"Well, thank God it's that and not the other."

"Are you okay?"

"I've never seen someone who's been burned to death."

Cork lifted his hand to shield his eyes from the bright low sun. "We don't know for sure that was the cause of death. That'll take an autopsy to determine."

"I wonder who it is."

"Who it *was*. According to Lindstrom and the night watchman, Harold Loomis, nobody should have been there. If I were Wally Schanno, I'd figure whoever it was, they were the victim of their own bombing, if it was a bombing."

"If you were Schanno." She looked at him, then quickly away. "I've heard a rumor. People are saying Wally Schanno won't stand for reelection in the fall."

"I've heard that, too."

"Are you thinking of running?"

"I haven't given it a lot of thought, Jo."

They were approaching the town limits. Cars, lots of them, moved past on the other side, headed toward the mill. Some belonged to the men on the first shift. Others were driven by the curious.

"But you have thought about it?"

"Some."

"Are you happy? Running Sam's Place, I mean."

They entered town on Center Street. Aurora was coming to life. People moved purposefully along the sidewalks and cars filled the streets. "The truth is, this morning I'm very glad I'm not in Wally Schanno's shoes."

They pulled into the drive of the house on Gooseberry Lane. Jo sat for a moment, then asked, "Would you tell me if you were thinking seriously of running?"

"We'd talk about it," he promised.
"That's all I ask."

History.

In a place like Aurora, where a man could spend his whole life, cradle to grave, his history was all around him, slapping against him like old newspapers in a wind.

Cork had a strong sense of that as he stepped into Johnny's Pinewood Broiler to get himself some breakfast. Breathing in the hot griddle scent was like breathing in the air of another time in his life.

"Well, I'll be." Johnny Pap smiled as Cork took a stool at the counter.

Johnny Pap was first-generation Greek and had run the Broiler since Cork was old enough to pay for milkshakes with the money he'd earned delivering newspapers. For most of Cork's life, a stop at the Broiler was part of his daily routine. A year and a half before, his routine had dramatically changed.

"Christ," Johnny said, leaning against the counter. "I haven't seen you in here since—well, must be since Molly died." As soon as the words escaped his lips, Johnny's face showed that he regretted them.

"Not since Molly died," Cork confirmed.

The moment seemed awkward for Johnny, considering the current state of Cork's marriage. But Johnny handled it well. He simply nodded toward the distant sky outside the Broiler and said, "Hell of a bang this morning. Heard those tree huggers really did a number at Lindstrom's. You know anything?"

"I was just out there."

"Yeah? Was it bad?"

Talk in the Broiler quieted as other customers turned to listen to what Cork had to say.

"To the mill, no significant damage. But someone died."

"No." Johnny pushed back in surprise. "Who?"

"They haven't ID'ed the body yet."

"One of us, you think?"

"Us?"

"Locals."

"As opposed to those outside agitators, you mean."

"Bingo."

"Like I said, Johnny, nobody knows. Say, what does a guy have to do to get some coffee and a short stack around here?"

Johnny shook his head slowly in puzzlement and dismay at this deadly turn the world around him was taking and he headed toward the kitchen.

The talk of the Broiler regulars—the county work crews, the shop owners, the locals—resumed, and most of it was about the incident at Lindstrom's. The talk Cork heard sided with the loggers. That didn't surprise him at all. In a town surrounded by and dependent in so many ways on national forest land, the federal regulations restricting the use of that resource were like slivers under the skin. Snowmobiles and SUVs were severely limited to marked trails. Game wardens packing firearms strictly regulated hunting and fishing. Felling timber, harvesting wild rice, even taking a goddamn crap in the forest was controlled by law.

Unless you happened to be Indian.

History.

The conflict between red and white was old and deep. Cork left the Broiler feeling a heaviness that weighed on him from the past. Because Tamarack County had been down this road before, and not that long ago. The last flareup had occurred only two years earlier. It had been about fishing rights, an issue over which the two cultures had been skirmishing for more than a decade. Jo had argued successfully before a federal judge on behalf of the Ojibwe, asserting that the Iron Lake Treaty of 1873 gave the Anishinaabeg the right to fish that lake and any other in the state without restraint. The judge had decreed that Ojibwe fishermen had the right to take, if they desired, the full limit of fish set by the Department of Natural Resources for the whole lake over the entire season, leaving nothing for other anglers. Resort owners had panicked. Much of the citizenry of Tamarack County, whose economic welfare relied heavily on the money from weekend fishermen, rallied round the resort owners, and threats of violence arose. Cork had been sheriff then and charged with the duty of ensuring the safety of those Ojibwe who chose to gillnet and spearfish. The conflict came to a deadly head one cold, drizzly spring morning at a place called Burke's Landing. Cork was escorting a group of Indian fishermen to their boats, down a corridor lined with angry whites. Jo was with the fishermen, as was Cork's oldest friend Sam Winter Moon. He'd brought them safely almost to the landing when a scared little man named Arnold Stanley, a resort owner driven to desperation by the fear of losing everything he had, stepped in front of Cork with a rifle in his hand. He fired once before Cork cleared his revolver from its holster and pumped six bullets into the little man, the final three while Stanley lay on the wet ground. Although Arnold Stanley's single shot had torn open Sam Winter Moon's heart, killing him almost instantly, the people of Tamarack County, incited in large measure by Hell Hanover's raging editorials, raised a hue and cry over the excessive nature of Cork's response. In a recall election, Cork lost his job as sheriff. His self-respect pretty much followed. And just about everything else in his life had unraveled from there.

As he stepped outside into the smoke-scented air, he had the frightening feeling that he—and all the others who called Tamarack County their home—were about to walk a bloody road again.

JOHN LePERE HAD BEEN WAKING SOBER long enough that even when he had one of the bad dreams, he woke fresh and strong.

And that night, he'd had a dream.

He woke early, at first light, pulled on his Speedo and his goggles, and hit the lake. Every day he swam, every day a little farther. He started when dawn colored the water with a cold, gray light, and he moved steadily, stroking his way north, heading out into the center of Iron Lake where the water turned dark and fathomless beneath him. He never tracked his distance. He swam for another reason, a reason that led—twisting and turning—ultimately back to vengeance.

When he drew abreast of North Point that morning, he paused and saw that the sun had risen, a feverish red through the smoke in the sky. The lake around him had turned a bloody hue. The same moment that he noticed the color of the water, he heard an explosion from the direction of Aurora. Beyond the town, a black column climbed into the sky like a snake out of a charmer's basket, but John LePere watched with only mild curiosity. Whatever the cause, it was the concern of other men. His only concern was keeping himself strong for the work that had become his life. As the siren in town sounded, calling the volunteer firefighters to their duty, LePere turned back and focused on cutting through the blood-colored water toward home.

He'd had the bad dreams so often over the years that he'd learned to keep himself from thinking about them by focusing on physical chores. By the time he'd showered and shaved that morning, he wasn't thinking about the dream at all. He dressed in clean creased jeans, a crisp white shirt, blue canvas slip-ons. He fixed himself breakfast—oatmeal with raisins, a sliced banana, brown sugar and milk, whole-wheat toast, and a tall glass of orange juice. He ate slowly, alone in the quiet of his small cabin on the shore of a cove off Iron Lake. When he'd finished, he did up the dishes. Finally, he lifted his Leitz binoculars from where they hung on a steel spike hammered into the cabin wall near the back door, and he walked out onto his dock. He settled himself in a canvas chair and watched the big log home more than a quarter mile north across Grace Cove.

His own cabin was simple. His father had built it in the space of a single summer when John LePere was six years old. LePere remembered that summer well—the building of the cabin and the feel of working with his father, a serious man who spoke little but never raised his voice or his hand to his son. The cabin was meant as a retreat whenever LePere's father tired of fishing Lake Superior for the herring and whitefish and lake trout that, for his living, he caught and sold to smoke-houses along the North Shore. Fishing on Iron Lake, he didn't care if he hung a line in the water all day and caught nothing. There, he fished for other reasons.

When his father bought the land in the late sixties, the price was cheap. The shore of Iron Lake was still quite empty, espe-cially along the eastern side south of the Iron Lake Reservation. Much had changed in thirty years. To build the big log home—the only other dwelling on Grace Cove—Karl Lindstrom had had to pay a fortune for the land, LePere had heard. Lindstrom bought everything up to LePere's property line. He even tried to buy LePere's land, offering better than a good price, but John LePere had refused to sell. Between the cabin and the Lindstrom home lay woods full of birch and aspen and a few magnificent spruce. The property line ran along a little stream—all dirt and rock now in the long, dry summer—called Blueberry Creek. Before Lindstrom bought most of the cove, it had been called Sylvan. Lindstrom had changed the name to Grace Cove, after his wife. LePere didn't know what sylvan meant, and although he liked the word *grace* attached to the beautiful inlet, he hated the ease with which money changed a thing that had been set on maps and in people's thinking for over a hundred years.

The great home, built of yellow pine logs, lay in the long shadows of spruce and birch, and LePere, although he hated to admit it, liked the look of the place, especially on cool mornings when it seemed to rise out of the mist of the cove like something from a dream.

There was no mist on the lake that morning. As with every morning for weeks, the air was already warm. The water was a perfect mirror of the hazy blue sky, and across the real and the reflected ran a black smudge rising up from somewhere far across the lake, beyond Aurora.

When the woman came from the house with her boy, LePere lifted his field glasses to watch. She was dressed for sailing, in a white top, khaki shorts, canvas deck shoes, and a red visor pulled over her long, honey-colored hair. The boy wore a light blue polo shirt, jean cutoffs, and black Converse tennis shoes. A few feet out the back door, the woman stopped, smiled, and said something to the boy. They started racing toward the dock. The boy was awkward, a graceless runner. The woman, LePere could tell, let him win. There were never any other children about. The boy seemed to have no friends. Because of the time the boy's mother spent with him, LePere guessed she understood this, too. Maybe she contributed to it. Sometimes the people you loved were the ones you most betrayed with your weakness, something LePere understood well.

They went to the dock where two boats were tied up—an expensive twenty-eight-foot sloop named *Amazing Grace* and a small dinghy with a sail. They stepped aboard the dinghy. The woman pointed toward the stern and began talking to the boy, giving him a sailing lesson, LePere guessed.

At that moment, LePere heard at his back the creak of the springy boards on his own ancient dock. He lowered the field glasses, but before he could turn, a nylon cord looped around his neck and drew taut.

" 'Round here," the voice growled into his ear, "this is what we do to an Injun who stares at a white woman."

The cord cut off LePere's breathing. He shoved himself up

and back, stumbling against the man who'd grabbed him from behind. LePere tried to twist, feeling the blood gather in his head, pounding in his ears, but the grip that held him was too powerful. He swept his left leg around, hoping to knock his assailant off balance. No good. Lightning flashed across his vision. Then, as suddenly as it had been drawn about him, the rope was loosed. LePere felt himself pushed free.

Wesley Bridger laughed, whooping hard. "Goddamn, Chief, you gotta be careful. Hell, you were so intent on that broad's hooters the U.S. Cavalry could've galloped up behind you and you never would've heard 'em."

LePere rubbed at the raw skin over his throat. "Wha—" His throat felt all kinked up. He forced down a swallow. "What the hell, Wes?"

Bridger picked up the field glasses that had fallen on the dock and peered through them at the dinghy. "You know, Chief, in the SEALs we learned more'n forty ways to kill a man. I could've employed a good three dozen on you just now. Here." He handed the field glasses back.

Wesley Bridger was tall, and although he was lean, every inch of him was taut. He was like a man constructed of steel cable with a thin layer of suntan slapped over it. LePere didn't know how old Bridger was, but there were more than a few gray hairs in his black mustache and he'd made reference once to losing his virginity in high school while he listened to Pablo Cruise. His age didn't matter. There was a part of the man that age, and the wisdom that went with it, would never touch.

Bridger shoved the cord into the back pocket of his Wranglers and watched the woman and the boy step back onto the deck of the sloop. "You know, Chief, the rich are different from you and me. I think it was Scott Fitzgerald said that. He sure knew whereof he spoke. You ever seen her up real close? I always wondered if those hooters were real. But I guess they must be. If she'd laid out the money to pump them hooters up, she'd've laid out the dough to cut back some on that honker of hers. Two amazing hooters and one hell of a honker. What a combination, huh?" He smiled at LePere and a lot of silver flashed among his teeth. "Got any cold beer?"

LePere was watching the woman and the boy again. With

Bridger there and making such a commotion, he kept the field glasses at his side. He needn't have. Neither the woman nor the boy looked his way. "You know I don't keep alcohol here. It's too early to be drinking anyway."

"Fuck you, Mom. How about a Coke?"

"In the fridge."

Bridger turned and headed toward the cabin whistling "Witchy Woman."

LePere sat back down on the canvas chair and brought the field glasses to his eyes again. The woman had a rope in her hand now and was showing the boy how to tie knots. When LePere was a boy, his father had taught him the same knots, probably.

Bridger strode back onto the dock, guzzling a can of Coke. In his other hand, he held a paperback book.

"*Superior Blue,*" he said, holding the book up so that the shiny cover caught fire in the morning sunlight. He nodded toward the woman in the dinghy. "This is the book she wrote. You read it?"

"Yeah. What of it?"

"You'd better be careful, Chief. People are going to think you're stalking her."

LePere didn't answer. Bridger rolled the can of cold Coke across his forehead, which was already beginning to glisten with sweat from the heat.

"Life's full of irony, don't you think, Chief? I mean, here she is, only a few hundred yards away, and she doesn't even know who you are. Hell, she doesn't even know you exist. Doesn't even suspect that you hate her guts."

"I don't hate her," LePere said.

"No?" Bridger shook his head. "You are one strange mother-fucker, Chief." He glanced across the water. "Show's over."

The boy let go the mooring lines. The little engine began to sputter and the woman steered the boat toward the opening of the cove. Once they were on the main body of the lake, LePere knew she would cut the engine and lift the sail. And if there were wind, they would fly. But even the rich couldn't command the wind.

Bridger turned and started off the dock. "Well. You ready for another day at the salt mines?"

*   *   *

Bridger drove, one arm resting in the open window of an old green Econoline van. They were headed toward Aurora, driving along the state highway that edged the southern shoreline of Iron Lake. The trees there were mostly evergreen, and the air carried the sweet bite of pine pitch.

"Hear what happened at Lindstrom's mill?" Bridger called over the wind.

"No."

"Somebody blew the fuck out of it."

"Protest?"

"Got me, Chief. All I know is it woke me up before I was ready to be woke up. I was dreaming about this little bar I used to go to in San Diego—"

"Anybody hurt?"

"Who am I? Walter fucking Cronkite?"

LePere settled back and let the air and the shadows of the trees and the smell of the pine wash over him. Lindstrom. More trouble for an already troubled man. LePere felt no pity.

"So . . . Chief—you give any more thought to what we talked about yesterday?"

"What *you* talked about."

"Whatever. You think about it?" Bridger watched the road.

"No."

"Easy money, Chief."

"It's crazy."

"Every great plan has some element of craziness to it. That's what makes it great."

"You must've been reading that biography of Patton again."

"Great man," Bridger said. "Look, I can tell you've been thinking about it." He leaned near to LePere and whispered like the voice of the devil. "A cool million."

"Only a million? Why not two?"

Bridger straightened up and pounded the steering wheel, grinning. "Hells bells, why not? The risk is the same."

They passed a sign on the road that said CHIPPEWA GRAND CASINO ¾ MILE TO A JACKPOT OF GOOD TIMES AND GOOD FOOD.

"You see, that's the point," LePere said. "You're thinking the way white people think. More, always more. Never happy with what they have."

"Tell me you'll be happy just cleaning toilets the rest of your life."

LePere stared out the window as they turned onto a beautifully paved road that led through a stand of young white pines to the casino. "It's too risky," he finally said. "People could get hurt, Wes. We could go to prison. Besides, we're on the verge of something big already."

"What we're on the verge of is destitution. My luck ain't held at the tables lately. If we have another hefty diving expense, I can't cover it."

"We stay with diving the wreck. We're so damn close to the answers. I know it. And that'll pay off big, sooner or later."

"You got more patience than brains, Chief. But that's okay." Bridger reached out and punched his shoulder gently. "You got time to think about it. The postman always rings twice." He pulled his van into the casino lot and parked it. They stood beside the van a moment before separating.

"We're still on for the dive tomorrow," LePere said.

Bridger smoothed his mustache and considered. "You'd go alone if I said no, wouldn't you?"

"Yeah. I'd go alone."

"Jesus. And you call me crazy. What time?"

"I'll pick you up at five A.M. We can be out on Superior by seven."

Bridger winced. "Make it seven. We'll be on the lake by nine." He saw the unyielding look on LePere's face. "For Christ's sake, Chief, that wreck's been there for a dozen years. It ain't going anywhere."

"Six," LePere countered.

Bridger threw his hands up in surrender. "All right. Six it is."

They headed in opposite directions, Bridger to the gaming floor, where he'd spend most of his day at a blackjack table, and LePere to a door marked EMPLOYEES ONLY. After he'd signed in at the security desk, he went to the locker room and changed into his dark blue jumpsuit. The other custodial staff were already heading out. He joined them, joking with them as they split off toward their own areas. He pulled his cart from a closet on the east end of the casino and headed to his first stop, the men's room on the first floor east wing. He put out the CLOSED FOR CLEANING sign and stepped inside.

A large bald man in shorts and a loud Hawaiian shirt stood at the third urinal, his stance wavering. When LePere stepped in, the man looked up from his business. His hand traveled along with his bloodshot eyes, and a stream of urine splashed over the wall. He watched the yellow flow make its way down the wall and puddle on the floor, then he grinned stupidly at LePere and zipped up. He started toward the door, reaching into his pocket as he came. When he was abreast of LePere, he said, "Sorry 'bout that, Geronimo." He pulled a red five-dollar casino chip from his pocket, tossed it onto LePere's cart, and stumbled out the door.

WHEN CORK FINALLY ARRIVED at Sam's Place, his daughters
already had things well under control.

Sam's Place was an old Quonset hut set on the shore of Iron
Lake, just outside the town limits of Aurora. Long ago, the
structure—a leftover from the Second World War—had been
purchased by Sam Winter Moon. Sam had turned the hut into
a clean little joint where, during spring, summer, and fall,
he'd served burgers and shakes and cones through a small
window. His customers had been mostly boaters who motored
up to the dock Sam built. When Sam Winter Moon was killed
at Burke's Landing, the old Quonset hut had passed, via Sam's
will, into Cork's possession. And when, immediately after
that, Cork's life fell apart, Sam's Place had become his refuge
and his vocation. He'd learned how to flip a pretty mean
burger.

North of Sam's Place, behind a chain-link fence, was the
long brick rectangle where Bearpaw beer had been brewed
since 1938. South, stood a copse of birch and aspen that hid the
ruins of an old foundry. In its day, the foundry had cast the
metal for a good number of the double-bladed ax heads used to
clear the magnificent white pines that had been the glory of
the great North Woods.

Except for the haze from the burn of the forest fires up north
and the black smudge from the fire at Lindstrom's mill, the day
was beautiful. A perfect day for sailing, and already a lot of
boats were on the lake.

Sam's Place was divided into two parts. In the rear half was a kitchen, a small bathroom, and a living area furnished simply with a table and two chairs handmade from birch, a desk with a shelf for books, a couple of lamps, and a bunk. Sam Winter Moon had lived there first, then Cork in the worst part of his life. The front of the Quonset hut contained the freezer, grill, deep fry, ice milk machine, and stacked cartons of food and paper goods. As Cork entered, he saw that it contained all of his children as well.

"Daddy!" Stevie cried. "I'm helping."

"I can see that, buddy. Good for you." He smiled at his daughters. "Thanks, guys."

Jenny said, "No problem, Dad." She was busy with the ice milk machine.

"We're going to need ones," Annie told him, looking up from the register.

His daughters were growing in a way that made him proud. Jenny had recently abandoned purple hair and a fierce desire to pierce her nose. Over the last year, she had worked her way through every volume of *The Diary of Anaïs Nin*. Her sixteenth birthday was less than a month away; she intended, once she'd finished high school, to move to Paris, live on the Left Bank, and write great works of literature.

Annie, eighteen months younger, redheaded, and freckled, was the star pitcher on her softball team. For as long as she'd had the ability to conceive a future for herself, she'd wanted to be a nun.

"What was all the excitement this morning?" Jenny asked.

"Some trouble at the Lindstrom mill."

"What kind of trouble?" Stevie asked. He'd opened a small package of Fritos and was munching.

"Well." Cork hesitated, but he knew they'd all hear soon enough. "There was an explosion and a fire. Someone was killed."

"Who?" Annie asked.

"We don't know."

"We? You mean *they*, don't know. Sheriff Schanno and his men." Jenny looked at him in the same way her mother did whenever she caught Cork in a slip of the tongue.

"Right," Cork said. "That's what I meant."

Stevie appeared troubled, his small face intense and focused as his mind worked. "He got blowed up?"

"They're not sure, buddy. He might have died in the fire."

"He got burned up?"

Cork felt his stomach turn as he watched his son work on that one in his small head. "Tell you what," he threw in quickly. "Let's you and me go to the bank and get some small bills so we can do business today."

Stevie brightened. "Will I get a Tootsie Pop?"

"If they don't give you one, we'll change banks. How's that?" He hefted his son onto his shoulders. "Hold down the fort, you two."

"We're on it, Dad," Annie said.

When Cork returned almost half an hour later, a beaten-up Econoline van stood parked in the graveled lot of Sam's Place. The van was a dull green and wore a thick coating of dust. Painted on the side, barely visible now beneath the grit, was a huge white pine. Scripted in red letters under the pine were the words SAVE THEM AND WE SAVE OURSELVES. The van carried California plates.

A young man lounged against the counter at the serving window. He appeared to be in his early twenties; he had curly blond hair, wire-rimmed glasses, a light green T-shirt with the sleeves rolled high up on his biceps, cutoff jeans, and hiking boots. He laughed as he spoke with Jenny. Near the picnic table on the grass that edged the shoreline of Iron Lake, a woman about Cork's age leaned on a carved wooden cane and stared across the glimmering blue water. When she turned and walked to the picnic table, her gait was slow and appeared to cause her a good deal of pain. She relied heavily on the cane.

The young man slid money to Jenny and received in return a white sack and two shakes. Cork, as he headed toward the door, heard the final exchange between the two of them, French words he didn't understand. The young man took the sack and shakes and joined the woman at the picnic table. They talked quietly, then opened the sack and began to eat.

"Dad," Jenny called to Cork as he came in. "That guy. He studied in Paris, at the Sorbonne."

"He *says* he studied at the Sorbonne," Annie pointed out. "Sister Amelia warned me that men will say whatever they think you want to hear."

Jenny fisted her hands on her hips. "Yeah? And what would that dried-up old cow know about men? The nearest she ever came to being with a guy was that Halloween Stuart Rubin got drunk and put on a Richard Nixon mask and trick-or-treated at her door stark naked. You know what she said to him?"

"Everybody knows what she's *supposed* to have said."

"What?" Stevie asked.

Jenny smiled down at her brother. " 'Thank you, Lord.' "

Stevie's right cheek bulged around his Tootsie Pop. "Huh?"

"Never mind," Cork said to him. "Why don't you help your sisters get some more cups out and ready to go. I'll be in the back with the books," he told the girls.

Cork sat at the desk in the back part of Sam's Place and pulled out the ledgers he used to track the finances of his business. So far, in terms of profits, the summer had been stellar. The heat drove people early to the lake, and when they got hot on the water, they often headed toward the little stretch of shoreline at Sam's Place where the big red pine shaded the picnic table. Cork paid his daughters a good wage, and not just because he loved having them around. They were excellent help. Annie possessed such a sense of responsibility that God, on the seventh day, could easily have turned his new creation over to her and napped without a worry. Jenny had a mystique and a skill with people that kept them talking with her through the serving window long after they'd been given their order. Studying the numbers in his ledgers and listening to the laughter of his children in the other room, Cork was fairly certain that—even full of smoke and fire—this summer would be the best since he'd taken over Sam's Place.

A knock at the door of the Quonset hut pulled him from the desk. He found Celia Lane and Al Koenig standing on his doorstep.

"Morning, Cork." Celia smiled brightly. She was a small, energetic woman dressed in gray. She chaired the committee for Tamarack County's Democratic-Farmer-Labor Party. Al Koenig, a big pot-bellied man who managed the Perkins restaurant on Center Street, was her cochair. "May we come in?"

Cork stood aside.

Celia, who'd never visited Cork at Sam's Place before, glanced around. "Austere," she commented. "I'm sure you're glad to be back with your family."

Cork waited, wordless. People in politics loved to talk. You never had to wait long. But it might be a long time before they came to a point. And Celia, once she began, talked in a line no straighter than a sloppy drunk could have walked. Cork hadn't asked them to sit. They didn't seem to notice, or if they did, didn't seem to care. After a couple of minutes, Cork broke in.

"What is it you want?"

Celia and Al exchanged a cautious look. Al said, "We want you to run for sheriff come November."

Cork offered them no reply.

Celia jumped in. "You had to have heard. About Wally Schanno, I mean. He's not standing for reelection."

"You know that for a fact?"

"On good authority," Celia said. "From what we gather, the Republicans are going to run Arne Soderberg."

"Soderberg?" Cork let his concern show.

"Exactly," Al said.

Celia began again, a convoluted line of words, talking party, talking politics, aspects of the job as sheriff Cork had never much cared for. He'd been a law enforcement officer first and foremost, and although he'd been a Democrat all his life, the Democratic-Farmer-Labor Party had simply been the way to the job. That way had always been a little like stumbling through a minefield. He wasn't fond of Celia or Al or most of the men and women who became absorbed in politics in the county. He didn't feel badly about not liking them. After the killings at Burke's Landing, not one of them had stood by him during the recall that opened the door for Wally Schanno to take his job.

As Celia went on and on, Cork became aware of the sound of voices raised outside Sam's Place. Annie stuck her head in the room. "Dad, you'd better get out there."

Cork moved quickly out the door and around to the front of the Quonset hut. He paused a moment to take in what he saw.

A shiny black Ford F10 pickup had pulled into the lot and parked beside the green van. The faces of two children poked out the driver's-side window of the truck. Their eyes were big and scared. Their father, Erskine Ellroy, had the young man who'd spoken French to Jenny pinned up against the front wall of Sam's Place. Since he was eighteen, Ellroy had been a logger. With his huge upper body and biceps, he could have arm-wrestled a grizzly. He had a thick black beard and as angry a face as Cork had ever seen on a man. He had the kid by his T-shirt and he'd nearly lifted him off his feet. The kid offered him no resistance.

"You little son of a bitch." Ellroy's face was shoved so near, the long black hairs of his beard brushed the kid's downy chin. "You come here where you don't belong, where you don't understand a thing about what's going on, and all you do is screw with people's lives. What do you care, right?"

"I care about the trees, man." The kid's voice came out weakened from the press of Ellroy's massive body against his chest.

"Fuck the trees."

"You are," the kid managed bravely.

Cork glanced at the woman who stood near the picnic table leaning on her cane. She watched with great interest and although the kid seemed in real trouble, she appeared not at all inclined to interfere.

Ellroy threw the kid to the ground. "Get up."

Looking up at that great angry body towering above him, the kid was clearly afraid. Hell, Cork would have been afraid. But the kid stood up anyway.

"Question for you, nature boy. How're you going to save the trees from a hospital bed?" Ellroy made a fist and cocked his right arm. The kid made no move to avoid what was coming.

"Erskine."

"Stay out of this, O'Connor."

"Question for you, Erskine. How're you going to feed your kids from jail?"

"One, O'Connor. Just one good one." His fist was back but still in a holding pattern.

Cork stepped out of the shadow of Sam's Place into the sunlight. He slowly approached Ellroy and the kid. "Criminal assault, Erskine. Witnesses. Open-and-shut case. You'll go down, I guarantee it."

"The hell with you, O'Connor. You're not the sheriff anymore."

"I don't have to be to know you're making a big mistake, one you'll regret. This tree business'll be over soon. You'll be logging again, making regular payments on your mortgage. But you lay into that man and you'll be in jail a long time after the rest of this is done. Think about it. Think about your kids there." Cork nodded toward the black pickup and waited until Erskine had looked where his children watched, frightened. "Hitting this man won't end the tree business, but it could take you away from your kids a long time. Is it worth that?"

Ellroy hesitated. A hot breath shot from his lips. He shoved the air in front of him as if pushing the whole business away. "Fuck it."

"If you came for food, Erskine, go ahead. It's on me."

"Screw you and your food." Ellroy stomped back to his vehicle. The tires of his pickup spit a lot of gravel, and a thick plume of dust followed him as he sped over the tracks into town.

The kid turned to Cork, pissed. "I didn't need your help. I could've handled him."

"I didn't do it for you." Cork looked toward the woman with the cane who seemed only to be waiting. "I'd be obliged if the both of you would take your food and eat somewhere else. You're not exactly helping my business here."

"We're finished anyway." The kid said it coldly. He moved to the picnic table, took the half-eaten meal, and threw it in the trash barrel. He escorted the woman with the cane to the van, got in, offered Cork a last hard look, and moved the van out.

Celia Lane and Al Koenig flanked Cork on either side.

"You're a natural, Cork," Al said.

"People would vote you back in a minute," Celia added. "Think about it. That's all we're asking. Just think about it."

They slid into their car and followed where the others had gone, down the short gravel road that led into town, kicking up more dust in their passage. Cork felt a tug at his leg and looked down. Stevie held on to him, looking scared. Usually, he was a boy full of questions. Now he was silent. Cork knelt and held him.

Jenny and Annie came from Sam's Place. They were quiet, too, watching where everyone had gone.

43

Jenny cautiously put a hand on his shoulder. "Are you going to run for sheriff again, Dad?"

"I don't know," he answered. "I honestly haven't given it any thought."

Until now.

He watched as the dust slowly settled on the road.

The bastards.

6

Isaiah Broom worried Jo O'Connor. Long before she'd ever visited the Iron Lake Reservation, she had seen him, many times in many places. Not Broom exactly, but men just like him. Angry deep down, and with the slow-fuse potential for real destruction.

Broom sat halfway down the long table in the conference room of the Alouette Community Center that housed the tribal council offices. Broom was an elected representative on the council. With him at the table were the other elected members: George LeDuc, chairman; Judy Bruneau, secretary; Albert Boshey, treasurer; and representatives Roy "One Swallow" Stillday, Edgar Gillespie, and Heidi Baudette. Thomas Whitefeather, one of the two hereditary chiefs of the Iron Lake Band of Ojibwe, was also there, in an advisory capacity. The only man not present was Charlie Warren, the other hereditary chief and a man who, like Whitefeather, commanded great respect on the reservation. The council members spoke with much feeling about the incident at Lindstrom's and the potential of its impact on the situation with Our Grandfathers. Although no one was sympathetic to Lindstrom, they were aware of the damage the violence could do to their own position in the controversy. Jo noted to herself that Isaiah Broom was uncharacteristically silent.

Near the end of the discussion that, in typical Ojibwe fashion, had gone on for hours, George LeDuc summed up the proposed position of the Iron Lake Ojibwe.

"We will issue a statement." He looked toward Jo, who, they all understood, would draft the wording. "We will say that we are not responsible for this violence. In no way do we condone it. We are, and always have been, committed to a solution based on the law. This Eco-Warrior doesn't act for the Iron Lake Anishinaabeg." His dark eyes moved around the table and were met with nods of approval. Until they fell on Isaiah Broom.

"Bullshit," Broom said.

George LeDuc crossed his big arms. "You could've said that real easy before, Isaiah. Instead, this whole time you sat there all wood eyed like some kind of decoy duck."

"Wouldn't have done any good to talk, George," Broom said. "You knew the outcome before you called us here. We all did." He stood up, all six feet four inches and two hundred sixty pounds of him. Although he was a logger, one of many independent Ojibwe contractors, he was a man deeply committed to observing and preserving Anishinaabe traditions. He'd run against George LeDuc for the position of council chairman, but his passionate—some said militant—rhetoric on many of the issues had ultimately worked against him. He was not yet forty, but his broad face was lined in such a way that he looked much older. He wore a black ball cap over long black hair that was pulled back in a braid. He had on a black T-shirt with HONOR TREATY RIGHTS printed in white across the chest. "What you're all worried about but ashamed to admit is the casino," he charged. "You're worried about pissing off the white people who might decide not to come and throw away their money."

"We're businesspeople, Isaiah," LeDuc reminded him. "We've got to consider the impact of all this on the casino business. But that's not our only concern, and you know it."

"You want to know what that casino is?" Broom took a moment for his eyes to encounter every face in the room. "A blanket with smallpox."

He shoved his chair back and slowly walked the length of the room. Through the long windows, a playground was visible. Half a dozen children were playing in the morning sunlight.

"That casino kills us," Isaiah Broom went on. "It makes us weak and afraid to fight like warriors for the things sacred to us. There is a warrior out there right now and he is doing what we should be doing. We should embrace him. We should honor him. But here we are, ready to condemn him. Once, we were a people not afraid to fight with our bodies. For too long now we have fought only with words. We've crouched like cowards behind the false shield of laws we didn't make but must obey." He leveled an unkind gaze on Jo. "We have become just like the enemy."

"There's no enemy here," Heidi Baudette said, "except foolish action."

"Foolish? To act like a warrior is foolish?"

George LeDuc responded, "To call up the ghost of a time none of us remember and can't bring back anyway is about as useful as offering us all an empty quiver, Isaiah. Things change. The People have changed. We're still warriors in the sacred fight to protect Grandmother Earth, but we fight as modern Shinnobs with the weapons Kitchimanidoo has given us—our brains, our determination, and our friendship with those who understand and use the law on our behalf."

"The law," Broom said coldly. "The white man's law is like the Windigo. You all know the Windigo. A cannibal with a heart of ice that feeds on the Anishinaabe people. And you remember how to kill the Windigo? A man must become a Windigo, too. If it is one of the People who did this thing at Lindstrom's, then I am proud, because it means we have a Windigo on our side."

Thomas Whitefeather shook his head. His face was dark and wrinkled as a dry tobacco leaf. In his early years, he'd been a trapper; later, he'd been a photographer who'd chronicled Ojibwe life until arthritis crippled him so badly he could barely walk. "Sometimes, Isaiah, you remind me of a cicada. A very big sound from a very small thing." With a gnarled finger, he tapped his forehead.

Broom saw that others in the room were smiling at the old man's remark. He looked as if he were about to snap at Whitefeather, but respect restrained him. He returned to his chair and sat erect and silent as the council voted to issue a statement disassociating the Iron Lake Ojibwe from the action at Lindstrom's. Although Broom's was the only vote against, Jo could tell by the looks on the faces of some of the council members that they believed there was a good deal of truth in the words Broom had spoken. Broom held back as the other council members left. He looked across the table at Jo.

"You know the law, but you don't understand war," he told her.

"What I understand about war," Jo said, "is that usually a lot of innocent people end up hurt. I don't think anyone wants this to become a war, Isaiah."

"This is already a war. The innocent are already dying. The problem is that you close your eyes to the reality. Trees are slaughtered every day. The water is poisoned. Our food kills us. And instead of fighting back like warriors, we cringe behind laws you claim will protect us."

"The law does protect." But even as she said it, she knew the truth was not that easy. The law often failed those who needed it most. In the history of the Ojibwe Anishinaabe people, the law had more often been their enemy than it had been their friend.

Broom threw his hands up as if he were arguing with a child. He rose and headed toward the door, where George LeDuc stood watching. As he passed LeDuc, Broom said, "The council doesn't speak for all the Shinnobs on the rez. If Charlie Warren had been here, his voice would have been loud, and the others, they would have listened. He's a man who understands what it is to be Anishinaabe, understands our sacred duty to Grandmother Earth."

"Charlie Warren wasn't here," George LeDuc pointed out. "But it wouldn't have mattered anyway. We would have listened to him with great respect, and we would have done what we did, because it was the right thing."

"One way or another," Broom declared, "Our Grandfathers will be protected."

"Isaiah," Jo called to him.

He turned back.

"Be careful who you say that to. Advice from someone who knows the law."

He only stared at her, and she knew that to Isaiah Broom her counsel was useless.

By late afternoon, Jo and George LeDuc had agreed on the wording of the statement, which LeDuc issued to the press on behalf of the Iron Lake Ojibwe. The sun in the western sky was copper colored as Jo headed home, and everything around her was cast in a hard copper hue. She switched on the radio and listened to the five-o'clock news. Forest fires burned out of control. The blaze near Saganaga Lake was worsening. Firefighters from as far away as Montana and Maine were prepared to fly in to help if requested. Jo had never seen a summer like this. She wondered if anyone had.

The house felt empty when she stepped inside. The window air conditioners were on, and the cool of the living room was a relief. She set her briefcase beside the door.

"Hello!" she called. "Anybody home? Rose?"

"In here!"

Jo headed to the kitchen.

Rose stood at the sink washing fruit. She wore white shorts and a sleeveless white blouse. Her feet were bare. A glass of iced tea sat on the counter beside her, dewy drops trickling down the sides.

"Too hot to cook, so I'm just going to fix up a big fruit salad for dinner." When she saw Jo, she stopped preparing the fruit and wiped her hands on a dishtowel. "You look absolutely beat. How about some iced tea?"

"Milk and cookies is what I need."

"Sit down. I'll get it."

Rose pulled a couple of her homemade cookies from a cookie jar shaped like *Sesame Street*'s Ernie. She took out a half gallon of Meadowgold from the refrigerator and poured milk into a blue plastic glass. She brought them to the kitchen table and sat down with Jo. "Talk to me," she said.

Jo knew that on the outside, it probably appeared to folks in Aurora that Rose had given up her life for others—first for their mother during the seven years between the stroke that left her paralyzed on her left side and the stroke that killed her, and then for Jo and Cork and the children. Sometimes Jo felt guilty because the presence of Rose in the house made her own professional life so much easier. But in truth, she'd never felt any bitterness from her sister, never any regret. Rose seemed to be the robust embodiment of an enviable and endearing goodwill, a personal grace that was certainly deepened by her spirituality but had, in fact, always been there.

Rose never seemed empty, never unable to give. To the church, to the community, to Jenny and Annie and Stevie, whom she hadn't birthed but had certainly nurtured. With the children, Rose had a special bond. Often Jo came into a room—usually the kitchen—and found her sister in quiet conference with one of them. The talk ceased the moment Jo entered, and she understood that Rose was a confidant to the children in a way that she, as their parent, could never be. And Jo knew there was no one Cork admired more than Rose.

She ate her cookies and sipped her milk and told Rose everything—the bombing, the body, the council meeting. Finally she confessed to Rose her concern that Cork might consider running for sheriff again.

"What are you afraid of?" Rose asked. "Really?"

Jo stared at the crumbs on her plate. "I like things the way they are right now. I don't want anything to change. We seem to be heading toward happiness again."

Rose waited, her wide, freckled face full of calm.

"I feel like we're all still wounded," Jo stumbled on. "I think we need more time to heal."

"Does Cork know how you feel?"

Jo got up and carried her glass to the sink.

"You haven't told him," Rose surmised.

"It's not that easy."

They heard the front door open and the sound of Stevie's laughter. A moment later Cork and Stevie came into the kitchen, Stevie holding up proudly a string full of sunnies.

"Look what I caught."

"Wonderful," Rose said. "Where are you going with them?"

"To clean them," Stevie replied.

"Not in my kitchen. Downstairs to the basement. You can use the laundry sink."

"Come on, buddy." Cork opened the basement door and followed Stevie down.

Rose smiled after them, then turned to her sister. "This family means too much to him. He wouldn't do anything that would jeopardize it. Just talk to him." Rose returned to washing the fruit.

Jo headed upstairs to change her clothes. In a few minutes,

Cork stepped in. She could smell the fish on him all the way across the room.

"How'd it go on the rez?" he asked. He pulled off his shirt and tossed it into a wicker hamper near the closet.

Jo sat on the bed and bent down to buckle her sandals. "We put together a statement denying any connection with the Army of the Earth or any knowledge about Eco-Warrior. We criticized the action. And we did our best to distance the Iron Lake Ojibwe from any threat of violence over Our Grandfathers."

"How'd Charlie Warren take that?"

"He wasn't there. But Isaiah Broom had a huge problem with it."

"That's because he probably is this Eco-Warrior."

"Don't joke."

"Who's joking?" Cork dropped his jeans and reached into the dresser for some shorts.

"You wouldn't be saying that if you were sheriff."

"No?"

Jo stood up. "You'd be reserving judgment until you had more facts. Even then you'd say it was up to the court to decide guilt or innocence."

"But I'm not the sheriff anymore." He grabbed a red T-shirt and tugged it on.

They were at the edge of a subject they never talked about—the events that surrounded Cork's fall from grace in Aurora. To talk would risk opening old wounds, discussing events that had hurt them terribly, that had nearly torn them apart. Although Jo felt all these things constantly between them, dark and restless, she was afraid that to look at the past straight-on might be deadly to her marriage. Cork had never seemed eager to talk either, and Jo believed his own silence on the subject of their past indiscretions meant a mutual—though unspoken—agreement not to dwell on hurtful history.

"I'm going to go down and give Rose a hand with dinner," she said. When she reached the bottom of the stairs, Annie came in the front door. "Where's Jenny?" Jo asked.

"Sean showed up at Sam's Place. He said he'd help her close and then bring her home."

Sean was Jenny's boyfriend. Jo knew Cork had a grudging

liking for the boy and didn't mind his dropping by to give Jenny a hand.

"Mom," Annie asked, "did Dad tell you?"

"Tell me what?"

"We almost had a fight at Sam's Place today. Dad broke it up, and some people there asked Dad to run for sheriff."

"People?"

"Yeah, like party bigwigs or something."

"They want your father to run for sheriff?"

"Yeah. Pretty cool, huh? Where's Aunt Rose?"

"In the kitchen."

Annie made a beeline in that direction.

Jo was waiting at the bottom of the stairs when Cork came down. "Could we talk? In my office?"

Although Jo practiced out of an office in the Aurora Professional Building, she maintained a casual office at home as well. Cork followed down the hallway and looked at her with apprehension when she closed the door behind them.

"Annie told me there was some trouble at Sam's Place," she said.

Cork sat on the edge of her desk. "Nothing I couldn't handle."

"She also said some people talked to you about running for sheriff."

"Yes."

"When were you going to tell me?"

"After I'd thought about it some."

"This morning, you promised me we'd think through something like this together." She could feel the anger rising, her voice growing taut. She didn't want to be that way, but she couldn't seem to stop herself.

Cork's response was edged with anger, too. "I told you we'd talk before I decided anything, and I haven't decided anything."

"Cork—" she began, but before she could finish the phone rang. They both looked at it. It stopped immediately, which meant someone else in the house had answered.

She moved away from the door, her eyes scanning the shelves of law books that lined the walls. No answer there, she knew. She wanted to walk toward Cork, to put herself nearer to him, but there was something unyielding inside her that kept her from it.

"I just . . ." She faltered, tried again. "I'm just afraid—"

A knock at the door interrupted her. "Mom." It was Annie, speaking from the other side. "The phone's for you."

"Can you take a message?" Jo called back.

"It's Sheriff Schanno. It sounds important."

"I'll take it in here, honey."

Jo headed to the desk. Cork moved himself out of the way.

"Yes, Wally?" She listened a moment. "You're sure?" A moment more. She closed her eyes. "I understand. And thanks." She hung up.

"What is it?" Cork asked.

"They've positively identified the body at Lindstrom's."

"Who is it?"

Jo took a deep breath. "Charlie Warren."

7

During summer in the north country, the sun seemed to linger forever. The light near dusk was like one final exhalation that breathed gold onto the pines and tamaracks, the birch and aspen, and everything seemed to hold very still as the sun let out its long last breath. Cork loved summer evenings in Tamarack County, loved those moments when the earth itself seemed to pause in its turning. Yet, as he drove to the Lindstrom mill and saw the light on the trees and heard the hush of the woods, inside he felt none of the serenity these things normally brought to him.

Jo hadn't wanted him to come, but he'd made her understand there was no way she could keep him from it. She hadn't said a word the whole way. Outside the gates of the mill, a few protestors still lingered. They sat comfortably on canvas chairs and talked, their protest signs lying in the long rye grass beside them. Cork recognized the kid who'd been at Sam's Place and the woman with the cane who'd accompanied him. Isaiah Broom was there, too. They stopped their talk as Cork drove by, and they eyed him as if he were the enemy.

Gil Singer, the deputy at the gate, let them through easily. As he had earlier that day, Cork parked beside the Land Cruiser Wally Schanno drove. There were a few other vehicles, mostly county sheriff's cars. The mill seemed pretty much deserted. Schanno stood near the burned-out cab of the logging rig. He was leaning a bit, and he reminded Cork of a stiff old tree in a hard wind. As Cork approached with Jo, he saw that, in fact, Schanno was bent to listen. From beneath the blackened chassis, two legs protruded.

Cork started toward the rig, but a voice behind him called him back.

"Can't go there, O'Connor." Karl Lindstrom was wearing the same clothes he'd worn that morning. He looked beat. His eyes were deep-sunk in their sockets. His stiff, military bearing had wilted visibly. "Nobody goes beyond this point except the police."

Schanno looked up and, seeing the small gathering, came over. "Cork, Jo."

"Long day, Wally," Cork said.

"Yeah." Schanno looked over the burned area in back of him. "Had my men out here most of it, and Alf Murray's volunteers, doing a quadrant search."

"Did you find anything?" Jo asked.

"Lots of pieces of things."

"No other explosive devices?"

"No."

"Thank God for that," Lindstrom said. "But I've still got to shut the mill down for a couple of days at least until they've finished with the investigation and we can get this mess cleaned up."

Cork turned back toward Schanno. "Quick ID on the body, Wally."

Schanno poked a thumb north. "Found Charlie's truck parked in the woods half a mile that way. I had the medical examiner compare his dental records with the victim's teeth."

"Do you have any idea why Charlie Warren would have been here, Mr. Lindstrom?" Jo asked.

"You mean besides blowing up my mill?"

"I wouldn't make accusations at this point," Jo cautioned. "You didn't know Charlie Warren."

"Right." Lindstrom gave her a sour look. "The only time I ever spoke with him, he told me basically I was about to stick my financial dick into Grandmother Earth, and if I did, he would see to it that it got cut off."

"Charlie Warren was outspoken," Jo said, "but he wasn't a violent man."

"Then you tell me what he was doing out here, Ms. O'Connor."

Cork asked Schanno, "Did you talk with the night watchman?"

"At length," Schanno replied. "He makes his rounds every hour. Carries a key that has to be turned in alarm boxes at various locations. He was about halfway through, on the far side of the mill, when the blast occurred."

Lindstrom said, "Harold Loomis's job is to prevent vandalism and major theft. This is a big mill. It wouldn't be hard for one man to climb the fence and hide himself."

"Did you check the perimeter of the fence?" Cork asked.

Schanno nodded. "Nothing conclusive. Ground's too hard for prints."

Jo asked, "Has the medical examiner determined the cause of death?"

"Asphyxiation. Then he burned."

"Trapped in the explosion," Cork guessed.

Schanno gestured vaguely in the direction of the debris. "When that LP tank went, it demolished the shed instantly. Whatever he was doing inside, Charlie was caught."

"For Christ's sake, he was watching the truck where he'd planted his damn bomb," Lindstrom said.

Cork gave him a hard stare. "I know it looks pretty bad, but anybody who knew Charlie Warren wouldn't believe for an instant he'd do something like this."

Jo changed the subject. "Have you told Charlie's daughter, Wally?"

"I sent Marsha Dross out before I called you."

"That brings up an interesting question, Sheriff," Lindstrom said. "Why did you call Ms. O'Connor?"

"Jo's the attorney for the Iron Lake Ojibwe," Schanno answered with an obvious effort at patience. "I also called George LeDuc. I believed these people had a right to know this particular development."

"Okay." Lindstrom seemed to accept it, although not happily. "Then what about him?" He jabbed a finger at Cork. "What's he doing here? Unless you're allowing him privileges in some ex officio capacity, he's got no business here."

Schanno didn't seem to have an answer for that one. He said,

"Look, Karl, it's been a long day for you. I suggest you head on home and get some rest."

"I've got a cot in my office. I have no intention of leaving here tonight."

Schanno looked at Cork and Jo. "Maybe it's time you left."

For the moment, Cork ignored him and watched the legs under the burned chassis grow into the whole body of a man who stood up and came toward them. He was a lanky fellow with an affable smile and a dark, receding hairline. He wore a short-sleeved denim shirt and jeans, both smudged heavily by soot.

"Cork, Jo," Schanno said, "this is Agent Mark Owen. He's an expert on arson and explosives. Agent Owen, Cork and Jo O'Connor."

"FBI?" Cork asked.

"BCA," Agent Owen replied.

Cork glanced around. "I thought you guys were going to bring up your mobile crime lab."

Owen pulled a rag from his back pocket and wiped his dirty palm before offering his hand in greeting, first to Jo, then to Cork. "Multiple homicide in Goodhue County last night. The last twenty-four hours in this state have been a bitch."

Cork's attention was grabbed by a man walking toward them from the shed where several deputies were still carefully sifting the blackened debris. Cork put him at just over sixty; he was of medium height and build and had gray hair. He wore a gray suit and tie, a neat figure amid all the chaos of the mill yard. He moved with the air of a man in no particular hurry.

"This is Agent David Earl," Schanno said, when the man had reached them. "Agent Earl, Jo and Cork O'Connor."

They shook hands.

"Are you BCA, too?" Cork asked.

"That's right." He took a pack of Marlboros from the pocket of his suit coat and tapped out a cigarette that he lit with a silver lighter. He blew a flourish of smoke and considered Cork. "O'Connor. I knew a sheriff up here, must be nearly forty years ago. His name was O'Connor, too."

"My father."

"A good man, as I recall. You in law enforcement?"

"He used to have my job," Schanno said.

Earl smiled and shrugged as if to say, *Politics.* "What do you do now?"

"I—uh—I run a hamburger stand."

"And you're here because?" He looked to Schanno for an answer.

"Chauffeur," Cork replied quickly. "For my wife. She represents the Iron Lake Ojibwe."

Earl shifted his gaze to Jo. "It must be the Warren fellow brings you here. Tragic business."

"Do you have any idea how the explosion happened?" Jo asked.

"Some. Sheriff?"

"Go ahead," Schanno said. "The whole county'll know soon enough anyway."

With the hand that held his cigarette, Earl gestured, giving his partner Owen the floor.

Owen finished wiping the soot from his hands, then stuffed the rag in the back pocket of his jeans. "We're still gathering evidence, of course, but I'll tell you what I suspect. It was a low-order explosive, smokeless powder, probably, encased in a steel pipe. The igniter was simple. A timer, probably a cheap clock, connected to a battery—my guess would be a nine-volt cell—wired to a camera flashbulb with the protective glass removed. The clock hits the right time, completes the circuit, battery fires up the flashbulb, the heat from the filament wire ignites the powder, and *boom.*" As he'd warmed to his subject, one he was obviously passionate about, his hands had begun to create pictures in the air to illustrate his words. "Now, normally a bomb of this kind would produce mostly fragmentation. But this bomb had something special. I think the pipe was coated with a chemical, a flammable gelatin or maybe even model airplane glue, which is quite flammable. The chemical ignited in the explosion so that the fragments, as they dispersed, were burning. At least one of these burning fragments sheared a valve on the LP tank, ignited the escaping gas, and that's when the really destructive explosion occurred."

"Don't let Mark fool you," Earl said with a slight smile. He tapped the ash from his cigarette. "He's not as smart as he seems. Same MO's been used in several other bombings recently in Vermont, Washington State, and California. Heavy equipment was the target in those incidents, as well."

"You're not saying it's the same person?" Lindstrom said.

"Not necessarily," Owen replied. "The device is simple enough, really, that a high school student with access to the materials and the Internet could have made it."

"There's someplace on the Internet that explains how to build bombs?" Jo asked.

"Unfortunately, yes," Owen replied. "The Army of the Earth that the caller this morning mentioned. It's the most militant of the environmental groups. It maintains a Web site with exactly the kind of information necessary to construct the device I've described."

"Great," Cork said. "It could be anyone from sixteen to sixty."

Earl dropped his cigarette to the ground and used the toe of his shoe to put out the ember. He took in the destruction of the shed and mill yard. "I really hate the Internet."

"The gelatin or airplane glue or whatever is a new addition," Owen went on. "It's got to make you wonder if part of the purpose here might have been to start some fires. This is, after all, a lumber mill. A lot could be destroyed. Still, I don't think the device was meant to hurt anybody."

"Why?" Jo asked.

"Look at the timing."

"You mean detonation when Harold Loomis was farthest from the blast," Jo said in clarification.

"Technically speaking, it wasn't a detonation," Owen said. "It was a deflagration. A slower form of explosion."

"By a whole thousandth of a second," Earl said. "Mark loves to show off."

Owen smiled boyishly. "Just keeping the record straight, Dave. I wish we'd been able to question Mr. Loomis immediately. It would have been best to test his hands and clothing for residue."

"You don't suspect Loomis of doing this?!" Lindstrom seemed on the edge of outrage.

In a reasonable tone, Earl said, "It would have been good to be able to eliminate him completely as a suspect, that's all."

"Does that mean you don't think Charlie Warren was responsible for this?" Jo asked.

Schanno answered, "It means we don't really know what happened, and we've got to consider all the possibilities."

"Not Harold Loomis," Lindstrom insisted.

"Look, Karl," Schanno said, "even taking into account his age, Loomis seems to have observed very little and remembered even less."

Lindstrom looked as if he'd hit some kind of wall. "I don't get it. I'm threatened. My mill is attacked. Outside that gate are a lot of people who aren't sorry in the least that this has happened. But here you are, questioning my employees. Christ, is this the way justice works in Minnesota now?" He didn't wait for an answer but turned and stomped across the yard toward the mill offices.

"We should be going," Jo said. "Wally, I appreciate the call."

"We've all got to live together here, Jo," Schanno replied.

It was nearing dark when they left. The protestors had called it a day. The road in front the mill was empty. Cork and Jo were quiet for much of the drive into Aurora. As they neared the first traffic light, Jo asked, "What would Charlie Warren have been doing there?"

"Anyone's guess at this point," Cork replied.

"Karl Lindstrom seems so ready to believe it was Charlie who planted that bomb."

"Given the way things look, if I didn't know Charlie, I'd probably suspect him. Karl doesn't know the Anishinaabe people except as someone on the other side of this logging issue. And he's under a lot of pressure."

The light turned green and Cork drove on. The street lamps were just starting to flicker on. In Knudsen Park, a game of softball was already being played under stadium lights.

"You grant Lindstrom a lot," Jo observed.

"I don't have any reason not to. I don't represent anybody."

Jo watched the softballers and said quietly, "Lindstrom was right about one thing. You shouldn't be involved in this."

"Aurora's a small town. Everyone's involved in this."

"Not the way you are." She looked at him. It was too dark for him to see her face clearly. "You shouldn't have been there tonight. Even Wally Schanno couldn't defend that one."

They were quiet the rest of the way home. Stevie was still up and Cork volunteered to put him to bed. He read for a few minutes—*James and the Giant Peach*—but Stevie was so tired he was asleep after one page. Cork turned on the night-light and turned off the lamp. He stood a while looking out the window. Stevie's breathing was soft and steady at his back. Through the branches of the elm tree in the backyard, a gentle wind blew, the breathing of the night. The dark air smelled of smoke, of the distant fires. Cork left the room. As he headed down the hallway, he heard Jo and the girls talking downstairs. There was a moment of soft laughter. He got himself ready for bed and lay on top of the covers. He thought about that morning, the moment he'd opened his arms to Jo and they were about to make love. It seemed like a long time ago. He felt more tired than one day should have made him. He waited. Jo didn't come up. At last, he fell asleep, so deeply he didn't know if she ever came to bed.

8

LePere had strong, hot coffee in a metal thermos, and he handed the thermos to Wesley Bridger as the man got into the truck.

"You look like hell," LePere said.

Bridger steadied his hands and poured coffee. "I'll be fine. It's this getting up before the goddamn birds."

"It's the whiskey before bed."

"Fuck you, Mom."

Bridger bent to his coffee as LePere kicked his old pickup into gear and took off. Coffee splashed down the front of Bridger's shirt.

"What the hell're you doing?"

LePere smiled at the road ahead that was just beginning to glow with morning sunlight. "Hot shower."

Despite the coffee, Bridger slept most of the way. After an hour, LePere hit Illgen City and turned south onto Minnesota State Highway 61. On his right, the hills that formed the southern tip of the Sawtooth Mountains were bathed in the gold of a beautiful morning light. From the base of the Sawtooths, Lake Superior spread east, dark blue water running unbroken to the horizon where it fused with the softer blue of the sky.

Clear day, LePere thought. *Perfect for the dive.*

Bridger shifted, opened his eyes, blinked at the sun that struck him full in the face.

"Hungry?" LePere asked.

"Toast, maybe. Soak up some of that battery acid you call coffee."

They stopped at a small restaurant in Beaver Bay. LePere ordered two eggs over easy, hash browns, wheat toast, a side of ham, and orange juice. Bridger rubbed his face with his hands and scratched at his grizzled jaw as the waitress, a young woman with patient brown eyes, stood with her pen poised over her order pad.

"Ah, hell," Bridger finally said. "Gimme a stack of cakes, bacon, coupla eggs scrambled. You got home fries here?"

"Yes."

"Gimme some of them, too."

"We're diving," LePere reminded him. "If you eat all that, you won't need weights."

Bridger scowled at him, then at the waitress. "And coffee. Lots of it."

The restaurant was filling up. A few locals, it seemed to LePere, and a lot of tourists. A family—man, woman, boy—stepped in and waited to be seated. They were only a few feet from where LePere and Bridger sat by a window.

"Can we go swimming in the lake?" the boy asked.

"No way, Randy," his father replied. "The water's too cold. It's so cold, in fact, that the bodies of drowned people don't float to the surface. Lake Superior, son, doesn't give up its dead."

"Stuart," his wife admonished.

"Why?" the boy asked.

Ignoring the look from his wife, Stuart replied, "As a body decomposes, gases form inside it that make it float. It fills up like a balloon. But the water here is so cold, bodies don't decompose. They just lie there on the bottom of that big lake—"

"That's enough, Stuart."

"They say," he went on, "that at night when the moon is very bright and the water very still, you can look down and see all the dead dancing along the bottom." He gave his hands a ghostly flutter.

"That's enough." This time it was LePere who spoke.

Stuart stared at him, surprised. A smile tried to come to his lips, hoping the unhappy, powerful-looking man at the table was only joking.

"I was just . . ." he started to explain. He ended simply: "Sorry."

The family stood silently until they were seated. LePere sat looking out the window toward the lake that burned with a silver fire under the morning sun.

When the check came after breakfast, Bridger said, "Mind catching it?"

LePere dug for his wallet. "Luck didn't change, huh?"

"Went down to Black Bear Casino last night. Thought a different location might help. It didn't."

"Maybe if you stopped mixing cards and alcohol," LePere suggested.

"Just buy the damn breakfast, okay? The least you could do. I didn't get out of bed this morning for my own amusement."

LePere dropped a couple of bucks for a tip and paid at the register. As he stepped outside, he saw Stuart watching him from the window. Stuart looked quickly away.

Breakfast had awakened Wesley Bridger. He walked briskly to LePere's truck, then stood shaking his head at the old blue Dodge pickup with its homemade camper shell.

"How long you had this rust bucket?"

"Eleven years now." LePere climbed in.

"Time for a new one," Bridger said, opening the passenger door. "But then, cleaning toilets won't exactly cover monthly payments."

LePere pulled the truck onto the highway and continued south out of Beaver Bay.

Bridger reached for the radio and found a country station. He crossed his arms and settled back. "Those casinos really rake it in. Christ, middle of nowhere and the parking lot's always full, day or night. They must haul in a million bucks a day." He eyed LePere. "And you don't get one red cent?"

"Like I told you before, each casino is operated by a specific band." LePere checked his mirror and passed a slow-moving Buick with an old woman at the wheel. "The Chippewa Grand Casino is operated by the Iron Lake Band of Ojibwe. To get an allotment, you have to be an enrolled member of that band. My mother was a Cree from Canada."

"Even so, you'd think with all that bread there'd be enough to spread it around to every Indian in the state. The hell with that band stuff." Bridger's foot tapped along to Reba McEntire. "You're thinking, I suppose, that at least they gave you a job. Big deal. Cleaning the crap off toilet seats."

"I know where this is leading."

"All I'm saying is that no matter how you look at it, you're owed big time by somebody."

"And that's why you've come up with this new harebrained scheme. Because I'm owed big time."

"No, I came up with it because the very idea of holding a million bucks in my hand makes my dick stiff."

"You used to be sure we'd get a million bucks diving the wreck."

"We will." Bridger settled back and crossed his arms. "We will. But it'll be at the end of long, drawn-out litigation. Way my luck's been lately, I can't wait that long for a bankroll. Like I told you, we got any more heavy expense with this diving, we're shit out of luck."

"Maybe it's time you stopped gambling, Wes."

"It was gambling brought us this far," Bridger reminded him sourly. "Look, I'm just suggesting a different game, that's all."

"What you're suggesting isn't a game. We could go to jail."

"Like your life ain't a fucking prison now."

They approached a long ridge that stretched east, a dark wall rising in front of them. The ridge was crowned with evergreen and aspen, but its sides were bare rock, striated basalt cliffs that, at the eastern terminus, plunged more than two hundred feet, before touching the surface of the lake. It was Purgatory Ridge, the deep ancient lava flow in whose shadow John LePere had been born and raised. The highway cut under the ridge in a long tunnel, lit by bright lights. As LePere drove through, the tires of his old truck seemed to be singing one long note that echoed off the tunnel walls. When the highway broke into sunlight again, LePere immediately slowed the truck and turned onto a narrow lane of dirt and gravel. The lane wound a quarter mile through a thick stand of poplars until it came to a small house on a protected cove named for the ridge that towered above it. Purgatory.

The cove had a beach composed entirely of small stones rounded smooth by waves. LePere's was the only house. The only other artificial structures were a sturdy little fish house and a long dock where a reconditioned 36-foot Grand Banks trawler christened *Anne Marie* was moored. LePere parked the truck near the fish house and got out. He fumbled the key into the padlock on the door.

Bridger got out, too, and stretched. With a nod toward the little house, he asked, "How come you never go in the old place?"

"I go in."

"Just not when I'm with you."

"I don't like things disturbed."

"What is it? Like some kind of shrine?"

"Get your tanks," LePere said, and threw open the fish house door.

In LePere's youth, the fish house had been where his father cleaned the day's catch—ciscos, herring, whitefish—he sold to the markets and smokehouses along the North Shore between Grand Marais and Two Harbors. Jean Charles LePere had come back from World War II and four years in the navy with a love of big, open water. With the money he might otherwise have used for college, he bought the land on Purgatory Cove from an old Norwegian named Bugge. Along with it came the dwelling, the fish house, a leaky fishing boat, and yards and yards of tangled nets. He spent nearly a year repairing the buildings, making the vessel seaworthy, mending the nets. In the winter of the repairs, he met and fell in love with a beautiful young Indian woman named Anne Marie Sebanc who worked as a waitress in a little place in Knife River. During his second year of laying nets, he married her. Although the house was small and rustic, it became their home, and within a year, they had a son. John Sailor LePere.

For a long time, John LePere's life was wonderful. He remembered spending long days collecting agates on the shore of the cove and accompanying his father to the north shore towns where he sold the stones to souvenir shops while his father was selling fish. He remembered picnics atop Purgatory Ridge with the Sawtooth Mountains to the northwest, and to the east Lake Superior stretching flat and blue all the way to the end of the world. He remembered his father pointing out to him from that height where, under the silver surface, the fish ran and where was a good place to set a net. His father had loved fishing and loved the big lake. Yet it had been these very things that had killed him, that had plunged his wife into a dark confusion from which she never fully emerged and that had forced his sons to grow up too quickly and too hard. For much of his life, LePere had struggled to crack the truth at the heart of this mystery. What he'd finally come to accept was that the lake called Kitchigami was so vast and ancient and part of something so huge in its ultimate purpose that one human life—or two or three—mattered not at all. In that way, he'd come to think it was like God, who gave and took and offered not the slightest explanation for either.

Bridger pulled his equipment from the back of the pickup. He brought his tanks into the shed, where LePere filled them, and his own, from a compressor. They loaded everything onto the boat. Bridger loosed the moorings and LePere backed the *Anne Marie* away from the dock. The entrance to the cove was protected on either side by great slabs of igneous rock sliced from Purgatory Ridge by eons of weathering. Even in the harshest storm, the power of the waves was broken before reaching the cove. LePere headed the boat away from the cabin and out onto the great lake, slicing through water deceptively calm, water that had taken from him his father, his mother, his brother, everything that he'd ever loved, water so cold it could punch the heart right out of your chest and so unforgiving it absolutely refused to yield up its dead.

9

Near four a.m. he'd become aware of Jo moving in the room.

"You okay?" he'd asked.

She paused in a slash of moonlight that made her feet glow but left the rest of her in darkness. She took a long time to answer. "Just going for some Tylenol." And she'd slipped out the door.

He'd meant to stay awake, waiting for her return, but the next thing he knew the room was bright with morning light and Jo was still not beside him in their bed. He glanced at the radio alarm: seven-fifteen.

"Have you seen your sister?" he asked Rose, who was in the kitchen in her robe.

Rose yawned and pointed to the refrigerator. "She left a note."

Cork pulled the slip of paper off the refrigerator door.

Couldn't sleep. Gone to the office. Jo

"Did you hear her leave?" he asked.

"No." Rose held a white mug with THE WORLD'S BEST AUNT in red on the side, and she was watching closely the last few drips as the coffeemaker finished its business.

Cork heard the television come on in the living room. He glanced through the kitchen doorway and saw that Stevie was up and settling himself to watch cartoons. Cork stepped to the wall phone and dialed Jo's office number. After four rings, her voice message system kicked in. He hung up.

"Coffee?" Rose sipped from her big mug and already looked more awake.

"Thanks, I'll get it myself."

She watched him a moment, then asked, "Are you okay?"

"Fine," he said.

It was a lie. For he was remembering a time, not that long ago, when Jo had been restless and gone at odd hours and the reason for it was that she'd been in love with another man and had stolen time to slip into his bed. Cork looked out the kitchen window. Jo had left the garage door open. He stared at the empty place where her old Toyota usually sat, gripped his coffee cup tightly, and chided himself. He hadn't been guiltless. He'd been in love with someone else, too, and regularly visited her bed. That was all in the past now. Surely they'd put the hurt and the distrust behind them. Hadn't they?

He sipped his coffee and burned his lip. "Shit."

Rose had opened a cupboard to get some Bisquick. She paused, the box halfway between cupboard and counter. "You seem upset, Cork."

"I told you," he replied, so harshly that he surprised even himself, "everything's fine."

He left the kitchen. In the living room, Stevie sat on the sofa. He had his thumb in his mouth, an old habit that, even at six, still sometimes surfaced when he was very tired or very scared.

"Hey, buddy."

Cork had tried to put some lightness in his tone, but Stevie didn't look up from the television. Cork didn't push it. He headed upstairs to dress for his morning run.

He'd run his first marathon the previous fall in the Twin Cities and his second, the famous Grandma's Marathon in Duluth, the following summer. He'd taken to running at the same time he gave up cigarettes, and he'd done both these things because of a promise he'd made to a woman he'd loved who was not Jo. In those days, he'd lived alone at Sam's Place. During the long months of separation from his family, what he'd wanted most was to bring them all back together somehow. He'd believed—foolishly, he thought now—that once he was back in the house on Gooseberry Lane, they could simply pick up where the good part of their lives had left off. But every day, life changed people, and when it hurt them, especially, it changed them a lot and forever. He and Jo never talked about that part of their past, when he'd loved a waitress and Jo had loved a rich man. Both lovers were dead now, yet it was as if their ghosts remained, haunting the silences that often slipped between Cork and Jo. He longed to talk about these things, but always in the back of his mind was the image of his marriage as a wounded, limping thing. What was the use of touching the old hurts? Wasn't it better simply to let time heal them?

Normally on his morning run, he followed one of the roads that edged Iron Lake. That morning, however, his feet followed a different route, one that took him to the Aurora Professional Building where Jo had her law office. He went in, dripping sweat. Fran Cooper, Jo's secretary, looked up from her desk. Cork had known Fran his whole life. She'd been secretary of his senior class, got pregnant (rumor had it) the night of senior prom, and married Andy Cooper the following summer. They were still married and, from all appearances, still happy. The child that had been born to them was a Valentine's Day baby and was now in her second year of medical school at the University of Minnesota. Fran looked Cork over and smiled.

"I think you took a wrong turn in the home stretch, Cork."

"Looking for Jo," he replied, a little out of breath.

"Not here. She'd already come and gone when I got in this morning. She left a note asking me to reschedule her appointments for today. She's out at the reservation."

"Any idea why?"

"Her note didn't say. But dollars to doughnuts it's got something to do with Charlie Warren." She glanced down where drops of Cork's perspiration were turning the beige carpet gray. "You want some water or something?"

"No thanks."

"I keep telling Jo to get a cell phone, Cork." Fran shrugged as if she'd done her best.

Cork cut across Knudsen Park, heading for the lake. He turned and followed Center Street to the edge of town. He jogged along the Burlington Northern tracks to the access to Sam's Place and headed in to shower.

He kept a change of clothes at the Quonset hut, kept the refrigerator plugged in and defrosted, kept fresh linen for the bunk. He'd done these things without thinking about them, but as he showered that morning and put on clean clothes, he wondered if unconsciously he'd been keeping himself prepared in case things on Gooseberry Lane didn't work out. He was angry when he thought this. He stared at his face in the bathroom mirror.

"What is it you want, O'Connor? Make up your damn mind."

He called home, told Rose to have the girls drive the Bronco out when they came to work. Rose reminded him that she was helping the women's guild at St. Agnes most of the day and wouldn't be able to watch Stevie.

"Have the girls bring him," he said. "Tell him we'll catch another mess of sunnies."

By the time the children arrived, Cork had the grill fired up, the ice milk machine filled, and the oil in the deep fryer hot.

"There's plenty of change in the register," he told them.

"You sound like you're leaving," Jenny said.

"I am. Sorry."

"Don't forget," she cautioned him. "Mom and I are going to the library tonight."

"The library?"

"To hear Grace Fitzgerald read from *Superior Blue*. I won't be able to close."

Annie jumped in. "Me either. I've got softball practice."

"Stevie and I will close up." He ran his hand through his son's hair. "We'll have a guy's night out. What do you say, buddy?"

Stevie shrugged. "Okay. When can I fish?"

Cork looked to his daughters.

"Go on, Dad," Jenny said. "We'll take care of everything here."

"Thanks. Thanks a lot."

Cork drove to the Iron Lake Reservation. He tried not to think. There was only one reason he wanted to go, and he knew if he thought about it too much, he'd have hated himself. Not enough time had passed since the days when Jo had lied to him about the places she was going and who she would be with and what they would do. He'd believed her then. Against all

71

evidence. Now he had to see. He had to see her on the reservation. He hoped she was following up on Charlie Warren. But God help him, he had to know absolutely.

He pulled into Alouette a little before noon and stopped at LeDuc's store. Inside, he found George LeDuc standing beside the magazine rack at the broad front window, staring down the street.

"*Anin,* George," Cork said, using the traditional Anishinaabe greeting.

"*Anin,* Cork." The darkness in LeDuc's face came from more than just the genetic coloring of his skin. "You're the first person to walk through that door today who wasn't a reporter."

"Bad, huh?"

LeDuc shook his head. "I don't have any answers for them, except that Charlie Warren wasn't the kind of man to make bombs."

"What was he doing out there?"

"Got me." LeDuc walked to the counter where the cash register sat, reached into a tall glass jar, and drew out a stick of beef jerky. He offered it to Cork, who waved it off. LeDuc tore off a bit and worked the tough meat around in his mouth. "It was always Charlie Warren's voice advising us to be patient, be reasonable, be strong. This just doesn't make sense."

"Have you talked to your guests?"

Cork was speaking of the scores of tents that had been erected in the new park just north of town. The tribal council had voted to open the site to those who'd come to Aurora to join them in the battle to save Our Grandfathers. They represented a variety of interests and were almost entirely white.

"They didn't know Charlie Warren. When I speak with them, they nod, but I see distrust in their eyes." He swallowed jerky and took a deep breath.

Cork saw something in LeDuc's own dark almond eyes. "You don't trust them, either."

"We fight a different cause, Cork. They want all logging halted. We're just interested in protecting Our Grandfathers. They don't seem to care that if all logging is prohibited, we suffer, too."

Cork knew he was speaking of the mill in Brandywine, the other community on the rez. The mill was operated by the Iron

Lake Ojibwe and was supplied with timber cut by Ojibwe loggers.

"Like always, they have their own agenda. It's not really about helping us Shinnobs." He stepped back to the front window again and stared down the street. "Another thing. They don't often shower."

"George," Cork asked finally, "have you seen Jo?"

"Not today. I called her office and left a message. She out here?"

His stomach gave a little twist. "I thought so."

"Tell her we need to talk. If you see her."

"I'll do that."

Cork walked through Alouette. The distance from one end of town to the other was just over half a mile. A few years earlier, most of the three or four dozen houses and trailers in town were in desperate need of renovation or bulldozing. Now the influence of the casino could be seen in new siding and shingles and paint. Old cars still sat on blocks in the backyards, but there were new vehicles in the drives. And money didn't mean that a man who didn't cut his grass before would cut it now. Still, on the whole, Alouette wore a new look. Within the last two years, a big community center had been built, as well as a clinic run by the People and staffed by a doctor, a physician's assistant, and two nurses, all Ojibwe Anishinaabe. The businesses—LeDuc's store, Medina's Mobile station, and the Makwa Café—were all doing well and looked it.

The heat was oppressive. As much as possible, Cork stayed in the shade of the huge oaks that lined the street. When he didn't see Jo's car at the community center, he simply kept walking, moving numbly. At the northern edge of town, he paused and studied the gathering of tents that filled the new park. Among the old vans and Saabs and the four-by-fours parked in the lot were several vehicles with broadcasting logos across their sides. Cork saw a number of tent people speaking with reporters and posing for photos. The kid who'd nearly been pulverized by Erskine Ellroy was facing the lens of a television camera and pronouncing boldly, "If war is what they want, hell, we'll give it to them."

Cork shook his head. They could use a good lawyer.

As if the thought had conjured her, Jo pulled up in her Toyota and stopped.

"Cork, what are you doing out here?"

He didn't have a good answer for that one.

"Playing sheriff," she said finally, unhappily.

"Playing?"

"You know what I mean." She got out and stood beside him under the shade of an oak. The heat rose from the hood of her car in shimmering sheets, evidence that she'd been driving quite a bit. Her eyes shifted toward what Cork was watching, the kid talking to the television reporter. "Someone ought to be advising these people," she said. "If they're not careful, they'll end up doing more harm than good."

"Where have you been?" Cork asked.

"I wanted to talk with Charlie Warren's daughter, try to get some idea what possible reason there could have been for him to be at the mill."

Cork felt relieved. And ashamed. "How's she doing?"

"Holding up."

"Was she able to tell you anything?"

"Apparently, Charlie had become pretty secretive of late. Gone nights. Back around daybreak. No explanation. He was a little old for it to have been a woman, I think."

Cork leaned back against the rough bark of the oak. "It's hard to believe Charlie would be involved in the kind of thing that happened at the mill."

Jo watched as the kid finished the interview and shook hands with the reporter. "Schanno's people and the BCA agents turned up just as I was leaving. Warrants to search for evidence."

"They find anything?"

"No." She glanced to her right. "Speak of the devil."

A dark blue Bonneville approached them from the same direction Jo had come. As it pulled abreast, Cork could see Agent Earl at the wheel. Earl had been looking at the tent city, but as he passed, he turned his eyes on Cork and Jo. Recognition registered in them, but little else. Because Jo represented the Ojibwe, she was probably, in his estimation, part of the problem. And Cork? More than likely he was just a man who flipped burgers and had no business investigating anything. The car moved on, slowly traveling to the other end of town, then south toward the edge of the reservation.

Cork stood in the shade, very close to Jo, but not looking at her. He wanted to say something, something simple that would sum up what he felt, an equation factored from love and fear and darker things he could not name. But nothing simple came to him.

"Where to now?" he asked.

"Back to the office. You?"

"Sam's Place. Give the girls a break. They've been handling things by themselves a lot lately."

"See you tonight," she said.

"Not until late."

She looked at him, puzzled.

"Jenny said you're both going to the library to hear Grace Fitzgerald read."

"Oh, that's right."

"Stevie'll help me close up Sam's Place. We'll see you after the reading."

"Fine."

They kissed. Dryly. Jo got back into her Toyota and headed south.

Cork stepped out under the glaring sun. He realized he'd forgotten his promise to George LeDuc to tell her to stop by. He watched her car pass the store and disappear into the distance, wavy at first in the heat rising up from the pavement, then melting away altogether, as if it—and all it contained—were made of nothing but ice.

10

For two hours, standing on the flying bridge, LePere headed the *Anne Marie* south by southeast at a steady eighteen knots. The lake was calm, the passage smooth. He made for the Apostle Islands, which lay on the water in the distance like blue whales sunning. To the Anishinaabe people, many of the islands were sacred, homes of *manidoog*, spirits of the lake. To John LePere, they were gravestones marking the place where Billy and twenty-seven other good men had died.

Wesley Bridger snoozed in the cockpit on the stern deck. He wore sunglasses and had put on an old canvas hat for protection against the sun. LePere worried a little about Bridger. The man had been drunk on whiskey the night before. For a dive as deep as the one they would make that day, it was best to abstain from drinking alcohol for a good thirty-six hours beforehand. But Bridger knew that. He'd been the instructor who certified LePere.

Wesley Bridger was the closest thing John LePere had to a friend, and LePere owed him in a lot of ways. The man had come into his life the summer before. Their first connection was a mutual fondness for boilermakers.

LePere had been sitting in the casino bar after he'd completed his shift. He was on his second boilermaker when Bridger took the stool next to him.

"Hey, bartender, drinks for everybody, on me," he called.

The bartender had paused in wiping a glass and looked

unimpressed. "*Everybody's* him," he said, indicating LePere.

"Then give him what he wants."

"Boilermaker," the bartender said without bothering to ask LePere.

"Give me the same." He stuck out his hand. "Name's Bridger—Wes Bridger. And I just won me twenty thousand dollars."

LePere shook his hand but not with enthusiasm. A free drink was good; conversation wasn't. Bridger did all the talking. How he'd just hit town. Killing time now. Loved to gamble; did okay. Did LePere know any friendly women.

By the fourth boilermaker, LePere found his own tongue had slipped its rein. Before the evening was out, he'd told Bridger his life story, the whole tragic tale of the sinking of the *Alfred M. Teasdale.*

A couple of nights later, Bridger plopped on the stool beside him again. "Hey, Chief, what's shaking?" He slapped down an old copy of a magazine called *The Great Lakes Journal,* a slick publication with lots of photographs, and he turned to a page that showed a photo of LePere, younger by ten years, standing at the wheel of a Grand Banks trawler. The title of the article was "My Brother's Seeker." It was about how John Sailor LePere sailed Lake Superior in his spare time trying to locate the wreck of the *Teasdale,* hoping to find his brother's body in that coffin of a ship, hoping to give Billy a decent burial.

"You really thought your brother's body might still be there?"

LePere slowly spun his whiskey glass. "Doesn't matter what I thought. I gave it up."

"In favor of booze?"

"I just want to forget it, okay."

"But you can't, can you, Chief? Still have nightmares, I'll bet. Can't hold a job or maintain a relationship. Am I right?"

LePere tossed down a shot of Wild Turkey and followed it with a long draw on a chaser of Leinenkugel.

"Ever heard of PTSD, Chief?"

"What is that? Something makes your car run better?"

"Post-traumatic stress disorder. A lot of Vietnam vets suffer from it. But I understand it can happen as a result of almost any traumatic event. Like watching your brother and your shipmates drown."

"So my nightmares have a name. Big deal."

"Chief, why do you figure that boat went down?"

"Forget it."

"You think it went down just because it was an old bucket, right? Maybe missing a few rivets. A tragic accident just waiting to happen. Maybe that's what the shipping company bastards wanted you to think. You and the insurance company."

LePere had his beer glass almost to his lips, but he stopped and looked straight at Wesely Bridger. "I gotta go." He put his beer down and started to slide off the stool.

"What if it was murder, Chief? Cold-blooded, well-planned murder."

LePere's chest suddenly felt constricted and for a moment he couldn't breathe. He swung back and leaned on the bar.

" 'Nother boilermaker here," Bridger called to the bartender.

The glasses came; LePere didn't touch his drink. His mouth was dry, but he wasn't thirsty.

"Let me tell you a story," Bridger began. "My third year as a SEAL, I got tapped for an assignment. Me and two others. Top-secret stuff. We meet with these intelligence people and the deal is this: There's a freighter preparing to depart Singapore, flying the Libyan flag. She's loaded with phosphates or something, but that ain't all, because these intelligence guys want to make certain she doesn't reach Qaddafi. They can't do anything officially because they don't want to cause an international incident. So what they propose we do is go under that freighter and attach a line of explosives across the hull. They want us to rig the charges with remote electronic detonation capability. They figure to shadow that freighter, and when it hits high seas, detonate the explosives. They want to make a perforated line across the hull. They're hoping the stress on the vessel will make it break apart, like tearing a sheet of creased paper, and it will go down looking as if it had all been a tragic accident. I'm thinking these guys are fucking nuts, but they got rank, right? So we do it. Get the explosives and detonators in place, then we all follow that fucking freighter in a little boat of our own. Three days out, we hit rough weather. Encounter eighteen-foot waves. Guy who's in charge of this operation gives the order. One by one, the charges go off. We're monitoring their radio broadcasts, and we're holding our breath, wondering if they're aware of the explosions. But, hell, you been in gales. You know how noisy it is inside a ship that's being hammered by rough seas. And each charge by itself is nothing big. Anyway, they don't say jack about it over the airwaves. The ship, she don't seem to show any effects. Just keeps right on moving. Everybody's getting nervous, except the dude who planned the whole thing. He's telling us all to be patient. And sure enough, about twelve hours later, just as the storm's starting to let up, that big-ass freighter folds in half and goes to the bottom in a couple miles of ocean. Nothing in the final transmissions say anything about sabotage. It looks like a terrible accident caused by structural flaws and the fury of Mother Nature. Fucking ingenius."

During the whole story, LePere had been staring at his hands, which were gripping the top of the bar. "You're saying somebody sank the *Teasdale*?"

"I'm only saying it's been done before because I did it. And just think for a minute, Chief. That old scow was due to be scrapped. How much does the Fitzgerald Shipping Company get for a few hundred tons of scrap metal versus insurance on an ore carrier fully loaded? The difference is probably enough to tempt anybody to commit murder. I'd bet my left nut on it."

That evening, LePere had stumbled from the bar in a daze not due to the boilermakers. He spent a sleepless night reliving the sinking of the *Teasdale*, dredging up every detail, examining it with bitter care. He thought about the *boom* that awakened him, that had made the ship pitch so that he'd been thrown from his bunk. He thought about Pete Swanson, the coal passer they'd picked up in Detroit, a man he'd never worked with before, a man whose dying words were "I blew it." LePere had always thought Swanson was simply delirious. But maybe there was more to it. Maybe he was trying to make a confession before he died, before he went to hell for his treachery. By the time a dingy morning light crept through his bedroom window, LePere had decided.

After his shift the next day, he found Wesley Bridger at a

twenty-dollar blackjack table. In front of Bridger were several hefty stacks of green chips.

"I want to talk," LePere said.

Bridger waved him off. "Later, Chief. I'm on a roll."

"Now."

"Okay, okay." He gathered his chips, tossed one to the dealer, and stuffed the others in his pockets. He followed LePere to the bar.

"Why'd you come to Aurora?" LePere asked.

"Like I told you, Chief. Just kicking around. Doing a little gambling, that's all. I like the casino here."

"There are other casinos. Why here?"

Bridger signaled the bartender. "Jack Daniel's, on the rocks. Anything for you, Chief?"

LePere shook his head.

The whiskey came. Bridger knocked it back.

"Ever since I left the SEALs, I've been a gambler. Small-time stuff. Never had the kind of stake it takes to play in the big games. One day I'm in the dentist's office. Got me an impacted wisdom tooth. I'm in the waiting room, waiting for my turn in the chair, reading this magazine. *Great Lakes Journal*. I find that story about you and the ore boat that went down. It gets me to thinking about that freighter I had a hand in sinking. I figure if you were to find that wreck, at the very least you could probably prove negligence. But maybe you could prove murder. In either case, a jury is gonna give you a shitload of money. I figure it's worth the gamble. So here I am."

"To do what?"

"This is the deal. I stake you, Chief. I outfit that old boat of yours—we fix 'er up, make her seaworthy, give her some good sonar. I teach you how to dive and supply the equipment. When we find the wreck—and I guarantee you we will—and when we get the evidence to nail those bastards to the wall, you give me a percentage of whatever the jury awards you."

LePere looked at him and said nothing.

"Aren't you going to ask what kind of percentage?"

"You help me find that wreck, you help me prove the Fitzgerald Shipping Company murdered Billy, you can have it all."

Bridger laughed. "That's okay, Chief. I'm not greedy." He shoved his hand at LePere. "Deal?"

"Deal," LePere said. And they shook on it.

A half mile east of Outer Island, LePere approached a buoy and cut the engine. Bridger woke up, stretched, and yawned. He stepped to the gunwale of the *Anne Marie,* where he stood a while, studying the lake.

"Tie her up to the buoy," LePere called as he maneuvered the boat near.

Bridger grabbed the bowline in one hand and a gaff in the other. He hooked the buoy with the gaff, drew the boat up next to it, and secured the line. LePere shut off the engine, and the quiet of the lake settled over them.

"Damn fine day for a dive," Bridger declared. He threw off his hat and began to undress.

The water of Lake Superior was far too frigid for a wet suit. The men donned dry suits of insulated, vulcanized rubber that kept the water from touching them. The suits had boots and hoods, and under the rubber the men wore sweats to fight the cold they'd encounter one hundred and fifty feet below the surface. LePere strapped his knife to the inside of his lower left leg. He buckled weights about his waist. From his belt hung a nylon bag for collecting things and a powerful Ikelite to illuminate the depths. He hefted his air tank onto his back. An extra hose hung from the regulator, and this LePere plugged into a valve on the front of his dry suit. The hose would feed a layer of air under the rubber to help insulate the suit and keep him dry. He pulled on his mask and, last of all, a pair of insulated gloves. He was left with only a small area of exposed skin on his face between his mask and the edge of his hood. He glanced at Bridger, who'd held off putting on his mask and was staring at a boat anchored a few hundred yards away.

"Third time, Chief," Bridger said, sounding unhappy.

"Third time what?"

"Third time that white launch has been anchored there when we dive. I thought last time it was just coincidence. Got your field glasses?"

LePere climbed up to the flying bridge and grabbed the

binoculars from beside the wheel. He came back down and gave them to Bridger, who put them to his eyes.

"Too far away. Can't read the name or registration. I don't like it. Maybe we should hold off diving."

"I'm not getting this close and turning back. Come on, Wes. So what if they've been there before. They haven't done anything."

"Doesn't mean they won't. Look, Chief, if it's the Fitzgerald Shipping Company, and you can bet your ass it is, they've killed before. Adding a couple more dead men to the roster wouldn't mean anything to those greedy bastards."

"Do whatever you want. Me, I'm diving." LePere lifted the new video camera, a Sony DCR-VX1000 in a Gates aluminum housing. The camera and deepwater housing had set Bridger back more than two grand, but it was absolutely necessary to gather the evidence they needed. "Come on, Wes," LePere said.

Bridger hollered toward the launch, "Fuck you!" He lifted his hand and gave the distant boat the finger. "All right. I'm ready now."

LePere went over the side. A minute later, Bridger followed.

The previous summer, Bridger and LePere had begun the search for the *Alfred M. Teasdale.* Bridger had paid to equip the *Anne Marie* with sonar and they'd carefully swept the area northeast of the Apostle Islands where LePere believed the *Teasdale* might have gone down. It took them weeks. Then they found the bow. Unfortunately, it lay in over three hundred feet of water, too deep for scuba. They were forced to abandon the hunt for the stern when the foul weather of November set in. They began again in April. Two months later they finally found the rest of the *Teasdale,* all in one piece. The propeller had still been turning when the aft section of the ore boat headed off into the storm, carrying Billy away. The stern had traveled more than five miles before it finally sank, coming to rest at a steep angle on the rocky bottom off Outer Island. On the first dive, they'd attached a steel cable to the propeller shaft and spooled the cable to the surface, where they set the buoy to mark the site.

On this dive, LePere could feel how the hot, dry summer had warmed the upper layer of water, but he knew that in the darkness where they were going, warmth never penetrated. He followed Bridger down the cable. At ten feet, they passed a yellow marker that indicated the place where, when they surfaced, they had to hold for ten minutes while they decompressed. LePere was already beginning to feel the growing pressure of the water on his inner ears.

At thirty feet, Bridger switched on his Ikelite. The water illuminated in the strong beam was blue-green. Except for the suck and sigh of his own breathing and the constant putter of bubbles expelled from his hose, LePere heard no sounds.

At seventy feet, the atmospheric pressure had quadrupled. They were nearing the depth where, LePere knew, without scuba his ribs would collapse, crushing his lungs. He could feel the press of the deepening cold through the rubber of his suit.

The curve of the *Teasdale*'s stern and the ten-foot blades of the propeller loomed out of the dark at one hundred feet. The hull rested on its side, tilted down a rocky slope at a forty-degree angle. LePere checked the psi gauge on his regulator hose. He'd used one third of his oxygen just reaching the bottom. He had only ten minutes of dive time before he and Ridges had to start back to the surface.

The man in the restaurant in Beaver Bay had been right. At that depth, in that cold, the lake was like a great meat locker and the dead did not decompose. When LePere had first found the wreck, he'd spent all of the precious minutes of every dive searching the quarters, the galley, the boiler room, the maze of companionways, looking in vain for Billy's body. He'd carefully canvassed the rocks where the hull was cradled, but all he'd found there was the coal that had spilled from the gaping cargo hold. He'd known it was probably foolish, but he had to be certain. Now he dived for a different reason, something he might have argued was justice but felt very much like revenge.

Bridger let LePere take the lead, and they started down the sloping hull where, three hundred feet farther and fifty feet deeper, was the midsection with its severed edge.

LePere hadn't gone far when the rhythmic clank of metal brought him around. Bridger had stopped and was tapping his tank with his knife. When he saw that he had LePere's attention, he cupped his hand to the place on his hood where his ear would be, and he pointed toward the surface.

LePere listened. He heard it, too. A sound like the distant buzz of a summer cicada. A boat somewhere above them. Where exactly, LePere couldn't tell. Abruptly, the sound stopped. Bridger shined his light upward. He looked like a man hanging at the end of a luminous icicle. He gestured emphatically, urging them to surface. LePere shook his head just as emphatically. He had only a few minutes left, and he intended to use the whole time for the purpose that had brought them. He turned and started again down the hull, ignoring the angry banging of the knife against Bridger's tank.

His own Ikelite pierced the dark ahead of him. He took only a couple of minutes to reach the place where the hull ended suddenly in ragged metal. Slipping over the lip, he shined his light into the huge cavern that had been the hold of the ore boat. For a long moment, he hung suspended in the mouth of memory. The hold was empty now and black. But on that night a dozen years before when LePere stood at the edge of the sinking bow section, crying out Billy's name, the hold had been full of smoke and fire. LePere had stared into the belly of a beast, and the beast had answered his cries with its own deafening scream of rending metal. He'd watched, paralyzed, as the beast tried to mount the deck where he stood, tried to get at him, to crush his bones. Many times after that, in the lonely dark of a drunken night, LePere found himself wishing bitterly the beast had succeeded.

The beam of Bridger's light swung into the hold beside his own. Bridger signaled toward his watch. They didn't have much time. Using their lights, they began to inspect the plating along the edge of the opening. About halfway down the hull, Bridger pointed to an area of metal that appeared gouged, bubbled at the edges, and he gave LePere an enthusiastic thumbs-up. LePere turned on the camera and drifted slowly down, pausing to let the camera linger on those areas where Bridger indicated. Very soon—too soon for LePere—Bridger pointed upward. Time to surface. LePere checked the gauge on his regulator. The needle lay at 500 psi. Bridger was right. They should head up. LePere ignored him and kept at the work. Bridger grabbed him and yanked him away from the hull. He jammed his hand upward vehemently. LePere could guess what he'd have said if he could speak. But they were onto something, and there was so much more to film. He shrugged off Bridger's hand. With a disgusted gesture, Wesley Bridger washed his hands of his partner, turned away, and exited the cargo hold. LePere was alone in the great empty dark.

Although he was angry with Bridger for a moment, he knew the man was right. And he knew, too, that to jeopardize his diving companion was a selfish and ultimately cowardly thing to do. He turned off his camera, pointed his Ikelite where Bridger had gone, and followed.

He was thinking in an excited way about what he'd captured on the film, but he didn't think it long. As he swung under the ragged lip at the entrance to the hold, he felt himself pulled back, like a dog on a leash. Some part of his gear had snagged on the sharp teeth of the broken, twisted metal that surrounded the mouth of the open hold. He tried to turn back but found he couldn't. He imagined his air hose, hooked on a razor-sharp sliver, ready to be severed if he pulled too hard. Reaching back, he tried to feel what was hung up, but his camera and light encumbered him. He realized he was breathing hard. At that depth every breath took several times more oxygen from his tank than at the surface. He could feel the panic taking control. *Stay calm,* he told himself. He swung his light over his shoulder but couldn't turn himself to look. He strained to reach back, to feel the problem, only the camera got in the way and his thick gloves made his hands too clumsy. He let go of the camera and watched it drop slowly into the dark below him, then he took a precious few moments to peel off his gloves. Immediately the frigid water made the muscle and bone ache. He felt along his air hose, then his tank. Nothing. What the hell was hanging him up?

He checked the gauge on his regulator again: 300 psi. Even if he freed himself now, there wasn't enough air left to make a safe, slow climb to the surface. His only hope would be to inflate the vest he wore as a weight compensator and shoot himself upward to the ten-foot marker for decompression. There'd be hell to pay in a lot of ways, but at least he'd be alive.

Then the beam of another light struck him full in the face. Wesley Bridger maneuvered behind him, and a moment later LePere was free. They swam quickly up the hull. At the cable, they started toward the surface. Bridger stayed beside him, holding him back when he tried to go too fast. At thirty feet, LePere motioned toward his tank, then made a slashing motion across his throat, indicating that he was out of air. Bridger pointed toward his own mouthpiece and gave him the "okay" sign. They held at ten feet, sharing the last of the air in Bridger's tank. Finally they surfaced and climbed aboard the *Anne Marie*.

LePere shed his mask and gear and turned to his diving buddy. "Thanks, Wes." He offered his hand gratefully.

"Forget it." Bridger accepted LePere's hand. "Christ, you're freezing. Where are your gloves?"

"Had to get rid of them. The camera, too. I've got to go back down."

"Not today."

"I've got to get that camera."

"It's not going anywhere. One close call in a day is plenty."

The late morning was hot, the sun bright. Although it felt great standing on the deck of the *Anne Marie*, breathing in the sweet, plentiful air, LePere couldn't help thinking about the evidence he'd captured on film. He wanted it in his hands.

"What kind of SIT are we looking at?" he asked, speaking of the time interval required on the surface before he could safely make another dive.

Bridger had turned away and now knelt at the portable compressor they'd brought to fill their tanks for a second dive. "I said forget it." He stood up. "We couldn't go back down even if I wanted to, which I definitely do not. Somebody took the filter off the compressor, Chief. They were probably hoping you'd go down again. Wanted you to breathe dirty air. I told you those rich sons of bitches would do more than just watch us. That camera of yours must've made 'em nervous." He scanned the lake, but the white launch was nowhere in sight.

"We'll come back tomorrow," LePere said.

"I already told you. I'm in a big poker tournament down at Grand Casino Mille Lacs tomorrow. We can do it another day." Bridger glanced at him. "Ah Jesus, Chief. I can read you like you're thinking in neon." He stepped across the deck toward LePere, who'd never seen on Bridger's face a look so serious or afraid. "Promise me, God damn it. Promise me on your brother's watery grave here that you won't dive alone. Promise me, Chief."

The lake was dead calm. Over it hung a high pall scented with the vague smell of smoke. The sun was white, and it lit a pale fire on the lake all around the *Anne Marie*. John Sailor LePere looked at these things, then at Wesley Bridger. He smiled calmly and said, "I promise."

11

THAT EVENING, as she backed her Toyota from the driveway of the house on Gooseberry Lane, Jo took note once again of Jenny's attire. Black silk blouse, short black skirt, black stockings, black beret. Somehow, she'd acquired glasses with stern black rims.

"You look like you're going to a funeral in a Greenwich Village coffeehouse." Jo turned up Center Street, heading toward the library.

"I don't want her to think I'm a kid."

"There's absolutely nothing wrong with being sixteen and liking her book."

"I *love* her book, Mom." Jenny clutched the novel to her breast. "She writes with such a deep understanding of tragedy."

"I suspect that's because she's lived with tragedy, Jenny."

"To lose the man you love, and so mysteriously." Jenny stared down at the dust jacket of *Superior Blue*. The cover art showed the dark blue of Lake Superior curving away beneath a menacing blue-black sky. Caught at the edge of earth and air, as if trapped in the mouth of a huge blue monster, was a small sailboat with an empty deck.

"Believe me, Jen, tragedy's more appealing in the abstract than in the reality. It makes a good read, but it's awful to live through."

"Do you think there'll be a lot of people?"

"If I know Maggie Nelson, she'll make sure people turn out in droves."

Two dozen chairs had been set up in the meeting room of the Aurora Public Library. By the time Jo and Jenny arrived, all the chairs had been taken. Along with half a dozen other late arrivals, Jo stood at the back of the room, Jenny beside her. Most of the audience were women, but a few men had come.

"Mom, there he is," Jenny whispered. "The guy who talked to me in French yesterday. The one who went to the Sorbonne."

She pointed toward a young man standing against the wall on the other side of the room. Jo pegged him to be in his early twenties. A thin blond mustache dusted his upper lip. He wore scruffy jeans and a white T-shirt that wasn't exactly clean. Jo recognized him, too. She'd seen him only that morning being interviewed by a newsman at the tent city on the Iron Lake Reservation. He'd spoken ill-advisedly then. She hoped he didn't have any other ill-advised notions at the moment and was there only because he admired Grace Fitzgerald's book.

Maggie Nelson stood at the front of the room beside a table on which sat a display of copies of *Superior Blue*. Grace Fitzgerald was seated at the table, and next to her a boy of nine or ten, with the same honey-colored hair as she. The author wore a light green blouse, probably silk. A small gold cross hung on a thin gold chain about her neck. She was a striking woman, even more so because of her nose, a prominence that resembled a raptor's beak and that dominated an otherwise soft-featured and lovely face.

Maggie Nelson introduced the author. After polite applause, Grace Fitzgerald said, "First of all, I'd like to thank Maggie for hosting this event. I'd also like to thank so many of you for turning out this evening, although I suspect some of you are here mostly because of the wonderful food waiting for you afterward, courtesy of Fairfield's. Thanks, Jackie." She gave a brief wave to a slender, dark-haired woman standing at a table filled with trays of cookies and exotic-looking bars. "And finally I'd like to thank the Friends of the Aurora Library for sponsoring this event and so many others like it."

She sent a smile in the direction of Jo, for Jo headed that organization and had been the one who'd first approached Grace Fitzgerald with the invitation. Jo had liked the woman immediately and immensely. She found her intelligent—which she'd expected—and also gracious and full of wonderful humor. More important, she felt a kind of kinship with Grace Fitzgerald. In a town like Aurora where not even a dozen years of residence and work on civic organizations were a guarantee of acceptance, she felt as if she'd found someone who could be a friend, someone who, like her, might always be an outsider.

The book, the author explained briefly, was the story of a rich young woman who fell in love with a poor young man. Over the objections of the woman's powerful father, they married. The young man finally won the father over with his intelligence and integrity and his obvious love for the man's daughter. A child was born. Life was good. The future looked perfect. Then one day the husband sailed off, as he often had, for an outing on Lake Superior. He never returned. The sailboat was found, adrift and abandoned, but no trace ever of the man who'd sailed it.

Grace Fitzgerald read an excerpt, a scene in which the woman stood on the shore of Lake Superior. It was a cold winter day, months after her husband had vanished. Snow spit from a gray sky and gray waves washed at her feet with an incessant voice that was "the bleak whisper of a bleak forever." It was the moment she wrapped her heart around the cold truth: He would never come back to her. The voice of the water called to her. She considered the black unknown of death, something that seemed at that moment far better than the stark cold air that sustained her. She teetered, her foot poised to take that longest of steps.

Grace stopped reading. The room held its breath. But Grace Fitzgerald did not go on.

"I'd be glad to answer any questions," she said. "If you have any."

A hand went up from one of the chairs near the front. "Ms. Fitzgerald—"

"Call me Grace."

"Have you had any movie offers, Grace?"

"Honestly, I have no intention of letting Hollywood have my story. I'm sure they'd find a way to slip in car chases and exploding buildings."

Jo was surprised to see Jenny put up a hand. "Are you really related to F. Scott Fitzgerald?"

"Absolutely. He was my grandfather's cousin. I'm sure that's where I get whatever literary talent I have. And just in case you're wondering, I got my nose from my mother's side."

There was general laughter, polite.

"Grace," Maggie Nelson said. "You've written one of the most beautiful books about a man and woman in love. I guess we all know it's based on your own experience. Does Karl ever get, well, jealous of how you feel about your first husband?"

Grace Fitzgerald shook her head slightly. "They were good friends. Karl's been very understanding that way."

"Ms. Fitzgerald, I have a question."

It was the young man from the tent city on the rez.

"Yes?" The author smiled encouragingly.

"Your current husband rapes the land for his living. He slaughters the forests. He destroys the future for us all. You write about the death of one man. How about the deaths of thousands of other living things?"

Maggie Nelson stepped in quickly. "We're here to discuss other issues."

"The trees have no voice. For them, there are no other issues."

"You're not going to have a voice either in just a minute," someone up front called out.

The young man's face was red, burning with a fierce passion. He moved forward, talking quickly now. "The woman you just read about is thinking of killing herself. Your husband and those like him are killing us when they kill the trees—"

A woman stood and moved to block his way. Jo knew her. Paula Overby, a very large woman with easily enough bulk to squash the young man like a boulder on a beetle. "My husband puts food on our table cutting timber. He's no killer, you little—" She held herself back from finishing.

Jo, who was more than sympathetic to the cause of Our Grandfathers, found herself irked by the young man's intrusion and irritated that there seemed nowhere anyone could go anymore to escape confrontation. She was also worried that such tactics did more harm than good.

"That's all right." Grace Fitzgerald left the table and walked to the young man. She put a finger to her lips, looking at him closely, thinking. She was a woman with great presence, something Jo noted and appreciated. "I understand how you feel. I share your concern for the environment, I really do. My husband and I don't see eye to eye on this issue. A lot of issues, actually. But you know—what did you say your name was?"

"I didn't. It's Brent. Brent Hamilton."

"You know, Brent, I'd like to ask you to use a different venue to express your concern, because tonight, we're just here to have a good time. Have you read my book?"

"No," he admitted.

"It's about losing what we most love. So I do understand how you feel about the trees. I'd be more than happy to talk with you about them, but not tonight. Okay?"

She smiled, reached out, touched his shoulder.

He was silent.

"I think it's time for refreshments," Maggie Nelson said. "Thank you, Grace. She'll be signing up here for all of you who brought books." She slipped quickly between Grace Fitzgerald and the young man, took his arm, and with gentle force, guided him from the room. He didn't resist.

Jo and Jenny found themselves near the end of a line that formed for Grace Fitzgerald's signature. When they reached the author, she smiled at them warmly. "Hi, Jo."

"Hello, Grace. I'm sorry about the disruption."

"What disruption?" Her eyes, a brown so light they were nearly golden, fell on Jenny. "This must be the writer I've heard so much about."

Jenny reddened deeply. "Just poems, mostly."

"That's exactly how I started." She took Jenny's book. "How would you like this inscribed?"

"Whatever you want to put there is fine."

"Wonderful." Grace Fitzgerald bent and wrote in a florid script, "From one writer to another, good luck." She started to close the book, then bent once more and added something Jo couldn't quite see. She handed the book back to Jenny and laid her hand on the shoulder of the boy next to her. "Scottie, I'd like you to meet Ms. Jo O'Connor. She's a famous lawyer here. And this is her daughter, Jenny. My son Scott."

He seemed shy, looking up at her with his head slightly bowed. A smallish boy, with green eyes and a normal nose, he looked very little like his mother. Jo figured he took after his father, the man lost on Lake Superior. "Hi." He lifted his hand briefly.

"Hello yourself," Jo replied. She glanced behind her. "We're holding things up."

Grace Fitzgerald leaned toward Jo and spoke quietly. "I wonder if I could talk to you—soon."

"Sure. What about?"

"Professionally."

"You have my number. Just give me a call and we'll set something up."

"Thanks."

They skipped the refreshments and headed to the car. As they drove home, Jenny said, "I thought she handled that guy pretty well."

"I thought so, too."

"He seemed so nice yesterday. If I was Grace Fitzgerald, I would have just told him to bite me."

" 'Bite me'? What's that mean?"

"Oh, you know, Mom."

"No."

Jenny shrugged. "It means fuck off."

"I beg your pardon."

"You wanted to know."

Jo found that she was smiling, despite herself.

"What do you think she wants to talk to you about?" Jenny asked.

"I don't know."

Jenny was quiet a moment. "Mom, I thought she looked kind of worried. Maybe even scared."

"You know, I thought so, too, Jen."

"I wonder why."

"I guess when she calls me, I'll find out. By the way, what did she write in your book?"

Jenny opened the cover and read proudly, "Someday you'll be signing a book for me."

12

CORK WOULD HAVE MADE MORE MONEY keeping Sam's Place open after dark, but he liked his evenings free. At seven-thirty, he finished grilling a couple of Sam's Big Deluxes and whipped up a couple of chocolate shakes for two teenage boys who'd motored up to the dock. Then he flipped the CLOSED sign outward and began to shut the place down. Stevie had helped a good deal during the day, but after his own dinner—a hot dog, chips, and milk—he'd fallen asleep on the bunk in the Quonset hut.

Cork scraped the grill, emptied and cleaned the ice milk machine, cooled and poured out the fry oil, wiped down the prep areas, and swept the floor. He took the cash from the register and turned out the lights. In the back, he sat at the desk, counted the day's take, and made entries in his ledger. Finally he prepared a night-deposit slip, bundled the money, and shook Stevie gently awake.

"Come on, buddy. Time to hit the road."

Stevie was slow in getting up.

"Want a ride?" Cork asked.

Stevie gave a sleepy nod.

Cork turned his back to his son and knelt. Stevie wrapped his arms around Cork's neck and his legs around Cork's waist.

"Up we go."

He carried Stevie piggyback outside and locked the door behind them. By the time he got his son settled in the Bronco, Stevie was wide awake.

"Are we going home?" Stevie asked.

"First we go to the bank. Then to the store for some cigarettes."

Stevie seemed bewildered. "You don't smoke anymore."

"They're not for me. After that, how about a walk in the woods?"

Stevie looked at the long shadows cast by the setting sun. "Will it be dark?"

"When we're done. Do you think the woods are scary when it's dark?"

"Sometimes."

"Sometimes so do I. But I'll tell you what—I promise I won't let anything happen to us, okay?"

Stevie thought it over, his dark Anishinaabe eyes seriously considering his father's face. "Okay," he agreed.

And Cork felt, as he often did, the sweet weight of his son's trust.

Cork drove north of Aurora, following county roads until he came to a place in the Superior National Forest where a split-trunk birch marked the opening to a foot trail through a thick stand of red pines. He pulled off to the side of the road, locked up the old Bronco, and set off with Stevie through the woods.

It was twilight then. Normally the air under the pines would have been cool and sharp scented, but the heat was holding and the smell in the air came from the forest fires to the north. The undergrowth was brittle. Whenever Cork or Stevie brushed against the branches and brambles, they gave off a sound like the rattle of bones. Stevie held Cork's hand tightly and warily eyed the woods around them.

After ten minutes on the trail, Cork knew they'd passed onto Iron Lake Reservation land, the far northwest corner where there was only one cabin for miles. The cabin belonged to Henry Meloux, the oldest man Cork had ever known, although years seemed a feeble measure of a man like Meloux. He was a *mide,* one of the *midewiwin,* a member of the Grand Medicine Society. To many of the whites in Tamarack County, he was known as Mad Mel. Cork, however, had respected the man his whole life.

As they neared Meloux's cabin on the small, rocky peninsula

along a north arm of Iron Lake, Cork sniffed the air with concern. The pervasive smell of distant fire had suddenly grown powerful and immediate. Cork broke from the pines into a clearing that gave him an unobstructed view of the cabin and the lake. Beyond the cabin, tattooed against the pale blue of the twilight sky, rose a dark coiling. A column of smoke.

"Come on, Stevie."

Cork broke into a trot, holding himself back only for the sake of his son's small legs. They ran past Meloux's outhouse and cabin and followed a well-worn path between two tall outcroppings of rock. On the other side of the rocks, Cork halted so abruptly that Stevie ran right into him.

Henry Meloux looked up from where he sat on a maple stump tending a fire that blazed within a circle of large stones. He didn't seem at all surprised to see Cork standing suddenly before him, but when his gaze shifted to Stevie, he smiled as if the boy's appearance were the greatest of unexpected pleasures. On the ground just to the left of Meloux lay an old yellow hound, its head resting on its paws. The dog didn't move when the visitors arrived. His big brown eyes simply took them in with a blinking calm.

"*Anin*, Corcoran O'Connor," Meloux said.

"*Anin*, Henry." Cork moved around the fire nearer to Meloux. "You know there's a ban on open fires, even on rez land."

The old man stared at him as calmly as did the dog. "You are a born policeman, Corcoran O'Connor. Even when you are no longer paid for it, you tend to the law. If you want to arrest me, I won't resist. If not, then how about you hand me that cedar branch there." He nodded toward a pile of cut wood and branches nestled against the rock outcropping.

Cork handed Meloux the cedar branch. Stevie stayed near his father, shadowing Cork's every move.

The old *mide* added the branch to the fire and followed the embers upward with his watchful eyes. "I see that you have brought with you a little Corcoran O'Connor."

"This is Stephen. You probably saw him last when he was just about the size of a muskrat. Stevie, this is Henry Meloux."

"Come, Stephen O'Connor. Sit with me." Meloux patted the ground between him and the old hound.

Stevie looked up at Cork, who nodded his okay. The boy sat,

and the hound lifted his head and nuzzled Stevie's hand. His tail swept the dirt behind him.

"Can I pet him?" Stevie asked.

"I think he would like that."

"What's his name?"

"I have always called him Walleye."

"Hi, Walleye," Stevie said, stroking the dog's yellow fur. "Hi, boy."

Meloux watched the boy, and a broad smile added creases to his face as he spoke to Cork. "The blood of the People is strong in this one."

From his shirt pocket, Cork took a pack of Lucky Strikes and handed them to the old man. Meloux accepted, opened the pack, and drew out a cigarette. He held the others toward Cork, who took one for himself. Meloux thrust the end of a stick into the fire and when it was burning, he held the flame to the tip of his cigarette. He passed the stick to Cork, who did the same. For a few minutes, they smoked in silence. Stevie had been right. Cork had given up cigarettes. But the smoking now had nothing to do with an old habit.

"Why the illegal fire, Henry?" Cork finally asked. "It's hot enough already I can fry burgers on the pavement."

"Cedar fire," Meloux pointed out. "There's anger in the air."

"And you think one cedar fire will clear it away?"

"Can it do any harm?"

"It could burn down what's left of the forest."

"I have been a tender of fires for nearly two of your lifetimes, Corcoran O'Connor. Fire and me, we are old allies. Stephen." The old man leaned toward the boy. "Do you know your father has another name?"

"Liam," Stevie replied, looking pleased that he knew the answer.

"His father and mother gave him that name. But I gave him another when he was no bigger than you."

"What?"

"Ickode. It means fire. He tried to burn down his grandfather's school on the reservation."

"It was an accident, Henry," Cork said.

"Do I have another name?" Stevie looked at the old man eagerly.

"If you were given one, it was not by me."

Stevie's eyes swung to his father.

"No, buddy," Cork said. He could see the disappointment on his son's face.

"Let me sleep on it," Meloux offered. "Let me see what comes to me in dreams, Stephen. When next we meet, I will have a name for you."

Stevie brightened and returned his attention to Walleye.

Cork sat on the ground to the right of Meloux. "Henry, I came to ask you about Charlie Warren. You know what happened at Lindstrom's mill."

"I know."

"The authorities are thinking Charlie was responsible, that somehow he was the victim of his own bomb. I don't believe it for an instant, but I can't figure what he was doing out there."

Meloux added the ash from his cigarette to the ash at the fire's edge. "I knew Charlie Warren all his life. He was a strong spirit, a good man. I also think he would not do this thing." A loud pop from the fire sent sparks outside the stone circle. Meloux watched them closely until they died in the dirt.

Night was coming on. A yellow haze nested in the trees to the east, the rising moon. Stars seemed to have popped out in the sky as sudden as the embers that burst from Meloux's fire. Cork saw that Stevie was more interested in Walleye than in the deepening dark. There was something about fire, he knew, and the company of men that had for centuries chased away the monsters of the night.

Meloux spoke again. "I'm an old man. I don't sleep like I used to. Sometimes the tree frogs and me, we talk all night long. I don't mind being alone with the tree frogs. But some men need other company. Charlie Warren liked company. He also liked checkers, and checkers a man cannot play alone. Sometimes Charlie Warren shared his nights with a friend whose name is Jack Daniel. I would think about these things, Corcoran O'Connor."

Walleye suddenly stood, shrugging off Stevie's hand. His nostrils flared as he sniffed the air. He went rigid and a growl rumbled in his throat as he watched the place where the path from Meloux's cabin threaded between the tall outcroppings of rock. Stevie's own dark eyes, frightened now, looked there, too.

The woman paused as soon as the firelight hit her, and she held still between the rocks, leaning on her cane.

"*Anin*, Henry Meloux," she said.

"*Anin*," Meloux replied. "I have been waiting for you."

Her surprise showed. "You knew I was coming?"

He beckoned her. "Sit."

She walked forward, using her cane at every step of her right leg. She sat on a section of saw-cut pine situated across the fire from Meloux. It was only then that Cork realized Meloux had subtly choreographed the movements of his guests so that the pine section would be vacant when the woman, who could not easily sit on the ground, arrived.

Meloux spoke to Walleye, Ojibwe words, and the dog returned to the dirt and again cradled his head on his paws. Stevie, looking tired, laid himself against the big hound, who seemed not at all to mind the weight of his small companion.

"You know who I am, then," the woman said.

"I know. Joan Hamilton. Some, I've heard, call you Joan of Arc of the Redwoods. That is not a bad name to be called."

Joan Hamilton looked down at Stevie, whose eyes were drifting closed. Then she stared long and hard at Cork.

"Corcoran O'Connor," Meloux said.

"We've met," she said. "In a way."

Meloux's eyes went from one to the other, taking in what was between them. "Not a good way, I think."

"His business was disrupted yesterday morning. I suspect he blames me."

"Your presence has disrupted a lot of businesses," Cork said.

"Not intentionally. That man—you called him Erskine, I think—started it."

"That man has a family, a mortgage, bills," Cork told her. "The trees are his living. I'm not saying he was right, but I can understand why he was angry."

"You worry about one man. One family. I'm worried about the world."

"I think you should worry a little about the kid."

"Kid?"

"The young man who was about to paint Erskine's knuckles with his blood."

"My son, Mr. O'Connor."

"Your son? You seemed pretty willing to let Erskine manhandle him."

"I don't need to explain myself to you." She laid her cane across her knees. It was carved of some dark hard wood that reflected the firelight as brightly as if it were on fire itself. "For two reasons I didn't interfere," she went on suddenly. "My son is a man now, not a kid. He wouldn't have wanted me to step in. This was something that, as a man, he needed to deal with. Also, he's a soldier, in his way, and as a soldier he will sometimes be hurt. He knows that."

"Spartan," Cork said.

"You disapprove. That's because you don't understand this situation as we do. I've seen the greatest trees on earth brought to the edge of extinction, not just by greed but by complacency. We're killing the earth and ourselves with it. This is war, Mr. O'Connor, and what we're fighting for is nothing less than our survival on this earth."

The Army of the Earth, Cork thought, remembering the militant environmental group Eco-Warrior claimed to be a part of, and he studied carefully the woman on the far side of the fire.

She was, he guessed, about his own age. Her hair was mostly red, although in the light of the fire it seemed rich with veins of silver. Her eyes were narrow, colorless slits that allowed her to look out and invited nothing in. At one time, she might have been beautiful. Now there was something jagged and hard about her, and Cork thought of her like an arrowhead chipped from flint, well capable of killing.

Meloux sat quietly while the exchange took place. Cork was sorry that he'd let himself trade harsh words with the woman there where Meloux burned cedar to cleanse the anger from the air. He was well aware that the old *mide* hadn't asked the woman's purpose in coming. Meloux probably already knew, in the way he knew so many things. If not, his quiet was simply a sign of the patience that was an aspect of his spirit. Cork, for his part, was dying to know why she, an outsider, had come and who had guided her.

But there were to be no answers. The woman fell silent and Meloux looked at Cork in a way that was as powerful as a shove.

"*Migwech,* Henry," Cork said, thanking the old man for his

help. He stood up and stepped to Stevie, who lay asleep against Walleye. He lifted his son and started along the path that had led him to Crow Point.

"We fight for the world our children will inherit, Mr. O'Connor," the woman said at his back.

Cork turned to her. "A noble-sounding justification for almost anything. Always has been."

Before Cork could move on, Meloux called to him, "I have heard you might be sheriff again."

"Somebody's spreading a lot of hooey in this county," Cork replied.

"Too bad," the old man said. "I think it would be a good idea."

"I don't share your optimism, Henry. But I thank you for the vote of confidence. 'Night."

He passed between the rocks and out of the firelight.

An early moon had risen, nearly full. Without it, the dark of the woods would have been impenetrable. As it was, Cork walked in a silver light bright enough to cast shadows. His son was heavy in his arms, but Cork didn't mind at all. Stevie stirred in his sleep and his cheek brushed Cork's cheek, soft down against the rough stubble of a day's growth. Cork thought about the woman and how hard she'd seemed when it came to her son. He knew his own arms could not hold Stevie forever. Someday he would have to let go. He hoped he would be wise enough when that time came to know how to do it and strong enough to let it be done.

As he drove toward Aurora with Stevie asleep on the seat beside him, Cork thought over all that Meloux had told him about Charlie Warren. They were not big things. Probably they were pieces of information that many on the rez knew but, out of respect for Charlie Warren and an understandable distrust of law enforcement, had not shared with the BCA or even with Jo. Meloux thought the information was important, and so Cork considered it carefully.

Charlie Warren was the traditional chief of the Iron Lake Ojibwe, and his voice had always been important in the affairs of the People. He was in his seventies and his health had been failing and lately he'd retired from most politics on the rez. He was a man who often did not sleep at night, and who did not like to be alone with his sleeplessness. What would such a man be doing at Lindstrom's mill when the bomb went off?

When he put it together that way, Cork thought he might have the answer.

He stopped at the Pinewood Broiler and borrowed Johnny Pap's phone book to look up an address. Then he drove out to a small clapboard house near the Burlington Northern tracks northwest of town. Stevie slept so soundly that Cork decided not to wake him. He got out of the Bronco quietly and followed the cracked, weedy sidewalk to the front door. The house was mostly dark. Through the blinds, Cork could see a lighted television screen in the front room, and he could hear through the opened window the sound of a baseball game. He pushed the button for the doorbell, but nothing rang inside. He knocked. A moment later the porch light flicked on. Harold Loomis, the night watchman at Lindstrom's mill, appeared at the door.

"Evening, Harold," Cork said.

Loomis was a thin man. He was dressed in an undershirt and plaid shorts. He had a full shock of white hair and a nose like a lightbulb that had been screwed into his face. He held a glass filled with amber liquid and ice, and his lightbulb of a nose was pretty well lit.

"What can I do for you, Cork?" He pushed the screen door open.

"I just need an answer to a couple of questions."

"Sure. If I can give 'em."

"You like playing checkers?"

"Yeah."

"You ever play with Charlie Warren?"

Loomis blinked at him.

"I was just thinking," Cork went on, "that you and Charlie had a few things in common. Besides checkers. You served in the Korean War, right?"

"What of it?"

"So did Charlie."

"Lots of guys did."

"Not so many around here."

Loomis stared at Cork. His eyes were watery and rimmed

with red. It could have been from what was in the glass. Or lack of sleep. Or maybe even from grieving.

"Was Charlie Warren your friend, Harold?"

Loomis tried to maintain his stare, but he finally broke and looked down at the glass in his hand.

"Because if he was, they're saying your friend was responsible for the destruction out at Lindstrom's, that he botched things, Harold, and he killed himself with his own bomb."

"Charlie's dead. What difference does it make what anybody says about him now?"

"He was playing checkers with you that night, wasn't he? Maybe sharing a drink. Talking over old times. Exchanging war stories. Helping the night get by for both of you. I'm guessing neither of you wanted folks to know. You had a job to worry about, and maybe Charlie figured it wouldn't look so good, him hanging out at Lindstrom's, what with all the hullaballoo over logging right now. You know, Harold, it's pretty understandable."

Loomis stared at the ice melting into his whiskey.

"I'll bet it got lonely out there at night."

Loomis stepped out and let the door swing closed behind him. He walked to the porch railing, took a long drink from his glass, swirled the ice, drank again. He looked out at the night, and when he spoke, his voice was barely above a whisper. "We served in the same unit. After the war, coming home, we never had much to do with one another. Charlie, he had all that business out on the reservation. Me, I went back to my own life. But you get old, Cork. People you got anything in common with pass on. You get lonely. Charlie and me, we bumped into one another sometimes at the VFW. Got to talking about old times. Korea, you know. I liked him. Didn't matter he was Indian. Didn't matter to him I was white. Yeah, at the end, he was my friend."

"He didn't have anything to do with the bomb. He was just there to play checkers."

Loomis nodded. "He always left before the guys started showing up for first shift. The other night, I had my rounds to make. We were in the middle of a game. Charlie stayed in the shed while I headed out. I was on the other side of the mill when it happened." Tears piled up along the rims of his eyes. "I couldn't do anything. Honest to God, there was nothing I could do." He shook his head. "They find out about Charlie, I'm out of a job, Cork. I got no pension. I got no way to pay my bills."

"I have to tell somebody, Harold. I have to tell Wally Schanno. I'm sorry." Cork felt bad, but there was no way around it. "Look, it doesn't have to be done tonight. And I'll see if Schanno can do something about keeping the details confidential. I can't promise anything."

Loomis stared down at the old boards of his porch. He seemed dazed. The effect of the whiskey. And a lot more.

"Thanks for your help, Harold."

Loomis looked at him and a question seemed to surface from somewhere deep in his consciousness. "Why do you care about any of this? You're not the sheriff anymore."

" 'Night, Harold."

Cork left him standing in his doorway, the question unanswered.

13

JOHN LEPERE LEFT HIS SMALL CABIN and walked through pools of moonlight scattered among the trees that separated his place from the big log home on the other side of Grace Cove. He crossed the dry bed of Blueberry Creek that was the property line, then followed the curve of the cove until he came to a narrow sand beach, white in the moonlight. The beach was not a natural feature of the shoreline there. Lindstrom had had it constructed the year before when the log home was built. LePere carefully skirted the sand so that he would leave no tracks. He often trespassed this way. For years, when his was the only dwelling on the cove, he'd walked the shoreline unrestrained by concerns about boundary lines. Although he actually owned only a small parcel of the land, over the years he'd come to think of the cove as his. It was wrong thinking, he knew, but inhabiting the place alone for more than a decade had made it so. Then Lindstrom had come, changed the look of everything. LePere resented the man, his wealth, and his thoughtless trespass on LePere's life.

He moved onto the grass of the wide lawn, a lake of silver under the full moon, and he slipped into the shadow of a spruce. From the darkness there, he watched the house.

Lights were on in several rooms, upstairs and down. Occasionally, a light would switch off in one room and switch on in another as if someone inside were moving about. It was an illusion. No one was home. LePere had learned over time that the lights were simply part of the rich man's security system.

He left the shadow of the spruce and headed to the dock. The boards were new and firm, the posts thick and well anchored so that the dock didn't move at all under his weight. It had been built to withstand a hurricane, although Grace Cove was so well protected the surface was generally smooth as glass. LePere ran his hand along the lifeline of the sailboat tied up there, the one called *Amazing Grace*. The 28-foot Grampian sloop, a boat for big water, was a little large and ostentatious for Iron Lake, LePere thought. He'd seen Lindstrom take the sloop out on occasion. The rich man looked soft, but he was a good sailor. Even alone, he handled the boat well. At first, Lindstrom had taken his wife and the boy with him, but he'd barked orders impatiently, until one day the boy stood on the dock and refused to go. LePere had witnessed the scene through his field glasses. Now the boy went out only in the dinghy and only with his mother. The woman was a good sailor, too, firm with the boy, but patient. Except for the cold darkness inside him, LePere might have allowed himself to admire her style.

When he'd first learned who his neighbors on the cove were to be, he'd considered it ironic. Now he considered it destiny. Although he fully realized the Fitzgerald woman was not to blame for the sins of her father, he understood—in the way of a man who knew firsthand that life was anything but just—that if ever there were to be retribution, it would fall to her to pay.

He stepped onto the sloop. The mast gleamed in the moonlight like a clean, white bone. He liked the idea that with every step he was further violating Lindstrom's territory. For a moment, he considered breaking something small, just to leave a sign of his presence, to let the rich man wonder, but he held himself back. Although it would be hard to connect him to any vandalism, they would look his way. On that isolated cove, he was all there was for them to see.

Headlights flashed, blasting among the pine trees that lined the private road to the cove. LePere didn't move. It would be the woman and the boy. Lindstrom would come home later. He worked long hours. Barely ever were they all together as a family. He would come after the woman had gone to bed and the lights were out in her room. LePere figured that as man and wife, they seldom connected. There was something about the unhappiness the situation suggested that pleased him in a bitter way. The people who had everything were no happier than he.

LePere heard the garage door lift at the approach of the car. He saw the headlights swallowed and heard the garage door close. Silence returned to the cove.

Lights went on, purposefully now. LePere tracked them through the house, up the stairs, to the bedrooms. He saw the boy pass a window. Hung on the wall visible through the window was a poster LePere had long ago identified with his binoculars as Bart Simpson on a skateboard. A couple of minutes later, the boy passed again wearing boxers and a T-shirt. A light went on in the room LePere always suspected was the bathroom, stayed on long enough for the boy to brush his teeth, then went off. When next the boy appeared in his room, he was followed by his mother. She would stay a while, LePere knew. Probably she read to the boy, because she often carried a book. LePere figured it was the kind of thing he would have done, too, if he had a son.

By the time the woman left the room, the moon had risen high, almost directly overhead. LePere's shadow puddled around his feet. He was tired, thinking of heading home. But he stayed, watching the room he knew to be hers, waiting for her to prepare for bed. Often, they didn't even bother to draw their blinds. Grace Cove was so isolated and they seemed so secure in their privacy. Who was there to see them? He liked watching the woman as she settled into bed, propped her pillow, opened her book. All of it alone. Her husband had his own bedroom, on the other side of the house. In those rare times they were home together at night, he sometimes came and sat on her bed. They talked a while, but LePere had never seen them kiss. Sometimes after her husband had gone, the woman stared out the window in a way that reminded LePere of how he himself sometimes gazed across Lake Superior from Purgatory Ridge, looking for things that had existed long ago but had long ago been lost.

He was caught off guard when the door to the first-floor deck opened and the woman stood silhouetted in the light from within. She closed the door, descended the deck stairs, and came across the lawn toward the dock. He looked around him on the boat for a place to hide and finally crouched in the shadow of the cockpit, hoping desperately the woman would not board.

She passed the *Amazing Grace* and walked to the very end of the dock. LePere eased himself up and watched her. She stood with her back to him, looking over the water. Through the gap in the pines that flanked either side of the entrance to the cove, Aurora was visible, a scattering of lights far across a deep, black emptiness.

In the moon's silver light, she began to undress.

She kicked off her shoes, undid the buttons of her blouse, and let the garment fall to her feet. Her hands slid up her back between the sharp bones of her shoulder blades and below the fall of her yellow hair. She worked free the hooks of her bra, slipped the straps down her arms, and dropped the large lacy cups atop her blouse. Her hands disappeared in front of her, working at her waist. She tugged down her slacks, stepped out of them easily, and dropped them in the pile with her other things. She was left in panties whose color LePere could not tell by moonlight, but the fabric had a sheen to it, as if what covered that most secret part of her body had been cut from ice. With her thumbs, she hooked the elastic of the waistband and drew off the last of her clothing. She stood naked at the end of the dock, her hair and skin and shadowed clefts all poised above dark water. She raised her arms, dipped her body, and sprang from the dock, cutting the surface of the lake with barely a splash. As the woman breaststroked out into the cove, LePere left the cockpit, leaped the railing, and loped along the dock back to land. He made for the spruce where he'd hidden before, and he let the shadow suck him in. He glanced back to see if the woman had spied him. She lay on her back, gazing up at the moon, her body outlined in ripples of black and silver.

She didn't know John LePere was watching. She probably didn't even know he existed. And she could not possibly have known why, as he stared at her from the darkness, he unconsciously balled his hands into tight, bloodless fists as if he clenched in them something he was determined to hold on to, something invisible to anyone but him.

Jo was awake long after Cork lay sleeping beside her. She watched moonlight gather on the windowsill and spill into the room. The minutes of the alarm clock on the nightstand crept by like a procession of condemned men. At midnight, she slid from the bed and stood at the window, staring into the night. The branches and leaves of the big maple in the front yard shattered the light from the street lamp in a disturbing way, and the quiet of the night felt suffocating. She went to the rocker in the corner and sat down. When Stevie was a baby, Jo had spent many nights rocking him there. Cork had taken his turns, too, losing sleep as they dealt with ear infections, upset tummies, and nightmares. She didn't miss those sleepless nights, but she grieved their simplicity, when the comfort of holding was all it took to set things right. She wanted to do that now. Just hold Cork, and have him hold her, and in that simple way make everything all right.

He'd come home late with Stevie asleep in his arms, and he'd explained that they'd hiked through the woods to visit Meloux.

All this time? she'd asked.

He went on, explaining that they'd also visited Harold Loomis, and he related his talk with the night watchman. When he finished, he looked at her as if he expected praise because he'd solved the mystery of Charlie Warren at the mill.

Instead she'd asked, *What do you think you're doing, Cork?*

She hadn't meant her voice to be so cold, but it froze the happy look in his eyes and killed the smile on his lips.

She closed her eyes and heard her words again.

"Jesus, Jo," she whispered miserably. "What were you thinking?"

She felt sick with regret. She knew she had no one to blame but herself and no reason for the coldness except her own fear.

She leaned across the moonlit room and spoke softly, "Cork, I'm so sorry."

She wished that instead of chiding him, she'd been able to tell him how afraid she was, how everything still felt so fragile between them. The truth was that she didn't trust it was love that held their marriage together. She couldn't believe that after such grave pain as they'd given one another love could ever grow strong again.

That evening, with Stevie in his arms, Cork had only confirmed what she'd already guessed. He missed being a cop. For a long time, she'd sensed he was restless. She hadn't been sure what it was until the bombing at Lindstrom's mill had brought it into the open. It was so obvious now. She wanted to be able to support him if he chose to run for sheriff, but the prospect of an election concerned her, for selfish reasons.

More than a decade before when she'd come with Cork back to his hometown, she was the first woman to hang an attorney's shingle in Tamarack County. She'd struggled long and hard against a lot of prejudices directed at her as a woman and an outsider. She'd succeeded in establishing a good practice and an unimpeachable legal reputation, but it hadn't been without some cost. Because she'd often taken on clients no other attorney in the county would touch—among them, the Iron Lake Ojibwe—she frequently found herself at odds with the prevailing sentiments in Aurora. Although she felt respected, she also felt that most people held her at a distance, just waiting for the day when she'd screw up royally. What no one knew—no one except Cork—was that she'd already blown it big time. There was a long black moment in her history in Aurora, but she'd been able to hide it for almost two years. She was afraid an election, especially a bitter one, might dredge up that history for public display. In another, larger place, her mistakes would be little more than a footnote in the news. In a place like

Aurora, they could wash her life away. She and Cork never spoke about that part of their lives, their separation and what had precipitated it. They had—by tacit mutual consent, Jo believed—agreed to move on and let the past be buried. She was afraid that if Aurora knew the whole of her history, she and Cork would be forced to face the past straight-on. Under such scrutiny, could any marriage long survive?

All these things she wanted to tell Cork, but she was afraid to begin a conversation whose end she couldn't foresee.

She left the rocker, walked around the bed, and knelt near her husband. He was such a good man, so different from any other she'd ever known. Softer in a lot of ways. When she'd first met him, he'd been a cop on Chicago's South Side. He'd seen more than his share of brutal things, yet there was something good and beautiful at the heart of him that hadn't been touched by the brutality. Whenever she'd looked into his eyes, it was as if she could see all the way down to that beautiful heart.

His eyes were closed now, his breathing a little irregular. He turned, mumbled in his dreaming. Jo reached out and touched his cheek. In a voice so soft he could not possibly have heard, she promised, "I'll try, Cork. I swear to you, I'll try."

15

HE DREAMED OF HIS BROTHER alone in the hold of the *Teasdale,* swaying in deep currents as if he were dancing in an empty ballroom, and John LePere, when he woke, found himself weeping. He didn't give himself over to the fresh grief the dream brought with it but rose immediately in the gray of first light, hit the cool, gunmetal water of Iron Lake, and swam out his emotion. By the time the sun had risen fully, he felt nearly empty and almost clean.

He was on the road by seven A.M., winding his way down Highway 1 toward the north shore. He cruised through Finland, hit Highway 61, and headed south—across the Baptism River at Tettagouche, past Shovel Point and Palisade Head, past the big taconite processing plant at Silver Bay. The sun was hazy and copper colored. Under it, Lake Superior had taken on an unsettling hue and seemed to have assumed a foul mood as well. A strong wind blew out of the southeast. The water was full of whitecaps. Not a good day for a dive, but LePere was determined.

As he entered the tunnel beneath Purgatory Ridge, he poured the last of the coffee from his thermos and swallowed it down. When he broke into the light on the other side, he slowed, took a sharp left onto the narrow lane, and headed through the poplars down to Purgatory Cove.

He parked his truck at the house and got out. The southeasterly wind funneled through the opening to the cove, pushing the water against the rocky beach. The *Anne Marie* rocked restlessly at her mooring. LePere headed to the house, unlocked the door, and went in.

Bridger's accusation the day before—that LePere never let anyone enter—was true. No one but LePere had been inside since Billy died. As much as possible, he'd kept the rooms exactly as they'd been before the event that had destroyed his life. The stove was an old cast iron wood burner and was also the only source of heat. The table and chairs had been made by his father from birch trees that grew among the hills on the other side of the highway. His mother's careful needlepoint, done in the years before Billy was born, hung framed on the walls. In the bedroom that had been first his parents' and then his mother's alone, the chest of drawers was empty, but on top, among the old jars and bottles that had contained the lotions and scents she'd once used, sat a photograph in a gold frame. A wedding photo. The man was half LePere's age but had LePere's strong, stocky build and black hair. The young woman had beautiful Indian features, and the shine in her dark eyes was evidence of a happiness LePere could barely remember in her.

Whenever he stayed in the cabin overnight, LePere slept in the room he'd shared with Billy. There was a collection of agates on a small bookcase, the prizes they'd found along the lake shore and had chosen not to sell to the souvenir shops. On Billy's bunk was a first baseman's mitt, a gift LePere had sent from Cleveland his first voyage on the *Teasdale*. Over the years, LePere had kept the mitt well oiled. On the wall, in a wood-burned frame he'd made himself, Billy had hung a photograph of his big brother standing on the deck of the huge ore carrier, the forecastle rising in the background. The future had looked hopeful in those days, and LePere had a big grin slapped across his young face.

Twice a month, he changed all the linen, dusted all the surfaces, shook out the rugs, and swept the floors. Every fall before winter set in, he drained the pipes. Every spring, he took note of what needed painting or repair and he saw to it. He'd had good offers and could have sold the place easily, but he had no intention of selling. To John LePere, the cabin and the cove on which it stood in the shadow of Purgatory Ridge were beyond value.

He'd made concessions over the years. The cabin now had a

microwave oven, a coffeemaker, and a cordless telephone. He kept the refrigerator and food shelves modestly stocked. That morning, he started coffee dripping and went out to the fish house to fill his diving tanks from the compressor and to load his boat. He knew Bridger was right. Diving alone was risky. No, it was more than that. It was stupidly dangerous. But what he'd seen and filmed the day before had fired him up. He had to retrieve the camera. He couldn't wait for Bridger. With an eye to safety, he stowed backup of all his equipment, including an extra dry suit, in a locker below deck. He returned to the cabin to fill his thermos with hot coffee, then locked the door and went down to the *Anne Marie*. He cast off the lines and backed the boat out into the cove. At last, he headed through the passage between the rocks and into the open water of the lake. As soon as he left the protection of the rocks, the wind and waves hit the boat. He turned the bow of the *Anne Marie* south by southeast and headed toward the Apostles, where the truth lay more than twenty fathoms deep.

There were times, LePere knew, when Bridger believed him to be a little crazy. LePere might have believed so, too, if he hadn't been through the ordeal of the sinking. An experience like that changed a man. No one who hadn't been there would understand. And no one who had been there was alive except John Sailor LePere.

That night, more than a decade before, after the stern had sailed off into the storm and the bow had sunk beneath the waves, LePere curled himself into a ball on the raft. His back was against Pete Swanson, who lay still, those three words—"I blew it"—spilling from his lips. Skip Jurgenson, the third man on the raft, dug into the storage compartment, pulled out a hand flare, and lit it.

"John." He nudged LePere. "Warm up whatever you can. Come on, John."

LePere rolled over and sat up.

"Hold this." Jurgenson handed him the flare. "Don't let it drip on you. It'll burn like hell."

Jurgenson reached back into the storage compartment and brought out a flare gun and a flashlight. He shot off one of the flares.

"You wasted it," LePere told him, although he didn't much care. "In this weather, who could see it?"

Jurgenson hunkered back down. "Think anybody aft made it off?"

LePere didn't answer.

"Think anybody knows we're here?"

LePere thought about Orin Grange trying to send a message on a dead radio. He stared at the flare burning in his hands and decided there was no reason to tell Jurgenson what he'd seen. He felt numb, and it wasn't just the wet and the cold. Inside he was empty. Inside, he was dead. When the flare burned out, LePere lay back down, curled into a ball again, and refused to move. Finally, Jurgenson lay down, too.

The waves continued to build and to wash over the sides of the raft. Icy water, followed by a chill, bitter wind, hit LePere. He could hear Jurgenson screaming, cursing the cold. LePere wore only a pair of boxer shorts under his peacoat. Jurgenson was clothed only in pajamas and a hooded sweatshirt.

Near dawn, the storm abated. The wind died. The water calmed and the raft rode smoothly. The sun rose pale and without warmth. LePere tried to lift himself, but he'd been frozen in a tight ball all night and his joints and muscles seemed riveted in place by pain. After great effort, he managed to sit up. He took a look at Swanson. The man's face was sheathed with ice, and his eyes were frozen open. LePere knew he was dead. Jurgenson was not moving. LePere nudged him with his foot.

"I'm alive," Jurgenson rasped. He coughed long and hard, then slowly uncurled. He pulled himself up using the side of the raft. His face was gray. Ice covered his life vest. He looked at LePere through eyelids barely open. "How long?"

LePere wasn't sure what he meant. How long had they been on the raft? How long until they were rescued? How long before they would be dead from exposure?

"Let's light another flare," LePere suggested. "Warm up some if we can."

But neither man had the strength to move. Jurgenson fell into a coughing fit that obviously gave him a lot of pain. He slid back down onto the deck of the raft, folded his arms across his chest, and drew his legs up. "Tired," he said. It was the last word he ever spoke.

The sun crossed the sky. LePere drifted in and out of consciousness. Time was an impossible measure. As dark crept over the lake, LePere gathered what little strength he had and lifted himself to peer over the gunwale of the pontoon raft. Under the evening sky, the lake was as calm as he'd ever seen it, flat and smooth and shiny. A few stars glimmered in the east. Beneath them, LePere made out a small constellation of stars, better defined and moving. A vessel. He kicked at Jurgenson. The man didn't move. He tried to find the flare gun Jurgenson had dug out of the storage compartment, but it was not at hand and he had no strength for a search, no strength even to cry out above a hoarse whisper. He watched the lights sail off into the windless night and disappear. He lay back down, completely alone now. He was thirsty. His mouth was so dry he could barely swallow. But he didn't have the strength to pull himself over the side and scoop water from the lake. Instead, he picked at ice that had formed on his peacoat and put it in his mouth to suck on.

And that was when his father came to him.

LePere didn't recognize him at first. He was just a man sitting on the gunwale. His face glowed as if lit by a light just under his skin.

"Don't eat the ice, Johnny," he said.

LePere asked, "Who are you?"

"We've been waiting for you, and for Billy," he said. "But it's still not your time, Johnny."

"Billy? Is he okay?"

"You're the last one. The only one left. You've got to make it. You've got to set things right, son."

"Dad? Is it you? I thought you were . . . Is Billy all right?"

"Don't eat the ice, Johnny. It will lower your body temperature. It will kill you."

"I was so scared for Billy."

"Billy is with us. I've got to go. They're waiting."

"Don't go. Please don't go."

"I'll see you later. We'll all be together again, Johnny. I promise. Remember. Don't eat the ice."

He faded, the outline of him lingering for a few moments, then he was gone, altogether and forever.

Although he wanted to more than he ever had, LePere could not cry. He didn't have the water for tears.

It was another ten hours before a Coast Guard helicopter spotted him and he was plucked from the life raft that was drifting midway between the Apostle Islands and the Michigan shoreline. He was flown to a hospital in Ashland, Wisconsin. LePere had little memory of the rescue and of the hours that followed. Later, the doctors told him his body temperature was only ninety-four degrees when the Coast Guard brought him in. They were surprised he hadn't died with the others on the raft. When he was able to respond, the Coast Guard questioned him. He told them about everything except the visit from his father. That was something he'd never told anyone. For a while, the doctors thought they might have to amputate some toes that suffered frostbite, but in the end, LePere's body emerged whole from the ordeal. Everyone was encouraging. Everyone was amazed. *You're alive,* they all told him brightly. *You're alive.*

John Sailor LePere knew they were liars.

LePere didn't stop at the buoy that marked where the wreck of the *Teasdale* lay. That morning, he continued down the shoreline of Outer Island, looking for the white launch. He didn't know how the Fitzgerald Shipping Company had found out about the dives, but it seemed clear to him now that they were worried. In the rough water east of the island, there were no boats, but in the small bay near the lighthouse, LePere spotted a number of pleasure craft. None appeared to be the white launch. When he was satisfied, he headed out to the wreck. Alone and with the water so rough, he had a difficult time tying up to the buoy once he'd reached it. He suited up and spent a final moment checking the lake. Except for the Apostle Islands, the horizon was empty. He could see waves sending up spray as they crashed against Outer Island's rocky shore, but the white launch was nowhere in sight. LePere figured they probably thought no one in his right mind would dive on a day like that.

He went over the side and followed the buoy line that was drawn taut by the pull of the boat above. Under the surface, the water was calm and everything was quiet. LePere descended, switching on his Ikelite as the sunlight diminished. He listened to his own breathing and to the steady spill of his bubbles. At seventy feet, an eelpout swam through the light, winding its body in the direction of the Apostles.

In ten minutes, he'd reached the stern of the *Teasdale,* where he followed the hull down to the broken midsection. He dipped over the edge and headed into the darkness at the bottom. His Ikelite illuminated a river of coal that spilled from the open cargo hold, but nowhere on that river did he see the camera. His light swept over the rocky bottom the coal didn't cover; the camera was not there either. LePere searched the hold thoroughly and came up empty-handed. There were no strong currents that deep, nothing naturally occurring he could think of that could have moved the camera. The only thing that made sense was that someone had been there before him.

Shit. He'd have screamed it but for the mouthpiece feeding him air. He checked his regulator. He'd been down long enough. There was nothing more to see anyway. He turned and headed back to the buoy cable.

What greeted him when he reached the end of the stern was a sight more chilling than any cold the water could have pressed upon him. The buoy cable was rapidly snaking down from the surface. He realized that a hundred feet above him, the *Anne Marie* had either been stolen or set adrift.

Without a moment's hesitation, he inflated the vest that was his weight compensator, and he shot toward the surface. At sixty feet, the yellow marker for decompression dropped past him and then the severed end of the cable. He knew that when he neared the surface, he'd have to rely on his depth gauge and on his own judgment to hold at ten feet and then force himself to be patient as his body decompressed. It would do him no good if he saved the *Anne Marie* only to succumb to the bends. The darkness gave way to light. At thirty feet, he saw the surface and that there was no silhouette of his boat above or any sign of the marker buoy. He punctured his vest with his knife to slow his ascent. When the needle on his depth gauge hit ten feet and when his own sensibility confirmed it, he held.

John LePere had gone through the torture of more sleepless nights than he could remember, watching the seconds tick off a clock so slowly he seemed in another time dimension. Nothing he'd experienced before was like the hell of the minutes he spent with the empty surface just out of his reach. He tried to think what he'd do if the boat were gone for good. What if she were drifting too far and too fast to catch? Or what if she had been set adrift with a hole punched in her hull to scuttle her?

Not yet, he told himself at six minutes when it had already felt like hours.

He calculated the wind direction and tried to envision where the boat would hit if it drifted toward Outer Island. The shoreline was nothing but tall trees, hard rock, and wild surf. He could think of no safe landing.

He gave himself nine minutes. Probably not enough to be completely safe, but the hell with it. He broke the surface and caught a wave that lifted him high. He spotted the *Anne Marie* adrift a quarter mile northwest. Not far beyond it, the breakers slammed against the rocks of Outer Island. Fitted for diving, he was unfit to swim. He shed his gear, abandoning tank, weights, vest. Although it was cumbersome, he left his dry suit on, his only protection against the numbing cold of the lake water. LePere began to swim.

He used strong, even strokes, trying to pace himself, relying on what his body could do as a result of all those mornings he'd cut through the water of Iron Lake for miles. But Iron Lake was small and calm. The angry waves of Superior crashed over him, choked his throat with icy water, lifted his body, and threw it down. For a long time, he couldn't tell if he was gaining on the boat at all. He focused all his effort on trying to reach the *Anne Marie* before she hit the rocks, which kept him from worrying about what he'd do if he reached her only to discover the engine had been sabotaged or the rudder cable cut.

Twenty minutes of a harder crawl than he'd ever done brought him to within reach of the bowline that was still dragging the buoy. He grabbed hold and hauled himself in, hand over hand, until he could reach the diving ladder. Breathing in gasps, he climbed aboard. He could hear the roar of the breakers less than two hundred yards distant now. Quickly, he went to the helm station inside the deckhouse. The key was gone. He ran down the companionway to the forward cabin and grabbed the extra key he kept on a nail under one of the bunks. Back at the helm station, he jammed the key into the ignition. The engine coughed and didn't catch. LePere glanced toward Outer

Island. He was still more than a hundred yards out, but he saw in the trough between the waves, less than fifty feet to starboard and directly in the path the wind and waves were pushing the *Anne Marie,* the glint of light off the sleek, jagged rocks of a shoal.

He hit the ignition again. "Come on, baby," he whispered.

The engine caught this time. He swung the wheel hard to starboard and eased the throttle forward, narrowly missing an arm of dark rock just beneath the surface. He came about fully, nosed the *Anne Marie* into the wind, and put a safe distance between himself and the island. He idled the engine and checked the boat. Nothing had been damaged. The extra diving gear stowed below hadn't been touched. He hauled in the buoy and checked the cable. The line had been cut.

He hadn't seen the white launch, but maybe everything was different now. Maybe they would always use a different boat so he'd never know when they were watching, waiting to have another go at him.

They'd taken his camera. They'd tried to destroy his boat. They were clearly afraid.

Good, he thought, and he found himself smiling. That meant they had something to hide.

He headed the boat home with the wind at his back. It would be a while before he returned. Bridger's luck had been bad lately and he was low on money. On a janitor's salary, LePere would have to save carefully for months to put together the cost of a new camera and housing, but he would do it. He would do whatever he had to. They hadn't stopped him; they'd only delayed the inevitable. Next time he came, he'd be ready to take them down for good.

He reached Purgatory Cove in the early afternoon, eased the *Anne Marie* up to the dock, and cut the engine. He secured the lines and headed toward shore. When he saw that the door to the fish house was wide open, he made for it quickly, then stood staring at the chaos inside. It looked as if someone had used a sledgehammer and had a field day. The compressor lay in pieces. His diving gear and the equipment and supplies for the *Anne Marie* had all been damaged or destroyed. Turning toward the small house, he saw that the door there stood open, as well. He hit the porch at a run. Inside, he found the rooms torn apart. The cupboards had been cleared. Drinking glasses and blue crockery plates lay shattered on the floor. In his mother's room, the bottles had been swept off the top of the bureau and smashed.

They were after nothing. They'd already got the camera and the tape it held. LePere knew this was an attack on him. They'd come to destroy the memories the cabin held for him. His mother's careful needlepoint had been torn from the walls. The framed wedding photograph of his parents was thrown to the floor where a callous heel had ground the broken glass, shredding the picture that had been the most solid evidence LePere possessed that once, long ago, life had been good and full of promise. In the room he'd shared with Billy, the agate collection had been scattered. Billy's first baseman's mitt was gone altogether.

For years, John LePere had lived with loss. He'd endured nightmares that, with each visitation, brought fresh grief. He'd learned to walk among other men as if he were a whole man, too, although he felt hollow inside. As he knelt amid the wreckage of all that had once remained to him of happiness, he let out a howl like an animal in terrible pain. What filled that hollow inside him now was a raging sensibility that felt more beast than human.

He picked the telephone up from the floor. There was still a dial tone. He punched in a number. The phone at the other end rang five times, then the voice message machine kicked in.

"Yeah, this is Bridger. Leave me a message. And make it short, God damn it."

The line beeped.

"This is LePere. That crazy-ass idea of yours—you still want to do it, I'm in."

16

FRIDAYS WERE ALWAYS BUSY at Sam's Place. Because of tourists getting an early start on the weekend, business came heavily from the lake. By midafternoon, Cork had run out of hamburger buns. He left the girls in charge and took off for the IGA SuperValu in Aurora. As he started up the gravel road, he spotted Wally Schanno's Land Cruiser turn off Center Street and head toward Sam's Place. Near the Burlington Northern tracks, Schanno waved Cork to a stop and both men got out.

The day was hot and Schanno wore a gray Stetson to shade his face. "Glad I caught you, Cork."

"What can I do for you, Wally?"

"You can give me the benefit of your thinking. I spoke with Harold Loomis."

"Then you're pretty sure Charlie Warren had nothing to do with the bombing?"

"As sure as you are. I'm also pretty sure Loomis had nothing to do with it. He let us search his place. He has a good collection of baseball cards, that's about it. All of which leaves me without a primary suspect. The BCA agents have a couple of ideas. So do I. I was hoping you might have a few of your own."

"This kind of thing isn't my business anymore," Cork reminded him. "Besides, how would the BCA like it, knowing you were confiding in unauthorized personnel?"

"This is still my investigation. Anyway, I told them I was coming out to talk to you, that because you're part Ojibwe yourself, you'd probably have an interesting perspective to offer."

"How about letting me in on the official thinking?"

Schanno crossed his arms, hooked his big hands into the crooks at his elbows, and stared toward town. "We've come up with several possibilities. Agents Earl and Owen are inclined in a couple of directions. I'm inclined in another."

"What do they think?"

"Tree huggers. They've run checks on a bunch of folks out there at the tent city on the rez and some are particularly qualified in explosives."

"Who?"

"Joan Hamilton, for one. Joan of Arc of the Redwoods. You've seen that she walks with a cane. The result of injuries sustained when a pipe bomb went off in her car a couple of years ago. California authorities contended that the bomb was of her own making and went off accidentally. She claims she was set up by the logging companies. Her son majored in chemical engineering at Cal Tech, which probably makes him well qualified to know about explosives. And then there's Broom. Hell, he uses explosives all the time in that logging business of his, blowing stumps and whatnot."

Schanno gave a little time for all this information to sink in. The wild oats along the roadside were dry and full of grasshoppers. So near the tracks, the air was strong with the scent of creosote and hot oil. The only sounds were the buzz of the grasshoppers, the rustle of the dry oats, and the crunch of gravel as the two men shifted their feet.

"You said their thinking was in two directions, Wally."

"This is a bit further out," Schanno said cautiously. "And I'd just as soon you didn't mention it to anybody. It's not unheard of, I suppose. It goes like this. If you look at the bombing, one thing seems clear. The death of Charlie Warren was an accident. And the damage was limited to an area of the mill that wouldn't affect operations greatly."

"This is important because?" Cork asked.

"Every logging operation that Lindstrom's involved in right now is being hit with protest. Word is that he's having trouble getting enough logs. With all the money he spent renovating that mill, I'm betting he absolutely can't afford not to supply it with timber. Even if he wins the court battle, and a lot of peo-ple seem to think he will, he needs to win support for the cut-ting or he's going to encounter trouble at every turn. It would sure be helpful to him if public sentiment was against the tree huggers."

"You really believe he could have arranged this himself?"

"At this point, I guess I'm not about to disbelieve anything," Schanno replied. "As for me, I'm thinking we ought to consider this might be about something else altogether."

He removed the gray Stetson and wiped the sweat from the band with his handkerchief. He put the hat back on and dabbed at his face.

"I'm just thinking," he went on, "that this whole logging brouhaha might be a perfect opportunity for someone with a grudge to get back at Lindstrom. They got a chance to vent here and blame it on the tree huggers."

"What kind of grudge?"

"Could be an old one. Lindstrom family's been cutting in the woods up here for nearly a hundred years and they've never been known for their delicate ways. The Iron Lake Ojibwe, they've got the gumption and, with the casino revenue, the resources to fight back legally. But a lot of folks who got stepped on still don't. Now that Karl's moved himself up here and settled down, I'm wondering if maybe the chickens aren't coming home to roost. Or it could be something as simple as a fired employee. I've got Gil Singer running that one down."

Cork absentmindedly leaned against the hood of the Land Cruiser but jerked back from the sting of the hot metal.

"Well, what do you think?" Schanno asked.

Cork rubbed where he'd burned his arm. "I'm thinking you're overlooking another possibility."

"What's that?"

"Hell Hanover."

"Hell? I don't follow you."

"The Minnesota Civilian Brigade, Wally."

"The brigade's broke up."

"You really believe that? The firearms were never found. Charges were never brought. You watched a lot of men for a long time, but I don't think you ever really saw the heart of the brigade."

"Okay, so how would the brigade tie in?"

Cork circled so that the sun was not in his eyes. Schanno watched him from the shadow under the brim of his Stetson.

"It fits their agenda. Civil disorder. Fomenting unrest over an issue that is, at heart, all about federal regulation. What a coup to have a small war erupt over the leasing of federal lands. I can just see Hell using his editorial page to jump all over the issue. And you can't tell me Hell or one of the brigade doesn't know about explosives."

With the tip of his index finger, Schanno eased his Stetson up an inch as he considered. "Hanover, huh?"

"I'm just saying it's another possibility. Any chance of getting search warrants?"

"Based on what we have right now, any judge'd laugh us right out of the office."

"So what do you intend to do?"

"Wait, I guess. See what happens next. Maybe we won't have to wait long. Karl Lindstrom's called a press conference this evening."

"What for?"

"Word is, he's going to make some concessions. For whatever reason, he wants to speak from the steps of the middle school. Agent Owen's over there right now checking for explosives. And I've got men stationed all around there until Lindstrom's finished speaking. It's a pain in the butt, but he insists it's important."

Cork kicked at a big chunk of red cinder that had somehow migrated from the bed of the railroad tracks. There was something eating at him, but he wasn't sure if he wanted to push it. Finally he blurted it out.

"Why, Wally?"

"Why what?"

"Why are you keeping me in this thing?"

"I'm just seeking out expertise where it exists."

"Bullshit."

"Not entirely," Scahnno said. Then he said the rest. "I suppose you've heard I'm not running again in November."

"I've heard. Didn't know if it was true."

"It's true enough."

"Arletta?" Cork asked. He was speaking of Schanno's wife,

one of the kindest and loveliest women Tamarack County had ever produced. And one of the most tragic as Alzheimer's overtook her.

Schanno nodded and looked down. "I figure she's not going to get any better, and whatever time we've got left to us I want to spend doing what we love. Some traveling. Visiting the girls and the grandkids. You know, before it's too late."

"Sure."

"The party people, they've already decided they're going to back Arne Soderberg." He gave a dry laugh. "Soderberg, can you imagine?"

Schanno looked down at the badge pinned to his shirt pocket. He kept it polished, and in the sunlight it flashed on his chest as if on fire.

"Look, Cork, when I first took this badge from you, I figured there'd be bad blood between us. There could've been, real easy. But when you had the chance to nail my ass to the wall—and we both know what I'm talking about here—you didn't. You gave me a chance at, well, redemption. I owe you. Honestly, I can't think of a better man for sheriff. And I know I'm not alone. Lots of folks around here'd jump party lines if you were to run. Which I think you ought to."

"Arne's got a lot of mud he could dredge up and throw around," Cork reminded him.

"Unless I misjudge you, you can stand up to a little mudslinging. And the voters in Tamarack County, while they're awful gossips, wouldn't look kindly on that kind of campaign." Schanno reached out and opened the door to his Land Cruiser. "I'm just saying you should think about it, okay?"

"Sure. And thanks, Wally."

Schanno made a U-turn, his wheels cutting narrow swaths in the rye grass at the edge of the road. After the sheriff had gone, Cork stood in the sun a moment, listening to the buzz of the grasshoppers in the dry heat. The sound reminded him of the sizzling of a power line that was just about to blow.

17

FOR ALMOST AN HOUR, Jo had been sitting at her desk in her office in the Aurora Professional Building, staring at the legal pad in front of her and not seeing it at all. She'd been looking over a variance for the casino that was due to be renewed on January 1. That had got her to thinking about a New Year's Day from her own history when she was seventeen years old, during the first year her mother—whom she and Rose between themselves always called the Captain—was assigned to Fort Hood in Texas.

The Captain had seen the old year out with heavy drinking and had begun the new year in the same way. When they sat down to the ham dinner Rose had prepared, the Captain was unsteady and her face had that hard, mean look it often got when she was drinking. The television was tuned to a football game. Jo got up to turn it off.

"Leave it on," the Captain ordered.

Jo continued toward the television, turned the sound down to nothing, and returned to the table. She had no tolerance for the Captain anymore, and she wasn't afraid to confront her mother. By then, confrontation was the most characteristic aspect of their relationship. But for the sake of Rose, who'd worked hard to create something special for the new year, she held her tongue.

"I think we should tell something we've been grateful for in the past year," Rose suggested. "And something we're looking forward to in the new year."

"Fine. Lemme start," the Captain said. She leaned her arms heavily on the table. "First of all, I'm grateful I've got a daughter who could cook for the angels and a daughter who could argue her way outta hell." She raised her glass, full of Jim Beam, to both of them. "This past year—let me see. . . . I've been grateful the U.S. Army has seen fit to assign me to this military base in the most godforsaken part of the world and to put me and my family up in the worst excuse for base housing I've ever seen. I've also been grateful for waking up alone every fucking day and for never having to worry about a toilet seat being all dribbled on with a man's pee." She drank from her glass and thought a moment. "As for next year, well, I guess I'm just looking forward to a lot more of the same. Happy New Year, girls." She lifted her glass once more. This time, as she set her drink back down, her hand caught the edge of her plate and sent it flying. The room was quiet. The Captain stared where the broken plate and the food splattered across the floor. Rose stood to clean up the mess.

"Leave it," the Captain snapped.

Rose sat down.

"My turn," Jo said angrily. "You want to know what I've been grateful for all year?"

"The invention of condoms?" The Captain sipped from her glass and eyed her daughter over the rim.

"Like every year before, it takes me that much closer to getting away."

"So much for the past. What, pray tell, are you looking forward to?"

"Another year of busting my butt to get straight A's, to be the absolute best at what I do. Because when I get out of here, I'm going to the top. Which, believe you me, will take me about as far from you as possible."

The Captain raised her glass. "Here's to the future, kid. Godspeed."

Across the table, their glares collided like trains meeting head-on. They both turned toward Rose.

"I'm grateful," Rose began in the way she always did, quietly, addressing their angry gazes with unwavering calm, "that I'm never lonely, because I know a lot of people are. And even though it's not much, I'm grateful for the roof over our heads because some people sleep in cardboard boxes. I'm grateful that the soldiers coming back hurt from Vietnam have someone as skilled as my mother to take care of them. And I'm grateful I have a sister who knows so many things and helps me with my homework and talks to me when we're in bed at night. I'm grateful for what I remember of my father because they're good things." She paused a moment and a smile came to her lips. "As for this year, I'm looking forward to worrying less that I'm fat and have freckles, and worrying more about why God put me here in the first place." She sat back. Then leaned forward once more, quickly. "And I'm looking forward to finally being finished with geometry."

For a few moments, the only sound was the hum of the wind through the weather stripping on the front door. Then the Captain put aside her glass and reached her hands across the table to her daughters.

Later, they walked, all of them, arm in arm in flurries of snow that forever after made Jo think of white rose petals.

Her conflicts with the Captain never really ended. Her mother's bitterness was always there, just below the surface, hauled up swiftly and easily by whiskey on the rocks. Which was why Jo seldom drank and never to excess. She was afraid her mother was inside her, just under her skin. She often felt that if she let herself, she could easily self-destruct. There had been times in her life when she'd seemed right on the edge, but always something happened to bring her back. As if the angels Rose so fiercely believed in had interceded.

She looked up from her legal pad, surprised to see that the sunlight through the window had dramatically shifted and was crawling up the eastern wall. She glanced at her watch. After five. That meant Fran had already gone. She should be heading home, too. As she started to put her pad away, there was a knock at her office door.

"Come in."

Smooth as a big ball bearing and white as a new morgue sheet, Hell Hanover's head thrust in, followed by his limping body. "Afternoon, Jo."

"Helm. What can I do for you?"

"Just hoping you might be able to verify or put to rest a couple of rumors floating around town." Without being asked, he sat in the chair on the far side of her desk. In his hand he held a large brown envelope.

Jo folded her hands on her desk and said, "Run them by me and I'll see what I can do."

He smiled. A crack in an egg. "I understand Cork's been instrumental in the investigation of the bombing at Lindstrom's mill. Is that true?"

"Any question you have about the investigation should be addressed to Sheriff Schanno, don't you think?"

Hanover laughed, sounding genuinely amused. "Lawyers," he said, and shook his head. "Let me ask you another question, then. I understand Cork's thinking of running for sheriff in the November election."

Jo waited. "That's not a question."

"Is it true?"

"You know about rumors. Seldom any substance. But if you really wanted to know Cork's intentions, you'd just ask him, Helm. So what is it you're really here for?"

The look of amusement abandoned Hanover's face. "I want your help."

"*My* help? For what?"

"I want you to convince your husband of two things."

Jo sat back. "I can't imagine where this is leading."

"First, I want him to butt out of the investigation into the incident at Lindstrom's mill. And second, I want you to make him understand that running for sheriff again would be the worst decision he ever made."

For her own reasons, Jo agreed with Hanover's sentiments, but she disliked the man immensely, and it was only years of practiced self-restraint in the courtroom that kept her from telling Helmuth Hanover to go fuck himself.

"What difference could any of this possibly make to you?" she asked.

"That doesn't matter. I'd just suggest you do it."

Jo smiled now. "You're not still sore that he broke up your little Boy Scout troop? The Minnesota Civilian Brigade." She looked him over carefully. "Or is it that you're afraid he might have another go at it? You know, he never believed for an instant you all just dropped your dreams of glory."

"Like I said, it doesn't matter why. Just do it."

"Helm, what makes you think you can slither in here and dictate terms to me?"

She saw his cold blue eyes slide down to the envelope in his hand. Another thin smile broke across his face. Without a word, he handed her the envelope.

When she saw the photograph inside, she felt gutted, like some animal Hanover had stealthily tracked and finally brought down. For a moment, she couldn't breathe. In the silence of that moment, she heard Hanover give a little snort of victory.

"You just finished ridiculing my dreams of glory, Jo. What about your own?"

The photograph was black and white, taken at night with a camera using a starlight lens. It was a bit grainy because the image had been enlarged several times. Despite the poor quality, the composition of the photo was brutally clear. A hot tub lit by candlelight. A woman, naked, holding to the edge of the tub and bent slightly forward, her mouth opened in a little circle of ecstasy as a naked man entered her from behind. The woman was Jo. The man was not Cork.

"Where did you get this?" she asked when she could breathe again.

"I've had it for some time. I got it from his father"—he pointed toward the man in the photograph—"before the old goat croaked. This was exactly his kind of weapon. Me, I prefer military hardware. But a weapon is a weapon." He leaned forward. "The bottom line is this. Unless you convince Cork to stop sticking his nose where it doesn't belong and to refrain forever from being a candidate for sheriff, he gets a copy of that photo. A big eight-by-ten in a gold frame."

Jo stared at Hanover. "He's seen this."

"He knows?" Hanover shook his head in bewilderment. "I guess he's not nearly the man I thought he was. Doesn't matter. The conditions still hold, but the consequence is this. All of Tamarack County will see that photo. I'll make sure it's not possible for you or Cork to walk down a street here without someone whispering at your back. And I wonder what those children of yours would think of their mother, especially when they start hearing the word *slut* and your name in the same sentence."

"Get out."

"Look at it this way, Jo. Cork's a great fry boy. All you have to do is convince him to keep flipping those burgers."

"I said get out." Jo stood and flung the photograph at him. It simply fluttered to the floor where Hanover let it lie.

"That's all right. You can keep it. I have the negative." He turned and limped to the door, but he paused with his hand on the knob. "You know, Jo, I've stood by and watched you twist the law every which way to get what you want around here. In this, there is no law. There's only justice. At last."

"Hell," she spit out, using for the first time the epithet so many others had applied to him, "bite me."

Hanover exited, and she heard him laughing as he closed the door.

She found she was shaking with rage. She walked unsteadily around the desk and stood looking down at herself on the floor. The camera had captured her as she bent to the pleasure of a man she would never forget but whose memory she hated. She'd believed that part of her life was over forever and that she'd escaped. But history, she understood as she knelt and took the photograph into her hands, could never be undone. And in a place like Aurora especially, it was as inescapable as her own shadow.

18

A T SEVEN-THIRTY-FIVE P.M., Cork parked his Bronco behind the Aurora Middle School and headed toward the back entrance, which was near a Dumpster. He could see that Deputy Gil Singer had been posted at the door.

"How's it going, Gil?"

"Quiet, Cork. Back here anyway. Action's out front."

"I know. Couldn't find a place to park, so I came 'round back. You mind?"

"All right by me."

"Is that Lindstrom's?" Cork asked, pointing toward a new blue Explorer parked not far from his old Bronco.

"Yep."

"Is he inside the school?"

"You're batting a thousand, Cork."

"Mind if I go in?"

"Sheriff said to keep suspicious types out. Don't guess that includes you." He opened the door.

When Cork graduated thirty years earlier, the building had been Aurora's high school. A few years later, a large consolidated county school had been built just west of town, and the old high school, a beautiful structure of red brick, had become the district's middle school. The building was full of good memories for Cork. Whenever he walked the hallways, the smell alone—waxed floors and old lockers—took him back instantly across three decades.

Inside the front door, he found Karl Lindstrom in a heated

discussion with Bruce Mortenson, the operations manager for the mill. Cork held back until Mortenson lifted his hands in exasperation and declared, "Fine, Karl. Have it your way. It's your damn mill, after all." Mortenson stomped out the door.

Cork coughed discreetly. Lindstrom looked his way. "O'Connor." He actually seemed glad to see Cork.

"Evening, Karl."

Lindstrom stepped toward him, about to speak, but the front door swung open and Lindstrom's attorney Frank Wharton slipped inside. He handed Lindstrom a sheet of paper and said, "Everything's ready, Karl. Folks're waiting."

"Thanks, Frank. I'll be right there." Lindstrom glanced at Cork. "You have a minute after this so we can talk?"

"Sure."

Lindstrom looked down at the paper in his hands, took a deep breath, and pushed outside. Cork gave him a moment, then followed.

A standing microphone and speakers had been set on the steps of the school. Parked cars lined the street, and the front lawn was crowded. Newspeople with cameras and tape recorders had positioned themselves at the bottom of the steps. Hell Hanover was right there in the thick of them. Looking over the crowd, Cork saw that both sides of the logging issue were well represented. Sheriff Wally Schanno and several of his deputies flanked Lindstrom on the steps. Agents Earl and Owen of the BCA were there, too. Across the street was a small park, and Cork saw Jo standing there alone, her arms folded across her body as if despite the terrible heat, she was cold.

Lindstrom stepped up to the microphone and tapped it. "Can you all hear me?"

Someone near the back of the crowd shouted, "Loud and clear, Karl. Give 'em hell."

"I'm not here to give anybody hell," Lindstrom said, leaning to the mike. "Seems to me we've had enough of that already." He considered the paper in his hand, then let it fall. "I had remarks prepared by my lawyer so that I'd say all of this right, but I'm a little tired of legalese at the moment. I'd just as soon tell you straight out how I feel.

"I don't know how many of you remember the company's old logo with the slogan 'Lindstrom houses the world.'

Remember? It showed the globe inside a home built with Lindstrom lumber. Well, we don't house much of the world anymore. For a lot of reasons.

"A few years ago, my father was faced with a decision. Drastic changes had to be made to our Eagle River mill in Wisconsin to bring it in line with new state and federal environmental regulations and to make it competitive with products from foreign markets. My father chose to close that mill rather than fight the government and unfair trade policies. Two years ago, faced with a similar dilemma here in the last of the Lindstrom mills, I chose differently.

"As most of you know, I built a home on Iron Lake last year, built it with Lindstrom logs. This spring, my family and I moved in. We came up here because I wanted to be a part of this town. The Lindstrom name's been important in the North Woods for several generations, but the Lindstroms have never been around to see the effects of what they've done. Well, I'm here, and I'm taking responsibility for what we do. Over the last two years, I've completely renovated the mill. We've got the best technology in the business. I did this at great personal expense because I believe it's best for the environment and for the people here. As far as I'm concerned, there's no more beautiful place on earth than Tamarack County and no better people."

"You're doing great, Karl! Don't let 'em get you down!"

"Thanks. Thank you." Lindstrom turned away from the mike and coughed. While he was at it, he took a moment to gather his thoughts. "A lot of good people depend on the mill for their livelihood. And for the mill to operate, we need to cut trees. Recently, every logging operation we've undertaken has been plagued by sabotage. Sugar in the gas tanks of our heavy equipment and marks removed from the trees designated for cutting, to name just a couple.

"The controversy that's recently disrupted both the normal life of this community and the harvesting of timber for the mill isn't just unfortunate. It's personally very painful. I've always tried to work within the framework of the law in seeking a resolution, but there are those on the other side of the issue who haven't. The result has been a terrible tragedy. A senseless death.

"Because I want to end this animosity, I'm offering some concessions to those who are so opposed to our logging in the area of the Superior National Forest the Ojibwe call Our Grandfathers. Should Judge Rabin rule in our favor—and I have to tell you that I believe firmly she will—I promise that when logging resumes, not one of the Lindstrom loggers or any logging company with whom we subcontract will cut a single unnecessary tree from Our Grandfathers. I swear to you we'll do only what's necessary to create a logging road through the area that will give us access to the younger trees surrounding and intermixed with those beautiful old white pines. In addition, I absolutely promise that any white pine cut will be replaced with a white pine seedling that, as the years go by, will take its place tall and proud among Our Grandfathers.

"I wanted to make this announcement on the steps of the school because ultimately, what's important is that we leave our children a world that holds for them the promise of health, wealth, happiness, and harmony." He looked the crowd over slowly. "That's all I have to say. I'd be happy to answer any questions you might have."

Before Lindstrom could grant anyone a chance to speak, a voice boomed against the brick of the building.

"I have a question."

Cork and a lot of other people looked across the street and saw Joan of Arc of the Redwoods standing atop her dusty Econoline van with a bullhorn in one hand and her cane in the other.

"Why is your head in the sand? For a man who claims to be concerned about the environment, you're pretty ignorant of the fragile nature of ecological systems. You cut a road through Our Grandfathers and you'll damage the system that sustains them. You harvest the timber that surrounds them and you do the same thing. The point we've been trying to make is that any cutting in that area is a violation of nature. The consequences will be devastating."

"Our studies tell us differently," Lindstrom countered.

"Your studies tell you what you want to hear. I've seen studies like yours, and I've seen firsthand the slaughter they've justified."

"You're talking, I assume, about your experiences with the redwoods in California. Let me just point out that the decisions there are being made by people thousands of miles from the forests. I've chosen to live here. I've brought my family here. I make decisions as a member of this community, for the benefit of the men and women who look to the mill for livelihood and who are also members of this community. I respectfully point out that you don't live here and that when one way or another this is resolved, you'll leave. Build a house here. Raise a family here. Try making a living here. Then maybe you'll have the right to be heard here."

Loud applause met Lindstrom's remarks.

When things had quieted a bit, the woman put the bullhorn to her mouth again. "I'm a member of a larger community, Mr. Lindstrom, as are you."

Lindstrom leaned to the mike, but before he could speak, a loud *bang* interrupted him and made him jump—made everyone jump. Cork hunched down instinctively and glanced to the north side of the building where the sound had come. The crowd also ducked and moved helter-skelter in a shifting wave of brief panic. Wally Schanno had his firearm drawn. Along with two deputies, he quickly moved toward the side of the school. Agent Earl of the BCA had his own weapon in hand and had taken up a protective position next to Lindstrom. For the first time in a long time, Cork wished he were carrying a piece, too.

Evening quiet settled in again almost immediately. All heads were turned where Schanno and his men had gone. It took less than two minutes for the sheriff and his deputies to reappear. Gil Singer was with them. Schanno spoke briefly to Singer, who disappeared again, heading back—Cork supposed—to his post at the rear door.

Schanno approached the microphone. "It's okay folks. Just a firecracker. Somebody's idea of a joke. Not a funny one." He turned to Lindstrom but still spoke into the mike. "Did you want to say anything else, Karl?"

Lindstrom stepped forward and spoke in a shaky voice. "Thank you, ladies and gentlemen, for coming this evening. I—uh—I guess that's all I have to say."

"I haven't finished." It was the woman with the cane and the bullhorn.

Lindstrom ignored her, turned abruptly from the microphone, and vanished back inside the building.

The crowd began almost immediately to disperse. Schanno headed over to confer with the BCA agents. With the help of her son, who'd seemed to come out of nowhere, Joan of Arc of the Redwoods descended from the roof of her van and drove away. Cork left the steps and crossed the street to the little park where Jo was now standing with George LeDuc.

"What do you think, George?" Cork asked when he'd joined them.

"I could've done without that firecracker. And Lindstrom, he looked like he could use a change of underwear."

"What about his offer?"

"I don't know, Cork. Seems like he's trying."

"He's offering us a bone without any meat on it." Isaiah Broom came up behind LeDuc. It was the first Cork had seen of him that evening. "Once his machines and men are in there, they can do anything they want to. If you believe him, George, you're a bigger fool than I thought." That said, Broom turned and left.

George LeDuc watched him go. "Now there's a man could piss off a saint." He looked to Jo. "What do we do now?"

"There's nothing to do but wait until the ruling comes down. Then we'll see."

LeDuc bid them good evening and headed toward his truck. "I'm going to talk to Karl Lindstrom inside the school," Cork said. "Care to join me?"

"He might not want to see me," Jo replied.

"He seems in a very forgiving mood."

The microphone and speakers were being removed. The crowd had pretty much dispersed. Schanno was down by his Land Cruiser talking with a couple of deputies. Cork and Jo went in the front door. Lindstrom had leaned a hand against the wall, holding himself up. When the door opened, he jerked to attention, startled.

"Easy, Karl. It's just us."

Lindstrom still looked shaken. "That's okay. I was just . . . I'm just a little . . ." He stopped and seemed to pull himself together. "I'm glad you're here, Cork. You, too, Jo. I wanted to apologize for my behavior at the mill the other night. I was upset."

"Forget it," Jo said.

"You know, I've sunk every dime I have into modernizing that mill. I thought I was helping people, doing something worthwhile."

"You've kept a lot of people employed, Karl. That is important," Cork told him.

"Joan of Arc out there, she makes me sound like a monster."

Cork could see it hurt. The Lindstroms before him would have grinned and worn the epithet proudly. "Let it go," he advised.

"You're right." His eyes shifted to Jo. "You'll be receiving a formal outline of my proposal, Jo, but if you'd like one now, I've got a copy in my briefcase. It's in my Explorer."

"Where are you parked?" Jo asked.

"Out back."

"I'd like to see it, yes."

They walked together through the darkening hallways to the back door that was unguarded now. When they reached the Explorer, Lindstrom plucked from the windshield a folded sheet of paper that had been stuffed under the wiper blade. As he read the note, the color drained from his face. He looked at his watch.

"What is it, Karl?" Cork asked.

"Nothing. It's nothing. Listen, Jo, I'll get you that document later, all right?"

"Sure, Karl."

Lindstrom waited. It was clear he wanted them to move away.

"I'll give you a lift to your car," Cork offered to Jo.

He turned and headed to his Bronco. When Jo was beside him in the passenger seat, he backed the Bronco out and started it away slowly, watching Lindstrom in his mirror. Jo was watching, too. Lindstrom took an old leather briefcase from the Explorer, opened it, and reached inside. He drew something out and his hand went toward his waist under his sport coat. Then he slammed the door closed and started walking briskly across the football field behind the school.

"Did you see?" Jo asked.

"Yes."

Lindstrom had shoved a handgun into his belt.

"What's going on?" she asked.

"You know as much as I do." Cork turned off the engine and reached for the door handle.

"Where are you going?"

"After Karl. I don't know what was in that note, but it wasn't good news."

Jo grabbed his arm. "Cork, this isn't your responsibility. This is for Wally Schanno to worry about. Get Wally or one of his deputies. Please."

Lindstrom was halfway across the field. Cork knew if he delayed much longer, Lindstrom would be gone—wherever it was he was going.

"All right." He drove to the front of the building. No one was left outside. All the cars except Jo's Tercel were gone. The front lawn was as vacant as it usually was on a summer evening.

"Jo, I have to go."

"Why?"

Cork looked at her. She was right. There was no reason for him to do this. He was a man who flipped hamburgers now. Except everything in him was shoving him after Lindstrom.

"Go," she finally said angrily, and grabbed the door handle. "Just go if you feel you have to." She got out and slammed the door shut. "But if you find yourself in the middle of something—"

Cork didn't wait for her to finish. He raced the Bronco to the parking area behind the school. Lindstrom was just vanishing into a line of maple trees that edged the field behind the bleachers. Beyond the maple trees was Lake Shore Drive, and beyond the drive lay Iron Lake.

When Cork stepped out of the trees, he saw Lindstrom a hundred yards south, heading toward the marina. It was after eight. The sun sat on the western edge of Aurora looking tired as a bloodshot eye ready to close. Lindstrom moved quickly through the long shadows of the maples that lined the street. Every so often, he scanned the lake. He reached the bait shop at the marina, stopped, and stood staring at the docks where rows of sailboats and motor launches were moored.

Most boats had come in. A few persistent fishermen lingered far out on the water. The marina was empty. The bait shop had closed. As he approached, Cork saw Lindstrom take the paper from his pocket, read it again, then glance at his watch.

"Karl?"

Lindstrom jumped and his hand shot toward his belt under his sport coat. "Christ, O'Connor. What are you doing here?"

"You looked to me like a man with trouble on his hands. I thought maybe I could help."

"You can't, okay? Just go somewhere else. Anywhere else."

Cork nodded at the paper clenched in Lindstrom's fist. "What's in the note, Karl?"

"Just go away, O'Connor. Now." Lindstrom eyed his watch again.

"Do you have an appointment?"

"Oh, for Christ's sake—here." Lindstrom shoved the note at him.

It had been made from words and letters cut out of a newspaper and pasted onto a blank sheet of typing paper.

We are all dead men. Unless we talk. Take a boat ride on the *Matador*. Dock 3. Marina. 8:15. Meet you middle of the lake.

Eco-Warrior

"Now will you just get out of here?" Lindstrom pleaded. "I don't want to scare him away."

"You're not really going to walk into this, are you, Karl?"

"I'm not afraid." Although it was obvious he was.

"Karl, this is crazy."

"If there's really a chance to put an end to all this, I'm not going to pass it up."

"Whoever this Eco-Warrior is, he's already killed once."

"Everyone agrees that was an accident."

"Look, Karl, if he really wants to end it, the way to do that is to give himself up."

"You sound like a cop."

"I think like a cop. And I'm thinking this is a setup. Maybe you are, too, and that's why you brought the hardware you stuck in your belt."

"It's licensed."

"Fine. Wonderful. It's licensed. And you've got it with you

141

because you don't trust this situation either. Use your head, for Christ's sake."

"Shut up, O'Connor. Just shut up." He tipped his wrist and glanced at his watch. "It's almost eight-fifteen. I'm going."

Lindstrom started away, but Cork reached out to restrain him.

"Karl, it feels all wrong. Look." He waved his hand over the deserted marina. "Where is he?"

"Out on the lake. That's why I'm taking a boat ride."

"Maybe. And maybe this is all just a way of getting you out here alone. If he wants an easy target, that's exactly what you're giving him."

"Listen, O'Connor, if this really does have a chance of ending the violence and I turn away, how do you think I'm going to feel? How would you feel? You want to know the truth? I'm scared shitless. But I've got to know. You understand?"

He pulled away from Cork and walked to the dock third distant from the bait shop. The dock jutted thirty or forty yards into the lake and nearly every slip on both sides was filled with a vessel. Lindstrom, as he stood a moment in the red light of the setting sun, cast an elongated shadow across the boards in front of him. He put his hand at his waist inside his coat, and he walked forward.

Cork scanned the marina, trying to see everything—all three docks, all the moored boats. The long angle of the sunlight created so many shadowed enclaves that there were a hundred places for a man to hide. A slight breeze blew across the lake, and the boats rocked gently, creating the illusion of movement on every deck.

Lindstrom walked slowly, looking carefully right and left, reading the names painted on the bows of the vessels, seeking the one called *Matador*. Cork glanced at his watch. The hands were just now touching eight-fifteen. He realized Lindstrom's watch was running fast by a couple of minutes.

He shouted, "Karl!"

Lindstrom paused halfway down the dock and turned back.

The explosion blew a small sailboat at the end of the dock into a blur of smoke and fragments. The other boats there shoved back and tugged at their moorings like nervous ponies.

Splintered board rained down on the marina, peppering the water and Cork. Lindstrom was down.

Cork ran to dock 3 where Lindstrom lay on his back, not moving. When Cork reached him, he saw that Lindstrom's eyes were open and he was staring up at the sky.

"Am I dead?" he asked.

Cork shook his head. "Are you hurt?"

"What? I can't hear you."

"Hurt." Cork mouthed the word and felt his own body in pantomime.

"I don't know." Lindstrom tried to rise, but Cork kept him down.

"Stay there." Cork gestured with his hands. Then he put an imaginary phone to his ear. "I'm going to call you in. We'll have some paramedics here in no time."

"Huh?"

"Stay."

Cork raced back to the bait shop and used the pay phone outside it to call the sheriff's office. By the time he'd returned to Lindstrom, he heard the sirens already wailing.

19

HIGHWAY MAINTENANCE BROUGHT OVER BARRICADES, and Schanno's men set up a perimeter, blocking access to the marina. Even so, deputies Gil Singer and Cy Borkmann were having a hell of a time keeping the crowd back.

"I want every off-duty officer brought in," the sheriff instructed Deputy Marsha Dross. "And get some floodlights. It's going to be dark soon."

Agents Owen and Earl were out at the end of dock 3, looking at the water where only the mast of the *Matador* jutted above the surface. Captain Ed Larson, who headed up all the criminal investigations for the sheriff's department, was talking with Jack Beagan, the harbormaster.

Karl Lindstrom sat on the front seat of Wally Schanno's Land Cruiser drinking coffee from a disposable cup. He'd been treated by the paramedics for minor lacerations—splinters—but aside from a bit of quivering in his hand as he sipped his coffee, he seemed just fine.

Jo stood apart, observing everything darkly. She'd arrived after the sheriff's people and before the ambulance. As soon as she'd made sure Cork was all right, she turned stony and moved away from him. She hadn't said, "I told you so," but the sentiment came off her anyway, strong as garlic.

Cork was scanning the crowd. In the murk of twilight, the red-and-white flash from the lights atop the sheriff's department cruisers added to the chaotic, jittery feel of all those people pressed against the barricades. Cork recognized a lot of the faces. The understandably curious. He also saw Joan of Arc of the Redwoods leaning on her cane, shoulder to shoulder with Isaiah Broom. And Hell Hanover was giving Gil Singer a hard time, trying his best to work his way onto the scene. The cameras that had captured the news conference on the steps of the middle school were set up and rolling. Cork knew a circus when he saw one. And he was glad that for right now, it was Schanno who had to play ringmaster.

A pickup truck marked TAMARACK COUNTY SEARCH AND RESCUE nosed through the crowd. Gil Singer pulled aside a barricade and let it through. When it had been parked, Agent Owen began pulling diving gear from the back.

Earl left the dock and approached the Land Cruiser. Schanno, when he saw him coming, stepped to the Land Cruiser, too.

"Is your partner going to need a hand?" the sheriff asked.

"Mark's fine. He'd prefer to go over the area under the dock himself. He knows best what he's looking for." Earl leaned an arm on the open door of the Land Cruiser. He wore a white shirt that looked freshly ironed and a blue tie that was tightly knotted. "How are you feeling, Mr. Lindstrom?"

"I've been better."

Earl looked to the sheriff. "You'll be taking him down to the department for a complete statement?"

"When he's ready."

Ed Larson called out, "Wally?" He beckoned the sheriff with a wave of his hand and Schanno headed over.

"Mind if I ask you a few questions?" Agent Earl asked Lindstrom. He pulled a cigarette from a pack in his shirt pocket, then offered one to Lindstrom.

"I don't smoke."

"O'Connor?"

"Gave them up."

Earl shrugged and lit his cigarette with a lighter. "Mr. Lindstrom, you said the note was left on the windshield of your vehicle at the school."

"That's right."

"You're sure it wasn't there before you parked?"

"I'd have seen it."

"Probably. But sometimes people drive with parking tickets

145

on their windshield and don't seem to notice. I've done it myself."

"It wasn't there."

Earl turned to Cork. "You parked next to Mr. Lindstrom, didn't you?"

"Yes."

"Did you see the note?"

"No."

"Could it have been there and you just didn't notice?"

"It's possible. But I'm more inclined to believe someone put it there when that firecracker went off. It was a good diversion."

"I'm sure you're right." Earl took a long, meditative draw on his cigarette. "Why did you park in back, Mr. O'Connor?"

"It's okay to call me Cork. No room out front."

"Ah. Sure. And according to your statement, you followed Mr. Lindstrom because you thought he might be in some trouble. What made you think that?"

"The way he looked when he read the note. And I saw him take a handgun from his briefcase."

"If you thought there might be trouble, especially trouble involving the possible use of a firearm, why didn't you alert the sheriff?"

"Wally and his men were already gone by then."

"Of course. Mind if I take a look at that firearm of yours, Mr. Lindstrom?"

The handgun was sitting on the seat beside him. Lindstrom handed it to Agent Earl, who dropped his cigarette on the pavement and ground it out.

"Colt Commander forty-five. Nice piece."

"It was the sidearm I carried as an officer in the navy."

"Not standard military issue," Earl observed.

The weapon had a satin nickel finish and a walnut grip inlaid with gold initials.

"My father gave it to me when I graduated from Annapolis."

Earl released the magazine and inspected it. He sniffed the barrel. "Me, I was just a grunt. A kid in the mud in Korea. How about you? What did you do in the service?"

"Things I'm not allowed to talk about, actually. What does this have to do with what happened here tonight?"

"Nothing. Just shooting the breeze." He slipped the

magazine back in. "One round is missing. And it's been fired recently."

"I fired a test round this afternoon."

"You were expecting trouble?"

"One of the important lessons I learned in the service was to anticipate and be prepared for all contingencies. May I have my gun back?"

"Of course." He handed it over. "This particular incident seems to have been directed at you personally. Do you know anyone who'd have reason to want to harm you? Anyone who might have a grudge against you, or a deep animosity?"

"Who doesn't these days?"

Earl grinned, politely. "After you read the note, why did you choose to walk to the marina rather than take your vehicle?"

Lindstrom shrugged. "It's not far from the school. And—I don't know—I guess I thought I might be able to check the lay of the land, so to speak."

"Before you blundered into anything?"

"Something like that."

"You seemed to be thinking pretty clearly. Your military training?"

"Maybe."

"Did you ever think about informing Sheriff Schanno?"

"There wasn't time."

"Enough time for a leisurely stroll to the marina."

"Maybe I wasn't thinking so clearly after all. This isn't a situation I face every day. Besides, I thought . . ."

"What?"

"That maybe this Eco-Warrior really was interested in bringing an end to things. And if that was the case, I had an obligation to try."

"That's an admirable motivation, Mr. Lindstrom. When you checked the lay of the land, did you see anything?"

"No. Only Cork."

"And lucky for you, eh?" Earl turned to Cork and gave him a congenial smile. "You're part Ojibwe, aren't you?"

"Yes."

"How do you feel about Our Grandfathers?"

"I'd hate to see them cut. But not enough to kill a man over it, if that's what you're getting at."

Lindstrom put his cup down on the dash, hard. Coffee sloshed out, all over Lindstrom's hand and the clean interior of Schanno's vehicle. "Look, Earl. I don't like the way these questions are going. I'd be fish food right now if it wasn't for Cork. And as for any of us thinking clearly, well maybe we weren't. But you know, it's our asses on the line here. It's our businesses that are suffering. It's our community that's being torn apart. Who the hell are you to come butting into something you don't understand or care about?"

"One man's been murdered already, Mr. Lindstrom. And someone just tried to kill you. Murder is my business, and about that business, I care a lot. But I didn't mean to upset you. You've been through enough for one night. No more questions."

He stepped away. As he headed toward his partner, who was donning the diving gear, he lit up another Marlboro.

"Who the hell does he think he is?" Lindstrom asked.

"He's just doing his job, Karl."

Cork turned and looked toward Jo. She stared out across the lake, beyond all the confusion. It was dark enough for the halogen security light to have come on, illuminating the parking lot. Jo looked white, her skin frosted, and when her eyes turned to Cork, there seemed to be no warmth in them at all.

Schanno left Larson and harbormaster Jack Beagan and headed back to the Land Cruiser. Agent Earl came back as well.

"Beagan says *Matador* belongs to Stan and Bernadette Lukas," Schanno reported.

"Stan and Bernadette spend every July in Seattle with their son's family," Cork said. "The whole town knows that."

"Exactly," Schanno said. "I'm thinking whoever planted that explosive was counting on no one except Karl to step aboard."

"Did the harbormaster see anything suspicious around the boat lately?" Earl asked.

"Nothing."

"Makes sense. If the charge was set underwater, there wouldn't have been much to see," Earl said. "Mark will be able to tell us more after he's had a look."

"What about the note?" Schanno asked.

"I'll get it down to the lab in St. Paul tonight, but it will probably be a couple of days, at least, before they can tell us anything."

Schanno nodded but didn't look particularly happy about the time frame. "Karl, I want you to head on over to the hospital, get yourself examined. I'll have one of my deputies accompany you, take a full statement, and make sure you get home okay."

Lindstrom climbed out of the Land Cruiser and went to the waiting ambulance. Earl returned to his partner. Schanno shook his head.

"Ever feel like you're holding a bag full of scorpions and you know sooner or later you're gonna have to reach inside?"

"Wally," Cork replied, "I know that feeling well." There was nothing more for Cork to do there. He joined his wife. "If you're willing, I could use a lift back to my Bronco."

Without a word, Jo turned and started walking.

By the time they drove to the school, night had descended fully. The town was reduced to a skeleton, bones of light with a lot of dark between. Jo was silent, and Cork could feel the heat of her anger. There was a little flame in him, too, but he didn't want to feed it. What good would it do, both of them flaring? Silence, he decided, was better.

Jo finally spoke. "So. I guess you were right."

"About what?"

"Karl's needing your help. Everybody seems to think he'd be dead if it weren't for you. On the other hand, it could have ended with both of you dead. But then, that goes with the territory, doesn't it?"

"What territory?"

"Law enforcement." She paused the car at a stop sign, not long enough to be legal, and took off quickly. "When do you plan to make your announcement?"

"What are you talking about? What announcement?"

"Your candidacy. That's what all this is about, isn't it, Cork? Or should I say Sheriff O'Connor?"

"For crying out loud, Jo. Didn't I promise that we'd talk before I made a decision?"

"You've already decided. Look at you. Every step of the way

since the bombing, you've been there, ahead of everybody else. You're besting everyone at this game."

"It's not a game."

"Isn't it? People's lives are at stake, but the point of all this as far as Cork O'Connor is concerned is to show people what a great investigative mind he has, what a mistake they made when they let him go. Tell me, doesn't it feel good right here"—she reached across the seat and slapped him hard in the gut—"to know how great you are at all this?"

"It feels wonderful," he said, and shoved her hand away.

Silence descended again, and the two feet between them in the car felt to Cork like the empty distance between two stars. Jo drove the car around behind the school and pulled it up next to Cork's Bronco. Lindstrom's Explorer was still there.

Jo spoke quietly. "Haven't you been happy at Sam's Place?"

"I don't think that's the issue here. Look, Jo, what are you really afraid of?"

Her hands still gripped the steering wheel, tightly. "If you run, all the dirty laundry will be dragged out."

"Ah." Cork nodded. "You mean *your* dirty laundry. Because everybody already knows about mine." He looked away, across the football field. The moon was rising behind the deserted bleachers. Eventually the grass on the field would turn silver, but right now it was a sorrowful gray. Cork remembered a game against Hibbing his senior year when he intercepted a pass and ran seventy-five yards for a touchdown. He remembered the sound of all those people in the stands cheering for him and how, for a little while, he felt huge and invulnerable. "I can win, Jo."

"I know you can. And that's the hell of it." She sat back but still wouldn't look at him. "Everybody here loves you. You walk down the street and it's 'Hey there, Cork.' 'How's it going, Cork?' 'Good to see you, Cork.' Aurora's like a big family and you're a favored son."

"Prodigal son."

"That's my point. You've already been forgiven. What's a little extramarital affair? Men will be men. It's different for me. In fact, it's different for any woman here."

"I'd stand beside you."

"Right. We've both done so well that way in the past." Her voice was low and bitter.

"Don't measure everything against the past."

"What other measure is there, Cork? If you become sheriff, all I can see is us going right back where we were."

Cork stared at her hard, dark profile. "You're saying it was my fault?" Something—like the tip of a knife—seemed to prick his gut. "It was my job as sheriff that caused all our troubles?"

"No, that's not what I'm saying."

"Funny. It sure sounded that way."

"What I'm saying is that your job as sheriff often brought you into conflict with the interests of my clients. It brought us into conflict. I don't want that to happen again."

"Fine. Change your clientele."

"I can't do that."

"But it's perfectly all right for me to throw away something I might want."

"You're shouting."

"I'm pissed. Jesus. I just kept a man from getting his ass blown to bits. You know, it was like this before, Jo. No matter what I was going through, what you were going through was more important."

"That's not true."

"It feels true." He stepped out and shut the door hard behind him. "I think I'll stay at Sam's Place tonight." He glared at her through the window.

"Is this where I'm supposed to plead, 'Don't leave'?"

"Damn it." Cork swung away and went to his Bronco. He drove off, leaving Jo's Toyota sitting in the parking lot like an animal too stunned to move.

20

WHEN JO WALKED IN THE BACK DOOR, the women of the O'Connor household were gathered at the kitchen table. They were partaking of Rose's remedy for all emotional ills—milk and cookies.

"Where's Daddy?" Annie looked at her anxiously from under a spill of wild red curls.

"He's fine," Jo assured her. "He's just fine."

"Everybody's been calling," Jenny said. "Annie and I wanted to go to the marina, but Aunt Rose wouldn't let us."

Rose looked unperturbed. "I figured there was no need to add to the confusion."

"Your Aunt Rose was right." Jo headed to the refrigerator, opened the door, and leaned into the cool air that flowed out.

"What happened?" Jenny asked.

Jo felt weary, so weary she could barely stand. She took nothing from the fridge, closed the door, and leaned against the big appliance. "It appears that someone tried to kill Karl Lindstrom."

"With a bomb," Annie stated. "We heard it was a bomb."

"That's right."

"But Dad saved him."

"Did you hear that, too?" Jo asked.

"Sort of," Annie said. "He did, right?"

"Apparently."

"And he's okay?"

"Yes, Jenny. He's okay."

152

Rose took a plate full of crumbs to the sink. "Where is he?"

"He had some business to take care of."

"Police business?" Annie asked.

"He's not a police officer anymore, damn it."

Jenny's blue eyes grew huge. "Whoah, Mom. Chill."

Stevie came into the kitchen, in his pajamas, looking sleepy. "I woke up." He shuffled to his mother and leaned against her hip.

Jo put her arm around him. "We'll get you back to sleep."

Annie and Jenny exchanged a glance across the table.

"Is it okay if we go out for a little while, Mom?" Jenny asked.

"To the marina," Jo guessed.

"Please. We won't get in the way," Annie pleaded.

"There's nothing to see."

"Then there's no harm," Jenny said. "We'll just be wasting our time. We promise to be back by midnight."

"Eleven," Jo replied.

"Eleven-thirty," Jenny countered.

"All right."

The two girls left in a blur.

"You look beat," Rose said. "I'll be glad to put the little guy back down."

"That's all right." Jo bent and hefted Stevie in her arms. "Come on, kiddo. It's back to dreamland."

She laid him in his bed and covered him with a sheet. She kissed his cheek. "Want me to stay a while?"

"Yeth," he murmured.

That was fine by Jo. She sat down in the chair by the window.

"How about a song?" she asked, although she didn't feel much like singing him a lullaby.

" 'Are You Sleeping,' " Stevie said.

The night-light was on and it bathed everything in the room in a soft, warm glow. Jo began singing quietly, "Are you sleeping, are you sleeping, Brother John? . . ." Stevie closed his eyes. After a few rounds, Jo saw that he was breathing deeply. She closed her own eyes and wished someone would sing to her. Before she knew it, she was crying softly. She realized that what had happened—Cork's retreat to Sam's Place—was a move she'd been anticipating since the day, months before, when Cork had finally come back home. She remembered a statement she'd heard once about murder. After the first time, it was easy. Maybe all transgression was that way. Maybe once a marriage had been violated, it was forever flawed and at risk of breaking apart. Maybe it was inevitable.

She left Stevie's room and found Rose waiting at the bottom of the stairway.

"Where's Cork?" Rose asked. "Really."

"Gone. Back to Sam's Place." Jo sat down on the stairs. "Damn it, Rose, I screwed it up."

"Tell me about it." Rose wedged herself in beside her sister.

"Nothing to tell. We said things. Lousy things."

"I take it 'I love you' wasn't one of them."

"I don't understand it, Rose. In front of a jury, I say something and it comes out exactly as I mean it to. I say something to Cork and even if the words are right, they seem to come out all wrong."

"Maybe that's because you know the rules in a courtroom. Look, Jo, I've never loved a man, so I could be all wrong, but it seems to me one of the most important rules in love is honesty. If you're tripping up right now, maybe it's because you're trying to dance around something you need to say to Cork. Like, maybe, you don't really love him."

"Don't love him?" She looked at her sister with astonishment. "Rose, he's the best thing that ever happened to me."

"Have you told him that?"

"Not for a very long time."

"Why not?"

"I'm afraid."

"To say 'I love you'? Why? You're afraid he won't say it back?"

"Why would he? All I've ever done is hurt him."

"That's not true, Jo. Talk to him. Now. Tonight. He can't know what's in your heart unless you tell him. And until you do, you won't know what's in his."

"You really think I should?"

"I wouldn't have said it if I didn't think so."

Jo considered, then finally blurted, "I'll do it, Rose. Will you—"

Rose held up her hand. "Go. I'll take care of everything here. You take care of the rest."

Jo put her arms around her good sister. "You're the best."

"Tell me something I don't know."

Moonlight spilled generously out of the sky. It flowed across the lake and dripped white as milk from the trees along the shoreline. No lights were on in Sam's Place. Cork's Bronco was not there. Jo knocked on the door, tried the knob. She turned away and looked at the grounds. The buildings of the Bearpaw Brewery just north beyond the chain-link fence seemed stark in the light of the moon, vaguely menacing. Jo realized she was alone out there.

Where was Cork? He'd put himself at risk, waded neck deep into whatever it was that was going on in Tamarack County. Was he in danger?

Or was it something else, something Jo would rather not have considered? He'd loved another woman once. Maybe he'd found someone to love again.

"Would you blame him?" she asked herself aloud. "Jo, Jo, what have you done?"

She wandered to the dock, thinking hopelessly, *You let your sister raise your children. You've put yourself at odds with the whole town. You've driven your husband away. Again. But at least you're one hell of a lawyer, kiddo. Yes, ma'am—you've certainly won everyone's respect.*

"Until they see that photograph," she whispered to herself.

She sat down on the old boards of the dock, took off her loafers, and let her feet dangle. The cool water of Iron Lake felt good.

What was respect anyway? Something bright and shiny but cold to the touch. It didn't keep her feet warm in bed at night. It didn't rub her shoulders when she was tired. It didn't listen—ever. It felt like a mantel trophy, stiff and lifeless and self-serving.

She looked back toward the dark windows of Sam's Place. Where was Cork? She stood up, becoming afraid—not that she had driven him away but that maybe something had happened to him.

Headlights flashed on the road from Aurora. They came over

the railroad tracks and fixed on her, so that she felt exposed. The vehicle pulled to a stop with the lights aimed directly at her. She shaded her eyes, in vain, because she could see nothing behind the glare. The headlights died, but her eyes were blind now in the sudden dark. She heard footsteps approaching.

"Rose told me you were here."

Cork paused at the other end of the dock. She could see him now, standing in the moonlight.

"You went home?" she asked.

"Yes."

"Why?"

"For the same reason you came out here, I hope. Jo, I'm sorry."

"No, Cork, no. I'm the one who's sorry." And she was moving toward him, and against him, holding him so tightly the thump of his heart felt as if it were her own. "I'm so thoughtless sometimes. I didn't mean to be so harsh."

"And I didn't mean to stomp out." His arms about her made her breathless. "Jo, I don't want you to be afraid that I'd ever leave you again."

"I don't ever want to give you reason. I love you, Cork." She was crying now, with relief and with gratitude, and it felt so good and right, and although something was flowing out of her, it seemed to be filling her up at the same time. "If you want to run for sheriff, I'll be right there beside you. Only . . ."

"Only what?"

"You might not want me there. Wait here, Cork." She kissed him, then went to her car. When she came back, she held out her hand. "Hell Hanover paid me a visit this afternoon. He brought me this." The moonlight was bright enough that she knew Cork could see the horror she offered him. He had seen it before, a long time ago. And then he'd left. She was afraid he might leave again, but he had to know.

Cork looked at it, his face grave. "He's the worst kind of coward, Jo."

"He says you have to step back from the investigation of the bombing and refrain from running for sheriff, ever, or he'll make that photograph public."

Cork tore the photo in half.

156

"He'll have others," Jo said.

He brushed her hair softly with his hand. "We'll figure a way to deal with Hell Hanover."

"If people see that photograph, they'll think differently about me, Cork. And maybe about you."

"They've thought a lot of different things about me over the years. I can live with it."

She put her arms around him and her cheek against his chest. "You know what I'm concerned about most? The girls. What kind of example am I? What will they think of their mother?"

"They'll see that I love her, and they'll understand that's what's important."

"You do love me, Cork?"

"What is it?" he asked, hearing her uncertainty.

She released him, just a little. "In your sleep sometimes, you say her name."

"Oh, Jo. I'm sorry."

"Do you still love her?"

She was afraid he would turn away, address the hard truth in a way that would spare them both the discomfort of having to look into one another's eyes, but he didn't. He spoke in a voice soft and graceful as the moonlight.

"When she was in my life, she was all I had. But she's gone now, and now I'm here with you. And there's nowhere else I'd rather be, and no one else I'd rather be with. I do love you, Jo."

She kissed him with a yielding of herself that was frightening and wonderful.

"What I know about the goodness of men," she said to him, "I know because of you. You're the best thing that's ever happened to me." She turned and leaned back into his embrace while she stared out across the dark water and the path across it the moon had paved. "Cork, I saw my mother alone, watched her give up little pieces of herself to men who didn't care. I did that, too, once. It was the biggest mistake I ever made. The worst part of it was that I almost lost you."

"But you didn't. I'll be here. Always."

"That sounds like a wedding vow."

"No, this is a wedding vow." Cork turned her and took her hands. "I, Cork, promise to love you with all my heart and all my soul, to cherish you and only you until death do us part."

He waited. "If I remember correctly, this is where you come in."

She looked into his eyes, eyes that reflected moonlight, and she wanted to say so much. "I . . . Jo," she began slowly, ". . . promise to . . . to love, to honor, and to cherish you forever and ever. God, and the angels, and the stars in heaven as my witnesses, I promise I will. Oh, Cork, I promise."

Although they had been an impulse, the vows seemed as real and as binding to Jo as if they'd been said in a church. She leaned to her husband and their lips touched in a moment that felt sacred to her.

"What now?" she asked.

Cork looked toward Sam's Place. "The honeymoon?"

21

H<small>E SLEPT A LONG TIME</small>, and when he woke with Jo's arm draped over him, he felt as if he'd never slept better. He lay on his side, Jo full against him. Her breath stirred the hair on the back of his neck. Her breasts pressed between his shoulder blades. The bone of her hip dug into the cheek of his butt. One leg was sandwiched between his own. Morning sunlight streamed through the window over the sink in the back of Sam's Place. Everything had a golden hue. At that moment, Cork couldn't remember ever having been happier.

Then the phone rang.

He felt Jo wake with a start. Instead of separating from him, she tightened her hold.

"Don't answer it," she whispered.

"All right."

After five rings, the message machine clicked in.

"Sam's Place. Leave a message. I'll get back to you. Thanks."

"Cork, Wally Schanno here. Rose said you were out there. Give me a call. I'm at my office. It's important."

The quiet returned, and with it, Jo was wide awake. She kissed the back of his neck. "Don't call him yet."

He had no intention of doing so.

"I slept so well," Jo murmured. "Better than in ages."

"Me, too."

"I know why for me. I'm not afraid anymore, Cork. I don't care what Hell Hanover does. I don't care what people think."

"We'll figure a way to deal with old Hell."

She squeezed him. "I love you."

"And I love you." He rolled over, kissed her gently. "You wouldn't happen to be hungry, would you?"

"Famished."

They showered together. Then, while Cork fried up eggs and frozen hash browns, Jo made coffee and called her office to say she'd be in late. They ate outside at the picnic table. The sun was high above the trees on the eastern shore of Iron Lake, but its brightness was cut to a pale yellow by the haze thick in the sky.

"I wonder what Wally wants," Cork said.

"Time with Arletta, I imagine. He's a man who has put his priorities in place. And you, Corcoran O'Connor, will assume his office."

"I mean this morning."

"You've had the answers so far. He probably wants a few more from you." Jo's eyes swung away. "Well, look who's here."

Jenny bounced over the railroad tracks on her bike and pedaled to the picnic table. She was breathing fast. Under her white-blond hair, her forehead glistened. She looked at them both with concern.

"Aunt Rose told me you were out here."

"What is it?" her mother asked.

Jenny looked at them both and seemed relieved. "Nothing. You look so—happy."

Her mother laughed. "Kiddo, you don't know the half of it."

An hour later, Cork walked into Wally Schanno's office at the Tamarack County Sheriff's Department. Schanno wasn't alone. Agent David Earl was there, and Karl Lindstrom, and a man Cork had known a long time, Lucky Knudsen, a captain with the Minnesota State Patrol out of the Eveleth district office. Earl smoked a cigarette and sat on the windowsill, where the cross-breeze carried the smoke outside. The other men were drinking coffee.

" 'Bout time," Schanno said.

"And a good morning to you, too, Wally. Agent Earl, Karl. And hey there, Lucky. Been a while."

"Yah, well, ya know how it goes, Cork." He grasped Cork's hand and gave it a strong shake.

"How's Phoebe?"

"Pregnant."

"Not again?"

"Yah. Seems all I got to do is look at her. Twins this time, the doctor's saying." He shook his blond head, then smiled broadly. "Not bad for a big dumb Scandahoovian."

"What are you doing here, Lucky?"

Instead of answering, Knudsen nodded toward Schanno.

"I got a call this morning from the governor's office," the sheriff said. "The governor's offered the services of the state patrol and anybody else we need up here. He's worried things may get out of control."

Cork waited. He knew there was more to it than that.

"Coffee?" Schanno asked.

"No thanks."

"The deal is this, Cork. Karl is scheduled to speak this evening at the Quetico. The Northern Minnesota Independent Business Association's annual dinner. A hundred and fifty people in a large room. After what's happened in the last few days, I'd prefer the gathering were canceled. But I spoke with Jay Werner down in Eveleth—he's president of the association—and he insisted on going ahead, so long as Karl was willing. Well, Karl here is more than willing."

Lindstrom said, "My only concern is the safety of everyone else."

"And that's why I'm here," Lucky Knudsen put in. "Delivering the guv's promised manpower."

Schanno said, "I don't have enough deputies to ensure the security of something like this. But with Lucky's officers, we can probably do what'll need doing.

"Specifically, Agent Owen is out at the Quetico as we speak, securing the facility, which, with the help of the state police, will remain secured up to and throughout the event. We'll have an officer at every entrance and exit. Only authorized staff or guests with invitations will be admitted to the building. Because Karl seems obviously the target, I've prevailed upon him to wear body armor."

Cork nodded. A good idea. "So what am I doing here?"

"His idea." Schanno waved toward Lindstrom.

"I'd be obliged if you would be at the Quetico tonight,"

Lindstrom said. "I appreciate that yesterday you were willing to put yourself at risk for a guy who'd been pretty rough on you. I'm prepared to pay. Think of yourself as a hired body-guard."

"I'll be there," Cork replied without hesitation. "But you can forget about paying me."

"Thanks, Cork."

"Well, gentlemen," Schanno said, rising from his chair. "We have a lot to do between now and this evening. I suggest we get started. Karl, I'd like you at the Quetico a good half an hour before festivities begin. We'll get you suited up. And Lucky, when you know your roster, get back to me."

"Will do, Wally. See you this evening, Cork. Say hello to Jo."

Karl Lindstrom and Lucky Knudsen left Schanno's office, but Agent David Earl lingered a moment on his perch on the win-dowsill. He was looking at Cork, not happily.

"Something on your mind?" Cork asked.

"O'Connor, I know about Burke's Landing."

"That was a while ago," Schanno said from across the room.

"I've already expressed my concern to everyone else. I just want to be straight with you," Earl went on. "There's every intention of arming you this evening. I'm more than a little concerned about a man like you carrying a loaded weapon in a situation like this. But it's not my call."

He waited, as if expecting Cork to argue the point. Cork didn't.

"Well. Until this evening, then." Earl looked for a place to drop the last of his cigarette. Schanno offered him nothing, and Earl left, still holding the smoking butt.

"He doesn't know you, Cork," Wally Schanno said.

"He's probably not alone in his thinking, Wally. People haven't forgotten Burke's Landing. I'm sure the truth is that there are probably a lot of them who'd rather not see me ever strap on a gun belt or wear a badge."

"Doesn't matter who's in this job—some people are going to feel that way."

Cork walked to a window and stood gazing at the town. In the morning light, it had a quiet, peaceful look to it. Across the street, the bell tower of Zion Lutheran Church rose with simple grace. Beyond that were the stores on Center Street. And not far beyond that, the lake, cut by white sails and the white wake of motorboats. When he'd occupied that office, the view had been a reassuring one. He'd felt as if being sheriff were part of a larger concept, sometimes as difficult to understand and to justify as the mysterious ways of God and Kitchimanidoo, but the purpose of which was clear to him—to help people live their lives with peace of mind. It hadn't been an idea with a lot of grandeur to it, no more far-reaching than the boundaries of Tamarack County, yet it had been a part of who he was—until a few confused moments on a cold morning at a place called Burke's Landing had left two men dead and brought to an end much of the way Cork thought about everything.

Even in his bitterness afterward, he'd never blamed Schanno for taking the badge. It was just the circumstances; it was just the time. And since his fall from grace, Cork had managed to put his life back together again. Did he really want to be back in that office with that view? Hadn't Burke's Landing or the years since taught him anything?

"Lindstrom trusts you," Schanno said at his back. "And for the record, so do I."

W E'RE CLOSING EARLY TODAY," Cork said.

"When?" Annie asked.

"Now."

"Now?" Even Jenny, who usually was delighted to shave off a bit of her time at Sam's Place, seemed perplexed.

"But it's only five-thirty," Annie said. "And look. There are boats headed this way."

"Shut the serving window and put out the Closed sign," Cork told her.

"It's Saturday," she argued on. "People expect us to be open."

"If it will make you feel better, write a note and tape it to the window. 'Family emergency.' "

Jenny suggested, "How about 'Closed by order of the health inspector'?"

"Let's not go overboard." Cork began cleaning the grill.

Jenny got paper for the note, but Annie stood her ground. "What will people think?"

"Let it go, Annie," Jenny said. "It's not like it's a sin."

"Why are we closing?" Annie demanded.

"Family dinner," Cork explained. "It's been too long since we all sat down together."

"Does Aunt Rose know?"

"Yes. But it's your mother who's fixing dinner."

Cork caught the concerned glances the two girls exchanged. Jo was the worst cook on the whole Iron Range. Jenny pulled in the Closed sign. "We'll stay."

"You'll go home with me," Cork said.

Like a couple of condemned prisoners, his daughters set about the work of closing up.

Cork drove home slowly, taking in the beauty of a town he knew as well as he knew his own face. On Center Street, he passed businesses that had been there forever—Lenore's Toy and Hobby Shop, Tucker Insurance, Mayfair's Clothing, Nelson's Hardware Hank. He knew all the men and women behind the glass of the storefronts. Almost every corner brought together some convergence in his life. The smell from Johnny's Pinewood Broiler—the Saturday-night barbecued rib special—had been the same smell every Saturday night as far back as he could remember, and it never failed to carry him instantly across almost forty years to the days when his father was still alive, still sheriff, and Johnny's on Saturday night was practically a family ritual. Cork knew that if you lived in a place long enough, you understood it as a living thing. You knew it had consciousness and conscience. You could hear it breathing. You felt its love and its anger and its despair, and you cared.

"You're driving like an old lady, Dad," Jenny said.

"I love this town."

Jenny shook her head. "Me, I can't wait to leave."

"When you're gone, you'll miss it."

"Yeah, like I'd miss the clap."

"Beg your pardon?"

"Just an expression, Dad."

With Rose looking over her shoulder, Jo had surprised even Cork and done a fine job of preparing the food. Although the fare was simple—meatloaf, mashed potatoes and gravy, green bean casserole, and Jell-O with bananas—it had been so long since they'd sat down together as a family, the meal felt like an occasion. Cork couldn't remember the last time he'd seen Jo laugh so much. Midway through the eating, Rose lifted her water glass and said, "A toast to the best family an old spinster could ask for."

"What'th a thpinthter?" Stevie asked.

Annie fielded that one. "A woman who's too smart to marry."

Rose laughed. "For that, you're relieved of dish duty."

After dinner, Cork said, "Dishes are mine." No one argued.

Jo helped him. Then they sat on the porch swing together, watching Stevie play catch with Annie in the front yard. The ball, as it lofted, caught sunlight for a moment and glowed as it passed from the hand of one child to the other. In a very short time, children from other houses on the block had joined them, and Annie began to organize a game. Cork waved to his neighbors across the street, John and Sue O'Laughlin, who'd stepped onto their own porch to enjoy the evening.

"This has been the best day I can remember in a long, long time." Cork laced his fingers with Jo's.

"I wish . . ." Jo began. She stopped herself.

"What?"

"I wish you weren't going to the Quetico tonight."

"I'll be fine. It's Karl Lindstrom who's taking the chance. It's probably a good thing you'll be out at Grace Cove tonight."

Grace Fitzgerald was to have met with Jo at her office that morning, but Jo had lingered at Sam's Place with Cork and had called to reschedule. Grace was due to go out of town on Monday, so Jo offered to drop by that evening.

"Still no idea what she wants to talk to you about?"

"None."

"And even if you did, you couldn't tell me." He glanced at his watch. "Time I was going."

Jo wrapped him in her arms and kissed him. There seemed something a little desperate in her grasp, in the press of her lips.

"What's that all about?" Cork asked.

"I don't know. I just . . . I'm a little afraid for you."

"I'll come back. I promise."

"And besides, I don't really have a choice, do I?"

He weighed her words, her tone, decided it was not censure he had heard but concern. "If you really don't want me to go, Jo, I won't."

"Really?"

"Really."

"You'd never forgive me."

"Do you believe that?"

"No."

"Well?"

166

"Go. It's what you need to do."

"Thanks, Jo." He brushed her cheek with his hand.

He let the swing rock a few more times, listened a bit longer to the song of the children's laughter, watched a few more tosses of the dirty baseball that, arching through the evening sunlight, was turned to gold. And he thought that although life was far from perfect, it offered moments of perfection, and this was one.

Jo walked him to his Bronco.

"You take care," she told him.

"I will."

"I'll wait up for you."

They held one another. Their separation would be only a few hours, but it had the feel of a long parting, and Cork remembered happily, *This is love.*

" 'Bye, Daddy," Stevie yelled and ran to the curb.

As Cork drove away, he leaned out the window of his Bronco and called out to his children a father's wish and a father's blessing: "Be good."

The Quetico was a large resort and conference center set on the shoreline of Iron Lake a few miles south of Aurora. The main building was an enormous, multiwinged structure with a log façade. On the outside, it projected a relaxed, old North Woods persona. Inside, it was slick and modern, with vast conference rooms, an Olympic-size pool, and the best wood-roast restaurant in the state. There was a wide, sandy beach, a small marina, a number of luxurious cabins hidden among the pines, six tennis courts, and a nine-hole golf course for which Cork couldn't afford the green fees, even if he'd played the game. The sun, as Cork guided the Bronco along the winding drive, wasn't far from setting. In the late light, the last of the golfers trailed long shadows as they approached the final green. The parking lot was nearly full. Cork pulled his old Bronco into a space between a blue Mercedes and a shiny black Windstar.

In the main lobby, a sign set on an easel indicated that the dinner for the North Minnesota Independent Business Association had been rescheduled to the Hiawatha Room in the building due north. Cork followed the arrow, out of the main building and across the drive to another, much smaller, log-façade structure. Two uniformed officers of the state patrol were stationed just inside the door. The officer to the right had a dog on a leash. The dog and the officers considered Cork carefully. The friendliest look came from the dog. Beyond a small lobby area, double doors opened onto a large room set with tablecloths and silverware and white napkins folded like flowers in water goblets. A lot of guests had already been seated.

"Do you have an invitation, sir?" the officer without the dog asked.

"Looking for Sheriff Schanno," Cork replied. "Or Captain Knudsen. I'm Cork O'Connor. They're expecting me."

"Do you have some ID?"

Cork handed over his driver's license. The dogless officer reached to a walkie-talkie clipped to his belt and spoke into it. Cork heard Schanno reply, "I'll be right there."

A minute later, the Tamarack County sheriff stepped through a door left of the big dining room and beckoned Cork to follow. Beyond the door, Cork found stairs leading up and to the left. A wood-burned sign indicated the Hiawatha Lounge was that way. Directly ahead ran a long, narrow hallway paneled with knotty pine. Cork followed Schanno to an opened door at the end of the hallway where they stepped into a kind of green room, a preparatory place for speakers—several easy chairs, a water cooler, a table, plants, and through the windows a view of the pines that edged Iron Lake. In addition to the law enforcement present—Schanno, Agent Earl, and Lucky Knudsen—Karl Lindstrom was there, along with two other men in slacks and sports coats.

"Evening, Karl," Cork greeted him.

"Thanks for coming," Lindstrom said. He looked a little pale. In his left hand, he held a tumbler filled with ice and an amber liquid. He swung his empty hand toward the other two men. "This is Jay Werner, president of NMIBA. And you probably know Jim Kaufmann, who owns the Quetico."

Cork shook the proffered hands.

"I was just telling Sheriff Schanno we've got the largest attendance ever for this dinner," Werner said. "It's Karl, don't you know. The Lindstroms have been a name up here for a good long while, but Karl's coming north to live here, revamping the mill, knocking heads with those tree huggers, that's all made him special in folks' eyes." He gave Lindstrom a hearty clap on the shoulder.

Kaufmann, a slender, balding man of fifty, added, "We considered canceling, of course, but we all figured, hell, if Karl's willing, who're we to back down? Besides, this is more excitement than I've had since I left the marines."

A look passed among the law enforcement officers. This was different for them. Schanno said, "We're planning this to be no more than another boring dinner followed by a boring speech. No offense, Karl."

"None taken."

"You'll be at the head table with all these gentlemen, Cork," Schanno said.

"Wear this." Knudsen handed him a vest. Kevlar. "Karl's wearing one, too."

Lindstrom unbuttoned his dress shirt and revealed his vest. He shrugged and lifted his glass in a slight toast.

"You carrying?" Earl asked Cork.

"The only gun I own is a thirty-eight police special. A little clumsy for a sports coat."

"Let's get you something," Knudsen said. He spoke into his walkie-talkie.

"You doing okay?" Cork asked Lindstrom.

"Fine. Really."

Right, Cork thought, glancing at the drink in his hand.

"Between Lucky's men and mine, we've got all the entrances and exits covered," Schanno said. "I'm hoping the rest of this county is quiet tonight, because I've got just one cruiser and one desk officer covering everything else."

"What's with the dog out front?" Cork asked.

"Borrowed him from the office in Duluth," Knudsen replied. "Trained to sniff for explosives."

There was a knock at the door and Deputy Gil Singer entered, carrying a belt holster into which was nestled a Beretta 92F.

Cork put on the vest and clipped the holster to his belt. He shrugged his blazer back on. "I'd forgotten how comfy body armor is."

Lucky Knudsen's walkie-talkie crackled and a scratchy voice said, "Sir, they say they're ready to serve dinner now."

"We're on our way."

Schanno looked at Lindstrom. "You ready?"

Karl Lindstrom bolted down the rest of his drink. "I'm ready."

"Gentlemen," Schanno said and opened the door for them.

They went out together, Knudsen leading the way. In the banquet room, every table was full. Despite the air conditioning, Cork was sweating profusely. Lindstrom's face glistened, too, and he walked just a little unsteadily. They threaded their way through the tables, Werner and Lindstrom shaking hands as they went, until they reached an empty table at the front near a podium set on a raised platform. They took their seats, Cork and Agent Earl taking chairs that allowed them to face the guests. Wait staff had already begun to move among the crowd, delivering the first-course salads. Cork looked out over the gathering, men and women in fine dress, laughing and talking, bending to their food, lifting water glasses or wine. Nothing unusual.

He caught a glimpse of a waiter slipping back through the kitchen door. From behind, he looked like the young man at Sam's Place who'd nearly been pummeled by Erskine Ellroy. He felt a rush of adrenaline, and he kept his eyes riveted on the kitchen door. A few moments later, the waiter appeared, looking nothing like Cork had expected, nothing like the kid.

He was jumpy, he knew that. He glanced at Earl and saw that the BCA agent was eyeing him closely, probably guessing nervousness. Cork nodded toward the room, and Earl, after a moment, swung his eyes to his duty.

There were sheriff's deputies at every door. Cork told himself someone would have to be crazy to try something there. But whoever it was who'd tried to kill Karl Lindstrom the night before wasn't exactly what you would call sane.

23

Jo LEFT THE HOUSE SHORTLY BEFORE EIGHT P.M. Stevie was beside her in the front seat, playing with a Lego spaceship he'd built. She'd brought him because at the house on Gooseberry Lane there was no one to stay with him. Rose had gone to St. Agnes to help set up for a fellowship breakfast the next day. Annie had gone to the movies with her softball friends. And Jenny was on a date with Sean.

Grace Cove was ten miles from Aurora, around the south end of Iron Lake, up the eastern shoreline, a few miles below the Iron Lake Reservation. When Karl Lindstrom built the home on the isolated cove, he'd paved smooth the winding access road that had always been nothing but gravel and dirt. The drive threaded through big red pines and black spruce and branched just once—left, to a rutted gravel road that led to the only other cabin on the cove, a place owned by John LePere, a man of mixed blood whom Jo used to see occasionally at the county courthouse pleading guilty to drunk and disorderly. He never had an attorney and he never pleaded anything but guilty. She hadn't seen him there for a while. *Had he sobered up?* she wondered. She recalled that he was a quiet man, respectful in court. Strong and stocky, he reminded her of the pictures she'd seen of the early voyageurs, the hearty French Canadian fur trappers with their huge canoes. There was something else about him she thought she should remember, but she couldn't quite get hold of it before she saw the big log house that

Lindstrom built looming out of the twilight between the pines. Grace Cove lay behind it, a sweep of dark silver in the waning light.

Grace came out to meet her. She wore dungarees, a yellow T-shirt, and sandals. Her blond hair was pulled back in a ponytail. She looked relaxed. Also relieved, Jo thought. They embraced. Two friends. Or almost friends.

"Grace, this is my son Stephen. Stevie, this is Ms. Fitzgerald."

"How do you do, Stevie?"

"Okay," he replied and limply took her offered hand.

"My son Scott is upstairs in his room. He's playing video games. Do you like video games?"

"We have a Nintendo," Stevie said.

"I think you'll both do fine. Why don't you come on in?"

Like Stevie, Grace Fitzgerald's son was small for his age. The part of him most like his mother was the color of his hair. Other blood was strong in him, especially visible in his eyes, which were green as lily pads.

"What do you want to play?" Scott asked politely, although he was clearly in the middle of a game.

"I'll just watch," Stevie said. He stood a moment, then sat down on the floor beside the other boy. The mothers made their exit.

"Can I get you something to drink?" Grace asked. "I made sun tea this afternoon."

"I'd like that, thanks."

Downstairs, Grace went to the kitchen. Jo made herself at home in the living room, an expansive room dominated by a great fieldstone fireplace. The floor was dark polished oak. The walls were dark oak paneling. Dark beams ran across the ceiling and reminded Jo of the veins on a powerful animal. It was not, she thought, the home a woman would have designed for herself. She wondered if perhaps it had been created by Karl Lindstrom to pay homage to his family's source of wealth—timber. The heavy wood feel of it was lightened somewhat by huge windows that let in air and sunlight, and by light-colored area rugs laid on the floor like sun-struck clouds against a darker sky. To Jo, who was used to the chaotic comings and goings of the O'Connor household, the big place on Grace Cove felt heavy and quiet and too far removed. But maybe for a poet and novelist it was the perfect place.

Grace brought in the tea and a plate of lemon bars. "I'll offer the boys something in a while," she said. She sat on the sofa with Jo. "I have to tell you, until I met you I was afraid everyone in Aurora talked in monosyllables."

Jo laughed. "It's because you're a celebrity, a writer with a capital W. They're a bit afraid of you."

"If you prick me, I bleed."

Grace sipped her tea, then was quiet. The silence began to feel weighty and awkward to Jo, but because she'd come to listen, she waited.

"Thanks for coming out," Grace finally said. "I know it's pretty far."

"Not so far for these parts. And it sounded important."

"It is. To me." She looked at Jo, and seemed to decide it was time to take the plunge. "I'm leaving Aurora."

"So soon? You haven't really given it a chance."

"It's a lovely place, I'm sure. But it's not really the place I'm leaving. It's Karl."

Jo was caught by surprise. Although she hadn't known what to expect when Grace asked to speak to her, she hadn't considered it would be this. The sun had dropped behind the pines and spruce that curtained Grace Cove. The room seemed to have filled with a melancholy light. Grace leaned forward and set her glass on the coffee table.

"What do you think of my husband?"

Jo set her own tea glass on a coaster made of a varnished slice of some sapling, the few rings that marked its brief life hardened into a lovely, useless pattern. "I've dealt with Karl only professionally."

"You sidestepped my question, counselor."

"Sorry. I've found him in all our dealings to be smart, prepared, and—except for a brief period after the bombing at the mill—quite civil, despite our differences."

"Bright. Prepared. Civil. Not warm, personable, funny?"

"Grace, I haven't dealt with him in any but a professional way."

"Are there other people you deal with on a professional basis to whom you would ascribe the traits warm, personable, funny?"

"Of course."

"I rest my case."

"You can't. You haven't even presented it. Look, why don't you just tell me about it. All about it."

"It's a long story."

"I'm here to listen."

Grace looked around. "A little dark in here, don't you think?" She stood and turned on a lamp, crossed the polished floor to another lamp, and turned that on as well. She paused, staring out the window toward the dark wall of pines at the edge of her lawn. "It's lonely out here. My family house is near Chicago, right on Lake Michigan in a row of great houses. Karl grew up in one just down the shoreline. The Lindstroms called it Valhalla."

"You've known him for a long time, then."

"All my life. Our families belonged to the same clubs. Karl and I were always paired for social functions. The expectation, at least on our parents' part, was that we'd get married someday. Karl always thought so, too."

"But not you?"

She shook her head, walked to the coffee table, took up her tea, idly sipped.

"Karl had a tough childhood. His father had his mother committed when Karl was seven years old, and not long after that he divorced her. His father married four more times, all women of looks and little substance. He paid no attention to his son. Poor Karl practically lived at my house. My parents, at least, treated him kindly. I always knew Karl felt a way about me that I didn't about him, but I was able to maneuver around that. Our senior year in high school, he proposed to me. I turned him down, of course. He made threats."

"What kind of threats?" Jo asked.

"Oh, nothing dangerous. The 'I'll join the foreign legion and you'll be sorry' kind of thing. Well, he did. Or his version of the foreign legion. He applied to the naval academy and was accepted. He went off to Annapolis, and I went to Stanford. We saw one another occasionally when we were home for the holidays. I have to admit, Karl in his uniform was quite impressive.

Then the summer between my junior and senior year, my father hired a young man on the crew of his yacht."

"You fell in love, your father objected, you married anyway, and the young man proved in the end to be more than worthy. *Superior Blue.*"

"What I didn't put in the book was how Karl came back into my life."

They both turned at the sound of footsteps on the stairway. The boys came down.

"Mom, can we have something to snack on?" Scott asked.

"Sure. Okay with you if I give them some cookies?" Grace asked Jo.

"Fine. But go easy, Stevie."

"In the kitchen, Scott. You know where."

The boys went together. Jo watched them, smiling.

"Scott's good with him. Stevie's usually pretty shy."

"Scott's just happy to have another nonadult around. Or nonmom." She looked down at the tea glass in her hand. "Where was I?"

"Karl coming back into your life."

Grace nodded. "In some ways, the navy was the best thing that could have happened to him. Growing up, he had a father he could never please, whose love he could never fully win. I always felt sorry for him. He was such a lonely boy. The navy did something, toughened him, gave him, I believe, some concrete measure of himself, an acknowledgment of his achievements, things his father never did. There was something very attractive about him then. He had a powerful feel to him. He could walk into a room and take charge. It was as if he'd grown into the man he was meant to become. Very handsome, indeed."

"You were married then. To the poor but worthy man."

"It wasn't like that, Jo. I didn't drool over Karl. I was happy for him. He visited Edward and me whenever he was in town. The two of them got to be good friends. They both shared a love of the water, sailed a lot together.

"Karl left the navy to take over the Lindstrom business after his father died. Everything had gone to hell under his father's haphazard practices. He was working himself to death. That's when Edward convinced him to take a break, a two-week voyage around the Great Lakes, to relax. Unfortunately, at the last minute, there was a problem at one of the mills and Karl had to back out. Edward went anyway, alone, and disappeared in the middle of Lake Superior." She stopped for a moment, and Jo could see that time hadn't yet healed the wound. "Even though Karl was overwhelmed with his own problems, he dropped everything and was there for me. I was a mess. He was my spokesman to the press, my guide, my shrink, my business executive. He did what needed doing, what I couldn't bring myself to do. For almost three years."

"And then you married."

"Yes."

"You'd fallen in love with him?"

"No. Not like with Edward. I'd come to rely on Karl. And I thought Scott needed a father. It seemed the natural progression of things."

"And now?"

"Karl has tried. It's not his fault. It's just that . . ." She paused, reached again for her tea, but missed and nearly knocked the glass over.

"Just what?" Jo asked after things were settled.

"At the very heart of him, he's still a Lindstrom. He snaps at Scott. He makes decisions without discussing things with me and then he brooks no argument. Moving up here, for example. It's lovely country, Jo. I won't deny that. But I don't belong here. And Scott desperately needs other children around. I know Karl thought it would be good to get away from where so many memories haunted us both, but—"

"You let him build a home like this without really wanting it?" Jo said, interrupting.

"I have homes in New York City and Malibu, too. I can easily afford a home like this." She put a hand on Jo's knee. "I'm sorry. I didn't mean that the way it sounded. It's just that money wasn't the issue."

"I understand."

"Edward and I, we shared everything. Our thoughts. Our fears. Our hopes. I knew his soul. I knew absolutely that he loved me. This honker, for example." She squeezed the end of her nose as if it were a bicycle horn. "He loved my nose. Karl asked me a few weeks ago why I'd never considered having something done to it."

"I'm sorry."

"Karl shares so little of himself. A Lindstrom trait. When he does, it's not attractive. I've begun to feel as if I'm living with a stranger, although I've known him all my life. With all the problems over the logging issue, he's hardly ever here. When he is, he's still not really here." She turned away from Jo, moved to the window again, clasped her hands behind her. "So I'm leaving him. I'm going to ask for a divorce."

Jo put her glass down. "Are you telling me this because I'm a friend, or because I'm an attorney?"

"You do family law."

"Up here, I do everything. But you have attorneys, I imagine. Good, expensive attorneys."

"I don't want you to handle the divorce, Jo. That's not it. Just tell me what I'm facing."

"Legally?"

"That. And anything else you think I ought to know. This is scary. I haven't said anything to anyone, but I need to talk to someone."

"Does Karl know?"

"I haven't told him. But I can't imagine he doesn't know at some level."

"Have you thought about counseling?"

"I've suggested it several times. Karl's a Lindstrom, an ex-naval officer. He doesn't believe in help. That kind, anyway."

Something fell in the kitchen, a crash of glass on the floor.

"Scott? You guys okay in there?" Grace called.

Another sound followed, something high, but muted, a muffled cry. The women exchanged a quick glance and moved toward the kitchen. They'd taken only a step when two men pushed through the kitchen doorway. They wore ski masks over their faces, black leather gloves on their hands. Each gripped a boy. One of the men held a handgun. All the air seemed to rush from Jo's lungs, and something hot and too heavy to hold very long pressed down inside her stomach. Even so, she felt the briefest sense of relief to see that the firearm was pointed not at the children but at her. She tried to speak but felt paralyzed. The two intruders seemed momentarily stuck, too.

"Who the fuck are you?" the man with the handgun finally asked her.

"I was about to ask you the same thing. More or less." She was surprised that although she could barely breathe, her words sounded calm.

"Take whatever you want," Grace said. "Leave the boys alone."

"We'll take what we want, all right."

Jo looked at Stevie. Her son's dark eyes were wide, little holes full of terror, and his mouth was open as if in a soundless cry. Jo wanted to kill the man whose huge hand dug into Stevie's tiny arm.

"It's okay, Stevie," she said.

"Oh, but it ain't okay," the man with the handgun said. "Both of you turn around." He swung the barrel in a tight circle.

Jo hesitated and Grace also did not move. The man with Scott in one hand and the handgun in the other put the barrel to the boy's head. "Do it now," he said.

A sound escaped Grace's throat, not loud, but pitiful. It seemed to hit hard the man who held Stevie. "For Christ's sake," he told the other man, "get the gun away from his head."

"All right." The barrel swung toward a Tiffany lamp on a walnut end table. The shot shattered more than the glass of the lamp. Whatever had held Stevie silent broke, and he began to whimper.

"Shut up," the man with the gun said. Then to the other man, "Shut him up."

"Don't." Jo took a step.

The barrel of the handgun was aimed again on her heart. "Don't even think about it."

The man who held Stevie said, "Look, you do exactly as we say and no one will get hurt, I promise. What'd you say his name is?"

"Stevie."

"Okay, Stevie. You're gonna be fine. Just fine. But you have to do what I tell you, okay?" He waited. "Okay?"

Stevie watched his mother nod, then he nodded, too.

"Good man." He looked at Jo. "Turn around."

She did. Slowly. Followed by Grace. So that both had their backs to the boys and the men. Jo heard the sizzle of tape pulled from a roll. Glancing back, she saw that Stevie and Scott's hands were being bound with silver duct tape.

"You okay? Does that hurt?" Stevie's captor asked.

Stevie shook his head. Scott was secured, too, and a strip of tape went over the boys' mouths.

"Just tell us what you want," Grace insisted. "Whatever it is, you can have it."

The man with the gun said, "Put your hands behind your back. That's all I want. Right now."

The women were bound in the same way as the boys. Their mouths were taped.

"What do we do with these two?" Jo felt a light tap on the back of her head.

"Can't leave 'em. They come, too."

"What about the note?"

"On the glass coffee table. He'll find it. Everyone this way." The man with the firearm in his hand waved them toward the kitchen.

Milk lay in a puddle on the kitchen floor amid shattered glass. Cookies sat on the table, half eaten.

"Outside." The man with the gun held the back door open.

They stood on the back deck, in that time of day when the sun had deserted the sky, yet something of it lingered, the memory of light, just enough to illuminate dimly the landscape of the cove. The moon was rising, and stars lay scattered above the trees like pinholes in a dark ceiling.

"This way." The gunman motioned them to follow and headed down a flagstone path toward the dock. Behind him walked Scott and Stevie, then Grace and Jo. The other man brought up the rear. When they reached the edge of the lake, the gunman called over his shoulder, "We're all going to take a little dip." He waded into the water, calf-deep, and began to follow the shoreline. Jo understood. They would leave no tracks in the sandy bottom of the lake. Where the lawn gave way to woods, a small runabout sat on the water, the bowline tied to a sapling on the shore.

"Everybody in."

The other man steadied the boat and, because their bound hands made it awkward, helped them in. Stevie he lifted bodily and set gently beside Jo.

"Lie down," the gunman ordered.

The runabout was narrow. They all lay together, nearly on top of one another. The bottom of the boat smelled of fish gut and cut bait and damp wood. Although Jo nestled next to Stevie, she knew she offered him no protection. She heard the crinkle of a tarp flapped open. The next instant they were plunged in darkness. A hand tamped her butt, then her shoulders as the men tucked the edges of the tarp tightly about them.

"I'll take it from here," she heard the gunman say. He had a hard, unpleasant voice that made her think of a saw blade biting dry wood. "You know what to do."

"I know."

"Don't look so worried. We just stepped onto the yellow brick road." The gunman laughed.

The boat was shoved back. The engine sputtered to life. The runabout slowly came around, and Jo felt it carry them away, out of the small cove and onto Iron Lake.

On the shoreline of the cove, the man in the ski mask watched the silhouette of the boat and its sole upright occupant until they disappeared. He realized he was sweating like a pack mule, and he yanked the ski mask from his head. He ran a hand through his wet hair. The whole time, he'd been barely able to breathe, and he sucked in the night air greedily. He bent and felt the rocky bottom of the lake until he found the right stone, a round one that filled his hand. He wrapped the ski mask around it, bound it in place with duct tape, and threw it as far as he could out into the water of the cove. He took off his gloves and shoved them into his back pocket.

It hadn't gone badly, although the other woman and her boy had been a surprise. Still, they'd handled it. No one had been hurt. It bode well.

He kept to the water, following the shoreline past Blueberry Creek and finally to his own dock. He stepped onto the old board and slipped out of his sneakers. In the cabin, he put the wet shoes beside the back door to dry, changed his clothes, and finally went to the kitchen where he broke the seal on a fifth of Cutty Sark. He poured three fingers of scotch into a glass and stared at it.

John Sailor LePere had been sober for a long time. But he needed a drink now. Not to steady his nerves. Not to forget his losses. Not to escape his nightmares. He needed, that night, to be what Aurora, Minnesota, believed him to be. A drunken Indian who could no more manage a kidnapping that he could a raising of the dead.

"To you, Billy."

He lifted his glass to the empty room and he filled his throat with fire.

Cork parked his Bronco in the garage at ten-thirty P.M. He was surprised to see that Jo's Toyota wasn't there. Inside the house, everything was quiet. Lights were still on in the living room, and he heard the television turned down low. He found Annie asleep on the couch.

"Sweetheart." He shook her gently. "Why don't you go on up to bed."

She nodded, her eyes still dreamy.

"Did your mom come home?"

"Unh-uh." She shook her head. "Aunt Rose went to bed a while ago. Jenny's still out with Sean."

He watched her stumble up the stairs, then he sat on the sofa himself and stared at the television. MTV. A rap video. He wasn't watching. He was thinking about the evening at the Quetico.

He'd sat next to Karl Lindstrom during dinner. The man had barely touched his food. But he'd had a drink to his lips nearly the whole time. Although he seemed to attend to the conversation at the table, his eyes were clearly scanning the room, checking to see if Death had an invitation. Despite the air conditioning, he was sweating heavily as he rose to make his way to the podium. When he spoke, however, his voice and manner betrayed not at all his concern. He appeared relaxed, very much in control, and he delivered a pretty good speech about balancing the need for growth and profit against the absolute duty to ensure the integrity of the earth for future generations. The only allusion he made to his own recent brush with death was to say at the outset, "It is, indeed, a pleasure to be here this evening, appearing before you in *living* color."

Although he listened, Cork was carefully watching the large room. With Schanno's men and the state patrol posted at every door, it would have been suicide for Eco-Warrior to try anything. Still, you never knew.

Nothing happened. Lindstrom finished his address to huge applause, rejoined the men at his table, and proceeded to further calm his nerves with a couple more scotch and sodas. He'd had enough alcohol by the end that Schanno insisted on having a deputy escort him home. Lindstrom didn't argue.

Cork used the remote to kill the picture on the television. The house slid further into stillness. He looked at his watch. It was much too late. He went to the telephone table next to the stairs and pulled the address book from the drawer. Under *Grace Fitzgerald,* he found a number Jo had written. He reached for the phone and was startled when it rang just as he touched it.

"Cork O'Connor," he said into the receiver.

"This is Wally Schanno."

"Yeah, Wally. What's up?"

"I'm at Karl Lindstrom's place. Was Jo visiting Lindstrom's wife this evening?"

"As far I know. Why?"

"Cork," Schanno said, his voice hesitant, guarded, "it appears that Grace Fitzgerald and her son have been kidnapped. They're gone and somebody's left a ransom note. Jo's Toyota is still here, but there's no sign of her."

Cork's mouth went dry. "Stevie was with her," he said.

"I think you'd better get out here."

On the access, fifty yards from Lindstrom's log home, a state trooper barred his way.

"I'm Cork O'Connor," he told the trooper.

"Yes, sir. If you'd just park your Bronco to the side of the road here, I'll see that you're escorted in."

Law enforcement vehicles lined both sides of the road within twenty yards of the house. After that, there was nothing except one Tamarack County Sheriff's Department cruiser and Jo's Toyota parked in front of the garage. The doors of the Toyota stood open. In the glare from the yard light mounted above the garage, Cork could see that the car had already been dusted for prints. The trooper who'd been his escort turned him over to Deputy Marsha Dross, posted at the front door.

"I'm so sorry, Cork."

"What's going on?"

"Earl, the BCA agent. He's asked that the whole scene be secured. He doesn't want any more vehicles up here, or anyone inside the perimeter without his okay until he's released the scene. The sheriff will be here in a minute. He can explain." She wrote Cork's name on a log sheet and noted the time.

Schanno came to the front door and joined them outside.

"What happened, Wally?"

"I'll tell you what we know, Cork. I asked Marsha here to drive Lindstrom home from the Quetico. She delivered him." He looked to Dross for her to continue.

"He'd sobered up quite a bit by then. He went inside. I called dispatch to let them know I was on my way back. Just as I was getting ready to head off, Mr. Lindstrom came running out the front door, waving a piece of paper. I read the note and called it in right away."

"And secured the scene," Schanno added. "Did a good job."

"What did the note say, Wally?"

"It was signed Eco-Warrior, said basically that he had Lindstrom's wife and boy and if Lindstrom ever wanted to see them again, he'd follow instructions."

"What instructions?"

"Lindstrom will be contacted."

"Anything about Jo and Stevie?"

"No." Schanno glanced at Dross.

"What is it?" Cork asked.

"The only other thing the note said was no police."

"I was already here." Dross seemed to be apologizing.

"Where did Lindstrom find the note?"

"On the coffee table in the living room," Schanno said.

"Just like that? He walks in, finds the note, and hollers at

184

Marsha before she can pull away? He doesn't go to the kitchen first for a glass of milk? Doesn't go upstairs to find out if they're sleeping maybe?"

"Cork." Schanno hesitated a moment. "There was indication of some violence. Pieces of a shattered lamp all over the floor. We already dug a slug out of the wall."

"Where's Lindstrom now?"

"Inside. Waiting by the phone. The note didn't say when he'd be contacted with instructions."

Schanno seemed uncomfortable with his empty hands and he put them in his pockets. "Look, I'm thinking they were just in the wrong place at the wrong time and were taken along with Lindstrom's family."

"Can I talk to Karl?"

"Did you log him in?" Schanno asked Deputy Dross.

"Yes."

"Come on, then." Schanno led the way to the living room, speaking as he went. "Ed Larson's in charge of the scene, but I asked Agents Earl and Owen if they'd help. They've got more experience with this kind of thing."

In the living room, Karl Lindstrom sat in a brown leather easy chair staring at the telephone on a small table next to him. Cork saw residue from the dusting for prints on the doorjambs and furniture.

"This is the only area that's been cleared," Schanno told Cork. "We stay here until either Ed or Agent Earl releases the rest of the house."

Lindstrom looked up, looked bewildered. "Cork."

"Karl."

He'd sobered. The relief at not having encountered any violence during his address at the Quetico had been replaced by fear. And anger.

"The son of a bitch," Lindstrom said. "Our families, Cork. The bastard's gone after our families."

Through the doorway that led to the kitchen, Cork saw the light go out, and another, a strong focused beam, began to sweep the floor.

"Cork, you have any idea why Jo and Stevie were out here this evening?" Schanno asked.

"Jo came because Grace Fitzgerald wanted to talk to her.

185

Professionally. And Stevie? There was no one to watch him at home."

I should have been there, he thought, *protecting my son instead of Lindstrom.*

"Professionally? Any idea what about?"

"No."

"You, Karl?" Schanno asked.

Lindstrom sat forward, his hands working angrily over one another. "She didn't say anything to me about it. Does it matter?"

"We don't know what matters at this point," Schanno said.

Cork heard Owen's voice in the kitchen. "There. And over there. At least two good prints. Let's get some powder in here to enhance them and then get them photographed. We'll try to lift them after that."

Lucky Knudsen appeared briefly, glanced at Cork, and gave him a look full of concern. He picked up a fingerprint box and stepped back into the kitchen. Agent David Earl came down the stairs from the second floor. Ed Larson was with him. Larson was writing in a small notebook.

"Doesn't look like anything was touched upstairs," Earl said, "but let's have the likely areas dusted for prints anyway." He looked up when he reached the bottom of the stairs. "O'Connor," he said. Then he said, "I'm sorry."

"How'd they get in?" Cork asked, skipping amenities that meant nothing to him at the moment.

"Back door, Cork," Ed Larson said. "No sign of forced entry."

"She never locked the doors before she went to bed," Lindstrom said. "I told her whenever she was out here alone to keep the doors locked. She never did."

Agent Mark Owen stepped in from the kitchen, looking pleased. "We've got good footprints," he announced. "Someone stepped in the spilled milk and tracked across the floor. Too big for the boys."

"All you need now," Cork said bleakly, "is an idea where to find the shoe that fits it. Got one?"

Owen calmly replied, "It's a start, Mr. O'Connor."

"What do we do now?" Lindstrom looked to Earl for an answer.

"I've called the FBI office in the Twin Cities," Earl explained. "They're sending up a team and the equipment to set up a trap and trace on the phone so that when contact is made, we'll be ready. The ransom note is already on its way down to the lab in St. Paul. It'll have priority. In the meantime, we finish processing the scene. We'll talk to your neighbors and find out if anyone saw anything. Then we wait and see."

"Do Rose and the kids know?" Schanno asked Cork.

"Rose. She's waiting by the phone. I'll have to call her."

"There's a phone in my office," Lindstrom said. "Down the hallway there. It's a separate line."

"Okay if I go?" Cork asked Earl. "Want to process the room first?"

"Go ahead. But just use the phone."

When he was sheriff, Cork had believed that in a frightening situation, the presence of law enforcement was a comforting influence. He looked around him as he headed away from the living room, looked at the people who were going about their jobs, following established procedures, but who, in reality, were just as ignorant as he. Any comfort they offered was at best an illusion. At worst, it was something akin to a prayer for the dead.

25

THEY WERE ON A LOGGING ROAD—an old one, seldom used. Jo knew it from the way the vehicle that transported them dipped and jumped and from how often and hard the man who drove it braked, then slowly maneuvered right or left. Jo imagined the headlights slicing into the dark, glancing off pine trunks, the far end of the beams swallowed by deep night and dense woods. She imagined well because she'd been trying for nearly an hour to track—blindly—where they were headed.

In the runabout out of Grace Cove, she was almost certain they'd headed north. Not far. Ten minutes and the engine had been cut and the bow scraped bottom. The man in the ski mask pulled the tarp away and placed black cloth bags over the heads of Grace and Scott Fitzgerald. Then he took the two of them away. He'd come back immediately for Stevie. "I've got nothing to put over your head, boy. So close your eyes. If you open them, I'll poke 'em out with my knife." He'd shown Stevie a vicious-looking blade, and Stevie had clamped his eyes shut tight as clamshells. The man had lifted Stevie and carried him away. When he returned for Jo, he pulled a crumpled red bandanna from his back pocket, snapped it once to clear the crust, folded it, and bound it over her eyes. "Mess with the blindfold and your kid's history."

He didn't immediately take her to the others. She stood for several minutes, listening as he smashed a hole in the hull of the boat, started the engine, set it at idle speed, and sent the runabout back onto the lake. She assumed that in a few minutes it would sink, deep and without a trace.

He led her to a vehicle—a van, she guessed from the way he had her enter. He sat her on the edge, and she felt the rear bumper under her legs. He told her to slide back. After she scooted a couple of feet, she heard a double slam—two doors. He moved to the front, climbed in, and said, "Hold tight." Which, with her hands bound behind her, was a cruel joke. As the van lurched forward and took a hard right, she tipped over, falling against a large prone form she guessed must have been Grace.

At first, the road was smooth. Jo believed they were heading east. She lay on the floor of the van, which was covered with old shag carpet smelling of gasoline and dog. With the van traveling on the relative quiet of the paved road, she could hear Stevie whimpering, and she prayed he had his eyes shut. The van veered hard left—north—onto a road that, from the shudder of the undercarriage and the choke of dust, Jo figured was not paved. She tried to think what roads headed that way. There were several and all tunneled into the Superior National Forest. Fifteen minutes, and they turned again—east—and the ride became a torture of bumps that tossed her up off the carpet and brought her down hard. She tried to calculate miles but could only guess at speeds. Still, her sense was that they were east of the Iron Lake Reservation and just south of the Boundary Waters Canoe Area Wilderness.

They'd been in the van nearly an hour when it pulled to a stop. The man got out, came around to the back, and opened the doors.

"End of the line," he said.

He grasped Jo by the ankles and pulled her to the edge.

"Stand up," he ordered.

When she did, he grabbed her by the shoulders and positioned her to the side.

"Stay right there, gorgeous."

Jo heard him bring the others out. To Stevie he said, "Keep those eyes closed." Then there was a tearing of fabric and a moment later he said, "There, got your own blindfold now, kid. Everybody just hang tough."

Jo heard him walk away. She couldn't tell if anyone was with him. She tried to say Stevie's name, but the duct tape over her mouth made it impossible. He came back, then away, then back and away, then he returned a last time for Jo. He grasped her brusquely by the arm and led her along. They entered a structure—Jo could tell by the dank smell, the closeness of the air, the way the distant chirp of tree frogs was suddenly muffled. Under her feet, she felt brittle grass give way to dirt. He stopped her, put his hands on her shoulders, and shoved her back against a square post. His hands were large and powerful, and they forced her down so that her back slid along the splintered post. She cried out as slivers of wood needled through her shirt into her skin. Her butt hit dirt. He looped a rope tight about her and cinched her to the post so that her hands behind her were pinned between the small of her back and the wooden post. When he'd finished, he lingered near her. She could feel his breath on her cheek, and then his fingers at the top buttons of her blouse. His hand crept down her skin toward her breasts. He made a sound, as if contemplating a good meal. The rope that bound her to the post kept him from exploring further. Like a spider retreating, his hand withdrew.

"Okay, everybody, listen up. You're going to be here a while, so you might as well get used to the idea. Someone's going to be outside all the time watching you. Try anything and you'll be sorry." He chuckled. "Oh, hell, you're probably already sorry. But believe me, I can make you a lot sorrier. Moms, if you want your sonny boys left in one piece, you don't do anything but sit unless I tell you otherwise. I don't want you to make a sound, not even so much as a squeak. And, boys, if you get any ideas about playing heroes, if you try anything, I've got a knife the size of your arm and I'll use it to slice your mothers' tits right off."

Everything fell quiet. Jo listened intently. The dirt floor let him move silently and she couldn't hear him. She anticipated his touch again, but it never came. There wasn't a sound, not even Stevie crying, and that worried her. She wanted to hear him, to know that her son was all right. Or as right as he could be, given the circumstances. Outside, the engine of a vehicle turned over and caught. Jo couldn't tell if it was the van that had brought them. Maybe another vehicle had been there, waiting. He'd said someone would be watching them. She heard the bump and rattle of the undercarriage and the growl of the engine growing distant. In a few minutes, she heard nothing at all.

Her back, riddled with splinters, was on fire. Her shoulders ached from the way her arms were pinned behind her. She was filled with disgust thinking of the filth of his handkerchief across her face. She thought of trying to call out to Stevie, but if someone were watching it might get them all hurt. If it were only she, Jo would have fought to free herself. But there were others who could suffer from what she did. The man with the ski mask and the gun had bound her in many ways.

She heard a sound, very soft, to her right. She cocked her head and listened. It came again, a faint rustle, a scurry of tiny claws across wood. Some small animal had joined them. Jo knew it was probably something on the order of a ground squirrel. She wasn't worried about a creature that moved on four little legs. In those woods, the only animal that terrified her walked on two.

26

T HE CALL CAME AT SIX A.M. By then the FBI had arranged with the phone company for a trap and trace, and they'd set up equipment to record the conversation. Lindstrom put the call on the speaker.

"Karl Lindstrom," he answered.

"Listen carefully, Lindstrom. I want two million dollars for the woman and the boy. In hundreds, nonconsecutive, not new. And none of that invisible powder shit. You have twenty-four hours to get the money. I'll call tomorrow, same time, with instructions."

"Two million? I can't get that kind of money in twenty-four hours. It's Sunday, for God's sake."

"Twenty-four hours."

"I want to talk to my wife and son. I want to know they're all right."

"How 'bout I just send you a finger? Or maybe I do a little impromptu plastic surgery on that honker of hers. Send you the leftovers. Twenty-four hours, Lindstrom."

Cork whispered quickly, "Are Jo and Stevie with him?"

It was too late. The line clicked, buzzed, and the voice was gone.

"Did we get a trace?" Schanno asked.

"Just a minute." Special Agent Margaret Kay of the FBI held up a cautionary finger. She stared at another FBI agent, Arnie Gooden, who was one of the resident agents out of Duluth. Gooden held a cellular telephone to his ear.

"Got it," Gooden said a moment later. "Pay phone. Harland Liquors, County Road 11."

"You know where that is?" Special Agent Kay asked Wally Schanno.

"Near Yellow Lake," Schanno replied. "It'll take fifteen minutes to get a cruiser there."

"Is anyone at the liquor store you could call?"

"They're closed Sundays."

"He'll be gone by the time your men get there," Kay said. "But he may have left evidence behind, or maybe somebody saw him." She turned to Agent Gooden. "Did you hear that voice?"

Gooden nodded. "Electronic mask of some kind."

BCA Agent David Earl, who stood near the window, said, "We'll get the tape down to the lab in St. Paul right away, see if we can get anything from it."

"Can you get the money?" Cork asked Lindstrom.

Karl Lindstrom gave Cork a desperate look. "You think I keep that kind of cash around here? In a cookie jar, maybe?"

"I didn't mean it that way, Karl."

Lindstrom sat down, not by choice, it appeared. His legs just buckled. "Two million dollars. I don't have that kind of cash anywhere. Everything I have is tied up in that damn mill. Even if it weren't, I couldn't get at it until tomorrow at the earliest. Christ, it's Sunday."

"What about your wife?" Cork asked. His own legs weren't feeling too steady, and he needed badly to hear something that offered hope.

Lindstrom shook his head. "Prenup. I can't touch her money. Jesus. And I was the one who insisted on the goddamn thing."

"Mr. Lindstrom," Agent Kay said, approaching him. "Even if you had the money and gave it, that would be no guarantee of the safety of your wife and son."

Lindstrom looked up at her.

"Meeting a kidnapper's demands seldom results in the safe return of those who've been taken."

Agent Kay had come from the Minneapolis office with a cadre of other agents. Some of the agents were at Lindstrom's. Some were at the sheriff's department, where the FBI had established an operations and communications center. Special

Agent Kay was a tall, large-boned woman with hands that reminded Cork of catchers' mitts. She painted her nails a delicate pink. She wore tan slacks, a beige blouse, brown flats. She had, she'd informed them earlier, supervised investigation in nearly two dozen kidnap cases.

Now Cork asked, "Have you ever been involved in a kidnap for ransom?"

"No," she admitted. "But I do know the statistics."

Lindstrom stared at her. "Do you really think I care about the money? My God, if they asked for ten million, I'd give it to them if there was even the slightest chance of getting my family back safely." Lindstrom's eyes burned into her. "You've been here all night and I haven't heard one good suggestion from you so far."

"The state crime lab in St. Paul is working on the ransom note even as we speak. We'll make sure the tape of the call is analyzed immediately. I've communicated with Quantico and they're working up a profile of the kidnapper. With the help of Agent Earl and your sheriff, Schanno, we've already arranged to put under surveillance a number of likely suspects."

"Like who?" Lindstrom challenged.

"I'd rather not say specifically. If we end up needing to negotiate for the return of your families, we have a trained negotiator who can be here in person within an hour."

"Do you have any idea where my wife and boy are?" Lindstrom asked.

"No, Mr. Lindstrom, I do not."

"Or who has them or how to get them back?"

Her answer was to say nothing.

"See? You people are almost worse than no help at all." Lindstrom stood up and headed toward the telephone. "I'm going to call Tom Conklin."

"Who?" Kay asked.

"Chairman of the board of Fitzgerald Shipping Company. My wife's family sold the business, but Grace is still on the board. Maybe Conklin can help me get the ransom money."

"Do what you feel you have to, Mr. Lindstrom. We'll do what we need to as well."

Lindstrom wheeled. "If you fuck up, if you cause my family

to be harmed in any way, I'll . . ." He seemed at a loss for a way to finish.

"I understand, Mr. Lindstrom."

Schanno stepped up next to Cork and put a hand lightly on his shoulder. "Look, Cork, there's nothing you can do here right now. I imagine Rose and the girls will need you at home."

"Yeah."

"Get some sleep if you can."

"Call me if . . ."

"I'll call you."

Cork started to say something to Karl Lindstrom, but the man was angrily punching at the numbers on his telephone. Cork left quietly.

He stepped out into early sunlight, into air that smelled of evergreen and clean water. An evidence team was canvassing the grounds, looking for cigarette butts, footprints, anything that might have been dropped or thoughtlessly discarded. He walked down to the shoreline of Grace Cove and onto the dock where Lindstrom's big sailboat sat mirrored in calm water. The trees—mostly red pine and black spruce—walled the inlet, isolating it from the rest of the lake. It was an empty place Karl Lindstrom had chosen for his home. That was exactly what people came here for these days. Escape. Yet Lindstrom had escaped nothing. Something angry seemed to have followed him, something that had divided the county and now threatened what Cork held most dear. Not Lindstrom's fault, he knew, but he couldn't help resenting the outsiders that were so rapidly changing the face of all he loved.

He knew he was going to cry. Tears of helplessness, of anger and fear and desperation and despair. He kept his back to the house where the other men might have been watching. When he was done, he walked to his Bronco and headed home.

Rose sat alone at the kitchen table. She was dressed in a beige chenille robe, her road dust-colored hair unbrushed, rosary beads gripped in her right hand. She studied Cork as he stepped in the back door.

Cork walked to the coffeemaker, poured a cup of what Rose had made.

"They called," he said. "They're demanding two million dollars."

Her eyes fluttered as if she'd been struck in the face by a hard, icy wind. "For them all?"

"Of course for them all."

"They have Jo and Stevie? You're sure?"

"I'm not sure of anything, Rose." He sipped his coffee. It was cold. He didn't care.

"They?" Rose asked.

"What?"

"You said 'they' have Stevie and Jo."

"They. Him. We don't know."

The rosary beads clattered softly against the tabletop. Cork walked to the table and sat down. Rose had dark circles under her eyes.

"You look tired," she said to him. Then she said, "What do we do?"

Cork stared at her. He hadn't heard in her question any of the fear or hopelessness that threatened his own perspective.

"We start by telling the girls. They should know."

"All right," she agreed. "How do we get the two million dollars?" She asked as if she'd been questioning him about fixing the bathroom sink.

"I don't know. Karl Lindstrom . . ." He stopped because Lindstrom hadn't sounded certain, and Cork didn't want to build a hope that would crumble.

"If Karl Lindstrom can't?"

"I don't know, Rose. I just don't know."

"All right," she said.

Through the window, carried on a breeze that barely ruffled the curtains, came the sound of church bells. The morning Angelus was being rung at St. Agnes. Rose listened intently, as if the bells were voices that spoke to her. Cork heard the creak of the old floorboards above him.

"The girls are up," he said.

"They'll be getting ready for Mass." Rose reached across the table and put a hand gently on his. "Maybe you should come."

Cork hadn't been to a church service in more than two years. Not since Sam Winter Moon had been killed and Cork had lost his job as sheriff and Jo had asked him to leave the house. He'd felt abandoned in those days—by God and everyone else. Although he envied Rose her strength of conviction and was glad that Jo had seen so carefully to the children's spiritual upbringing, he couldn't in good conscience share their belief. He couldn't remember when last a word directed at God had passed his lips. Still, he believed prayers couldn't hurt, especially if prayed by those who believed.

"You go and pray for both of us," he told Rose.

Annie came down first, dressed in a green sleep shirt that reached to her knees and that was embossed in front with the words FIGHTING IRISH. "Where's Stevie?" she asked. "He's always watching cartoons by now."

For the moment, Cork ignored her question. "Is Jenny up?"

"Yeah." Annie yawned and stretched. "She's crawling down the stairs now." She went to the refrigerator, took out a carton of Minute Maid orange juice, and headed toward the cupboard for a glass.

Jenny came in wearing the black workout shorts she usually slept in and a wrinkled, baggy, gray T-shirt. Her white-blond hair was wild from sleep, but her ice-blue eyes—*her mother's eyes,* Cork couldn't help thinking—were wide awake.

"So . . ." She offered her father a devilish smile. "You and Mom must've stayed out at Sam's Place again last night. You weren't in bed when I got home, and Aunt Rose was pretty evasive."

"Sit down, Jen," Cork said. "You, too, Annie."

The girls looked at their father a moment, then exchanged a glance between them. Cork hated seeing the dark veil that dropped over both their faces. They did as he asked, sat at the kitchen table. They eyed their aunt and saw there, too, something worrisome.

"Is somebody—like—dead?" Jenny asked, not seriously.

"Just listen a moment."

A dark understanding seemed to come to Jenny. "Where's Mom?"

"Yeah," Annie added. "And Stevie?"

Cork didn't know how to tell them any way but outright. "They've been kidnapped."

"Right." Jenny laughed. When her father didn't, she asked, "That was a joke, wasn't it?"

197

"No joke, Jen."

"Kidnapped?" Either the word or the context seemed incomprehensible to Annie. "How? When?"

"Last night. At Grace Fitzgerald's home. From the note that was left, it's pretty clear that Ms. Fitzgerald and her son were the targets. Your mother and Stevie were just at the wrong place at the wrong time."

"They're okay?"

Cork couldn't tell if Jenny was insisting or asking, but he replied firmly, "Yes."

Annie still looked puzzled. "How do we get them back?"

"Mr. Lindstrom is working on putting together the money the kidnappers have asked for." He avoided using the word *demanded*.

"How much?"

"Two million dollars."

"He has it, right?"

"He'll get it, Jen."

Her eyes took on an unfocused look and moved slowly away from her father. She stared out the kitchen window. Annie looked down at the tabletop.

"You okay?" he asked them both.

"It's not fair," Jenny said, under her breath. Cork reached out to take her hand, but she drew away. Her eyes seemed full of accusation. "Everything was good again. Everything was finally right again. How could you let this happen?"

"We'll get through this," Cork said. "We'll get them back, I promise." He stood up and stepped toward her, wanting to take her in his arms, to give her the only comfort he could, but she shoved him away.

"How can you make a promise like that? You're not the sheriff anymore. What can you do?"

"Jenny—" Rose began, a soft admonition in her voice.

Jenny stormed from the kitchen, leaving behind her a question that cut to the heart of the matter as quickly and cleanly as a butcher's knife.

Annie put herself in her father's arms. "What can you do?" she echoed, holding to him desperately, her voice choked with tears.

He laid his cheek against her hair. "I don't know, sweet-heart," he said.

"I'll tell you what I'm going do." Rose stood up decisively. "I'm going to do what I always do on Sunday mornings. I'm going to church. And I'm going to pray my heart out."

Annie looked up at her father.

Cork offered her the best he could. "For now, that's about all anyone can do."

27

THEY HAD COME TO HIS CABIN IN THE NIGHT, just as Bridger predicted they would. Knocked on his door. Politely at first, then with a firm and heavy fist.

"Sheriff's department, Mr. LePere," they'd said to identify themselves. Two of them. A woman in a deputy's uniform and a man in a suit. He'd seen the woman before, at the sheriff's office in the days when he was routinely hauled in for drunk and disorderly. She recognized him, too. He saw it in her face when she caught the whiskey smell on his breath and saw the nearly empty fifth in his hand, most of which he'd poured down the sink hours ago.

"Yeah?" he said, feigning both drunkenness and anger. "Wha' the hell do you want? I may be drunk, but I'm drunk in my own house. There's no law against that so far as I know."

"Just to ask you a few questions," the woman said.

He swayed a bit as he stood in the open doorway. "Like what?"

"Have you been home all evening?" the man in the suit asked.

"Who're you?"

"Agent Earl. Bureau of Criminal Apprehension." He flashed an ID. LePere had caught the odor of cigarette smoke wafting off his clothing. "Have you been here all evening?"

"All evening," LePere said. "Me 'n' ol' Cutty 'n' Clint Eastwood." He stepped back, stumbling just a little, so that they could see the television and the video playing on the screen—*The Good, the Bad, and the Ugly.*

"Did you happen to look outside at all?" the deputy asked.

"Maybe I glanced now 'n' then."

"Did you notice any activity on the lake?"

"Can't see the lake from here. Only the cove."

"Did you see anything on the cove?"

"Loons, maybe."

"No boats?" the man asked.

"Boats, I'd've noticed. 'Less it was dark."

"How about on the road?" the man asked. "Did you see any vehicles moving along the road to the cove?"

LePere eyed the man as if he were a simpleton, and he lifted the hand in which he held the scotch bottle and pointed into the dark behind the intruders. "You take a look back there. Can you see the road? Hell, too many trees to see anything, even if I was looking. And I wasn't. Say, what's all this about, anyway?"

"We're trying to find some folks that may be lost," the deputy said.

"Well, you're looking in the wrong place. Only people out this way are me 'n' that big log home over there. We all keep pretty much to ourselves, 'n' we like it that way. Tha's why we live out here." He looked at them pointedly, to let them know his privacy had been invaded enough.

"I thought you gave up the drinking, John," the deputy said. She said it as if it concerned her.

"I gave up drinking lotsa times. What the hell business is it of yours anyway?"

"Sorry to bother you, Mr. LePere," the man in the suit said.

They left.

He'd seen lights the rest of the night. Around the big house. Down at the shoreline. In the morning before he left for work, he heard dogs in the woods between his place and Lindstrom's. He hadn't slept at all despite the bit of whiskey he'd drunk in order to make a good show. He hadn't taken his morning swim. He'd showered, shaved, dressed for his shift at the casino and gone to work as usual.

But he felt watched. Bridger had predicted that, too. Told him not to let it get to him. It was natural. As if Bridger did this sort of thing all the time.

John Sailor LePere went about his routine as naturally as possible, complaining of a terrible hangover every chance he got. Although it was Sunday morning, the casino was still doing a brisk business. LePere wasn't a particularly religious man, but there seemed something unsettling about a world in which so many people gambled on a day that was supposed to be kept holy. A commandment was being shattered, yet there seemed no punishment. God, John LePere had decided long ago, was asleep at the wheel. For a brief moment, he thought about his share of the ransom money—one million dollars. It was not money he would gamble away. It was to purchase justice, another thing that God, in his carelessness, had overlooked.

28

SHE HAD A SENSE OF MORNING. Of light. Of air moving as day pushed out the night. She heard birds, too, and that was a dead giveaway of dawn.

She was past aching. Or she hurt so much and in so many places now that she couldn't separate what hurt from what didn't. Her back, she was certain, had begun to fester from the splinters wedged under skin when her captor had forced her down the square post.

All night, she'd heard the van come and go. She'd decided there was no one watching when the man who'd brought them was gone. Whenever the van drove away, she'd felt along the ragged post, hoping to find a way to nick an edge of the tape, to begin the work of freeing herself.

She'd heard the others moving, shifting, making noises of discomfort. However, Stevie hadn't made a sound at all, and that worried her.

Fear had passed. What moved in to replace it was anger, a hatred that festered like the splinters on her back. *The bastards.* She wanted to get her hands free, to fill them with something big and deadly to smash the heads of the men who would hurt her child. She couldn't fathom why God would let this happen.

A little moan came from somewhere in front of her and to her right. Was it Stevie? She tried to speak, to offer her son some comfort, but words couldn't pass her taped lips, and the sound came out an unintelligible mumble, frightening even to her. God, she wanted to speak to him, and to have him reply, just to know that he was all right. She thought of the night before, when she'd put him to sleep with a song. How wonderful and simple that had been.

Jo began to hum, thinking the words in her head.

Are you sleeping, are you sleeping, Brother John, Brother John? Morning bells are ringing. Morning bells are ringing. Ding, dang, dong. Ding, dang, dong.

She stopped, hoping for a response that didn't come. *Oh, God, please let him answer. Let his little heart be strong.*

She tried again. *Are you sleeping, are you sleeping, Brother John, Brother John?*

Now she heard the resonance of another voice, but it wasn't Stevie's. It was Grace, who hummed with Jo, *Morning bells are ringing, morning bells are ringing. Ding, dang, dong. Ding, dang, dong.*

The two women paused. Once again, only a terrible, silent waiting filled the cabin.

Then she heard a smaller voice humming. *Are you sleeping, are you sleeping, Brother John, Brother John?*

It was Scott. Grace joined him, and Jo's voice became a part of the music, too.

Morning bells are ringing. Morning bells are ringing. Ding, dang, dong. Ding, dang, dong.

To hum was liberating, to fill the cabin with the nearest thing to talk they could achieve. They went through the round once again, Jo praying that she would hear Stevie. But at the end, he was still silent. A moment passed. Then a high little hum, like an echo of the round's final line, reached her—*Ding, dang, dong. Ding, dang, dong*—and her heart leaped. Stevie was with her, and he knew she was with him. It was so small a triumph, yet she found herself overwhelmed and weeping. She began the round again, and four voices joined in a sound Jo believed the angels would have envied.

The birds had been singing for a couple of hours before the van returned again. Jo could hear it a long way off, the undercarriage rattling as it bounced over what she still assumed was an old logging road. Her stomach tightened. The man was so vile. The van stopped; a door opened and closed; the morning fell quiet. For two minutes there was not another sound. Then he was next to her. He spoke no words, just warmed her cheek with his foul breathing. She'd have spit at him if her mouth hadn't been taped. He made a sound, a tiny snort as if he'd decided something. And his breath was no longer there.

"Oh, ho. What's this? Looks like somebody didn't listen when I talked. Hmmm. And you didn't even get very far. A lot of work for very little. And for what it will cost you."

Jo heard a muffled cry. Grace. *No,* she wanted to scream, but the tape constrained her to a pitiful wail. She struggled against the ropes that bound her to the post. It was a vain effort, but Christ, she couldn't just listen. What was he doing? Oh God, she didn't want to think.

Above the sound of Grace's crying another sound slowly rose. The bastard must have heard it, too, because he stopped his punishment and seemed to be listening. It was an engine. Above them. In the sky. The man moved quickly away and outside.

The plane sounded low and slow as if searching.

Oh, please find us.

It was directly overhead now. Jo wondered if the cabin were hidden among trees, or was it in a clearing?

Let us be in a clearing, please, God.

The engine seemed to hesitate. Jo held her breath. The plane kept moving, flying north, and she knew then that it hadn't been looking for them, that it was simply passing overhead, probably on its way to help fight one of the fires still burning in the Boundary Waters. She slumped back, feeling lost and abandoned.

He was among them again. She could smell him, an odor of sweat and whiskey and tobacco. "You and me have some unfinished business, Grace. But it will have to wait." Jo heard him leave; then his voice came back to them from outside the cabin. "Just relax. Enjoy the hospitality." And he laughed all the way to his van.

The air felt dead still after he'd gone. Even the birds seemed to have fallen silent. The only sound Jo could hear was the quiet weeping of Grace Fitzgerald.

29

THE AFTERNOON WAS SWELTERING. The air conditioner in the Bronco had broken. Cork figured the condenser was probably shot. He drove toward Grace Cove with the ninety-plus heat blasting at him through the open windows. Where the road to the cove split from the county highway, Deputy Gil Singer had been stationed to bar access to all but law enforcement. He wasn't especially busy, and in Cork's thinking that was good. The media hadn't got hold of the story yet. But they would. Somehow, they always did. *The longer they stayed out of it,* Cork thought, *the better.*

Gil Singer waved him to a stop, but only to say, "Sorry about Jo and your boy. We'll get the bastard; don't worry."

Cork knew the deputy was just blowing smoke. Schanno had said he'd call when, and if, he had anything more to offer, and Schanno hadn't called. Still, Cork appreciated the deputy's sentiment. Even a little false hope seemed better than none.

Lindstrom's big log home was at the center of an enormous amount of energy. In addition to the cars from the sheriff's department, the state patrol, the BCA, and the FBI, there was a Jimmy that belonged to the U.S. Border Patrol. A good number of uniforms were combing the shoreline of the lake, and others moved through the woods. A float plane—a Forest Service De Haviland Beaver—sat on the water of the cove. Seeing all this, Cork was amazed the media was still in the dark.

Inside Lindstrom's place, the air conditioning seemed to have been cranked to the max. Lindstrom was nowhere to be seen. A tall man in a starched white shirt and tie was talking on a cell phone. At one point, he said, "No, Governor, that won't be necessary." Schanno, Agent Earl, Lucky Knudsen, Special Agent Margaret Kay, and a couple of FBI agents whose names Cork didn't remember stood around the large mahogany dining-room table looking at a map spread between them. They were so intent they didn't notice Cork.

A toilet flushed down a hallway. A moment later, Lindstrom stepped into the living room. He walked slowly, slumped a bit, looking exhausted. He spotted Cork and gave him a grim nod.

"Did you talk with the Fitzgerald Shipping people?" Cork asked.

"I talked."

"And?"

At the table, the discussion stopped as Schanno and the others turned to listen to the men whose families were at the heart of the trouble.

"They're considering."

"Considering?" Anger cut along Cork's nerves, made his muscles tense.

"Very sympathetic, of course," Lindstrom said bitterly. "But there's no mechanism that allows for the kind of cash outlay we need. I tried Len Notto at Aurora First National and Jon Lynott at First Fidelity. They're somewhere in the Boundary Waters. Together. Some kind of annual thing they do. I've got a call in to a friend of mine at Chicago City Bank. I even tried an old school buddy whose family's loaded with railroad money. The problem is it's Sunday. Nobody's reachable. If I could just get back to this bastard and convince him nothing can be done until tomorrow." He closed his eyes a moment, then he sat down in a big leather chair and leaned forward in a defeated way. "I don't know what else to do now."

Cork moved toward the men at the table. He saw that the map on the polished mahogany was of Tamarack County, the huge blue of Iron Lake almost dead center. "What do you have?" he asked Schanno. "Anything?"

"Not much." Schanno sounded truly sorry. "After the dogs came up blank this morning, we tried the border patrol. Those guys can track a ghost across concrete. They found nothing. We're still checking the woods, but I'm pretty sure we won't find anything. The good part of that is that everything indicates this Eco-Warrior took them all and he kept them all."

Cork understood the implication. His wife and son were alive, not left dead somewhere, discarded like excess baggage. He appreciated it, the real hope it offered.

Agent Kay said, "We're fairly certain they were taken by boat. That probably means Eco-Warrior approached on water and took them the same way. We've got officers searching the shoreline for any evidence he might have left behind."

"The footprints Agent Owen lifted from the kitchen floor. Anything there?" Cork asked.

"A Vibram sole. Only about a million of those in Minnesota."

"What about the call from the public phone outside Harland Liquors?"

Kay shook her head. "It was too early for any witnesses to be around. We took fingerprints, but I doubt they'll give us anything."

"How about the notes he's left?" Cork looked at Agent Earl of the BCA. The man seemed uncomfortable.

There was quiet around the table. Then Lindstrom said from the other room, "Jesus, just tell him."

Earl put his hands on the polished mahogany and leaned on them heavily. "The note that lured Mr. Lindstrom to the marina. Do you remember what it said?"

"Not exactly."

"It began, 'We are all dead men.' When the crime lab ran it through the computer, they got a hit."

"A hit?"

"It matches text. The Bible. Exodus. Chapter twelve, verse thirty-three. The lament of the Egyptians after their firstborn are killed. This may be an indication that kidnapping the boy was what Eco-Warrior had in mind from the very beginning." He gave a brief, apologetic shrug. "If only we'd known a little sooner."

"Why would he try to kill Karl if he intended to kidnap his family for ransom?" Cork asked.

"The bomb went off before Mr. Lindstrom was in any real danger. We believe it was remotely detonated, to make us think he was the target."

"Because?"

Schanno fielded that one. "To focus all of our attention on Karl last night when he spoke at the Quetico. Left damn little law enforcement around to interfere with the plans out here. It appears he played us like trout on a line, Cork. Money was probably what he was after all along."

"At least it appears that way at the moment," Kay added.

Cork moved closer to the map. "Taken by boat. Any idea where?"

"Iron Lake's a big body of water," Special Agent Kay said.

"What do you think?" Cork asked Schanno.

"If I were Eco-Warrior and wanted to get them off the lake without being seen, I'd take them up north, maybe all the way to North Arm. A lot of sheltered coves there where they could be unloaded without anyone seeing."

"A long way to go in the dark," Cork said.

"There's that," Schanno agreed.

Cork looked to Agent Earl. "Any guesses?"

"Maybe a private cabin on the lake. With its own dock."

"Lots of those," Cork said.

"Exactly."

"How about you?" he asked Kay.

"I don't think they've gone far. Too many people to move without being seen."

"There are lots of back roads up here. You can drive miles without seeing a living soul," Cork told her. He looked again at the map. "Have you talked to John LePere?"

"Last night," Earl said. "He was drunk. Claimed he didn't see anything."

"Drunk?"

"I gathered that's not unusual."

"I thought he'd given up the booze," Cork said. "You check his place?"

"Why?"

"I'm just thinking, if Karl's family was Eco-Warrior's target all along, he probably had this house under surveillance for a while. LePere's place would be good for that."

"We checked all we could without a warrant," Earl said.

"Fuck the warrant," Cork snapped. "The lives of my wife and my son are at stake here. And his." He drilled a finger through the cool air at Lindstrom.

"Cork." Schanno spoke evenly. "You know we can't just waltz in wherever we want, much as we'd like to sometimes."

"Then get a warrant."

"We'll do what we can," Schanno promised.

Cork glared at the map. "What about the old landing on the rez?"

"Where's that?" Kay asked.

"Here." Cork put his finger on the map. "About two miles north, just inside the rez. It doesn't show on recent maps, like this one. The Iron Lake Ojibwe were the only ones who ever used it, but nobody goes there anymore since they built the new docks and landing in Alouette. A boat could still be put in there, and be taken out, and probably nobody around to see it."

"Get someone on it," Kay said to Schanno.

"I was just going to do that," Schanno said. Irritation grated his voice.

Cork stood a moment not knowing exactly what to do next, what to do with his anger, his frustration. He saw that Lindstrom had settled back in the big chair and closed his eyes again. Cork wondered if he'd slept at all.

"What if we can't get the ransom money?" he asked the men at the table quietly.

"It's like I've already said, O'Connor," Kay replied. "Paying the ransom is a guarantee of nothing."

"And if we give them nothing," Cork shot back, "what does that guarantee?"

Kay said, "We're doing our best."

Cork left the table. Schanno, who'd gone to send an officer up to the old landing, met Cork halfway across the living room. "Where are you going?"

"Home, I guess."

"I'll keep you posted," Schanno promised.

"Thanks." Cork looked at Lindstrom and saw the deep despair on his face. It was like looking into a mirror, and he didn't need to say a word.

Heading up the road away from Grace Cove, Cork had to swerve quickly to avoid an old pickup with a camper shell that swung fast around a blind curve and almost into his path. He caught a glimpse of the driver and he recognized John LePere. In the rearview mirror, he watched the pickup turn off the paved road and onto the rutted dirt and gravel that led to the only other cabin on the cove. He considered LePere, a man he'd often dealt with when he was sheriff. Like Cork, LePere was of mixed heritage. Although LePere kept to himself and seemed to have no friends in Aurora, Cork knew some of the man's history. He'd survived the sinking of an ore carrier many years before. The only survivor, Cork believed. And hadn't his brother been among the men lost in that tragedy? No wonder he drank. He made his home on Iron Lake now, but Cork thought he still had a place on Lake Superior, somewhere around Purgatory Ridge.

He wondered how thoroughly LePere had been questioned. Although the man had seen nothing the night of the kidnapping, perhaps he'd seen something before, someone on the cove who didn't belong there, someone watching the big house.

Let it go, Cork told himself. It was no good second-guessing. There was nothing but anguish in doubting the work of all those officers gathered around Lindstrom's table.

But what if they'd missed something? In every investigation, there was some error.

Cork whipped a U-turn and followed where the pickup had gone.

LePere hadn't made it inside his cabin yet. He must have heard the Bronco coming, because he stood in the shade on his porch watching as Cork pulled into the yard. Over his shoulder was slung a dark blue jumpsuit, the uniform of the custodial staff at the casino.

"Afternoon, John," Cork said as he stepped from the Bronco.

"Sheriff," LePere replied. Then he caught himself. "I mean—"

"That's all right." Cork waved it off. He put a foot on the bottom porch step and looked up at LePere in the shade. "I wonder if I could ask you something."

"I suppose."

"The sheriff's people were out here last night. Wanted to know if you'd seen anything out on the cove."

"If that's what you're wondering about, I'll tell you same as I told them: I saw nothing."

211

"Last night, maybe. But what about lately? Have you seen anyone out here who didn't belong?"

"You mean besides them?" He nodded toward the big home across the cove.

"Don't like your neighbors?"

"I don't like neighbors period."

"So. Have you?"

"Seen anyone out here? No." He looked toward Lindstrom's place. "Lots of cops. What's going on?"

It was remarkable that he didn't already know, but Cork figured he would soon enough. Pretty soon everybody would.

"A kidnapping there last night. Lindstrom's wife and son were taken."

"That so?"

"My wife and boy, too."

LePere thought about that and seemed surprised "Lindstrom's got money. But what would anybody want with your kin?"

"You heard about this Eco-Warrior?"

"I'm a long way from town, but I listen to the news."

"He grabbed Lindstrom's family for money. Mine just got in the way."

"They asking for a lot?"

"A lot."

"You going to pay?"

"I'm going to try, John. Wouldn't you?"

LePere let it slide.

"Whoever this guy is," Cork went on, "he's probably been watching Lindstrom's place for a while. I thought maybe he might have been careless. Maybe you saw him out here somewhere."

"Like I said, I've seen nothing."

Cork was squinting, looking directly up into the sun. He was hot. He wiped a trickle of sweat from his cheek. "Could I trouble you for a drink of water?"

LePere eyed him a while before answering. "Wait here." He went in the front door.

Cork walked around behind the cabin and to the dock. He studied the cove and Lindstrom's log home across the water. He turned and surveyed the woods that isolated LePere's place, that formed a wall all the way out to the point at the entrance to the cove. A man could easily slip among the pines undetected, post himself out there near the end of the point, watch Lindstrom's home without being spotted. Eco-Warrior had been smart about everything. There was no reason LePere should have seen him.

It was different being on this side of a crime. Frustrating. Frightening. He felt he ought to be doing something more, something substantial, but he didn't know what that was. Two of the people he loved most in the world were in terrible jeopardy, and there didn't seem to be a thing he could do about it. As sheriff, he'd often had to offer the only comfort he could— *We're doing our best*. That sounded so feeble from this side.

Think, he told himself desperately. *Think like you've been trained to think.*

Who was this Eco-Warrior? Was he really what he seemed? If the whole point of all that had gone before was to set up the kidnapping, it seemed too risky, too complicated. Why not just make the snatch, deliver the demand? Why all the theatrics? On the other hand, theatrics seemed often to be a part of terrorism.

Two million dollars. That was a huge leap from demanding the safety of Our Grandfathers. What were they after? What would the money do? Buy weapons? Bombs? A more sophisticated arsenal for their terrorism?

His thinking went immediately to Hell Hanover and the Minnesota Civilian Brigade. They could put two million dollars to good use. Hell had already threatened Jo to get Cork to back off the investigation. It seemed the newspaperman had a lot to be nervous about.

But what about Joan of Arc of the Redwoods? Or Isaiah Broom? Two million could finance the saving of a lot of trees after the fight over Our Grandfathers was finished.

And wasn't it possible, also, as Schanno had speculated, that Eco-Warrior was simply a cover for an old grievance? Or maybe now for simple greed?

"You're trespassing," LePere said at his back.

Cork turned. LePere had a glass in his hand. Water with ice.

"Sorry, John. I'm just trying to figure it."

"Some things are beyond figuring."

Cork took the water. "It's my wife and my boy. What am I supposed to do?"

LePere looked away. "I can't help you with that one."

Cork drank the water and handed the glass back. "The wind's up."

A breeze had risen, quite suddenly. The water on the cove began to ripple. Far west of Iron Lake, thunderheads began to mount.

"Rain maybe," LePere said. "Finally."

"Thanks for the water. If you think of anything, anything that seems like it might help, you'll let me know?" LePere only stared at him, and finally Cork started back toward his Bronco.

"O'Connor," LePere called after a dozen steps.

Cork turned back.

"Good luck."

Cork got in the Bronco and started away. There was a lot on his mind, but he found himself puzzling over a small detail. On the way to the dock, he'd passed LePere's garbage can. The lid was off. Yellow jackets and flies buzzed over what was inside. Paper, coffee grounds, discarded food. The odd thing was that there wasn't any glass. In Cork's experience, alcoholics generated lots of empty bottles.

30

JOHN LEPERE WATCHED O'CONNOR'S OLD BRONCO head off between the pines.

Damn.

It wasn't supposed to be this way. When O'Connor was sheriff, he'd always treated LePere decently, even in the days of the heaviest drinking. The man was part Shinnob, too, so he understood the difficulty of growing up mixed blood. LePere was sorry for the turn of events. Nothing was anything like he'd expected. Still, he told himself as he stepped back into his cabin, nothing really terrible had come of it. If it all ultimately went the way Bridger had planned, O'Connor would have his family back together in a couple of days. It would give him a greater appreciation of how precious were the people he loved, and all it would cost him in the end was a bit of worry. To LePere, who'd lost everyone he loved, that seemed a small price.

He took his field glasses from the hook beside the back door and stepped outside again. Across the cove, Lindstrom's home was a busy place. The shoreline was still crawling with uniformed officers, as were the dock and the woods. They'd come across Blueberry Creek, trespassed on LePere's land. That was fine. They'd find nothing, and they'd turn away. Although the ransom note had clearly said *no cops*, Bridger had called this one, too. "There'll be cops," he'd said. "A shitload. Don't let that scare you. We'll have them fooled. They'll be looking for that Eco-Warrior, and there's nothing to connect you with him.

You don't give them just cause, they can't do a thing. Just be cool, my man. Just be cool."

He returned the field glasses to their hook and went to the closet in his bedroom. From the shelf above the hangers, he took down a sleeping bag and a canvas pup tent rolled and bagged. He put these on the front seat of his truck. Back in the cabin, he filled a paper sack with food—bologna, bread, peanut butter, strawberry jam, American cheese, and apples. He dropped a butter knife in, as well, and a roll of toilet paper. He put the sack in the truck beside the other things. Finally, he filled two one-gallon plastic milk jugs with tap water and took them to the truck. After he'd locked the doors to his cabin, he headed the truck up the road. He pulled over when he reached the deputy stationed at the highway.

"There's cops trespassing all over my property."

The deputy took off his hat and wiped the sweat from the band. "Sorry about that, Mr, LePere. Would you like to talk to the sheriff?"

"No. Tell him he's welcome to trespass all he wants. I'll be back when it looks like I can have my privacy again."

The deputy eyed the gear in the front seat. "Sorry we drove you out."

LePere replied with an unhappy grunt and hit the highway. He breathed easier once he'd left the cove behind. All those cops made him nervous. He could hear Bridger's voice in his head, "Just be cool." It seemed easy for Bridger. All of it. LePere thought about the gun in the log home and how he'd been afraid Bridger would really use it. Which would have been truly tragic. But then, tragedy happened, didn't it? He'd never asked for or deserved the tragedy that had been his own life. As far as he could tell, it struck like lightning, without warning or just cause. Still, it would have been hard seeing it happen to the O'Connor woman or her boy. He knew her. He'd seen her sometimes when he was in court. She represented the Iron Lake Ojibwe, had represented them even before they had all that casino money. It was too bad she'd stumbled into the middle of all this. Too bad she had to be taken. But Bridger was probably right. They couldn't be left behind. And there was no harm done. When the money came, they'd be free again.

He followed the road, the old logging trail, toward the ancient trappers' cabin that stood just outside the Boundary Waters Canoe Area Wilderness. The old road was never used, and even if it were, the cabin couldn't be seen from it. You had to know where to look. LePere knew. And Bridger, now that LePere had shown him.

Dark was coming on as John LePere pulled his truck off the road, through a gap in the pines, and into a small clearing. Bridger was waiting beside his dusty green Econoline van.

"About time," Bridger said.

LePere stepped from his truck. "Any word on the money?"

"He'll get it, all right. I offered to send him a couple of body parts as incentive."

"You wouldn't."

"Damn straight I would. People do just fine without their pinkies, Chief."

LePere nodded toward the cabin, a run-down affair with a gaping doorway and no windows. "How're they doing?"

" 'How're they doing?' " Bridger's tone mocked him. "They're alive, Chief, and that's all you need to worry about. I'll spell you in the morning, after I've called Lindstrom with the next set of instructions." A long growl came from his stomach. "Goddamn, I'm hungry. Here." He handed LePere the handgun.

"What do I need this for? They're tied up, aren't they?"

"Insurance. In the SEALs, I learned the most valuable lesson of my life. Never underestimate the likelihood everything's going to go to hell, and be ready for it. They're all yours. You can do whatever you want with Lindstrom's woman, but don't touch the other one. I've already marked her as mine."

"What are you talking about?"

Bridger laughed. "Relax, Chief. Have a little fun." He gave LePere a hearty slap on the shoulder, and he got into his van. "See you in the morning."

He drove off, the noise of the van shattering the peace of an otherwise quiet evening.

The cabin was ancient. It was old even when he'd stumbled onto it with his father one day while they were searching for blueberries. The logs were cedar, the roof of cedar shakes. The door had long ago been lost and the chinking weathered away,

217

but even in the worst heat of the day, the cabin remained cool inside, shaded by the pines at the clearing's edge and open to the breeze.

The drought had turned the long grasses in the clearing to dry stalks, and they broke with a brittle crackle as LePere made his way toward the gaping doorway. Inside, the cabin was dark and dead quiet. It took a moment for his eyes to adjust. He saw that Bridger had left the duct tape in place around everyone's wrists and had taped their ankles as well. The Fitzgerald woman and her boy had black hoods over their heads. The O'Connor woman was blindfolded with a red bandanna. It looked as if Bridger had torn a strip of material from the O'Connor boy's shirt and bound it over the kid's eyes. All the prisoners—he balked at thinking of them in that way, but he couldn't find a more delicate word—had been separated from one another and bound with tight loops of nylon rope to the uprights that supported the roof beams. The two boys had their heads down and appeared to be sleeping. The women knew he was there. Their heads were cocked and they were listening. He surveyed the room and found no evidence of water or food. Hadn't Bridger fed them? Given them water? Had he even given them a chance to relieve themselves?

LePere knelt beside the O'Connor woman. She tried to pull away.

"Easy," he said. "I'm just going to take the tape off your mouth."

The duct tape stuck pretty well, and she grimaced as he pulled it off.

"Sorry," he mumbled. "You had anything to eat or drink?"

"No."

"How about going to the bathroom?"

"We've been like this since we got here." She seemed torn between anger and relief.

"All right," he said.

The boys were awake now, their heads up.

"Look, I'm going to take the tape off your mouths so you can eat something and drink a little water. If you have to relieve yourselves, let me know and we'll take care of that, too." He went to the O'Connor boy. "This'll hurt a bit, son."

The boy made a sound—"Owww"—as the tape came off.
"There. That better?"

The boy didn't answer. It was clear that he was scared shitless. LePere could tell from the urine smell that he'd wet his
pants already. Well, there was nothing that could be done
about that now.

He moved to the next boy, the Fitzgerald kid. He was surprised to find him quivering uncontrollably, and the smell of
urine was even stronger on him. LePere lifted the hood over
the boy's head just enough so that he could remove the tape
from his mouth. "You okay?" he asked.

The boy's breathing was deep, labored. LePere noticed a
fruity smell on his breath. The boy said nothing, but his
mother began making a ruckus. LePere lifted her hood a bit
and pulled the tape off her mouth.

"He's diabetic," she gasped. "He needs insulin."

"Ah, shit. How often does he have to have it?"

"Three times a day. And it's been almost two days now since
he had his last injection. Please, he needs insulin, and he needs
it soon."

"Christ." LePere stepped back, trying to figure the best
course. It wasn't supposed to be this complicated. Why didn't
Bridger know about the boy's condition? Or maybe he did and
just didn't care. He was a man LePere was disliking more with
every minute.

"All right, let's get some food and water in you," he growled.

"Could we go to the bathroom first?" the O'Connor woman
asked.

"Everyone need to go?"

"Yes," the Fitzgerald woman replied.

One at a time, he untied them from the wooden uprights, cut
free their hands, and took each for a turn out into the clearing.
He handed over the roll of toilet paper and allowed a minute or
two of privacy. He told them to call when they were finished,
and he warned each that he had a gun and he would use it.
They gave him no trouble. When they'd all taken their turns,
he bound their ankles, then went to his truck and brought
back food and water.

"Leave your blindfolds and hoods in place," he instructed
them. "I don't want to see anything exposed except mouths."

He opened the jug and they passed it around and drank, especially the Fitzgerald boy. He gave them food, dry bread and bologna that, with the exception of the Fitzgerald boy, they ate greedily.

"You're not like the other one," the Fitzgerald woman said.

"Who?"

"Your partner. He's a son of a bitch."

"I can be, too. Just don't test me."

"I feel sick," the Fitzgerald boy said.

"I'll get your damn medicine, okay?"

"It's not too late to end this," the O'Connor woman said.

"It's been too late for a dozen years."

"What does that mean?"

"Forget it. Look—where do I get this insulin?"

"I keep it in the cupboard in the downstairs bathroom," the rich woman said.

"I can't go near your place."

"Any pharmacy."

"Right. Soon as the police know your boy's diabetic, they'll be waiting for me when I walk in the door. Forget it. I'll figure it out. Everybody, hands behind you."

"Do you have to—" the Fitzgerald woman began.

"Just shut up and do it." He pulled her arms behind her and taped her wrists, then scooted her against the post where she'd been tied before. He bound her in place and taped her mouth. He did the same with each of the others.

"I'll be back," he said. "You all just sit tight and don't make any trouble. This'll all be over soon."

He left the water jug and the bag of food and headed back toward where he'd parked his truck among the trees at the edge of the clearing. The tall, dry stalks of foxtail and timothy snapped with a sound like small bones breaking as he pushed through. He turned back once. The cabin was a black square against a dark wall of trees that rose up into a sky grown murky with the approach of night. He was tired. The weight of what he was involved in seemed to have grown enormous. In addition to everything else, now he had the sick boy to worry about. Christ, maybe he should just let it be. What was the boy to him?

The thunderheads he'd seen earlier had continued to mount. Now there was lightning far to the northwest. As he opened the door of his pickup, he heard the low rumble of distant thunder, but he didn't pay it much heed. He was deep in thought. *Where the hell am I going to get insulin?*

31

INSIDE THE HOUSE ON GOOSEBERRY LANE, it was a day out of place, out of time. Even amid all that was familiar, everything felt wrong. The quiet of Sunday afternoon, usually so welcome, seemed drawn taut, wrapped around something sinister. Rose set out cold cuts for supper. No one ate. Cork wondered if he should head back to Lindstrom's, but what good could he do there? They had no answers. They offered no hope. And Schanno had promised that if anything developed, he'd let Cork know.

Near sunset, Cork stepped out and sat on the porch swing. Annie came, too, and sat with him. Rose drifted out, leaned against the railing, and stared west where thunderheads stumbled across the sky. Jenny joined them finally and stood on the porch steps with her arms crossed.

"I have to do something," she said. "I can't just wait anymore."

"The question is what to do," Cork replied.

"I want to kill somebody."

"No, you don't, Jenny," Rose said.

Jenny uncrossed her arms. "I do. I want to kill the people who'd do this kind of thing."

"Do you think they're all right, Dad?" Annie asked.

"Yes."

Jenny challenged him. "How do you know that?"

"In the absence of proof, you believe."

"I wish you were sheriff," Annie said.

"Why?"

"You could do something."

"Wally Schanno is doing everything he can."

"I trust you more."

"Thanks, Anne." He put his arm around her. "Come here, Jen."

His oldest daughter sat beside him on the swing, and he had both daughters in his arms. It hadn't been very long ago that he'd come near to losing his children, losing his whole family, losing everything he held most dear. They'd all had to struggle to hold together. He refused to believe that they'd come this far only to have happiness snatched away so cruelly. But then he'd never claimed to understand life. The only thing he knew absolutely was that he wouldn't think twice about sacrificing himself for those he loved.

"I'm tired of sitting, too," he said. "I think it's about time I did something."

"What?" Jenny asked.

"I'm going to start by talking to someone."

"Who?" Annie looked up at him.

"Henry Meloux."

"What can he do?"

"He always surprises me." Cork stood up.

"May I come, too?" Jenny asked.

"Me, too," Annie put in.

"I'd prefer someone to stay with Rose."

"That's not necessary, Cork," Rose said.

"That's okay." Annie left the swing and put her arm around her aunt's ample waist. "I think Dad's right. I'll stay."

Cork ruffled her hair affectionately. "Thanks, kiddo."

"It's almost dark," Rose pointed out. "You should go quickly."

Cork kissed his sister-in-law on the cheek. "Hold down the fort."

"Don't I always?"

The thunderheads had completely muscled out the stars by the time the Bronco left the town limits of Aurora. Lightning— a lot of it—played across the clouds, illuminating the face of a storm that had yet to break.

Jenny leaned forward and looked up through the windshield. "How come it's not raining?"

Cork said, "Maybe the air's too dry, or maybe it's too hot. I don't know."

They drove a while on a county road, the dark growing deeper around them, pierced only by the Bronco's headlights and by the startling bursts of lightning that were growing more frequent by the minute.

"When you and Mom split up," Jenny said after a time, "I used to lie in bed at night thinking of ways to trick you into getting back together. Like, you know, faking a deadly illness or running away."

"You never did."

"I was never sure what was the right thing to do, what would work. Is that how you feel right now?"

"Pretty much."

Jenny stared out at the darkness of the North Woods. "I wish you had your gun."

"Who would I shoot? It's only Henry we're going to be seeing."

"Just in case."

"Relying on your brain is better. First lesson I ever learned in law enforcement."

Jenny sat back and Cork felt her staring at him.

"How did you feel when your dad was killed?" she asked.

"That was a long time ago."

"But you haven't forgotten."

You never forget, he thought.

His father was the youngest sheriff ever elected in Tamarack County, and the best remembered. He'd been killed when Cork was thirteen. An old curmudgeon of a woman deaf as a post had stepped into the middle of an exchange of gunfire between the sheriff's people and some escaped convicts making for Canada. Cork's father put himself between the old lady and a bullet from a stolen deer rifle. The clock on the tower of the courthouse was hit in the fracas, and the hands had not moved since. Cork had only to look at the clock to be reminded of a moment that had changed his life forever.

"I was angry," he finally replied to Jenny's question. "I wanted to kill the men who'd killed him."

Jenny looked straight ahead. "That's how I feel."

"I understand," he said.

He turned off the county road and onto a narrow track of dirt and gravel.

"Do you think Henry Meloux will know what to do?" Jenny asked.

"Not necessarily. But I'm hoping that after I talk with him, I will."

By the time Cork parked next to the double-trunk birch that marked the trail to Henry Meloux's cabin, black clouds had gobbled the moon. Except for those frequent moments when lightning made the trees jump out at them, Cork thought it was the darkest he'd ever seen the woods. He took a flashlight from the glove compartment and gave it to Jenny.

"Go ahead and light the way. Just follow the path. I'll be right behind you."

The lightning was all around them by now. Cork knew there could be a lot of ground strikes. With the woods tinder dry, he believed that unless a good rain came with the storm, things could be bad. Unfortunately, the clouds didn't seem inclined to offer anything but the lightning that jabbed at the night and the forest. Cork stayed close behind Jenny as she made her way along the path. He was surprised at how quickly and nimbly she moved. A wind swept in with the clouds, and it shoved against the trees so the trunks bent as if something big walked among them. Although he didn't want Jenny to know, he was becoming very concerned about being in the woods.

When they stepped out of the trees and onto Crow Point where Meloux's cabin stood, Cork felt a moment of relief. In the flashes of lightning, he could see the dark cabin a hundred yards ahead. They'd gone less than a dozen strides in that direction when he heard a dull roar growing behind them. He puzzled for a moment, but as the sound grew in nearness and intensity, he suddenly understood.

"Run for the cabin," he shouted to Jenny, and he pushed her forward.

His daughter didn't question him. She took off at a hard run, the beam of the light she carried bouncing crazily ahead of her, mostly missing the trail. Twenty yards from the cabin, she stumbled and fell. The flashlight flew from her hand and when it hit the ground, the light went dead. Cork could hear the roar almost upon them. He grasped Jenny and pulled her to her feet. As they bolted over the last stretch of dark ground, the hail overtook them.

The stones were larger than any Cork had ever seen, big as his fist, and had plummeted thousands of feet. They hit with a force like hard-thrown baseballs. Jenny screamed and put her arms over head. She stopped dead still so that Cork, coming up fast from behind, almost knocked her down. He lifted her up and carried her forward. The hail struck Meloux's cabin with a deafening clatter that seemed to put into question the ability of the thick logs to withstand such a beating. Cork threw open the door and, shoving his daughter before him, stumbled into the dark inside. He grabbed an oil lantern from a wooden peg next to the door and a match from a box that sat on a small shelf next to the peg, and he quickly gave the cabin some light. Finally, he slammed the door against the hail. Still the stones came inside, breaking through the panes on the windows, bouncing across the old plank floor before finally coming to rest near the stove or under Meloux's bunk.

"Are you all right?" he called out to Jenny over the din of the stones striking the roof and the walls and the windows.

She looked dazed, but she gave him a slow nod.

Cork glanced around the cabin, a place he'd often spent time. The walls were hung with trappings collected over the long life of a man of the woods—a bearskin, a deer-prong pipe, snow-shoes, a toboggan. It was all familiar but somehow strange at the same time, for Meloux was missing.

As abruptly as it had struck, the hailstorm ended. The cabin grew very quiet.

"Is it over?" Jenny asked.

"For us," Cork said.

Jenny looked around. "Where's Henry Meloux?"

"I don't know. Henry gets around pretty good for an old man. He could be anywhere." He said it lightly, as if, of course, there were no reason to expect Henry Meloux to be waiting for them. Except Cork had every reason to expect it. Henry was always there when he was needed. It was part of the old *mide's* magic. "But it's odd that Walleye's gone, too. Walleye never leaves."

Cork felt a little uneasy being in Meloux's cabin without the old man there, without his consent. But he also felt something prickling, an old cop instinct. He stepped to Meloux's table, an ancient construction of birch. Laid out on the table were several large, soot-blackened stones.

"What are they?" Jenny asked.

"They're *madodo-wasinun*. Stones for a sweat. You know that Henry Meloux is a *mide*."

Jenny looked at him, not comprehending. "A mighty what?"

Cork smiled. "Not *mighty*—*mide*. One of the midewiwin. A member of the Grand Medicine Society. It looks as though Meloux has taken someone through a purification recently."

"What for?"

"A sweat can be for a lot of reasons. Atonement, for example. To help a spirit return to a state of harmony."

"Henry Meloux's spirit?"

"Maybe." But he wasn't thinking at all that it was Henry. He was remembering the visit Joan of Arc of the Redwoods had made to Meloux only a couple of days before. Had she come seeking the old *mide*'s help? His guidance, perhaps, in her effort to atone? Atone for what? The death of Charlie Warren?

"What do we do?" Jenny asked.

"We go back home."

He could tell from the look on her face that it wasn't what she wanted to hear, but she accepted it. Maybe like him, she felt too beat to fight it anymore.

Outside, the clouds were moving east. The sky to the west had cleared and above Iron Lake stars were reappearing. Cork found the flashlight Jenny had dropped. He tried the switch, but the light didn't come on. As they started back along the path, the moon slipped out from behind the bank of clouds and lit the way for them. It was moonlight, as moonlight had existed for millions of years, but it seemed, like everything else that used to be familiar, to have an eerie quality to it now. The ground was thick with melting hailstones, and when Cork reached the Bronco, he found its body pocked with dents. He started the engine and made a U-turn. Jenny switched on the radio. As they headed back toward Aurora, the news came on, and with it, a report that forest service authorities feared the lightning might have set new fires in the North Woods.

Cork shook his head. Henry Meloux had always told him that everything had purpose, that the Great Spirit oversaw all life with a profound wisdom. At that moment, Cork found it hard to believe. What in the hell could Kitchimanidoo be thinking?

32

SHE HEARD THE THUNDER coming from a long way off, and her first thought was *Rain*. She let herself imagine the feel of it, cool against her face, running down her festering back, quenching the fire there. She lifted her head, as if to greet the raindrops, and pain shot through the stiff muscles of her neck and shoulders.

Time and pain. They were two strands of what bound her. The hours dragged. Her body seemed to chronicle each minute with a new aching. She couldn't sleep, refused to let herself. She needed to be aware, even if it meant feeling everything. She needed to believe something might break for them, even if there seemed nothing she herself could do. Vigilance and hope. What other allies did she have?

The thunder grew nearer, big cracks that sounded as if they were splitting the earth. Blind, she pictured the forest shattered where the lightning hit, the ground scarred black. It wasn't a pleasant image and she tried to shake it. A strong wind rose in advance of the storm. She could feel the air pushed through the gaps in the old cabin, and she could hear the creak and groan of the trees as they bent. If there were rain, she knew it wouldn't be gentle.

The storm overtook the cabin. Lightning flashed so brightly that even through the disgusting cloth across her eyes she could see the night illuminated. Immediately after each bolt, thunder made the ground tremble as if, compared with what the heavens wielded, the earth under Jo was nothing. The lightning seemed to strike all around the cabin, frighteningly close. Although she'd thought that after what she'd already been through, nothing could scare her further, she was terrified.

Between the claps of thunder, she heard a growing roar, like a huge wave sweeping toward her. A few minutes later, hail hit the cabin. The din as the stones pounded the old roof and walls was deafening. The end of the world would be no less terrible, Jo thought. As frightened as she was, her greatest concern was for Stevie, for whom even a normal thunderstorm was a nightmare. She longed to be holding him, comforting him.

God, she prayed, more desperately than she ever had, *please help us.*

And the hail left. As suddenly as it had come.

In the quiet that followed, she heard Stevie whimpering softly.

"Are you sleeping," she hummed to him. She was relieved to hear his quivering little echo.

More time passed. Hours, it seemed. She was afraid for Scott. She thought she could hear him, his shivering almost audible. Was he coming back, the man who'd given them food and a bit of hope? His concern had seemed genuine, and his promise to return with the insulin had seemed sincere. Still, a man capable of kidnapping was probably capable of almost anything despicable. Maybe it was part of the plan, a sort of good cop–bad cop scenario. One terrorizes, the other gives hope, and in that way they keep the hostages caught in indecision, incapable of escape. The man who'd brought them to the cabin was vile, there was no doubt in Jo's mind. He was fully capable of the cruelty he promised. But the other was an unknown. And even if he meant well, what control did he have over anything?

She could barely keep her eyes open. For a moment, she closed them.

She was dreaming instantly. Of walking through a strange house. Looking for Cork, but unable to find him. She opened a door and something black leaped at her and she woke.

The dream turned her thinking to the house on Gooseberry Lane. It was the only place she'd ever lived that she let herself love. She could see Cork and Rose and the girls gathered at the kitchen table. She could see the worried look on all their faces. Imagining their helplessness made her want to weep, and she yanked herself away from that weakness. Instead, she imagined her family in council, considering action. Cork wouldn't sit by and let this happen. Jo didn't know what he would do exactly, but she knew that somehow he was working his way toward her. She wrapped all her hope around the solid belief that somehow he would come.

She was dreaming again. This time it was a horrible dream full of fire. She woke with a start and found that the air she breathed was full of smoke, so thick she could feel the texture of it in her nostrils when she breathed. She listened. No tree frogs or crickets. None of the usual night sounds. The only noise from outside the cabin was a dry crackle that sounded like a thousand feet marching across a bed of brittle branches. The march was accentuated now and then by the boom of a big bass drum.

Fire.

She began working her wrists desperately over the ragged edge of the post, trying to cut the duct tape that bound her. The smoke grew thicker, and the sound that only minutes before had seemed distant rose to a constant roar punctuated by the boom of trees exploding. The fire was moving rapidly toward them. She felt the current of the air shift as it was drawn in to feed an immense body of flame.

Please, God, no. Not this way.

Behind her back, her wrists covered a territory of only inches as she strained, twisting against the ropes. Then she felt the slight resistance as the tape snagged on a big splinter. She tried to calm herself, to focus on the delicate trick of notching the tape, for she knew that if she pulled too hard, the splinter would simply break off. She began to cough, and she could hear Grace and the boys coughing, too. The cough made it hard to be delicate with the tape. Sweat soaked the bandanna across her face. The air was growing hotter and moving faster as it was sucked in to feed a monster that was almost at the doorstep.

Please, God. Over and over again as she struggled, she prayed that simple, desperate prayer. *Please, God.*

But it seemed God had not listened, because the splinter broke away from the post, and Jo screamed through the tape that sealed her mouth, cursing an end that was too cruel to believe.

Then she felt a hand on her ropes.

"Don't move."

Jo recognized the voice of the man who'd gone for the insulin.

A knife blade slipped between her breasts and quickly severed the rope. Jo leaned forward and his hands were at her wrists, cutting them free. He moved to her ankles as she pulled the bandanna from her face. The cabin was filled with smoke made luminous by a pulsating glow that came through the doorway. The man moved to Grace and Scott. As he freed them, they pulled the hoods off their heads. Last, he bent over Stevie, who ripped the strip of cloth from his eyes as soon as his hands were free.

"Come on," the man shouted over the roar and boom of the fire. He headed out the door.

Grace was right behind him, holding onto Scott's hand. Jo followed with Stevie in tow. Outside, smoke thick as fog rolled off a tide of flame that had engulfed the trees on the far side of the clearing, a little over a hundred yards away. Sparks had ignited fires in the tall, dry grass that surrounded the cabin. The man who led them ran a crazy zigzag between islands of flame. Stevie's small legs couldn't keep up and he fell. Jo turned back and scooped him up in her arms. When she turned around, the fire had closed in front of her, blocking her way. She sprinted left, toward the only gap she saw. She cleared the wall of fire just as the flames licked at her heels. She saw a truck with a camper shell parked among the trees at the clearing's edge. The tailgate was down. Grace and Scott were sliding inside. The man was gesturing furiously for Jo to hurry. When they reached the truck, he lifted Stevie and tossed him in back. Jo leaped in beside her son and the man slammed shut the tailgate and dropped the door of the camper shell, locking them inside.

The fire moved with incredible speed. Already it had eaten the cabin and the whole of the clearing and was now racing through the crowns of the pine trees along the logging road. Jo knelt and peered through the rear window of the cab and through the windshield beyond. The man jumped in behind the wheel. Over his right shoulder, Jo could see that the tiny corridor of road ahead of them was solid fire on both sides. The man glanced back and in the glow of the flames, Jo looked into his face and he into hers. He turned away, jammed the truck into gear, and gave it gas. The tires spun on dry dirt, then caught. The truck hit second gear and the flaming corridor at the same time. Jo dropped and clutched Stevie to her. Fire splashed against the sides and rolled off the tailgate. The air inside the camper shell grew so hot it threatened to sear her lungs.

Then they were out. Beyond the flames. Through the back of the camper shell, Jo could see fire touching the sky, but as she turned and peered ahead through the rear window of the cab, all she could see beyond the windshield was lush woods, dark and cool. The truck bounced wildly over the old road as the man kept pushing for speed, putting distance between his truck and the fire. Jo's head slammed against the roof. She hunkered down beside Stevie.

They didn't stop for miles, until they came to a place where the logging road opened onto well-graded dirt and gravel. They were still in deep woods, but by then the fire was only a distant glow against the night sky behind them. The man behind the wheel pulled over and killed the engine. Immediately, Jo slid to the tailgate and tried to open it. The inside latch was broken. She heard the man in the cab cry, "Shit!" and felt the pickup shake as he pounded angrily on the dashboard. He threw the cab door open, and kicked the side of the truck. "Shit! Shit! Shit!" he screamed. Jo slid back to Stevie and took him in her arms.

The tailgate dropped, and the rear window of the camper shell lifted. A flashlight beam shot in at them.

"Here. Your damn medicine," the man said. He threw a plastic bag into the light.

In the beam of the flashlight, Grace dumped the contents from the bag—several syringes in individual packets and a small box. She took a bottle from the box, opened a syringe, and jabbed the needle into the bottle's thin membrane covering. Scott offered her his leg and she drew back the cuff of his shorts to expose the top of his thigh.

"Could you hold the light a little steadier, please?" she asked.

"Just poke him, for Christ's sake."

She slipped the needle into Scott's skin and slowly depressed the plunger. When she was finished, she put everything back into the bag, then looked directly into the light. Her eyes were blue and shiny. "Thank you, " she said.

"Give me the stuff."

She slid it to him across the bed of the pickup. He rolled her the duct tape.

"Now," he said, "tape his wrists behind him."

"Please—" Grace began.

"Just do it," he yelled.

She pulled off a long piece of tape and used her teeth to tear it from the roll. She took her son's hands, guided them behind his back, and bound his wrists. "Are you all right, sweetheart? Does that hurt?"

He shook his head.

"Tape his mouth." When she'd done as he'd asked, he said, "Now you." He jabbed a finger into the light, pointed at Jo. "Tape her the same way."

Jo did so, bound Grace's wrists and ankles and put tape over her mouth. "I'm sorry, Grace," she said.

"Now you. Turn around."

Jo scooted toward the tailgate, turned, and put her hands behind her. He taped them.

"You come down here, too, boy," he said to Stevie.

Stevie didn't budge.

"Come here, boy, or by God, I'll shoot you where you sit."

"You'd save us only to kill a child?" Jo shot back at him.

Behind the light, the man fell silent. He stepped away from the truck and looked up at the night sky a while. Jo heard him whisper, "Jesus." When he came back and spoke, the harshness was gone. "I'm not going to hurt you, son, I promise."

Still, Stevie did not move. The man lowered the beam. Jo studied his face and saw only weariness there. "You won't hurt him?" she asked.

"I won't hurt him."

"Come here beside me, Stevie," Jo said.

Stevie hesitated.

"Come on," Jo urged him. "It will be all right, I promise."

Slowly, Stevie crawled to his mother. The man bound his small wrists with a single loop of tape. He didn't bother with Stevie's ankles or his mouth.

"You last," the man said, and he closed up Jo's lips with duct tape.

"Everybody scoot together," he said when he was done. He sounded exhausted. "And hold tight. There's still some rough road ahead."

They huddled against one another. The man closed the camper shell, raised and locked the tailgate. A moment later, the truck started off.

They weren't free, but they weren't dead either, and they'd come close to that. Jo knew there was a lot of reason to be hopeful. Unfortunately, she knew there was, perhaps, even greater reason to be concerned . . . For she had looked into the man's face and had recognized him. And he knew it.

NOBODY WANTED TO GO TO BED. Separating, going to their own
rooms, lying alone with their fears seemed impossible. The girls
brought down their pillows and blankets, curled up at opposite
ends of the sofa, and slept. Rose, in her robe, napped in the
recliner. Cork sat in the easy chair, but sleep did not come. He
couldn't stop thinking, even though his thinking took him
nowhere. He stared at the telephone, hoping Schanno would
call with something. The phone refused to ring. Finally he got
up and touched his sister-in-law's shoulder very gently. She
jerked awake.

"Sorry," he whispered. "I'm going back out to Lindstrom's."

"What can you do there?" Rose asked.

Cork had no good answer. But Rose nodded and said, "I
understand."

Even with the moon already high in the sky, the night
seemed dark. Cork followed the highway around the southern
end of Iron Lake, then headed north along the eastern shore.
He turned onto the drive to Grace Cove and saw a line of headlights racing toward him from Lindstrom's place. As he pulled
to the side of the road, two dark green Luminas he knew to be
FBI vehicles sped past, followed by the Bonneville that
belonged to the BCA. Bringing up the rear was Wally Schanno
in his Land Cruiser. Schanno's vehicle skidded to a stop beside
Cork's Bronco. Schanno rolled his window down, and he
hollered, "Get in! Things are happening!"

Cork wasted no time complying, and the sheriff's Land

Cruiser shot off, following the others, who were headed north toward the reservation.

"What's going on?" Cork asked, buckling in.

"The agents that had the Hamilton woman and her son under surveillance reported a visitor about an hour ago. Didn't get an ID. A few minutes later, their van peels out of the park on the rez and heads to Isaiah Broom's place. FBI's had Broom under surveillance, too. Hamilton, her boy, and their visitor all go inside. Five minutes later, Broom rushes out and him and the Hamilton kid load the back of Broom's pickup truck with what appears to be crates of dynamite. Then they hook up a trailer carrying a Bobcat, and they all head off again, this time to George LeDuc's place. That's where they are now."

"Dynamite," Cork said. "Are they sure?"

"They seem to be."

Schanno's radio crackled. "Come in, Miss Muffet, do you read me? Over."

Cork heard a voice he recognized as Agent Kay reply, "Loud and clear. What's shaking?"

"They're on the move again, headed your way. LeDuc's not with them. He's just standing by his pickup. He seems to be waiting."

"Cordell's team stays with LeDuc. You follow the others. "

"Ten-four."

Kay's voice again: "Earl, Schanno, did you copy that?"

Earl said he did. Schanno spoke into his mike, "We stay on this road and we'll run into 'em headlong in a few minutes. We need to disappear. Over."

Kay was silent on her end of the conversation. Cork said, "Have them pull off at the old landing. It's just ahead. The aspen will hide the cars."

Schanno relayed Cork's suggestion.

"That's a ten-four," Kay said.

They entered the turnaround at the landing, the same access that might have been used to take Jo and Stevie and the others off the lake after the kidnapping. An evidence team had got a tire imprint that indicated someone had been there recently, at any rate. They maneuvered until they were positioned to head quickly back onto the county highway, and they killed their vehicle lights.

"Dynamite and George LeDuc," Cork said. "This isn't adding up, Wally."

"Take it easy, Cork. Let's just see what develops."

In less than five minutes, Broom's pickup zoomed past, flying way over the speed limit. The dusty green van with its faded evergreen tree on the side was right behind it.

"Let's give them plenty of room," Kay said. Half a minute later, the FBI cars pulled out. Earl and Schanno followed.

Cork said, "The road's always deserted this time of night. A caravan like this one they're going to spot for sure no matter how far back we stay."

"Not my call, Cork," Schanno replied.

Cork could see the red taillights of the van and pickup less than half a mile ahead. The distance began very suddenly to increase.

"They've made us," Kay said over the radio. "Hit your lights and make some noise. We're going to bring them down."

"This is Captain Lucky Knudsen. I've got a couple of cruisers ready to move into a barricade position on your command, Miss Muffet. Over."

"Do it, Captain."

"Ten-four."

From the radio came yet another voice Cork didn't recognize. "Miss Muffet, this is Cordell."

"What is it, Cordell?"

"LeDuc's been joined by half a dozen men. They've piled into the back of his pickup and they're on their way, heading straight for you."

"Stay with them. We'll be ready on this end. Over and out."

A few minutes later, Cork saw the red-and-white blink far down the shoreline where the state patrol had established a position. Ahead, the van and the pickup slowed, then pulled to a stop a hundred yards shy of the barricade. The cars in pursuit closed in swiftly from behind and parked in a spread so that the two suspect vehicles were fully illuminated in the glare of eight headlights. The doors of the Luminas sprang open, and federal agents, weapons drawn, took up covering positions.

Special Agent Margaret Kay shouted, "This is the FBI. Exit your vehicles with your hands raised."

After a moment's pause, the door of Broom's pickup swung

open, and the big Indian emerged with his hands high and a sour look on his face. The driver's door of the van also opened, and what appeared to be a rifle barrel jutted out.

"Drop your weapon," Kay ordered.

"It's not a weapon, you imbecile," Joan Hamilton yelled. "It's my cane." She eased herself out and stood on the asphalt, leaning on her cane, her free hand lifted high.

Another figure slid carefully out of the van after her, his old hands raised toward the sky.

"Henry?" Cork uttered, dumbfounded to see Meloux there.

"Turn around and place your hands on your vehicles," Kay commanded. "And keep them there." When they'd complied, she called out sternly, "Brett Hamilton, step out of the van now."

No one came forth.

"Tell your son to come out, Ms. Hamilton. We don't want anyone hurt."

"He's not with us."

"We know he is."

"What you people know wouldn't fill a thimble."

Kay waved her agents forward. Two men approached the back of the van, weapons readied. When they popped open the rear doors, it was clear that Brett Hamilton was not, in fact, present.

Kay said, "Gooden, you and Stewart take Broom."

The two agents moved to Isaiah Broom, who leaned with his hands on the cab of his pickup truck. They patted him down, then began to question him. Kay and the other agents walked to Joan Hamilton and Henry Meloux, Cork and Schanno following like shadows.

"Frisk them," Kay ordered.

Cork stepped forward. "Henry—"

"Sir, step back," an agent named Hauser instructed him.

"This man's no criminal, for Christ's sake."

"Sir, I won't ask you again."

Schanno put a restraining hand on Cork's arm. "Let them do their job."

"What's this all about?" Joan Hamilton asked.

"You were attempting to elude officers of the law."

"We didn't see you."

"You can argue that in court. Where's your son?"

"I told you, he's not with us."

"My people saw him." Kay gestured to one of her men. "Brian, take Sweeney and Jensen and sweep the trees and brush along the roadside. He can't have gone far. And be careful."

"He's not armed," the Hamilton woman said, her voice betraying her concern.

"David, take Ms. Hamilton to the car and talk with her. Jeff, you've got Mr. . . . ." She glanced at Cork.

"Meloux," Cork said. "Henry Meloux."

She nodded and the agent drew Meloux aside. Kay went to the rear of the van and looked in. BCA agents Owen and Earl stepped up beside her, along with Cork and Schanno.

"I'd love to search it," Kay said.

"The explosives in Broom's truck seem good probable cause for the stop," Earl offered. "And it was clear they were attempting to elude us."

Gooden left off his questioning of Broom and joined the others at the back of the van.

"What's his story about the dynamite?" Kay asked.

"He uses it in his business."

"That's true," Cork confirmed. "He clears trees, blows a lot of stumps."

"A strange hour to be blowing stumps," Kay said.

Gooden went on. "He says he was going to use it to fight a fire that's burning in those old pines, Our Grandfathers."

Kay turned to Schanno. "Have you heard anything about a fire up there?"

"No."

"Let's see what the others have to say."

They all told the same story. That Meloux had come to Joan Hamilton warning of a fire that threatened Our Grandfathers. They'd gone to Broom because he had the materials, equipment, and expertise to help. Finally, they'd enlisted George LeDuc to round up more hands to fight the blaze.

"It's certainly consistent with everything we've seen," Schanno observed.

"It might also be consistent with a conspiracy to plant more explosives in the name of Eco-Warrior," Kay pointed out.

"So the pertinent question is whether there's actually a fire burning in the area of Our Grandfathers," Earl concluded.

Cork said, "If Meloux claims there's fire, then there's fire."

"I'll check with the Forest Service," Schanno volunteered, and he headed back to his Land Cruiser.

Cork walked to the FBI car where Meloux was being held. "You okay, Henry?"

Meloux answered with a shrug, but he looked tired and sad.

"There's fire, isn't there, Henry?"

"Sometimes," the old man said with a slow shake of his head, "I wonder what Kitchimanidoo can be thinking."

Schanno returned and Cork followed him back to the van. "Nothing," Schanno reported. "The Forest Service has had no reports of fire anywhere near those old trees."

"All right," Kay said. "Let's search the van."

Gooden and another agent put on gloves and entered the vehicle.

"Margaret," one of Kay's agents called from his Lumina. "Cordell radioed. LeDuc's truck is just down the road. It'll be here in a minute."

By now, Lucky Knudsen and his men had joined the gathering of law enforcement around the pickup and the van. Kay spoke to all the officers in a general caution. "This could get tense. I expect everyone to exercise reasonable restraint."

Cork looked around him, and what he saw made him afraid. In the glare of the headlights that lit up only a small area of the night around them, a lot of people with guns stood together in a loose, unorganized confederation that represented the white man's law. That they believed what they were doing was right didn't offer Cork much hope. The truckful of Indians who were approaching undoubtedly believed that an important, perhaps even sacred, responsibility lay on their shoulders, and they, too, believed that right was on their side. He could feel the tension as the officers around him silently watched the headlights coming. And he couldn't help thinking of that moment not very long ago at Burke's Landing when Death, invoked by a misguided belief in righteousness, had stepped from behind a gentle curtain of morning rain and senselessly struck down two men.

LeDuc's pickup slowed and stopped in the dark on the road

fifteen yards back of the spread of cars that had penned in Broom and Hamilton and Meloux. As George LeDuc stepped from the cab, the FBI car that contained Agent Cordell's team closed in from behind. LeDuc froze, blinking in the glare of their headlights, trying to make sense of the whole scene. Cordell and two other agents leaped from the car and leveled their weapons. The men in the back of the pickup—a half dozen of them, all with the powerful upper bodies of men who logged timber—stood up, holding weapons of their own. Axes and chainsaws.

Special Agent Margaret Kay called out, "This is the FBI. I want you men to empty your hands."

None of the Anishinaabeg made a move to comply. Cork recognized them all. Jesse Adams, Hollister Defoe, Bobby Younger, Dennis Medina, Eli Dupres, and Lyman Villebrun. All were loggers, either independent contractors or working for the Ojibwe mill in Brandywine, and all of them lived on the rez. More importantly to Cork, they were all good men with families.

"I'm George LeDuc, Chairman of the Iron Lake Tribal Council," LeDuc shouted, angrily standing his ground.

"I know who you are," Kay said. "And I repeat: You men in the truck, empty your hands."

"The hell we will," Bobby Younger hollered back. "You put down your damn guns."

"Look at them," Cork said to Kay. "Those aren't weapons they're holding. They're logging tools, for Christ's sake."

"Cork? Is that you?" George LeDuc yelled.

"It's me, George. Just be cool."

"What's going on?"

"Stay back, Mr. O'Connor," Kay ordered.

Cork ignored her and strode into the beam of LeDuc's head-lights. "Where were you headed, George?"

"Our Grandfathers. Word is there's a fire burning up there, and we intend to put it out." LeDuc peered beyond Cork. "We could use Isaiah there, and that Bobcat of his."

"Have your men empty their hands and we'll talk about it," Kay offered in a stern voice.

Cork walked near to LeDuc.

"A lot of badges, Cork. What the hell's going on?"

"A big misunderstanding, George. I think the men should put down those saws and axes; then we can talk and clear this whole thing up and you can be on your way."

LeDuc's face was still taut with anger, but his dark brown eyes offered Cork their trust. He gave a nod. "Put 'em down, guys," he said over his shoulder.

The truck bed rumbled with the clatter of sharp, heavy tools laid to rest. The federal agents, who didn't yet holster their firearms, moved in.

Kay approached LeDuc. She flashed her ID and said, "I'm FBI Special Agent Margaret Kay. We have reason to be concerned about the explosives Mr. Broom is transporting in his truck."

"He uses dynamite all the time," LeDuc replied. "Everybody knows that."

"Agent Kay," Gooden called.

She held up a hand to LeDuc, a sign to wait, and she went to the van. Gooden showed her something, and she called BCA Agent Mark Owen over to confer. After that, she spoke briefly with Earl and Schanno. When she returned to where LeDuc and Cork waited, Agent Owen accompanied her. "Show them," she instructed him.

Owen held up a clear evidence bag. It contained a small length of iron pipe capped at one end. "We found this in a hidden compartment built into the floor of the van. There's more. Powder, fuse, detonators, airplane glue. Everything necessary to construct the kind of bomb that killed Charlie Warren."

Kay cast a grim eye on Cork and LeDuc, then she called, "Cordell, read them their rights and bring them all in."

"They must have a sick kind of radar."

Lindstrom stood at the window in Wally Schanno's office looking down at the parking lot. The media were gathering, newspaper and television journalists. Schanno had two deputies out front to keep them at a distance.

Lindstrom shook his head. "They're like bugs that feed on misery."

LeDuc and the men who'd been with him in the pickup had been put in a large holding cell. Isaiah Broom, Joan Hamilton, and Henry Meloux had been separated from the others and were being questioned individually by the FBI. An APB had been issued on Brett Hamilton, who hadn't yet been apprehended.

A big metal thermos sat on the sheriff's desk, and Lindstrom and Schanno held mugs full of coffee. Cork, who felt as if he'd talked LeDuc into that jail cell, was angry. "Wally, George and those men had nothing to do with anything, and you know it."

"It's out of my hands," Schanno replied. "This a federal investigation now."

"This county's on the edge of something tragic. Pulling in those men may be all it will take to push everyone, white and red, over the line."

Lindstrom turned from the window. He'd come from Grace Cove as soon as he'd received word. He looked drawn out, beaten down. "They were helping Broom and the Hamilton woman. The evidence in the van is pretty damning. Maybe they did have a hand in the bombings, Cork. Maybe they took our families. People can fool you."

"Not these people," Cork said. "And certainly not Henry Meloux. Wally, you want to hold onto Joan Hamilton, fine. Even Isaiah Broom. But for Christ's sake, let the others go. While they sit here, Our Grandfathers burn."

"Damn it, Cork, I talked to the Forest Service—" a tired Schanno began to argue. He was interrupted by Agent Kay, who stepped into the room.

"Ms. Hamilton is ready to make a statement. However, she's asked that the two of you be present." Her eyes moved between Lindstrom and Cork.

"Did she request an attorney?" Schanno asked.

"She's waived her right to counsel. Gentlemen, if you'd come with me." Kay led the way.

Joan Hamilton sat erect at a small table in the room the sheriff's department used for serious questioning. It was wired for sound and had a two-way mirror set in one wall. Cork had lobbied for the money to create the room during his tenure as sheriff. Although the funds had been allocated, he'd lost his job before construction began. When he stepped in with Lindstrom and Kay, it was the first time he'd set foot there, and he was struck by how cold and sterile the bare walls felt. Joan of Arc was staring at her hands clasped near a microphone in front of her on the walnut table. Her eyes lifted when Cork came in, but nothing else about her moved.

"Sit down," Kay said to the men. When they had, she instructed Joan Hamilton, "Please state your name for the record."

"Joan Susan Hamilton."

Her voice was far more subdued than the time Cork had heard it challenging Lindstrom from atop her van as she shouted into a bullhorn.

"Ms. Hamilton, do you wish to have legal counsel present during your statement?"

"No."

"Are you giving this statement of your own free will and under no duress?"

"Yes."

"Go on, then."

"They told me about your families," she said to Cork and to Lindstrom. She fell silent and stared again at her hands. Eventually, she took air in deeply and confessed, "I am Eco-Warrior. I admit that. No one else knew, not even my son. I acted entirely alone. But I had no part in the taking of your wives and your children. Someone has used Eco-Warrior as a cover. I swear this to you."

Cork said, "If you are Eco-Warrior, you're responsible for Charlie Warren's death. Why should we believe that you wouldn't kidnap our families?"

"Charlie Warren was an accident. A terrible accident. I intended to attack the mechanisms responsible for the destruction of the trees. Machines, not people."

"Am I a machine?" Lindstrom asked caustically. "You nearly killed me at the marina."

"That wasn't me. After what happened at the mill, I realized Eco-Warrior was a mistake and I decided that was the end. I thought about issuing a statement denying the incident at the marina but figured it wouldn't do any good."

"You still haven't given us a reason to believe you," Lindstrom said.

"This hip of mine that is such a torment." She touched herself there. "Despite what you may have heard, that wasn't my doing either. Someone tried to kill me. One of the big lumber companies, I believe. Or maybe several acting together. I know how awful it is to be the victim of violence. I would never target a human being that way. You must believe that I had nothing to do with what's happened to your families."

"Why are you telling us this?" Cork asked.

"To free you, so that you can look in a more fruitful direction. I'm a mother. I know what it is to worry about my child." Although she remained rigid and erect, something about her seemed to have given in, given up.

"Is that all?" Lindstrom asked.

"Yes. I wanted you to know. I wanted you to hear it from me."

Kay said, "I'm going to need a more formal statement. Gentlemen, I believe you've heard what you need to." She opened the door for them.

In the hallway, they were joined by Schanno, who'd been watching through the mirror. "What do you think?" the sheriff asked.

Cork said, "She always struck me as a pretty tough cookie, but she seems to have broken pretty easily."

"The feds have her dead to rights now on the mill bombing," Schanno pointed out.

"What about the kidnapping?" Lindstrom asked. "Do you think she's telling the truth?"

Schanno shrugged. "A good liar can make you believe the sun is blue. She knows she'll be charged in Charlie Warren's death. If she is, in fact, responsible for the kidnapping, maybe she's stalling, hoping to use the whereabouts of the hostages as leverage in bargaining with Kay."

"And if she's not responsible?"

"Then someone else is."

"And we're no further than we were before. Wonderful," Lindstrom said bitterly.

"I'm sure Agent Kay will keep the pressure on her. We'll find out soon enough if there's more to know." Schanno couldn't disguise that he was more hopeful than certain. "In the meantime, Karl, maybe you should go back out to your house and stick by the phone. Just in case."

"What about Meloux and LeDuc and the others?" Cork asked. "You're not going to hold onto them, are you, Wally?"

"I don't know, Cork. Seems to me they were clearly involved with Broom, who, don't forget, was carrying a significant amount of explosives in the back of his truck. There's still the question of why they tried to elude us."

"The fire," Cork said vehemently. "They were trying to save Our Grandfathers."

"The Forest Service says there's no fire."

"I told you, if Meloux claims there is, then there's fire."

"There's fire," Deputy Marsha Dross said, striding toward them down the hallway. "We just got word. A big blaze is heading right toward Our Grandfathers. The Forest Service has a crew on its way up there right now."

Schanno gave Cork a look of apology. "I'll tell you what. Isaiah Broom stays for a while. That man still worries me. But I don't see any reason to hold onto the others. Let me talk to the feds. Then you can take Meloux home, all right?"

"Thanks, Wally."

Cork and Meloux slipped unaccosted through the media people outside. The reporters were looking for the face of authority—Schanno or some other law enforcement officer—or for the face of tragedy—a glimpse of Joan of Arc of the Redwoods. When he reached his Bronco, Cork felt as if he'd escaped a nest of snakes.

"You okay, Henry?" he asked when they got inside.

"Why would I not be okay?"

"I know that wasn't a picnic in there. I hate the thought of them throwing you in jail like that."

"A lot of good Indians spend time in white men's jails, Corcoran O'Connor. Not many get out so quickly."

"You knew, didn't you, Henry?"

"What did I know?"

"That Joan of Arc killed Charlie Warren. That's what she came to see you about the night Stevie and I were with you on Crow Point."

"She came to see me because Charlie Warren was dead, yes."

Cork could feel that Meloux had made a subtle sidestep. Cork held off starting the engine and looked keenly at his old friend. "She confessed to the bombing, Henry. Even though it was an accident, she did kill Charlie Warren. Didn't she?"

"In a meadow, sometimes, I will see a killdeer flutter across the ground very near me, pretending her wing is broken. She does this, places herself in danger, for the best of reasons."

"To draw you away from her nest," Cork said. He thought about it a moment. "Are you saying Joan of Arc is protecting her son?"

"I am only telling you about a bird."

"The sweat. That wasn't for her. It was for her son."

The look Meloux offered Cork was really a question.

"I was at your cabin this evening," Cork explained. "With my daughter. Looking for you. Hail hit and Jenny and I took shelter inside. I saw the *madodo-wasinun* on the table. The stones for the sweat. I didn't mean to trespass."

"I do not have a lock on my door because there is no one who is not welcome. Why were you looking for me?"

Cork told the ancient *mide* about the kidnapping. He confessed to feeling helpless and hopeless.

"I am sorry," the old man said. "That is a heavy burden to shoulder." He was quiet for a moment. "What did you expect me to do when you came to my cabin?"

"I don't know, Henry. It's just that whenever I talk to you, things seem clearer."

Meloux nodded and thought for a while. "I do not have any answers. I will tell you what I would have told you at my cabin. You have a choice, Corcoran O'Connor. You can keep company with despair, or you can choose a different companion."

"I'm tired of despair, Henry."

"Then abandon it."

"Just like that?"

"Just like that."

Cork turned himself over to his trust of Meloux. And almost immediately he felt something vital flowing back into him. He got out of the truck and began to pace the parking lot, unable to contain his energy. The old man stepped out and watched him.

"What about the Hamilton kid?" Cork said, mostly to himself. "If he was responsible for the mill bombing, could he have done the other things, too?"

"I think he is not yet a man in many ways," Meloux said.

"To steal women and children is no small matter. That takes a dark heart and the balls of a warrior."

Cork stopped. "Hell Hanover."

"The scribbler?"

"He's more than that, Henry. And he threatened Jo already."

"I have heard he is a man who loves weapons."

"Why do you say that?"

"These woods have been friendly to the Anishinaabeg for a very long time. These woods see everything and speak to a man who knows how to listen."

Cork puzzled a moment. "Are you talking about the cache of weapons the Minnesota Civilian Brigade hid? Do you know where they are?"

The old man gave a slight shrug.

"Why didn't you ever say anything, Henry?"

"It was a business between white men. Now it involves you and Jo O'Connor and little Stephen."

Full of gratitude, Cork faced Meloux. "Henry—" he began.

The old man cut him off. "It is time we acted."

"We?"

Henry Meloux grinned. "A good fight is something I have always loved."

"I think we may need some help in this, Henry."

There was a commotion at the front door of the sheriff's department. LeDuc and the Ojibwe loggers from the rez wordlessly shoved their way through the reporters and headed toward the far end of the parking lot where LeDuc's towed pickup had been left.

Meloux eyed Cork and nodded approvingly. "I think Kitchimanidoo is finally listening."

For John LePere, the drive to Purgatory Ridge was like a slow trip to hell. He had a lot of time to think, and what he thought was that no matter how he looked at it, he was screwed. They were all screwed. The O'Connor woman had seen his face, and it was obvious she'd recognized him. As he negotiated the dark, winding highway that led to the north shore of Lake Superior, his own thinking was taking a lot of twists and turns, trying to find a way that could keep things from ending badly. Was there a way to deal with the O'Connor woman, to strike a bargain that would avert disaster? No matter how he looked at the situation, no matter how he imagined Bridger and himself playing things out, it seemed clear that someone had just rolled snake eyes.

Christ, this wasn't the way it was supposed to have been. Bridger had planned it so carefully. A quick, clean snatch of the Fitzgerald woman and the boy. Hostages for no more than a couple of days. Hooded the whole time so they would be blind to their captors. No one would get hurt. And even if they did (Bridger had put it to him), did LePere really care? Had the Fitzgeralds cared when Billy and twenty-seven other good men lost their lives in a storm churned up by the Devil himself? Had they even noticed?

Bridger had laughed and slapped him on the shoulder. "Don't worry," he'd said. "The scheme is very clever, very clean and very safe. I promise, Chief."

Except Bridger hadn't counted on the O'Connor woman and

the boy. He hadn't known about the diabetes. He couldn't have predicted the fire. All his life, LePere had been offered nothing but disappointment and despair. Why should this situation be any different?

When he finally turned south onto Highway 61, he saw that although the sky above Lake Superior was clear, the brightness of the moon and stars was drastically cut by the high smoke from all the fires. The whole world was burning, it seemed to him, and it was only a matter of time before everything around him was turned to ash.

Beyond the lighted tunnel that ran under Purgatory Ridge, LePere turned onto the narrow lane that led through the poplars down to the cove. He pulled up to the old fish house and parked. He dropped the tailgate, lifted the door of the camper shell, and shined the beam of his flashlight inside. The women and the boys were huddled together, pressed up against the cab, eyeing him as if he were a monster about to gobble them up.

"You'll be safe here." They inched forward. He cut the tape that bound their ankles, and he helped them down from the bed of the pickup. "This way." He opened the door of the fish house, turned on the light, and ushered them inside.

The fish house was ten feet wide by fifteen feet long. Waist-high tables were built against the long sides. The floor was solid maple planking with a drain dead center. There was a washbasin and cupboard at one end and half a dozen built-in shelves at the other. Three days before, after he'd found the fish house broken into and his equipment destroyed, he'd installed bars over every window and put a new heavy-duty lock and hasp on the door. He'd cleaned out the useless materials from inside, so that except for a couple of empty wooden crates and a few items on the shelves, the fish house was bare. There was plenty of room for his "guests."

"Sit on the floor," he said.

The Fitzgerald woman tried to speak through the tape over her mouth. LePere pulled the tape off.

"Scott needs food."

"You gave him the insulin," LePere said.

"He needs food now."

LePere had to admit the boy didn't look so good. "Anything special?"

"Fruit. Or peanut butter and jelly on bread. Sweetened cereal. Almost anything."

"All right." He took the tape off the O'Connor woman's mouth. "What about you and your boy?"

"Water," she replied. She looked down at her son, whose mouth LePere had refrained from taping. "Stevie, do you want anything?"

The boy stood hard against his mother, barely as tall as her waist. He shook his head.

"Maybe some peanut butter and jelly. And some milk," his mother suggested to LePere.

"Sit down," he told them. When they had, he said, "I'll be back." He turned out the light, locked the door behind him, and headed across the yard.

He'd also cleaned his little house on Purgatory Cove after it had been trashed. The only obvious signs of the destruction were the bare places on the walls where his mother's needle-point had hung. LePere went to the phone and dialed Bridger's number in Aurora. He got the answering machine.

"Fire burned down the cabin. I've got our friends. We're visiting Anne Marie." He hung up, wondering where the hell Bridger could be at that time of the morning.

From the food he kept in the kitchen, he fixed sandwiches and put them on a tray. He put a carton of milk, a jug of water, and some old Welch's jelly jar glasses into a paper bag, and he carried it all out to the fish house. He set the things on a table-top and turned the light back on.

"Okay," he said. "One at a time. You first." He cut the tape from the wrists of the diabetic boy and handed him a sand-wich. The boy began to eat.

"Where are we?" the O'Connor woman asked.

He didn't see any point in not telling her. "The north shore. A couple of miles out of Beaver Bay."

"What kind of place is this?" the rich woman asked.

"This is a fish house. My father's. He was a herring choker."

"Herring choker?"

"A fisherman," LePere explained. "He caught herring in a net. To get them out, he had to grab them around the throat and untangle them. Herring choker." He poured water from the jug into one of the glasses and offered it to the boy, who'd

252

finished eating. When the water was drunk, LePere took the glass. "I'm going to tape your wrists again."

The boy put his arms behind him and leaned forward.

"Why us?" his mother asked.

LePere didn't answer. He finished taping, then turned to the O'Connor boy. "Now you."

When the boy's hands were free, LePere gave him a sandwich. The boy only looked at it. "Not hungry?"

"He likes to drink his milk along with his food," the O'Connor woman said.

LePere shrugged and poured the boy some milk. The boy began to eat, sandwich in one hand, milk glass in the other.

"Why us?" the Fitzgerald woman asked again.

LePere was tired and didn't feel like going into it. "If you ask me again, I'll tape your mouth shut."

The women ate a little and drank some water, each in her turn. LePere had the duct tape in hand, ready to bind the rich woman's hands again when she said, "How much?"

"How much what?"

"To let us go. How much? I can pay you whatever you want."

His face burned with anger. He stared at her, a woman who'd lived her life in luxury, who'd always been able to buy her way out of trouble. He wanted her to know, to understand as profoundly and horribly as he did, that there were some circumstances money could not alter.

"What is it you want?" she pressed him.

"The dead alive again."

"I don't understand."

"Of course you don't. But you will." He stepped behind her and pulled her arms back roughly.

"Please," she said. "You're hurting me."

"Hurting you?" Something snapped inside him. He jumped away and yanked the gun from his belt. "Be glad I'm not killing you."

"John." It was the O'Connor woman, speaking to him quietly. "She didn't mean anything. She's just scared. We all are."

LePere stared down at his hand and saw that it was trembling. He was surprised—and frightened—to see his fingers wrapped around the gun and to know that he'd drawn it

253

without thinking. What else might he do without thinking? He looked at the O'Connor woman. It was her voice that had grounded him, and the fact that she'd spoken his name. He put the gun back in his belt.

"Your hands," he said to the rich woman. Then he added, "Please."

She put her arms behind her and said not another word as he bound her wrists. He went to the door. "I'll check back in a while." He turned the light off and slapped the lock in place.

He didn't go to the house. He walked down to the small dock where the *Anne Marie* was tied. The hailstorm earlier had swept across the North Woods and headed east so swiftly that nothing at all could be seen of it now in the distant dark where black sky and black water met in an indistinguishable horizon. Purgatory Cove and the great lake beyond it were very still. LePere remembered summer days with Billy, challenging one another to jump from the dock into the water of the cove that, even in August, was cold enough to cramp every muscle of his body in an instant. Billy was always the first to go. Not only would he hit the water but he'd also swim out a distance, mocking his older brother, who seldom did more than jump in and climb quickly out. Billy tolerated the cold better than LePere ever could. It seemed all wrong that Billy was the one the lake had taken.

As he had so often—and so pointlessly—over the years, LePere tried to fathom the reason he'd survived the wreck of the *Teasdale* when, by all rights, he should have been the one dancing with the other dead at the bottom of Kitchigami. In the still of the night, a thought occurred to him, the first clear understanding he'd experienced in a very long time. He *should* have been dead. From the moment he climbed aboard the little pontoon raft on that angry lake, he'd felt dead. And after that, for more than a dozen years, he'd walked dead through every day.

John LePere understood that in the dangerous game he'd become part of, the hand that had rolled snake eyes that day was his own.

35

As soon as the sound of John LePere's footsteps receded from the fish house, Jo slid herself against the wall and began the struggle to stand.

"What are you doing?" Grace whispered.

"My best to get us out of here. I'll need your help. You've got to stand up, too."

"What about us?" Scott asked.

"Until I tell you, just stay put," Jo replied. "That would be the biggest help."

Jo managed to get herself on her feet. With her ankles taped, she was forced to hop to maneuver to a window. In a moment, Grace had joined her.

"See him?" Jo asked. "There on that little dock." She nodded toward a figure, pale in the moonlight, beside a large boat. LePere was standing very still, staring out at the cove. "Tell me if he moves this way."

Jo left Grace to her duty and hopped toward the shelves built into the wall at the far end of the fish house. She didn't know what she was looking for exactly, but the bit of equipment stored there offered hope. In her hurry, she lost her balance and toppled against one of the long wooden tables that ran along the sides of the single room. Her face came near the tabletop that held a thousand scars from knife blades, and she caught the ghost of an odor, the old smell of fish that had soaked into every fiber of the wood. She righted herself and, more carefully, made her way across the floor.

"You called him by name," Grace said very quietly. "You know him."

"Don't you?"

"Should I?"

"His name is John LePere. He's your neighbor on the cove." She bent toward the shelves, trying to see by moonlight what they held.

"I've never seen him up close. I always had the feeling he resented us being there."

"It looks like he resented you a lot more than you thought."

"Mom?"

"Yes, Scott."

"I talked to him once."

"When?"

"A while ago. I was down by the creek and he was there, too. He seemed nice."

"People aren't always what they seem, Scott."

The items on the shelves were a diverse collection of boating equipment, diving gear, and general materials. At first glance, nothing that would help.

"I'm sorry, Jo," Grace said.

"For what?"

"If you hadn't come out to my house, you wouldn't be in this mess."

"Not your fault there are monsters in the world, Grace."

Jo tried to stoop without falling over. She wanted a better look at the bottom shelf.

"Do you think they're looking for us?" Grace asked.

"I know Cork is."

"How do you know?"

"Because I know Cork."

"You love him." Grace sounded envious.

Stevie whispered, "I want Daddy." His voice was on the edge of tears.

"We'll get you back to Daddy," Jo promised.

She saw something, like a large white feather, where the moonlight fell on the lowest shelf. She wobbled a bit as she lowered herself to her knees, but she made it down safely. Her heart seemed to give a loud, joyous thump when she saw that it was no feather but the clean steel blade of a knife. She began to work her way around so that her back was to the shelf, and she had a shot at grabbing the knife handle. Leaning back, she pushed her arms as far as her sore shoulders would let her, and she touched the knife. Her fingers scrabbled to find a hold.

"Yes!" she whispered triumphantly.

"What is it?"

"A knife. I've got a knife."

She rocked back slowly and pushed herself up, trying to stand from her kneeling position. She'd almost made it when she lost her balance again and fell against the shelves. Her shoulder bumped a paint can, which fell to the floor with a clatter.

"He's coming back," Grace whispered sharply.

Holding desperately to the knife, Jo hopped toward the place next to Stevie where she'd been sitting when John LePere had left them. She was keenly aware that if she fell, she risked a terrible wound in her back. Grace had already resumed her position next to Scott. Jo was not quite to Stevie when she heard the crunch of LePere's feet on the gravel outside the fish house. She hopped once more, a long, dangerous move that brought her up against the wall. The lock clicked open and the metal hasp clanked as it was unlatched. Jo dropped the knife and let her body slide down quickly, her butt covering the blade.

LePere stepped in. He turned the light on and looked carefully at Jo and the others. "I thought I heard something."

"I was uncomfortable," Jo said. "I was trying to get into a different position."

He nodded but seemed distracted. He said to Jo, "I want to talk to you." His eyes shifted to Grace. "And you."

He took out his pocket knife and cut the tape around Jo's ankles. He moved to Grace and did the same. Jo was thinking fast, trying to figure what to do with the knife hidden under her. Stevie bumped against her and she caught the look in his eye. As LePere helped Grace to her feet, Jo slid left and Stevie followed, hiding the knife with his own little body. Jo glanced down at her son. *Good boy,* her look said.

LePere stepped to Jo, helped her up, and said to the boys, "They'll be back." He indicated Jo and Grace should preceed him. When they were all outside, he turned and locked the fish house. "Follow me." He led them to his tiny house, opened the door, and said, "Inside."

When John LePere switched on a lamp, Jo was surprised by what she found. It was a cozy place, well kept. There was a good feel to it, to the way everything seemed to have a proper place to be. She'd always thought of men alone as a little barbaric in the way many of them lived comfortably with disorder and dirt.

"Sit down."

He indicated a small sofa with a floral design. When they were seated, he left them, went into another room, and came back in a few moments with a stack of newspapers in his hands.

"I want you to understand why I'm doing this."

He put the newspapers on the clean surface of the coffee table, moved behind Grace, and cut free her hands.

"Read," he said, and he pointed to the newspapers.

Jo, too, read what LePere had offered them. They were old newspapers, old by a dozen years. The date on the first was November 19, 1986. The headline read ORE BOAT SINKS IN SUPERIOR; CREW FEARED DEAD. The story reported that the ore carrier *Alfred M. Teasdale,* bound for Duluth harbor, had foundered in a terrible gale on Lake Superior and had apparently sunk with all hands aboard. Winds of ninety miles per hour had been recorded at the weather station on Devil's Island and radio reports from other vessels on Lake Superior indicated the gale had produced thirty-foot waves. The last communication with the *Teasdale* had been at eleven-thirty-seven P.M., nearly a day and a half earlier, when the captain reported to the Coast Guard station at Duluth that he was altering the ship's course to seek shelter in the lee of the Apostle Islands. Because no other communication occurred, it was assumed the ore carrier had made it safely and was waiting out the storm. Official report of the ship as missing wasn't made until nearly thirty-six hours later. The search was being carried out in a large area centered on the ship's last known location north of the Apostle Islands. The Coast Guard held out little hope that anyone had survived.

"Now this one," LePere said, and he handed them a second paper.

It was dated the next day, November 20, 1986. The headline read, SOLE SURVIVOR OF SHIPWRECK FOUND. The article reported that the Coast Guard had located a single pontoon raft from the lost ore carrier *Alfred M. Teasdale*. Three men had made it onto the raft before the ship went down, but only one man had survived the long ordeal of the wait to be rescued. John Sailor LePere had been found, barely alive, as the raft floated in open water nearly twenty miles from the area believed to be the site of the sinking. LePere had been flown by Coast Guard helicopter to Ashland, Wisconsin, where his condition was reported as serious.

"Here." LePere handed the women another paper.

It was dated November 22, 1986. SOLE SURVIVOR TELLS TERRIFYING TALE was the headline.

Grace Fitzgerald let the paper lie unread in her lap. She looked up at LePere. "What does any of this have to do with us?"

"With you," LePere replied brusquely. "The *Teasdale* was owned and operated by the Fitzgerald Shipping Company. She was an old carrier, too old. She should have been scrapped long before that last passage."

"The article says the storm was one of the worst ever on Superior."

"No other ships were lost." LePere slapped the remaining newspapers down on the coffee table and leaned toward Grace. "The *Teasdale* had help in its sinking."

"I don't understand."

"Explosives," LePere said. He grabbed a newspaper and tore away part of a page. He took out his pocket knife and unfolded the blade. "Small charges set in a line across the hull." He poked a line of holes with the tip of his knife across the piece of newsprint. "Then you wait for a storm, the kind of storm that happens all the time on the Great Lakes in November. And when it comes, you detonate the charges all at the same time." With the blade, he cut dashes where he'd poked holes. "The waves twist the hull up and down, and eventually, the ship breaks up." He tore the paper in half along the line he'd made. "And it looks like a terrible accident."

"That sounds awfully far-fetched," Grace said.

"Believe me, it's been done before."

"But why?"

"Insurance."

Grace Fitzgerald's face grew hard. "You're saying my father or his agents would have conspired to cause a tragedy like this for the insurance money? Obviously, you didn't know my father, Mr. LePere."

"I have proof. Hard proof."

"I don't believe it."

"I located the wreck. I've been diving it, filming the damage to the hull. The proof is there. But someone's been watching me. A few days ago they tried to kill me. They destroyed all my equipment."

"And you think it was someone from Fitzgerald Shipping."

"No one else would have cared."

"I can't believe this."

"Believe it." LePere stormed from the room and came back with a framed photograph. He nearly threw it at Grace Fitzgerald. She glanced at it, then at LePere. "My brother Billy," he said. "The last picture I ever took of him. He went down on the *Teasdale*. He was only eighteen years old."

Grace took a longer, more careful look at the photo. The boy—for he was a boy, long and angular in his face and limbs, with a body that was held awkwardly, as if he hadn't yet grown into it completely—was smiling. He stood on a small dock, with a cove at his back, and a high, dark wall of rock rising beyond that. "I'm sorry," she said.

"Sorry doesn't bring back the dead."

She glared up at him. "But money does? I assume that note you left for my husband was a ransom note."

He snatched the photo from her hand. "I needed the money to continue investigating the wreck, to prove Billy was murdered. That all those men were murdered."

Grace studied him for a minute, her brown eyes hard, her long nose lifted. "How much are you asking?"

"Two million."

"My husband will have trouble getting it."

"Hell, you're a lot richer than that."

"I am. But he's not. And he can't touch my money. We signed agreements before we married."

"He's no pauper."

"All of his assets are tied up in the mill. On his own, he can't come up with more than a few hundred thousand."

"You're lying."

"My life is at stake here, Mr. LePere. And my son's. Why would I lie?"

"Nobody's going to die."

"But we know who you are."

"Yeah." The anger seemed to wash from him. His shoulders sagged and he closed his eyes a moment. "That's what I wanted to talk to you about." He stepped to a chair, a bentwood rocker, and sat down. He stared at his brother's photograph, held delicately in his hands.

"When I was on that raft, something strange happened to me, something I've never told anybody about."

He told them the story of his ordeal on the raft. The huge waves, the freezing water, the fierce bitter wind. The men dying one by one until he alone was left. Then he told them what he'd never told anyone else. "My father came to me. My dead father. He sat on the edge of the raft and told me it wasn't my time to die. He said he and my mother and Billy were all waiting for me, but it wasn't my time." LePere was up now, pacing, the muscles of his face taut with emotion. "I tried to drink that memory away, along with all the other memories about the sinking, but it wouldn't go. I couldn't figure out why it wasn't my time, why out of all the good men on that ore boat, I was the only one spared. I spent nearly a dozen years lost in figuring that one out. But I finally did." He stopped pacing and faced Grace. "I'm supposed to find the truth."

Jo held up her taped hands. "Was this a part of it?"

He seemed genuinely sorry. "No, things just went . . . wrong. Look, I want to make a deal."

"We're listening," Jo said.

"Your lives in return for a promise that the wreck of the *Teasdale* will be fully investigated and that nothing that's found will be covered up."

Grace Fitzgerald said, "I promise."

He ignored her, but he looked steadily at Jo. "I know you. I've heard your word is good."

"I give you my word, John. But you understand, you will be prosecuted. There's nothing I can do about that."

He sat again in the rocker. "How does that saying go? Know the truth and the truth will set you free. For a long, long time, I've felt like a man in prison. You find the truth and it won't matter what they do to me. I'll still be free."

Grace asked cautiously, "Will you let us go now?"

"I can't. But soon."

"Why?" Jo asked. "The other man?"

"He's not a good man," Grace said.

LePere nodded his agreement. "But I owe him."

"And how do you intend to repay him?" Jo asked.

"We go through with the ransom. He takes the money—all of it—and disappears. After he's gone, I set you free, and I take the rap."

"I told you, my husband may not be able to raise the ransom."

"Then we'll take whatever he can give and that will have to do. For me, it was never about money."

"What about your partner?"

"I'll take care of him."

"Never trust a man who'd hurt a child or a woman."

"He hurt you?"

"Not me. Grace."

He gave Grace Fitzgerald a questioning look and she nodded.

"It won't happen again, I give you my word."

"Let us go," Grace tried again. "I promise we—"

LePere didn't let her finish. He stood up and cut her off, saying, "Your sons will be worried."

Jo and Grace pushed themselves up from the sofa. LePere opened a kitchen drawer and took out a roll of gray duct tape. "Turn around," he said to Grace.

"Is that still necessary?" she asked.

He just stared at her. His dark eyes were tired but firm. Grace turned around. He taped her hands and led the two women outside.

The moon pushed their shadows ahead of them across the yard to the fish house. LePere stepped in front and took a moment to fumble the key into the lock. As the door swung wide, Jo thought how like a gaping mouth was the darkened opening, waiting to swallow her again. The moment the thought occurred to her, she was startled to see a small silver tongue flick out from that black mouth and lick at John LePere's belly. LePere grunted and stepped back. The tongue darted again. This time Jo realized that it was the knife blade, glinting in the light of the moon. She didn't have a chance to cry out, to move at all before LePere snatched the boy and lifted him off the ground. Boy and man struggled briefly, the knife thrust high above them, the sharp, clean steel fired by moonlight. The blade fell and lay on the ground, still glowing as if white-hot. The boy became a dark, empty sack in the powerful grip of John LePere.

"Let him go," Grace Fitzgerald cried, for it was Scott whom LePere held.

Then another form shot from the fish house and hit LePere low. The man stumbled but did not go down. The small dark figure attached itself to LePere's legs and little grunts escaped as he tried to topple a man nearly two times his height and several times his weight. The boy in LePere's grasp resumed his own struggle, flailing his arms and legs wildly.

"Stevie," Jo called out. "It's all right. Let the man go."

And Grace ordered, "Scott, stop. He's not going to hurt us."

All the parts of John LePere, who seemed to have become many-headed and many-limbed, grew still. He put Scott down and the boy ran to his mother. Stevie let go his hold and he, too, joined his mother. LePere bent forward—slowly, it seemed—and picked up the knife. The blade threw a reflection of moonlight across his eyes. He looked at the boys.

"That was a brave thing to do."

His left hand went to his stomach. Jo could see a dark staining on his shirt.

"You're cut," she said.

He tugged his shirt tail loose from his pants and took a look beneath. "It's only a nick." He stepped into the fish house and turned on the light. "Everybody back inside."

They filed past him. He taped the boys' hands again, but he didn't bother to tape their ankles or their mouths. He looked at the shelves of equipment from which Jo had taken the knife.

"There may be something else in there that tempts you. Please don't. It will be over soon," he promised. "And you'll be with your families again."

"One thing," Grace said.

"Yes?"

"The other man. Don't leave us alone with him."

"I give you my word."

He put them in the dark and locked the door. Jo listened to his slow step as he crossed the yard to his house, to that place that once had held family for him but never would again.

36

THE SUN WAS JUST RISING as Cork approached the turnoff to Grace Cove. He'd left Henry Meloux at the cabin on Crow Point less than an hour before. It had been a long night, and warrior though he was, Meloux was an old man and very tired. George LeDuc sat on the passenger's side of the Bronco. He was nodding, nearly asleep, the night's labor having taken its toll on him as well. Cork pulled a small prescription bottle from his shirt pocket and popped the tab with his thumb. Using his forearms to manage the steering wheel, he tapped two white tablets into the palm of his hand. He tossed the tablets into his mouth and swallowed them dry. He snapped the lid back on and returned the bottle to his shirt pocket. That would keep him for a while.

Cy Borkmann, a long-time deputy, was posted at the turnoff. He raised his hand and Cork rolled the Bronco to a stop. Borkmann was a portly man with a double chin that quivered like the wattle on a turkey whenever he talked. He stepped to the Bronco and leaned a fleshy arm on Cork's door. "Hey, Cork. You been home yet?"

"No. Why?"

"Word leaked to the newspeople. They're all over Lind-strom's place, and yours. They've been coming since before sunrise. We tried to keep 'em out, but hell, they come by boat and hiked through the woods and even had a helicopter drop somebody on the back lawn. This is big news. Sheriff finally gave instructions to go ahead and let anybody with a press ID through. They're liable to swarm all over you soon as you drive up."

"Thanks for the warning, Cy."

Cork pulled away. Where the road splintered off toward LePere's cabin, he turned in.

"What are you doing?" George LeDuc asked.

"I'm going to park out here and walk in. I don't want to drive into a zoo." He glanced at his watch. "It's only five-twenty. Kidnapper's call is supposed to come at six. We've got time."

He pulled to the side of the road and parked in high weeds. It was LePere's land, but he didn't figure the man would mind much now. His privacy had already been shattered. LeDuc followed Cork through the woods, across a dry creek bed, and finally onto the wide lawn that surrounded the big house. As Borkmann had said, the place was a circus. Cameras had been set up to shoot the log home from several angles. Newspeople stood about, talking with one another or trying to talk to the officers posted at every door. Fortunately, no one seemed to take much notice as Cork and George LeDuc made their way across the grass. At the back door, a state trooper blocked their way.

"I'm Cork O'Connor. I'm supposed to be here."

"May I see some ID, sir?"

Cork showed him a driver's license.

"And you, sir?" the trooper asked LeDuc.

"He's with me," Cork said. "He needs to be here, too."

The trooper considered George LeDuc, but not for long. A number of reporters were headed their way, and it was clear the trooper had already had enough of the media. "Go ahead." He stepped aside and let them pass.

The kitchen smelled of breakfast, of sausages, eggs, hash browns, and coffee. Several empty foam containers sat on the table along with a couple of big white sacks with JOHNNY'S PINEWOOD BROILER printed boldly across the side. Cork figured Schanno had arranged for it. The Broiler supplied the meals for prisoners at the jail. Although he'd eaten almost nothing since Jo and Stevie had been taken, not even the smell of the Broiler's good food made him hungry.

The officers were gathered in the living room, awaiting the call. Agent David Earl of the BCA sat in a leather easy chair scribbling in a small notebook. FBI Special Agent Margaret Kay held a cup of coffee in her hand and leaned over the shoulder of Arnie Gooden, who was checking the equipment set up to record the next ransom call. Lucky Knudsen sat with his arms folded, staring, as nearly as Cork could tell, at the rainbows on the dining room wall formed by sunlight that fractured as it passed through the crystals of the chandelier. Wally Schanno was speaking into a walkie-talkie.

"Where have you been?" Schanno asked when he saw Cork. "Cy said you'd come by him a while ago."

"Did an end run around the media," Cork said. "I didn't particularly want to talk to anyone. Looks like all hell's busted loose."

"I knew it would sooner or later." Schanno glanced toward a window where the curtains were open to the front lawn. The craziness that had descended there was clearly visible. "I've put them off for a while, but somebody's going to have to give them something substantial pretty soon. The whole county knows now anyway. The department's been flooded with calls, folks claiming they saw everything from Big Foot to Elvis out this way."

Cork spotted a pot of coffee sitting on a tray along with disposable cups. He headed over and poured himself some. "Coffee, George?" he asked.

LeDuc shook his head.

"Cy told me the press is camped at my house, too," Cork said to Schanno.

The sheriff nodded dolefully. "I'm sorry about that, Cork. I sent Deputy Dross over there to help Rose out."

"I'd better call."

Karl Lindstrom stepped out of a doorway down a short hall and walked slowly toward the living room. The man's appearance startled Cork. Karl was a Lindstrom, a fighter, but the man approaching Cork looked so beaten down that there was no fight left in him. His eyes were bloodshot and tunneled deep into dark sockets. He walked like an old man, sucked dry of life, limp skin over fragile bone. Three feet from Cork, he stopped, and it was a moment before he spoke.

"I'm sorry. I couldn't get the money. I tried. I don't know where else to turn. I don't know what else to do."

Special Agent Kay spoke to him quietly across the room. "I've told you, Mr. Lindstrom. You can negotiate."

"With what?" Anger—a spark of life—burned in his words.

"The promise of money. Tell them you'll have it but you need more time. If it's money they're after, they'll wait. And then something will break for us, I'm sure of it."

Lindstrom looked at her, his face gone empty again. "I'm so tired."

"Karl." Cork put a hand on his shoulder. "We have the money."

Every face turned to him.

"You know George LeDuc," Cork said.

"Of course." The look Lindstrom gave LeDuc was full of puzzlement. In all their dealings, the two men had been adversaries. What could possibly be the purpose of the Indian's presence in this business that was no business of his?

"George has promised us the money," Cork said.

Lindstrom squinted, as if he hadn't quite heard or didn't quite believe. "How?"

LeDuc replied, "I've asked the manager of our casino to put it together. You'll have it pretty soon."

Lindstrom's look did not change. "Why?"

"Because it's what people should do," LeDuc told him. "Wealth in and of itself isn't an Ojibwe value. The value for us lies in how the wealth is used."

Lindstrom seemed stunned, truly stunned. "I . . . don't . . . know what . . . to say."

Cork had a suggestion. *"Migwech* would be just fine, Karl."

"Migwech?"

"It means thanks."

Lindstrom's arm slowly rose and he reached out to George LeDuc. *"Migwech,"* he said, as he shook the Ojibwe's hand. "I will repay you, I give you my word."

"We'll speak of that later."

"Is that where you've been all night?" Schanno asked Cork. "I've been trying to get in touch with you."

"It's better you don't ask, Wally. But listen. I was at the clinic on the rez. Adrianne Wadena, the physician's assistant out there, agreed to give me something to help me stay awake.

When we got to the clinic, we found that somebody had broken into the place."

"Drugs?"

"That would be my first guess. She's doing an inventory, but you'd best get someone out there to check on it."

"Thanks, Cork. I will."

Cork walked to where Arnie Gooden was fiddling with the recording equipment with Kay looking over his shoulder. "You're set up for the call?"

"Phone company's helping with another trap-and-trace," Kay replied. "But this time we're better prepared. We've located all the public phones within a twenty-mile radius. One hundred seventeen. Of those, forty-eight are situated outside business establishments. We have enough agents and officers to cover thirty-three, and they're in place now. Chances are very good we'll spot the caller."

"And?"

"If it seems appropriate, we'll make the arrest."

"That doesn't necessarily ensure the safety of our wives and children."

Kay breathed out deeply. "What does, Mr. O'Connor?"

She was right, and Cork let it go. "Anything more on the ransom notes or any of the evidence you've gathered?"

"I'm afraid not. We're following up any reasonable reports that come to the sheriff's department and hoping something might turn up there. For now, that's the best we can do."

Cork said, "Thank you. I appreciate what you're doing."

She smiled. Slight but definite. Like everyone else, she looked pretty well beaten.

"I need to call home," Cork said to Schanno.

"The phone in my office," Karl Lindstrom said. "Or my cell phone." He took a small unit from his pocket and offered it.

"I'll use the one in your office, thanks." He headed away.

Rose sounded tired but as if she was holding up. "They came early, Cork. Before it was even light. Those reporters, they're . . ." She searched for the word.

"Vultures?" Cork offered.

"I was going to say sons of bitches."

"How are the girls?"

"Exhausted. They finally fell asleep a little while ago. I'll wake them if you want to talk to them."

"Let them sleep. But I've got some good news for you to give when they wake up. We have the money."

"Oh, Cork." Her voice died in a moment of tears. "Thank God."

"And the Iron Lake Ojibwe."

"I don't understand."

"I'll explain it all later. I have to go. The kidnapper will be calling soon. Take care of my girls, Rose. I'll be home when I can."

"God be with you, Cork."

Lindstrom had drifted to the window and stood now in sunlight, staring out at a lawn that up until that morning had been a beautiful expanse of empty green. Cork joined him. He could see reporters snapping pictures of him and Lindstrom together, but he didn't care. He caught sight of what looked like a dry white stone, bobbing through the crowd. The shaved head of Hell Hanover. Cork felt his stomach tighten. He had business with Hell, and he would see to it very soon.

"This is my fault," Lindstrom said.

"Don't do that to yourself, Karl."

"It is my fault. I've been so worried about that damn mill and the great Lindstrom name that I let go of what was really important. I should have been here that night."

"Nobody could have known."

"Why is it you don't think about taking care of what you love until it's too late?"

"It's not too late, Karl. We're going to get them back."

The man turned to him, and Cork thought he saw something spring to life again in the dark where Lindstrom's tired eyes had tunneled. "I think I believe you."

The phone rang.

"This is it," Special Agent Kay said.

Lindstrom walked quickly to the phone. He waited to pick up until Arnie Gooden gave him a thumbs-up. He put the call on the speaker.

"Lindstrom here."

"Do you have it?" Once again, the true voice was hidden behind a grating electronic mask.

"Yes."

There was a long pause. "You have it?"

"I told you, yes."

"Son of a bitch." Even the mask couldn't hide the fact that the caller was chuckling.

"What now?" Lindstrom asked.

"The drop will be tonight. After dark. I'll call at nine P.M. sharp with delivery instructions."

"Not delivery," Lindstrom said. "Exchange."

"That will be arranged."

"I want proof my family is all right. And O'Connor's."

"Or what?" the voice chided. "Until tonight, Mr. Lindstrom." The line went dead.

"Did you get it?" Cork snapped at Agent Arnie Gooden, who was in contact via cell phone with the telephone company.

"Just a minute. Yes. It came from a public phone at 3414 Harbor Avenue . . ." His face clouded. ". . . Duluth."

"Duluth?" Lindstrom repeated.

"Damn," Kay said quietly. She turned to Arnie Gooden. "Give Duluth PD a call. Ask them to secure the phone booth until we can get an evidence team down there." She looked at Agent David Earl. "That was smart."

"Yes. But . . . did you hear? He sounded surprised when Lindstrom indicated he had the ransom money. What do you make of that?"

"I don't know." Kay rubbed her temple. "He's put off the drop until after dark. That makes sense. Hoping to be invisible."

Schanno said, "Somebody needs to give a statement to the press out there."

"I'll talk to them," Lindstrom said, his voice at the edge of a threat.

"I'd rather you didn't," Agent Kay said. "I'll do it." She turned to Agent Earl. "You're welcome to accompany me out there. Represent the interest of the state."

"All right," Earl said.

Kay looked at Schanno. "We have some plans to make. I'll need your help."

"Whatever it is, you've got it."

When Kay moved toward the front door, Cork said quietly to

George LeDuc, "Meet me at the Bronco in a few minutes. I'll give you a lift back to the rez."

"Where are you going?"

"To shake hands with the Devil."

Cork let himself out the back door as the reporters flowed to the front lawn in response to the appearance of the agents from the FBI and BCA. He slipped among the throng, which was focused on Kay and Earl. Kay stood on the front porch, the sun in her eyes, blinking at the upturned faces.

"Ladies and gentlemen, I appreciate your patience . . ." she began.

Cork found Hell Hanover without any trouble. From behind, he leaned to the man's ear and spoke softly. "Got an exclusive for you, Hell."

Hanover turned and his face showed genuine surprise. "O'Connor. What do you want?"

"I've got a story for you. An exclusive."

"About your wife and boy being snatched?"

"No. About your ass and keeping it out of jail. Meet me at Sam's Place in an hour." He slipped away before Hanover could object.

Hell Hanover's maroon Taurus wagon rumbled over the tracks near Sam's Place and pulled to a stop in the empty parking area. Hell sat a moment looking things over. He opened the car door, swung his stiff artificial leg out, and stood up. His right hand shaded his face against the low morning sun, and once again, he carefully took in the lay of the land. He appeared wary of what he might be walking into, and with good reason. A year and a half earlier, he'd been careless in a confrontation with Cork, and that carelessness had nearly sent him to prison. He dropped his hand, limped to the door of the Quonset hut, and knocked. He saw the door was already slightly ajar, and he pushed it open fully with his artificial foot.

"O'Connor?" he called inside.

When he received no answer, he glanced behind him and to both sides. His left hand slipped under his wrinkled sports coat to the small of his back and came out with the butt of a small handgun nestled in his palm.

"O'Connor?" he tried again. Then he made the mistake of stepping inside.

Cork left the window of the serving area up front in Sam's Place. He'd been watching Hanover through a small hole cut in the middle of a poster featuring Sam's Big Deluxe Burger. He stepped silently to a position just inside the doorway that separated the living area of the Quonset hut from the serving area of Sam's Place. He was holding a baseball bat, the Louisville Slugger he'd given Annie for her last birthday.

The floor of the old Quonset creaked under the weight of Hell Hanover, and it was easy for Cork to track the man's position. Hanover went straight to the place Cork wanted him and he stopped. Without needing to look, Cork knew Hell was staring at the photograph—mended with tape and hung over the kitchen sink—of Jo naked and making love to another man. Paper-clipped to the photo was a note on which Cork had written in big red letters, I DON'T GIVE A DAMN, HELL."

The moment the floorboards ceased to call out Hanover's progress, Cork made his move and rushed through the doorway. Before Hanover could react to the sound of footsteps, Cork swung Annie's Louisville Slugger and connected with Hell's left forearm. Hanover cried out in pain; his handgun clattered to the floor. Cork used the tip of the bat as a baton and lunged, catching Hanover square in the stomach. Hell went down to his knees, gasping for air. Cork kicked the handgun clear of the bald man's reach.

"You know," Cork said, standing over him, breathing pretty hard himself, "for a guy who wants to lead an armed revolution, you're a piss-poor strategist."

"I'll have you . . . arrested," Hell threatened between gasps.

"And rely on the system you want to destroy? I don't think so, Hell. Besides, you'd lose. You trespassed and pulled a gun. I'd take that to a jury any day."

Hanover had wrapped his good arm around his stomach and was struggling to look up at Cork. "What's this all about?"

With the toe of his shoe, Cork tapped the handgun that lay fallen on the floor. "A little thirty-two, Hell? A whole military arsenal to choose from and you pick a prissy weapon to carry."

"It's licensed."

"Playing it safe, I see. Worried you might go to jail?"

"What do you want, O'Connor?"

"An exchange."

Hell slowly got to his feet. He stopped nursing his stomach and gingerly felt the forearm that had taken the full force of the Louisville Slugger. "Jesus, I think you broke it."

"It's only the beginning of what I'll break unless we strike a deal."

"You said exchange. What are you talking about?"

"Jo, Stevie, Grace Fitzgerald, and her boy. In exchange for your stockpile of illegal arms."

"I don't know what you're talking about."

"Wrong answer." Cork swung the bat again and connected with Hanover's good leg just below the knee. Hell went down again, screaming.

"You're crazy, O'Connor."

"Absolutely. Crazy enough to kill you right now, Hell. I want my family back."

"I don't know anything about your family, God damn it. I didn't have anything to do with this abduction thing."

"You tried to use that photograph to force me to back off investigating Eco-Warrior. Why?"

Hanover tried to stand again, but his leg gave out and he ended up back on his knees. "Because it was a situation that could explode in the face of government at every level. Jesus, it was a dream and I wanted it to happen." He felt his leg and grimaced. "Oh, shit."

"Two million dollars, Hell. That's how much the ransom demand is. Two million could buy you a hell of an armory for that little militia of yours."

"I don't have a little militia. You saw to that, remember?" He gave Cork a look more sour than painful. "Are you going to kill me, O'Connor? Then why don't you just do it? Bash my brains out or whatever it is you have in mind."

Cork put the bat against Hanover's head. "I haven't slept in two days, Hell. My wife and my boy are in the hands of some madman. If you think for a minute that I wouldn't kill you, think again."

"Look, what do you want from me? I didn't take your family. Your wife and boy were abducted Saturday night, right?

Saturday night I was covering the volunteer firefighters' picnic over in Tower. A hundred people saw me there."

"Some of your militia, then."

"If I had a militia, O'Connor, consider the ranks. You think there's anybody brilliant enough to carry off this kind of thing? Jesus, you beat the fuck out of me for nothing."

Cork stepped back, but he didn't put the slugger down. "Not for nothing. We still have to deal with that photograph."

Hanover looked at the photo hanging above his head. "You'd kill me over that? I don't think so." He grinned, as if he had Cork beaten.

"Blackmail for blackmail," Cork said. "Little Sun Lake."

At those last words, Hanover's face changed. The grin died, and his eyes took on a hunted look.

"That's right," Cork said. "I found your cache of arms out at Little Sun Lake. And I moved it. Every crate of AK-47's, every Skorpion submachine gun, every CS grenade, every round of ammunition, all of it. Now it's *my* cache. But unless I'm sorely mistaken, your fingerprints are all over everything, and probably the prints from a lot of the rest of the Minnesota Civilian Brigade. ATF would have a field day with that. You'd go to prison for a very long time."

Hanover's only reply was an unflinching glare.

"And don't think that taking me out sometime will solve your problems, Hell. I had a lot of help moving those weapons. If I'm ever harmed, the ATF will have the location of the cache within half an hour. You're a free man only so long as no one else ever sees that photograph or any copies of it or any similar evidence of indiscretion you might have stashed somewhere. Understand?"

Hanover took a few ragged breaths before he was able to reply. "Yeah, I understand."

"Good. Now get out."

Cork moved back, but Hanover didn't rise. "I'm not sure I can walk."

"Here." Cork handed him the Louisville Slugger. "Use it as a cane. But I'll keep the thirty-two for now." He lifted the handgun from the floor.

Hell Hanover struggled to his feet, leaned heavily on the

wooden bat, and slowly thumped his way outside. He eased into his Taurus, grunting painfully as he did so.

"Leave the bat," Cork called.

Hanover dropped the Louisville Slugger on the ground, closed the door, and started the engine. Without glancing once in Cork's direction, he left.

Cork stood in the doorway of the Quonset hut, his body quivering as it dealt with all the adrenaline that had been pumped into it in the last fifteen minutes. He'd been ready to kill Hanover in cold blood if the man had given him any indication he had anything to do with the kidnapping of Jo and Stevie. Although he hated Hanover and everything he stood for, Cork believed that in this instance, he was innocent.

He stared at the empty parking area. The grass at the edges was brown from drought. The grasshoppers were legion, feeding everywhere, the sound of their brittle wings buzzing in the heat. But Cork wasn't seeing or hearing them. He was deep in thought, wondering desperately, *If not Hell, then who?*

37

Wesley Bridger showed up late in the morning. He parked his van next to LePere's small house and went inside.

"What the hell happened, Chief?"

John LePere sat at the little dining table, a cup of coffee in his hand. He was pretty tired, but he didn't want to sleep, not until he'd dealt with Bridger. He leaned his elbows on the table-top and gave the man a long, steady look. "Something in all your careful planning you never counted on," he replied. "Fire. Nearly killed us all."

"The others? They're okay?"

"They're okay."

"Well, hey, Chief, where's the damage? You did a good job." He walked to LePere and gave him a hearty slap on the back. "Mind if I pour me a cup of that java there? Been a long night for me, too."

"Where've you been?"

"Preparing, Chief. Getting things ready. They've got the money." Bridger poured himself some coffee and let out a rebel yell. "They've got the fucking money."

"The Fitzgerald woman wasn't sure her husband could get it."

"Unless he's lying his ass off, he's got it. And we'll have it tonight." Bridger lifted his cup in a brief toast. "Time to start celebrating. Start imagining what it's going to feel like being a millionaire."

LePere put his cup down. "There's something we need to talk about."

Bridger pulled out a chair, turned it backward, and plopped himself down. He drank his coffee and addressed LePere over the chair back. "Yeah? And what's that?"

"I'm not taking any of the money."

Bridger laughed. "That's a good one."

"I'm serious."

"I don't get it."

"I don't want the money."

"You sure took a hell of a risk for nothing, then."

"They saw my face, Wes."

Bridger stared at him and blinked. Then he threw his cup against the wall. "Fuck me." He stood up and kicked over the chair. "God damn it. How the hell—"

"The fire. It happened while I was getting them away from the fire. It couldn't be helped. It wasn't their fault."

"Shit." Bridger kicked the floral sofa. He closed his eyes and thought a moment, shaking his head angrily, as if all he could see were blind alleys. "So, how does this translate into you not taking any money?"

"You take the money. I take the rap."

Bridger snorted ruefully. "You started drinking again?"

"It's the only way."

"No." Bridger glared at him. "It's not the only way."

LePere understood what he meant. "These people are going back to their families, Wes."

"They go to their families. You go to jail. And what about me? I just slip off into the sunset with two million dollars?"

"That's it."

"You think they're going to let it go at that? These are rich people, Chief. You fuck with rich people and they have all the resources available to fuck you right back, and better. And the cops? You think they're not going to make your life a living hell until you tell them about me?"

"They'll try. But I've been in hell a long time now. There's nothing they can do that'll make it any worse."

Bridger walked back to the table, leaned close to LePere, and spoke in a conspiratorial whisper. "There's more to it than you're telling me, am I right?"

"They've promised to investigate the wreck, to find the truth."

Bridger stepped back in mock amazement. "And you believed them? Chief, you are one stupid half-breed."

"Don't call me that."

"Christ." Bridger walked away in disgust. He headed to the door but didn't go out. He just stood looking at the fish house. "I guess the die's been cast, huh? You've crossed your own little Rubicon." He took a breath and faced LePere. "But we go through with the drop tonight?"

"Yes."

"All right. Your funeral." He came back and offered his hand. "Sorry about the half-breed thing."

LePere didn't take his hand. "One more thing. Until this is over, you stay away from them."

Bridger dropped his arm and gave LePere a quizzical look.

"You hurt the Fitzgerald woman."

"I scared her a little." Bridger shrugged, then smiled sheepishly. "All right, I scared her a lot. But, hey, she was trying to get away."

"Just leave them alone."

Bridger solemnly held up a hand. "You have my word." He turned and started away. "I've got more arrangements to make for tonight. I'd best get moving." He paused at the door. "You're sure about all this?"

"I'm sure."

Bridger made a gun of his thumb and forefinger and shot an imaginary round at LePere. "You're some piece of work, you know that, Chief?" He stepped outside. A minute later, the van pulled away and headed up the narrow lane to the highway.

John LePere felt good. The hardest part was over—dealing with Bridger. He left the table and went into the kitchen. He put some bananas in a sack and filled a plastic jug with cold tap water. Outside, the air was warm and carried the smell of smoke. LePere crossed to the fish house and unlocked the door. The women looked up as he entered. The boys were asleep, chins resting on their chests.

"I thought you might be hungry, maybe could use a drink of water," he said quietly. He put the sack on the floor. The jelly glasses were sitting on the table and he filled them. He offered a drink to Grace Fitzgerald. She nodded and he put the glass to her lips. "Your husband has the money," he told her. A trickle ran down her chin and he wiped it away.

"I can't imagine where he got it," she said.

"If two million would have saved Billy, I'd have moved heaven and earth to get it."

"Scott needs another injection," the Fitzgerald woman said.

"I'll get the stuff." He looked at Jo O'Connor. "You want a drink before I go?"

"No, thanks."

When LePere returned, Scott Fitzgerald was awake. "I'm going to cut your hands free so you can give him the shot," LePere said to the boy's mother. He severed the tape and pulled it off her wrists, then put the packaged syringe and the medicine into her hands. He stood back and watched. The boy took the shot without flinching. LePere reached out for the syringe so he could dispose of it.

As she put it in his hands, the Fitzgerald woman said, "If ten million could have saved Edward, I'd have given it."

LePere was caught by surprise and it took him a moment to place the reference. "Your first husband, right? The lake got him. I read your book. He sounded like a stand-up guy."

LePere put the syringe down a small slot in a metal box on the wall that had been a repository for old razor blades in the days when his father sometimes used the basin in the fish house to shave. "Do you remember him?" he asked her son.

"Not really," the boy said.

"Maybe you're lucky. It hurts a lot if you do."

"You move on with your life, Mr. LePere," the Fitzgerald woman said.

"Yes." He tapped the metal box to make sure the syringe had dropped. "But you never forget, do you?" He turned and looked down at her. "I watched you a long time on the cove. You're different from the person I thought I saw."

"Different how?"

"Doesn't matter. I was way off base." He picked up the roll of duct tape. "I need to bind your hands again."

"Do you have to?"

"It won't be much longer. I'm sorry." He bound her, then asked her son, "Are you hungry?"

"Yes."

"How about a banana?"

"Okay."

He cut the boy free and waited while he ate. "What about *your* son?" he asked the O'Connor woman.

"Mostly, he needs to sleep."

He tossed the banana peel outside and taped the boy's wrists again. "I'm tired. I need some sleep, too. I'll check back in a while. The windows are open and the breeze is up. You should stay cool."

LePere locked the fish house and drifted down to the rocks that separated the cove from the lake. He sat down, trying to take it all in, trying to memorize every detail. In another day, he would be looking at bare walls and iron bars, and he wanted to remember home. He gazed up at the great ancient lava flow called Purgatory Ridge, the dark, striated cliffs that were the backdrop for his best memories. He closed his eyes, and the silver-blue circle of water that was the cove was there, bright in his mind, and hard beside it, the little house. The popple and aspen along the shoreline were green now, but he could remember them aflame in fall, their autumn leaves scattered across the water like shavings of gold. Last, he turned and looked at the lake that had been there for a thousand lifetimes before his and would be there a thousand lifetimes after. He'd often hated the lake, blamed it for what had been taken from him. But the truth, he knew, was that the lake was simply what it was, vast and indifferent. It asked nothing and yielded to no one, and if you journeyed on its back, you accepted the risk. In its way, it mirrored life exactly.

Facing the prospect of prison, John LePere felt free and alive for the first time in more than a dozen years.

The sound of a powerful inboard motor woke him. He lay on his bed, listening as the thrum grew louder and entered the cove. He jumped from his bed, went to the window, and watched as Wesley Bridger cut the engine and guided a sleek motor launch up to the dock. LePere put on his shoes and headed down to the water.

Bridger tossed him a line. "Tie her up."

"Where'd you get this?"

"Borrowed her. Just for tonight. They'll never miss her, believe me."

"What for?"

Bridger jumped from the boat. He held his ski mask in one hand and a heavy-looking metal flashlight in the other. As soon as his feet were squarely on the dock, he slipped the mask over his head. "Let's go up and talk to our guests."

"Why?"

"We'll give 'em the good news." He put his arm around LePere's shoulders in the way of comrades. "Everything's set for the exchange. Don't you think they'll want to know? Also, I owe them an apology, Chief. I was pretty hard on them."

It was early evening. LePere realized he'd slept much longer than he'd expected. The air felt good, cooler. Something in the wind had changed.

At the fish house, as LePere undid the lock, Bridger asked, "Chief, I just want to check. Are you sure about all this? I mean, taking the whole responsibility on your shoulders while I'm free as a bird with a two-million-dollar nest?"

"It's been a long time since I've been as certain of anything, Wes."

LePere opened the door and took a step inside. He didn't even feel the blow to the back of his head. He simply dropped into darkness.

38

THE GIRLS LOOKED BATTERED, tired beyond weeping, and older by far than their years. And Rose, for all her courage and faith, looked ready to yield to despair.

"When you give them the money, they'll give Mom and Stevie back, right?" Jenny pressed him.

Cork chewed on a ham-and-cheese sandwich that Rose had put together for him. He barely tasted the food, and he ate only because he knew he had to keep his own strength up. "Yes, Jen," he said. "I believe they will." He glanced at Deputy Marsha Dross, who leaned against the wall near the kitchen doorway. She was a slender woman of medium height, had short brown hair, and was as smart as any law enforcement officer Cork had ever known. He saw her eyes shift away because she knew the true uncertainty of the situation. He saw, too, how tired she was. Like all the law officers involved, she'd put in long hours with little sleep. She didn't do it because it was her job, Cork knew. She did it because it was the right thing to do and because it might help. Cork was truly grateful.

"How will you give them the money?" Annie asked. She sat at the kitchen table with her father and Jenny. Rose stood at the kitchen sink, washing a few dishes. Wet silverware in the dish drainer caught the rays of the early evening sun and scattered flames of reflected light across the walls and ceilings.

"I don't know, Annie. We'll have to wait for the call this evening. At nine-thirty."

"Can't they, like, trace the phone call and catch him?" Jenny asked.

"They've tried. Whoever it is, he's smart."

"But he'll give them back, right?"

"I told you, Jen. I believe he will." Cork pulled himself back from the anger that her persistent question and his persistent lie drove him toward. "We have every reason to believe he'll do just what he's promised."

"The FBI deals with these situations all the time," Rose offered. "They have things well in hand, I'm sure."

The girls looked to their father for confirmation. He wiped his mouth with a paper napkin and stood up. "I need to get back out to Grace Cove."

"The coffee's almost ready." There was a subtle plea in Rose's voice. *Don't leave,* she seemed to say. Cork understood how heavy was the weight she carried, holding up the hopes of the girls while she suspected the true gravity of things, isolated in the house on Gooseberry Lane, besieged by reporters, with nothing but her faith to sustain her.

"I have to go, Rose," he told her. "I'll keep you posted."

She gave him a silent nod.

Cork hugged and kissed his daughters.

"When we see you again, you'll have Mom and Stevie, right?" Jenny asked.

"We'll be a family again," he promised.

Cork headed out of Aurora and around the southern end of Iron Lake. There had been a breeze earlier, a hot one. Now the air was still and sitting heavy on the North Country. Something was ready to break. Cork felt it like an ache in his bones.

He'd tried all afternoon to put everything together in a different way, hoping to see something he hadn't seen before. With Hell Hanover out of the picture, and with Joan of Arc and Isaiah Broom in jail, the most obvious possibility lay in Brett Hamilton, the son of Joan of Arc of the Redwoods. As far as Cork knew, he was still at large. If what Meloux had intimated was true, if the kid really was Eco-Warrior, then he'd killed once already. What more did he have to lose in kidnapping?

Yet the feel was all wrong. Meloux believed a man who'd

kidnap women and children had to have a black heart and the balls of a warrior. The kid had balls. Cork had seen that in the way he'd faced Erskine Ellroy in the parking lot at Sam's Place, ready to take a beating for his beliefs. But the same incident seemed to demonstrate both a selflessness of spirit and a concern for the sanctity of life that was incompatible with a heart black enough to put women and children in jeopardy.

He couldn't say why exactly, but Cork's thinking kept coming back to John LePere. Part of it was that he wasn't convinced LePere was the drunk he'd appeared to be, and part of it was that LePere's land on Grace Cove would have been the perfect area from which to observe Lindstrom's home in planning an abduction. The problem was that LePere, like the Hamilton kid, seemed a different kind of man than would be involved in kidnapping. In his days as sheriff, Cork had prided himself on knowing the people of Tamarack County. He believed he'd learned to take the measure of a man pretty accurately. LePere had been a heavy drinker once. Sometimes when he was drunk he argued. Once in a while, he fought. But it was the booze that did that, and probably the disappointment life had handed him. He was no saint, but neither was he a devil who'd steal a man's wife and child for money. Or so he'd seemed to Cork.

Still, Cork felt strongly that LePere knew more than he was telling, and if so, two obvious questions presented themselves: What did LePere know, and why was he silent?

Gil Singer was the deputy now posted at the turnoff to Grace Cove. Cork pulled over and called out to him, "Still a zoo at Lindstrom's?"

"Only the hearty remain, Cork. Heat drove the rest of them back to their hotel rooms. You doing okay?"

"Holding my own, Gil. Have you seen John LePere lately?"

"Cy told me LePere took off earlier, complaining cops were all over his place like flies on shit. Haven't seen him since."

Cork started to pull away, but Singer hailed him down.

"By the way, the sheriff had me out on the rez this morning checking out that break-in at the clinic. All that was missing was some insulin and syringes."

"A diabetic burglar?"

"Strange world, Cork."

"Thanks, Gil."

He parked on LePere's property, but instead of hiking directly to Lindstrom's, he walked to LePere's cabin. The man's pickup was gone. The place looked deserted. Cork headed around in back and to an outbuilding that was just large enough to hold LePere's truck. The door was locked. Cork peered through a dusty window. Hand tools—a shovel, a pick, a long-handled ax, a couple of kinds of rakes—hung on the walls. A stack of old tires stood in a corner. Mostly, the shed was empty. He checked the dock, stepped down into a rowboat tied there, bent, and looked for anything that might have been left by someone taken against their will. The boat appeared clean.

"O'Connor."

Cork turned, fast enough that he almost lost his balance and fell into the lake. Agent David Earl stood on the dock looking down at him.

"I already checked the boat," Earl said. "Nothing."

"What are you doing here?"

"Same as you, I imagine." Earl reached out a hand and helped Cork back onto the dock. "I came out after I heard the news."

"What news?"

"You don't know?" Earl pulled a pack of Marlboros from his shirt pocket and tapped out a cigarette. He started to offer the pack to Cork, but drew it back. "That's right. You gave them up." Earl lit the cigarette with a Bic lighter and blew smoke over the dock. "Brett Hamilton's dead."

The news jolted Cork. "How?"

"It seems that after he eluded the FBI, he made a beeline back to the tent city on the reservation, recruited a dozen other activists, and they headed out to stop the fire burning Our Grandfathers. They got there before any firefighters and didn't know what the hell they were doing. One of them got himself trapped under a falling tree full of fire. Hamilton put himself in danger cutting the guy free. The guy got out. Hamilton didn't." He pursed his lips and sent out a stream of smoke. "Just when you think you've got someone pegged."

Cork thought about Joan Hamilton, Joan of Arc of the Redwoods. She was a hard woman, shaped even in her crippled walk by her choice of wars. But she was still a mother, a parent who'd tried to sacrifice herself for her son, her only child who was dead now. Cork looked up at the sky, and he let a moment of deep sorrow pierce the armor of his own concerns.

"How does that bring you here?" he finally asked Earl.

"I've been thinking—who's left? I stand in Lindstrom's big log house and all there is to see is this place. Now, that doesn't mean John LePere has any connection with the abduction, but it's odd that he saw nothing. If not that night, then before. He strikes me as a man extremely protective of his privacy. I'm guessing he'd know if someone were out here who shouldn't have been."

"I talked with him. He denied it."

"He's an alcoholic. Denial is everything."

"Alcoholic?" Cork said. "Follow me." He led Earl to the garbage can near the shed, lifted the lid, and released a cloud of black flies. "What do you see?"

"Besides garbage?"

"Booze doesn't flow from the tap in the kitchen sink. Where are the bottles?"

"Why pretend to be drunk?"

"Good cover, especially if people are predisposed to believing it. I've known John LePere a long time. Not especially well, but enough to wonder how he'd get himself mixed up in something like this."

"Two million dollars is a lot of incentive."

"At great risk. That's the thing. Whoever did this is risking everything. John LePere's got a good job at the casino. And a nice place here, for a man who likes to live alone. He has a place on the north shore, too. Kidnapping just doesn't seem to fit."

"Maybe because we don't have all the pieces." Earl dropped his cigarette and ground it out under his heel. He glanced at the cabin. "I can't go in there. I can't even be aware of someone going in there."

"Maybe it's time you left," Cork suggested.

"I think I've seen everything here I want to see."

After Earl had gone, Cork tried the back door of the cabin. As he expected, it was locked. He returned to his Bronco and took a heavy-handled screwdriver and a pair of cotton gloves from the tool kit he kept in back. He put the gloves on and used the handle of the screwdriver to break a pane in the back-door window. It was simple, then, to reach in and undo the lock on the door handle.

LePere's place surprised him. In his experience, bachelors were generally sloppy housekeepers, especially if they were heavy drinkers. LePere kept a clean home. Cork wasn't sure exactly what he was looking for. Whatever it was, the tidy kitchen—where not even a crumb lay on the counter—seemed unpromising. He stepped into the main room. It was furnished sparely, in the way of a man who seldom had to accommodate visitors. An easy chair with a standing lamp for reading, a small dining table with two chairs, a Franklin stove, a four-shelf bookcase—full. A tasteful, braided area rug in shades of brown covered the old floorboards in front of the stove. On the walls, LePere had hung several framed photographs, all black and white. Cork checked the only bedroom, went through LePere's small closet and chest of drawers. In the bathroom, he looked inside a little Hoover portable washer. Back in the living room, he stood a while, hoping to be struck by something that felt out of place, but nothing hit him. He crossed to the nearest photograph on the wall. It was of a man and boy standing in front of a cabin under construction. Written in white in the lower right-hand corner were the words SYLVAN COVE, 1971. The boy looked to Cork to be a very young John LePere. He assumed the man, who had his arm proudly around the boy's shoulders, was LePere's father.

Cork moved to the next mounted photograph. A teenage John LePere stood on a dock alongside a boy a few years younger. Behind them lay a curve of silver-gray water backed by a huge ridge of solid, dark rock. The boys were smiling broadly. In the corner, in white, had been written PURGATORY COVE, 1979.

The photograph that hung nearest the stove showed John LePere in a peacoat and wearing a watch cap. He stood in a crow's nest, his hand shielding his eyes, as if he were intent on scanning the horizon. On the mast below him was a gigantic letter *F* illuminated by huge electric bulbs. In the corner of the photograph, the penned explanation read "When the radar fails. *Teasdale,* 1985." A grin played across LePere's face, and it was clear he was clowning for the camera. Cork knew LePere's tragic history—sole survivor of the wreck that took the lives of the rest of the crew on the *Teasdale*. He tried to place the year, and believed it probably wasn't long after the picture had been taken. He considered for a moment what the big lighted *F* on the mast below LePere might be all about, but he quickly let go of his wondering because it had nothing to do with the reason he was in the cabin.

He went over everything once more, and once more he came up empty-handed. He left the cabin by the same door he'd entered. Outside, the sun was resting on the tops of the trees along the western shore of the cove. Cork checked his watch. Eight-thirty. In another hour, the kidnappers would call, and what now seemed like the only hope for saving Jo and Stevie and Grace and Scott would present itself.

39

JOHN LEPERE CAME OUT of a dream of his father holding him tightly. His father's clothes smelled of fish, a smell LePere loved. When he opened his eyes, he found that he was inside the old fish house and he was bound with rope. The air was hot and close and filled with a fish odor that ghosted up from every board.

"He's coming to." It was a woman's voice.

His eyes focused in the dim light, and he saw that the two women and their sons were watching him. "What happened?"

"Your *friend*," the Fitzgerald woman said bitterly.

LePere remembered everything up until coming into the fish house. "He knocked me cold?"

"He hit you with a big flashlight," the O'Connor woman explained. "We were afraid you might be dead."

The back of his head hurt. He tried to wiggle free of his bonds, but the rope was so tight that it bit painfully into his muscles and cut off the circulation so that his hands were numb. He was hog-tied, several coils looped around his arms and chest, his hands pulled behind him and secured to his bound ankles.

"How long have I been out?" he asked.

"Two or three hours," Jo O'Connor replied.

LePere looked toward the door. "Has he been back?"

"No. He took a bunch of things from the shelves that he apparently thought we might try to use to escape, and he left. We haven't seen him since."

290

"Did he say anything?"

The Fitzgerald woman gave a short, unhappy laugh. "He looked down at you and said something about landing a big-mouth bass. Who is he?"

LePere hesitated before he said, "His name is Bridger." Between the stuffy air and the rope that squeezed his chest, he could barely breathe. "It's hot in here."

"Your friend Bridger shut all the windows," Grace Fitzgerald told him. "I guess he was afraid we might scream and be heard."

"There's no one to hear you out here," LePere said.

The sound of gravel underfoot came from just outside the door, and then the rattle of the lock being undone. Wesley Bridger stepped inside and switched on the light. "Back among the living, Chief?" He held a filet knife in a gloved hand. LePere recognized the knife as one from the kitchen in his cabin on Iron Lake.

"What's going on, Wes?"

"Just dropping a few more crumbs for the cops to follow."

"I don't get it."

"You never did. And that's been the beauty all along." Bridger looked everyone in the fish house over carefully. "Who goes under the blade of old Doc Bridger? Let me see."

"What the hell do you think you're doing?" LePere demanded.

"Just following the plan. Mine, not yours." He laughed when he saw the look on LePere's face. "You look so lost, Chief. Let me explain a few things." He grabbed an old wooden crate, turned it over, and sat down. He tugged the glove off his left hand and tested the tip of the filet knife against his thumb. When he'd easily drawn blood, he smiled and wiped the blade clean on his pants. "Chief, it never was what it seemed. That wreck you're so goddamned interested in was never anything to me except a door to your trust."

"What was so important about my trust?"

"Two million dollars." Bridger opened his arms toward the women and the boys. "See, Chief, I knew about you and the *Teasdale*. And there you were, right across the cove from the last of the Fitzgeralds. All I had to do was stir up the hate that was bubbling inside you."

"It was a lie, all that about the *Teasdale* being sabotaged?"

"Not all of it. I did help sink a Libyan freighter. So I suppose the *Teasdale* could have been sabotaged in the same way, but it really didn't matter. I gave you what you wanted, someone to blame for all your misery. Oh, and by the way, it was me who destroyed all your equipment here. I needed you to be desperate enough to agree to help me."

"There never was a boat watching us when we dived?"

"It's been my experience that if you tell someone the grass is full of snakes, even a crooked stick looks dangerous." A mock sadness came into his voice. "And now, the unkindest cut of all. You were always going to die, Chief. Just like them." He nodded toward the others. "You see, the only way for two people to keep a secret is if one of them is dead." Bridger stood up. "Time to spill a little blood."

"No," LePere said.

Bridger laughed. "Relax. I want only a little blood. The cops will look your way eventually, and I need enough blood to let them know you brought your hostages here. What happened to the women and children after that"—he shrugged—"will always be a mystery. So . . . who will it be?"

"Take my blood," Grace Fitzgerald said.

"Ah, you saw me looking at young Scotty there, didn't you? I wish I'd had a mother like you. Maybe I'd have turned out differently. What do you think?"

"Just do it," the Fitzgerald woman said.

Bridger put the glove back on his hand and reached behind her with his knife. She gave a small gasp. He lifted the blade that was bright with a glistening of crimson. "You'll bleed a bit more onto the floor, but it's only superficial, Grace. And I wouldn't worry about infection. There's not really going to be enough time for germs to get a foothold." He walked back to the door. "I need all of you mobile for a while longer. If you're inclined to believe in God, I'd start right now making amends."

"You enjoy this," the O'Connor woman said.

"More than you can imagine."

He hit the light switch and locked the door. The fish house was quiet and filled with a blue evanescence that crept in through the windows. Twilight, LePere knew. It was nearly time for the ransom to take place. He heard the engine of the van turn over. A moment later, the vehicle rattled away toward the highway.

"Ms. O'Connor, do you think you can move?" he asked.

"Some."

"There's a metal box on the wall next to the washbasin. Sometimes my father used the basin to clean himself and to shave after he was done with the day's catch. He put his used razor blades in there so nobody would get cut with them. So far as I know, he never emptied it."

The O'Connor woman worked herself into a standing position and hopped across the floor. She knelt, then lay down, and positioned herself near the wall. She lifted her legs, tried to reach the box, and had to readjust. It was an awkward position that, with her hands bound behind her, put a lot of strain on her shoulders, and LePere heard her grunt in pain as she raised her legs again toward the box.

"Just kick it?" she gasped.

"That," LePere said, "and pray."

40

THE DECISION HAD ALREADY BEEN MADE before Cork arrived, the decision that made everything go bad.

Two million dollars had been delivered to Lindstrom's home on Grace Cove at seven-twenty P.M. It had come in bundles of hundred-dollar bills, packed in two large metal cases, and accompanied by Lucky Knudsen and three additional state troopers. George LeDuc had come along as well, bringing with him a simple, no-interest agreement for repayment that Karl Lindstrom signed. Afterward, the two men shook hands. Not a single attorney was present.

By the time Cork had hiked from LePere's cabin to the big log home, the worst heat of the day had passed, and the media were again out in full force. Still, he entered the house without drawing much notice. Inside, he found Lindstrom, and the agents of the FBI and BCA, Lucky Knudsen, and Wally Schanno all gathered around the dining-room table. The metal cases that contained the ransom money were open. Also on the table were two empty black cases the same size as those that held the money. Kay glanced at her watch and said, sounding a little put out, "Mr. O'Connor. I'm glad you're finally here."

Cork let her peevishness slide. He walked to the table and looked at the cases full of hundred-dollar bills. Although he'd never seen so much in one place at one time, he didn't think of it as a lot of money. To him, it was the possibility of Jo and Stevie in his arms again. Yet, no matter how many millions it might have been, he didn't trust it. In the transaction ahead, in the commerce of human lives, there were no guarantees, no warranties, no legal recourse. If things went bad, there was just dead.

"What's going on?" he asked, eyeing the empty black cases.

"I was in the process of explaining the plan," Kay said.

"What plan?"

"We've been trying to reach you."

"You've just reached me. What plan?"

Kay held up an electronic device about the size and shape of a deck of cards. "This is a Global Positioning System transmitter. It's designed to be hidden in this case." She reached into one of the empty cases and flipped open a small compartment that was hidden in the thick lining. She put the transmitter in place and closed the compartment door. "You see? It's not obvious in any way. It may allow us to follow the money once it's been picked up after the drop. We're hoping it will lead us to where your wife and son and Mr. Lindstrom's family are being held."

"Can it be detected electronically?" Cork asked.

"Well, yes. But the kidnapper would need some pretty sophisticated equipment for that."

"The kidnapper's been prepared so far," Cork pointed out.

"Do you have a better idea?" Kay's eyes were a clear green and at that moment rather sharp in their regard of Cork. She hadn't had a decent interval of sleep since she'd arrived, and it was beginning to show.

He glanced at the hollowed face of Karl Lindstrom. "You've agreed?"

Lindstrom nodded once. "Like she said, Cork, it's a chance at least. I don't know what else to do."

"Wally?" Cork asked.

Schanno shrugged. "I'm out of my league here, Cork."

Cork looked to Agent David Earl, who stood back a little from the others. "What about you?"

"I think unless you have a definite suspect in mind . . ." Earl paused, probably wondering if Cork had found anything substantial at LePere's cabin. "I think," he began again, "that if it were my family, I'd be willing at this point to try anything. And probably to put my trust in nothing. I wish there were more to offer you, O'Connor."

Although it wasn't dark yet, the curtains had been drawn across the windows. The dining room was lit by lamps and the light from the chandelier. By most standards, the dining room was large, but to Cork the walls seemed too close and the room airless.

"All right," he finally said. "How's it going to work?"

Agent Kay explained that as soon as she knew the drop site, she would have it surrounded by officers with night-vision equipment. When the kidnapper attempted to make the pickup, a decision would be made whether to apprehend at that point. If the determination were made not to detain the kidnapper, a car with tracking capability would be ready to follow. When movement ceased, the area would be quickly secured and, it was hoped, the hostages located and freed.

"We're planning in the dark in a lot of ways," she admitted. "And I won't bullshit you. There's a good deal of risk involved. Well?" She looked at Cork and Lindstrom for final approval.

Lindstrom spoke first. "It seems to me we go with the plan. It's that or just give him the money and hope for the best. And, believe me, I'm not inclined in the least to trust this person. What about you, Cork?"

"Let's go after him," Cork replied grimly.

First Jo had exhausted herself trying to kick loose from the wall of the fish house the metal repository full of old razor blades, then Grace Fitzgerald had done the same. The screws that anchored the metal box were sunk deep into hard wood, and in the end it was the strength of the two women that had finally yielded. The fish house, filled for a long while with the desperate thump of shoe soles against wood and metal—a sound that offered some hope—fell into silence. The light through the closed windows was fading. Eventually darkness would close in.

Darkness and silence, Jo thought. *Like a grave.*

Although she was tired and sore, she kicked herself mentally beyond the temptation for despair. For Stevie's sake. "How long before this Bridger comes back?"

"If he sticks to his plan," LePere replied, "the drop will be made at ten o'clock. He'll do some maneuvering then to make sure he's not followed. Give him an hour, hour and a half to get back here. So we have maybe two and a half hours, at best."

"Two and a half hours," Jo said. Not much time, but it was something. "All right."

"Do you have an idea?" LePere asked.

She didn't. Except not to remain on the floor like someone already dead. She scooted to the wall and pushed herself into a standing position. Grace followed her example, saying, "I'm with you, whatever."

Jo looked the room over carefully. She wasn't seeing anything she hadn't seen before, but she was trying to see it in a different way. The nearly empty shelves, the long tables where for years fish had been gutted and cut, the windows. She paused, thinking for a moment it might be possible to break a window and to use a shard of glass to cut free. Unfortunately, the windows were all too high to reach—too high for someone like her, anyway, someone with her hands bound behind her. She eyed the washbasin, the slender wooden cabinet above it, the floor drain. She came back to the washbasin and the cabinet above it.

"Your father, when he shaved, what did he use for a mirror?"

LePere closed his eyes, remembering. "He had . . . something . . . inside the cabinet."

"Glass?" she asked.

"I don't remember."

Jo hopped toward the cabinet. She put her belly against the washbasin and leaned toward the cabinet door. There was a wooden knob on the left-hand side that she intended to take between her teeth and use to pull the door open. As she leaned, she realized she wasn't quite tall enough to reach. She resettled herself and leaned forward again. This time, she lifted her feet off the ground as she set her weight full on the edge of the washbasin, hoping the fixture would hold for a few seconds while she got her teeth around the knob on the cabinet door. Unfortunately, the basin shifted. Jo fell forward, hit her head on the wall, and tumbled to the floor.

"Are you all right?" Grace asked.

"Mommy?" Stevie called in a frightened voice.

"I'm fine, honey," she said. "Mommy's just fine." In the growing dark, she turned her gaze toward Grace. "You're taller than I am."

As Jo worked herself up, Grace Fitzgerald hopped to the washbasin.

"Careful," Jo cautioned her. "It's not as solid as that damn razor blade box."

Grace was able to keep her feet on the ground as she took the knob between her teeth and pulled the cabinet door open. The shelves were empty, but a glass mirror had been affixed to the inside of the door. Grace looked at it, then at Jo. "How do we break it?"

Jo surprised herself with a slight smile. "In a situation like this, it's best to use one's head. Can you open the door all the way?"

Putting her long nose to good use, Grace nudged the door so that it swung clear of the basin. Jo hopped into position with the back of her head against the glass.

"Oh, Jo, be careful," Grace cried.

Jo closed her eyes and tapped her head against the glass. Nothing. *Harder,* she told herself. Again, nothing. *Damn.* She threw her head back and heard the glass shatter, and she tensed for the feel of it cutting her.

"Let me see," Grace said.

Jo turned her head.

"There's no blood."

Jo realized she was holding her breath. She let out a deep sigh of relief. "Okay. We're getting there. Now, Grace, can you get a piece of the broken glass off the floor?"

Grace knelt, then went down on her butt, and slid to where shards littered the old wood planking. She lay on her side, rolled a bit so that she could sweep her fingers across the floor. "I've got one. It's pretty fragile, I think, but the edges feel good and sharp."

"Grace, I'm going to lie down with my back to yours. I want you to try to cut the tape that's around my wrists."

Jo maneuvered herself to the floor and edged backward until she felt Grace Fitzgerald's bound arms touch her own. She repositioned herself—careful of the shattered glass under her—so that her wrists were even with Grace's hands. She waited. "Well?"

"Jo, I'll be cutting awfully close to your wrists. I'm afraid if I slip—"

"Do we have a choice?" Jo broke in.

"All right. But, Jo, if it goes wrong . . . I'm sorry."

"You'll do fine, Grace."

She made her words sound strong and positive, although she knew that the skin at her wrists was very thin and the glass very sharp and it wouldn't take much of an error for an edge to slice right through to an artery.

"Here I go."

Jo closed her eyes. A moment later, she felt the prick of a jagged edge. "That's me," she told Grace quickly.

"Sorry. How's that?"

"I don't feel anything. You must be on the tape now."

The process was awkward and slow, mostly because Grace was reluctant to put a lot of pressure against the duct tape. As it turned out, she wasn't concerned just about Jo.

"Are you all right?" Jo asked, hearing small, painful grunts from Grace.

"I may be doing more damage to my fingers than the tape," she answered. "The glass is getting slippery. And I don't think it's from sweat."

"I can feel the tape beginning to give. Can you stay with it?"

"I'd cut off a finger if I thought it would get us out of here. Unhhh."

"What was that?"

"Nothing."

"Mom?" Scott called out with concern.

"I'm fine. Just fine. How you doing, kiddo?"

"Feeling a little sick."

"Hang on, sport. We'll all be out of here in a minute."

Grace took a deep breath. Jo felt again the cut of the glass on the tape, and the grip around her wrists loosened dramatically. She forced her hands apart, breaking the last of the tape that held her. She sat up quickly, picked up a piece of broken glass, and cut her ankles free.

"Now you," she said to Grace.

The light had faded almost completely. The fish house was filled with a deep, dismal gray that was all the narrow windows would admit of twilight. Although color was nearly impossible to tell, Jo knew that in a stronger light, the dark that dripped over Grace Fitzgerald's right hand would have been bright red.

"Oh, Grace," she whispered gently.

"Just cut me loose."

Jo did, carefully and quickly. "Let me see."

Deep slices scored Grace's palm and fingers. All the wounds bled freely and all looked severe enough to require stitches to close them. Under normal circumstances, her injuries would have been at the center of concern. As it was, she pulled her hand back and said, "Now my ankles."

Jo cut the last of the bonds that held Grace prisoner, then freed Scott and Stevie. Before she turned her attention to LePere, she tore a wide strip of material from the tail of her blouse and gently wrapped Grace's bleeding hand.

"Thanks," Grace said.

"No. Thank you." Jo put her arms around Grace and thought how, aside from Rose, she'd never felt such love for another woman. "You're remarkable."

"Just desperate," Grace said with a smile. "Come on. We still have to get out of this damn place."

Jo set to work on the ropes that bound LePere. Stevie snuggled next to her and took hold of the loose tail of her torn blouse for comfort. She paused a moment in her cutting and gave her a son a kiss on the top of his head. "We'll be home soon," she promised.

When he was finally free, John LePere sat a moment rubbing where the ropes had bit deeply into him. Although he was a little wobbly, he stood and headed quickly for the door. He tried his shoulder as a battering ram.

"I just finished making this place like a fortress," he told the others. Then he cursed himself.

"The windows," Jo suggested. "Maybe we can squeeze through."

LePere looked doubtfully at the nearest window. "There's only five or six inches between each bar."

Jo glanced down at Stevie, who still clung to the tail of her blouse. He was so small for his age. "What if one of us *could* get through? Is there a key to the lock?"

"In a drawer in the kitchen."

Jo knelt and spoke to her son quietly. "Stevie, you know how I sometimes call you a little monkey?"

He nodded.

"I want you to be a little monkey for me, okay? I want you to squeeze through that window"—she pointed—"and help us all get out of here. Can you do that for Mommy?"

Stevie stared up at the high window. His face was full of fear. "I don't want to."

"I know you don't," she said softly. She smoothed his hair.

"But there's no one else who can do it. And your daddy will be so proud of you when we tell him how brave you were and how you saved us all."

"I don't want to," he said again.

"Maybe Scott," Grace suggested.

LePere reached up and used the span of his hand to measure the distance between the bars. He used that same measure to assess the width of Scott's head and chest. "I don't think so." He looked down at Stevie. "As it is, it will be tight for him."

Jo hugged her son and spoke calmly but seriously. "The man who wants to hurt us all will be back soon, Stevie. Unless we get out, he *will* hurt us."

"He'll kill us," Scott said.

Jo stared into Stevie's dark, frightened eyes. "Yes. He will kill us. But you can help us. And you're the only one who can. All you have to do is climb out that window. I know you're afraid, sweetheart. We're all afraid. If I could do this, I would. But no one can do it except you. Can you do this for me, little monkey? And for Daddy and Aunt Rose, who are waiting for us to come home?"

She hated herself for putting such pressure on her small son, hated the whole situation, but none of this was of her choosing, and there seemed no other way. She held Stevie close to her and she whispered, "Please."

She said no more. Stevie was rigid in her arms. Finally he whispered back, "Okay."

LePere raised the window glass. All that lay between them and freedom were the bars and the question of Stevie's ability to slide through.

"I'll lift you up to the window, son," LePere told him. "All you have to do is squeeze through. Then I'll tell you what to do from there."

Jo kissed her son, then gave him over to LePere, who picked him up easily and lifted him to the window. Stevie took hold of the bars and pulled himself toward them. His head made it through. LePere supported him while he turned his body to align his shoulders and chest with the gap between the bars. He began to wriggle forward. He'd gone less than a foot when he stopped.

"What's wrong?" LePere asked.

"I'm thtuck."

"I'm going to give you a little push," LePere told him.

"Owww!"

"Wait." Jo grabbed LePere's arm. "Stevie, we're going to pull you back." To LePere, she said, "Gently."

"Owww!" Stevie cried as LePere drew him back. "I can't get my head out."

LePere supported Stevie with one hand and reached up with the other to assess the situation. "It's his ears," he reported to Jo. "They won't come back through the bars. He's stuck. Really stuck."

"Hang on, Stevie. We'll get you out."

Jo tried to keep the panic out of her voice. Fighting against anger, frustration, fear. Fighting against time. She looked up into the dark gathered above her, descending, and she spoke in a bitter whisper as if someone there were listening.

"Why?"

THE CALL CAME AT NINE-TWENTY-SEVEN P.M., after dark had swept over most of the sky. There was still a narrow strip of washed-out blue along the western horizon, more like the memory of light, but it would soon be gone. Cork stood at the window looking across Grace Cove as Lindstrom reached for the phone.

"This is how it will be," the voice—masked electronically, as it had been during each previous call—said over the speaker. "Take your cell phone and the money and get into your Explorer. No cops along for the ride, understand? Drive south. Keep your speed at forty. I'll direct you as you go. Try anything—hide a cop somewhere, screw me over in any way—your family's dead. And O'Connor's. Dead, dead, dead. You have five minutes to be on the road."

As soon as the caller hung up, Kay asked Arnie Gooden, "Did we get a trace?"

"1911 Cascade Trail, Yellow Lake, Minnesota. Phone's in the name of Minda Liza and Robert Levine."

"Yellow Lake. Ten miles south of Aurora," Cork said. "Wally used to be the police chief there. You know these two?"

"Yeah. She's Latvian. He's gay. Odd couple, but nice folks. They spend a lot of time in Europe buying expensive art. Whoever this guy is, I'm guessing he broke in and used the phone."

"He'll be gone by the time we get there, but let's send an evidence team down anyway," Kay said to Schanno. "Mr. Lindstrom, it sounds as if all this is going to go down on the run. Don't worry. We'll be behind you, but far enough back not to be spotted. You have the cellular I've given you so we can be in communication the whole time. If anything happens, if we get out of touch, we'll still be able to track you and the money via the transmitter. I want to reemphasize that you will not attempt anything on your own. Make the drop and go. Do you understand?"

"Yes."

"Fine. Everybody ready? Let's go."

"I'm going with Karl," Cork said.

"You heard the guy, Cork," Schanno said. "No cops."

"I'm not a cop, Wally. Not anymore."

"I don't think it's a good idea—" Kay began.

"Let him go," Earl said.

Kay glanced at the BCA agent, then at Lindstrom. "Any objection?"

Karl Lindstrom had taken a money case from Lucky Knudsen. It looked heavy in his hand. "It's his family, too," he said. "He wants to come with me, he comes."

"Yellow Lake," Lindstrom said. "That means he's not watching us." They were heading south on County 11, per the kidnapper's instructions.

Cork glanced at the speedometer. "He said to keep it at forty. He's probably driven the route and timed it so that he can direct us blind. I'd bet he's headed to the drop site right now."

Lindstrom's cell phone, which was sitting on the seat beside him, chirped. Lindstrom picked it up and listened. "All right," he said, and broke the connection. "We're coming up on Bone Creek Road. We take it east."

Cork looked behind him, but he saw no headlights. On the cellular supplied by Special Agent Kay, he tapped in the number she'd given him. "Bone Creek Road," Cork said. "We're taking it east."

"We're half a mile behind you," Kay said. "Just keep the line open and give us the instructions as you receive them."

The phone on the seat next to Lindstrom rang again. Lindstrom answered. "Yeah?" He held the phone in this right hand and the steering wheel in his left. The road dipped toward a bridge over Bone Creek. As the Explorer crossed the bridge, the headlights picked up the eyes of a deer frozen in the middle of the road.

"Christ!" Lindstrom dropped the phone and grabbed the wheel with both hands. He swerved left, just missing the buck, and nearly ran off the road. Cork slammed against the passenger-side door. The cellular Agent Kay had given him whacked the window hard. "My phone," Lindstrom shouted. "I lost my cell phone." While he brought the Explorer back under control, Cork was on the floor, groping for Lindstrom's phone. He grasped it from where it had lodged under the accelerator pedal, and he put it to his ear.

"He's gone," Cork said.

"Shit."

"Did you get the next instruction?"

"South on Shipley Road, I think."

"That's coming right up. There!" Cork hollered, and pointed at a narrow dirt lane almost invisible beneath a canopy of arching pines.

Lindstrom hit the brakes. The Explorer went into a slide. He brought it around smoothly, however, in a clean one-eighty that ended with the nose of the vehicle pointed back in the direction from which they'd come. Without hesitating, Lindstrom leaned on the accelerator, hit the turn onto Shipley Road, and, to make up time, kept the speedometer just above forty.

Cork tried the cellular with which he'd been communicating with Agent Kay. He couldn't get a dial tone. "It's dead," he said. "We've lost them."

"Remember, they can still follow us via the transmitter."

Cork considered the kidnapper's directions thus far. "He's working us southeast, toward the back side of the Sawtooths."

"What's that mean?"

"I wish I knew."

They crossed a major road, County 13.

"Are you sure we weren't supposed to turn there?" Cork asked.

"I don't know. I didn't hear him say anything about it, but then I was worried about not killing us right about then."

The phone rang. Cork was beginning to hate that noise. Lindstrom picked it up. "No, I didn't hang up. We almost hit a deer, for Christ's sake." Lindstrom listened. "Yeah, I under-stand." He put the phone down. "Next left. Private road."

The wooden sign at the crossroads indicated they were headed toward Black Spruce Lodge on Goose Lake. Cork didn't believe that was their ultimate destination. Too many people around. He was right. Within two minutes, the kidnapper called again.

"I understand," Lindstrom said after he'd listened a moment. He put the phone down. "Logging road on the right."

It wasn't much of a road, and keeping the speed at forty tested both the suspension on the Explorer and the durability of Cork's spine. But they weren't on it long. Lindstrom got another call, and in a moment, they turned onto a paved county road. Almost immediately they were confronted with a long bridge. Cork knew the place. The bridge spanned the Upper Goose Flowage, a wide, slow sweep of water that con-nected Goose Lake with Little Red Cedar Lake just south. Lindstrom pulled into the parking area of a small picnic ground along the flowage.

"What now?" Cork asked.

"He said to wait."

Almost immediately the call came. Lindstrom listened, then turned out the headlights but kept the engine running. A moment passed as Lindstrom listened further. "It's only Corcoran O'Connor," he said into the phone. "No, you said no cops. O'Connor's not a cop. And, Jesus Christ, you have his family. . . . All right, all right." Lindstrom put the phone down. "He knows you're with me."

"He's here somewhere. Watching."

"He says to leave the money behind the trash cans."

Cork had seen them in the flood of the headlights when Lindstrom pulled in, two cans side by side, painted green and bearing the U.S. Forest Service emblem.

"I hope you don't want to try something," Lindstrom said.

"No. Do as he says."

Lindstrom took the cases from the backseat and got out of the Explorer. He walked to the trash cans, put the cases behind them, and returned to his vehicle. The phone rang. Lindstrom answered and listened. "Yes, I understand."

"What about the exchange?" Cork asked.

"What about our families?" Lindstrom said into the phone. He got an answer and replied, "What assurance do we have?" He closed his eyes and then he hung up. "We drive away. Just keep driving east. If everything's okay, he'll call with their location in fifteen minutes."

"That's it?"

"What else can we do?"

"We sit. And when he calls again, we negotiate until he gives us our families. The money's almost within his reach. He'll be greedy."

"Cork . . ." Lindstrom began, then stopped. "All right."

They sat a minute. The phone rang.

"No deal," Lindstrom said when he answered. "No more threats. No more promises. Just give us our families, now." Lindstrom listened, then he looked slowly down. "Cork?"

Cork followed Lindstrom's gaze. Dead center on Lindstrom's heart was a small red circle not much larger than a BB.

"Laser sight," Lindstrom whispered. "He says we head out now or we both die and he takes the money anyway."

Cork looked hard at the dark outside the Explorer.

"The beacon." Lindstrom sounded a little desperate. "The others can follow the beacon, Cork."

"All right," Cork said.

Lindstrom backed the truck out of the parking area, turned onto the road, crossed the bridge, and kept on going. After a quarter of a mile, the highway curved, and a small private access cut off to the right.

Cork said, "Pull in there and park."

"What?"

"That private road."

"He said to keep moving."

"He can't see us. And we're too far for him to hear. Unless he's got radar or something, he won't know."

Lindstrom turned onto the narrow dirt road and parked among thick pines.

"Call Agent Kay. Find out about movement of the case."

"What if the kidnapper tries to call?"

"He said fifteen minutes."

Lindstrom dialed the number Kay had given him. "It's Lindstrom. We made the drop. Is the case moving?" He looked at Cork and shook his head. "We're about a quarter mile past the drop site, pulled off the road. The kidnapper said he'll call in fifteen minutes with the location of our families." Lindstrom nodded at something that was said. "All right." He hung up. "They're stopped a half a mile short of the bridge, waiting to see which way the case moves. They're positioning cars above and below us to stop him if they decide to make the arrest now. They'll call us when they know."

Cork looked at his watch a dozen times over the next few minutes. He seemed to be in a warp where seconds dragged out into hours. After five minutes, he opened the door to the Explorer.

"Where are you going?"

"I can't sit."

He walked to the road and looked at the empty curve behind them. The moon hadn't yet risen above the Sawtooth Mountains, and the night was dark. Tall pines walled the highway on either side. When he looked up at the narrow swath of sky above him, he felt as if he were looking at another road, one across the heavens and covered with a dust of stars. *Where is this all leading?* he wondered. *Where is the end?*

He didn't feel comfortable with the time. He hurried back to the Explorer. "Any word?"

"No."

"I don't like it. Call Kay."

"It hasn't been but a few minutes."

"If he's smart, he grabbed the money and ran. Get on the phone. Find out if the case is moving."

Lindstrom did. According to the beacon, the case hadn't budged.

"I don't like it," Cork said. "Do you have that Colt Commander you were carrying at the marina?"

"The glove compartment."

Cork reached in and pulled out the Colt. He checked the clip.

"What are you doing?" Lindstrom asked.

"Something's not right. That case should have been snatched by now. I'm going back to see."

"Cork, if you screw this up, he'll kill them."

"He might anyway."

Cork was out of the Explorer and heading toward the road. He heard the other door of the Explorer slam, and Lindstrom was quickly beside him. "We're in this together. I'll take my gun back," Lindstrom said. "I'm probably a better shot with it than you. But you might want this." He handed Cork a flashlight.

They kept to the road until they were within a hundred yards of the flowage, then Cork moved into the cover of the trees. He wished there were a moon, something to cast light. As it was, he couldn't make out the picnic ground at all, even when they were just across the bridge from it, no more than forty yards.

"He has night-vision equipment," Cork whispered. "That's why he could see us so well when we parked."

"Which means he has all the advantage," Lindstrom said. "When we come across the bridge, he's sure to spot us."

Cork could hear the easy trickle of water below them. He knew that because of the drought, the usually deep flowage had been reduced to a shallow ribbon. "Let's go under the bridge."

He crept down the bank. At first, the ground was hard and rocky. Halfway across, he stepped among reeds and into mud up to his ankles. His feet came out with a loud suck. He paused and listened. All he could hear was Lindstrom breathing very near at his back. He went ahead, through the running water, through the muck on the far side, and finally again onto hard ground under the bridge embankment. Lindstrom brushed his shoulder. Cork went down to his knees and crept up the slope. At the top, he laid himself flat on the ground and peered across the parking area. He could just make out the trash cans.

"What now?" Lindstrom whispered. He had the Colt steadied in front of him with two hands, in a prone position for effective firing. *Thank God for his military training,* Cork thought.

"Can you see anything?" he asked.

"The cans. Barely," Lindstrom replied.

Cork wasn't sure at all what to do next. He didn't want to risk rushing in. On the other hand, he felt in his gut that something was already wrong, and the sooner he knew what it was, the better. Then he heard the trash can rattle, and Lindstrom drew back the slide on his weapon. A moment later, the quiet of the picnic area was shattered by the crash of metal as one of the trash cans fell over. Lindstrom pulled off a round. Cork flipped on the beam of the flashlight. Caught with his handlike paws full of litter, paralyzed by the light, stood a fat raccoon. Out of the natural mask nature had given the little thief, two eyes blinked. The raccoon dropped to all fours and scurried away.

"We might as well see what there is to see." Cork stood up.

Lindstrom followed him to the trash cans. The cases were still on the far side. Lindstrom picked one up. "It feels empty," he said.

Cork shined the light as Lindstrom set the case on the ground and opened it. The money was gone. In the center of the case, pulled from its hidden compartment, lay the transmitter. A note was with it. Lindstrom lifted the paper well into the light so they both could read what was written there.

The note said, "They're dead. They're all dead."

43

It was Scott, Grace Fitzgerald's young son, who finally suggested the means for freeing Stevie from the grip of the bars on the fish house window.

John LePere had stood on an empty wooden crate and tried to force the bars apart. Unfortunately, he'd done a good job in choosing the hardware to make the fish house secure, and the bars wouldn't budge. He took a section of old board—three feet of two-by-four—wedged it above Stevie's head, and attempted to pry at least one bar loose from the bolts that anchored it to the window frame. He ended up splintering the board. Jo did her best to comfort Stevie, but as time dragged on, her little boy gave in to his terror. He was sobbing uncontrollably when Scott said quietly from behind the huddled adults, "What about this?"

He held out to them a can he'd found on the nearly empty shelves—motor oil for marine engines, one of the few items Bridger hadn't removed. "Maybe you could slide him through," he suggested.

Jo took the can and gave Scott a grateful hug. The boy looked away, embarrassed. "Stevie," she said. "I'm going to take your shirt and pants off, sweetheart, and then I'm going to put something really slippery all over you. It will feel icky, but I think it will help you squeeze out of those bars. Okay?"

Stevie was still sobbing, but he managed to choke out, "'kay," so that Jo knew he understood.

"That's my good boy."

LePere supported Stevie's body while Jo unbuttoned and removed her son's shirt. She unsnapped his jeans and pulled down the zipper. She had to pull off his shoes to get his pants off. At last, she took a shard of glass from the broken mirror and made a slit in the cardboard side of the oil container. She poured the viscous fluid over his back and rubbed it completely along his sides and chest and stomach. Finally, she dripped the last of it down the bars that held her son prisoner.

"Okay, I think we're ready. Here goes, honey." She gave LePere a sign and he lifted Stevie so that the boy could turn his shoulders. Gently, LePere eased him forward. Stevie made a hurting sound. LePere glanced at Jo, who nodded for him to continue. LePere's face was contorted with concern as he worked Stevie through the bars toward freedom. Once his chest was clear, Stevie nearly shot through the window. LePere held tightly to his ankles.

"I'm going to let you down slowly," he called to Stevie. "As far as I can. Then I'll let you drop. I'll tell you before I do that." He inched forward until his arms were through the bars up to his shoulders. "Okay, Stevie. I'm going to let go. You shouldn't drop more than a couple of feet. Roll when you hit the ground. It will help."

Jo heard a small thump as Stevie fell. She shoved up beside LePere on the crate. "Are you okay, sweetheart?"

Stevie didn't answer.

"Stevie?" she called. She tried to see below the window. The moon had just begun to rise over Lake Superior and in its light the ground looked silver as if covered in frost. She couldn't see her son. "Stevie, answer me." Her voice was cold with a desperate fear.

They all turned suddenly as the door to the fish house rattled. Stevie cried from the other side, "I can't get it open, Mommy."

Jo rushed to the door and pressed herself against it. "That's okay, Stevie," she said, nearly weeping with relief. "That's okay."

"What do I do?" he called in his small, frightened voice.

Run, she wanted to tell him. *Run fast and far.* But there was another mother and child, and Stevie was their only hope.

"He needs to get into the house," LePere said to Jo. "If the door's locked, there's a key on a nail under the top porch step."

Jo dropped Stevie's clothes through the window and as he put them on, she explained very carefully to him what he had to do. She heard the crunch of his little feet on the gravel as he hurried away, then she heard nothing. She hopped onto the crate at the window. From there she could see the whole scene—the dock, the cove, the dark profile of Purgatory Ridge, and the house, all coated with moonlight. In the sky to the west, above the Sawtooth Mountains, Jo saw flashes of light. A minute later, she heard the distant growl of thunder. She couldn't see Stevie at first. Then he emerged from where the dark of the front porch had swallowed him, and he ran back to the fish house.

"It's open," he told them.

"Inside the house," LePere said, this time addressing Stevie directly through the door, "there's a kitchen area. As you face the sink, there are drawers on the right side." He paused and glanced at Jo. "Does he know right and left?"

"He knows."

"Okay, Stevie. In the top drawer on the right-hand side is a ring of keys. There's a key for the lock on this door. Bring the ring and I'll help you find the right key. Okay?"

"Okay," Stevie said.

Atop the crate at the window, Jo watched her son cross the yard again. The light of the moon gave him his shadow as a companion.

"How much time do we have before Bridger comes back?" Grace asked.

"Not much," LePere replied. "How's he doing?"

Jo said, "I can't tell. I think he's in the house, but I don't see a light on."

LePere slapped the wall angrily. "The switch is in an odd place. Damn, I should have explained that to him."

"Find it, Stevie," Jo whispered.

As soon as she said it, she wanted to take it back. For she saw headlights swing toward the cove from far up through the trees near the highway.

"He's back," she said. "Bridger is back."

At that moment, the light in the house came on, making the place like a bright beacon in the dark on Purgatory Cove.

AGENTS OWEN AND EARL of the Minnesota Bureau of Criminal Apprehension stayed at the bridge over the Upper Goose Flowage to help the FBI oversee processing of the crime scene. Wally Schanno and Lucky Knudsen coordinated a search of the area that included Goose Lake and Little Red Cedar Lake. Both lakes had resorts and public campgrounds on their shores, a lot of ways to access the water. Everyone agreed that the kidnapper had probably made his escape via one of the lakes and had driven the back roads from there. What they didn't say was that a search would take time and, even if it uncovered something, would probably be too late to do any good.

There was no reason for Cork to linger. With Lindstrom and Special Agent Margaret Kay, he returned to Grace Cove in the meager hope that the kidnapper might make contact again. Also, it kept him from having to go home where Rose and his daughters would be waiting and hoping. Cork didn't know how to face them, what to say.

Kay made calls on her own cellular, reporting. She looked drawn and tired. She made a final phone call and spoke in a soft, loving tone. Cork thought about the gold band on her finger. She'd put her own life on hold, had gone without sleep, had done her best to bring about a safe resolution. Cork knew it wasn't her fault, the way things worked out. The phone in Lindstrom's living room was still set up for a trap-and-trace. Agent Arnie Gooden sat near it with his recording equipment ready. He looked drowsy. Lindstrom had slumped into an easy chair, and he sat staring at the silent phone. He seemed dazed. Exhausted. Empty. Cork felt the same way. So tired he could barely see straight. It wasn't just exhaustion, he knew. It was what happened when you were empty of everything, when the last bit of hope had finally run out of you. It was like sucking exhaust from a tailpipe. All you wanted to do was give up, close your eyes, and sink into whatever would keep you from thinking. Sleep. Death. Whatever.

"I need to call home," he said.

Lindstrom raised his eyes slowly. "And tell them what?"

"I don't know, Karl. Okay if I use the phone in your office?"

Lindstrom gave a small shrug. Cork took that as a yes. He walked down the hallway. The big house and its grounds were nearly empty. To maintain security for the ransom drop, the media had been cleared away before the caravan of cop cars had left to follow Cork and Lindstrom. Except for one officer posted in a cruiser in the driveway, all the law enforcement officers present earlier had been called to help search the area along the Upper Goose Flowage. In the quiet of the house, he could hear thunder rumbling in from the west. On the way back from the drop site, he'd heard a weather report on the radio. A storm was on its way, bringing heavy rain, the first in months. He didn't care.

Cork sat at the cherry wood desk in Lindstrom's office. His head ached, a pounding that threatened to blind him. Three times he reached for the phone and three times he drew his hand back. He had no idea what to say to Rose, the girls.

I couldn't save them. They're gone. They're gone forever.

He couldn't say that over the phone. Nor could he yet bring himself to leave Lindstrom's home.

The clock on the wall read ten to midnight. Cork wanted to turn the hands back, do it all differently, be in all the right places at all the right times. He wanted a second chance at the last few days. The last few years. He wanted not to have failed them, all the people he loved.

His eyes drifted over the photographs mounted on the wall around the clock. Lindstrom in a naval officer's uniform aboard a military vessel of some kind. Another with Lindstrom and Grace Fitzgerald together on a boat—clear blue water, a great white sail full of wind. In another, he recognized a very young Grace Fitzgerald, a teenager. Recognized her because of her distinctive nose. She stood next to a white-haired man. They had their arms around one another, smiling. Father and daughter? Cork wondered. They were posed on the deck of a great ship. High above them, visible on the forward mast, was a big, glowing *F*. Cork wondered if the old man were still alive. No. Otherwise, he'd have given Lindstrom the ransom money. Grace Fitzgerald's father was lucky. He was dead. Beyond feeling loss. Beyond being hurt.

Christ, stop it. Cork yanked himself back from self-pity. *What are you doing? Don't let go of them yet.*

Meloux had said he had a choice. He could keep company with despair or he could choose a different companion.

Cork stood up. He needed to think clearly. He went to the bathroom just down the hallway and closed the door. Turning on the cold water, he splashed his face. He had to get rid of the headache, clear his mind. In the cabinet above the sink, he found a bottle of Excedrin. He shook out a couple of tablets, popped them in his mouth, and swallowed the aspirin with tap water. As he was putting the bottle back, something caught his eye. Syringes. There were a number of them on one of the shelves, each in an individual packet. Next to the syringes was a bottle of medication. Insulin.

Hadn't Gil Singer told him the only thing stolen from the clinic on the rez had been insulin? Who was the diabetic in Lindstrom's home?

Cork went to the living room. Gooden had closed his eyes and lay back, sleeping. Kay had settled herself at the dining-room table and had put her head down; she seemed to be napping, too. Lindstrom was still staring at the phone.

Cork held up the bottle and asked Lindstrom in a whisper, "Who?"

"Scott," Lindstrom replied. He followed Cork's lead and kept his voice low.

Cork beckoned him to follow, and they went to Lindstrom's office. Cork closed the door. "Last night, the clinic on the rez was broken into. The only things taken were insulin and syringes."

Lindstrom thought it over. "For Scott? Why?"

317

"The kidnapper cared about keeping him alive. He risked a lot to keep your boy alive."

"Until tonight," Lindstrom pointed out dismally. He sat at his desk, mirroring none of Cork's enthusiasm.

The thunder was growing louder. It followed very quickly the lightning flashes visible through the window. The wind was up, lifting the curtains high. Cork went on thinking out loud as he paced the room. "It's probably someone who knows the rez clinic, someone who's been treated there."

"Indian?" Lindstrom said, considering. "Isaiah Broom?"

"Not Broom," Cork said. "He's still in custody. And he was arrested heading off to fight a forest fire. That doesn't sound like the action of a man in the middle of a two-million-dollar ransom negotiation. No, not Broom. Maybe not even a full-blood Anishinaabe. Only enough to be treated at the clinic."

Cork paused in front of the photographs on the wall. He was staring at the one that showed Grace Fitzgerald and her father on the ship. He pointed to it. "The big *F* in this picture. What's that all about?"

"Means the ship was part of the Fitzgerald fleet. All the Fitzgerald freighters carried that big lighted *F*. You could identify a Fitzgerald ship from miles away, even at night. Why? Is it important?"

"There's a photograph in John LePere's cabin. He's on a ship with the same big letter below the crow's nest. Do you know anything about LePere?"

"What's to know?"

"He was on an ore carrier about twelve years ago that went down in a storm on Superior. All hands were lost except for him. His brother died on that ship." Cork stared at the photo on Lindstrom's wall. "I'm betting it was part of the Fitzgerald line."

Lindstrom stood slowly, the exhaustion in his face giving way to a glint of understanding. "LePere." He squinted at Cork. "Revenge?"

"Maybe. Or maybe in his thinking, some kind of long overdue and just compensation." Cork started pacing again, fast. "Gil Singer said LePere headed off yesterday, claiming he was driven away by all the activity on the cove. A good excuse for a man known to be reclusive to disappear."

"Disappear where?"

In his mind, Cork pictured another photograph he'd seen in LePere's cabin, the one labeled PURGATORY COVE, 1979.

"I'm betting the north shore," Cork said. "A place called Purgatory Cove. It's just south of Beaver Bay."

"You're betting lives," Lindstrom reminded him. When Cork didn't back down, he said, "All right. Let's go."

"We need to talk to Kay," Cork said.

"The hell with the FBI. Everything they've handled has turned out badly. I'm going to do this my way. Are you in?"

"We need to talk to someone," Cork insisted.

"Why? So they can drag their feet while they get their writs and warrants? Kay will want evidence, something solid. Do you have anything, anything she could take to a judge?"

Lindstrom was right. Cork didn't have anything substantial. Only a gut feeling and the fact that everything seemed to fit.

"I'm sick to death of waiting," Lindstrom said. "Are you coming?"

Twenty-five years of law enforcement made Cork hesitate.

"Look," Lindstrom argued, angrily now, "if you're right about LePere, what's the nearest law enforcement office?"

"Cook County sheriff in Grand Marais."

"How long would it take them to get to Purgatory Cove, providing they believed us and were willing to go?"

"Half an hour, forty minutes."

"If we put the pedal to the metal, we can make it in forty-five. If we leave right now."

Cork looked at the door. "They'll miss us."

"You tell them you're going home. I'll tell them I've got to sleep." He threw his hands up in exasperation at Cork's hesitation. "Jesus, you've been ahead of all these people. You've been right all the way down the line. I trust you, Cork, more than I trust any of them. It's *our* families we're talking about. The ones *we* love. In the end, who has a greater right to act?" He paused, then shoved away Cork's reluctance. "Fine, do whatever you want. Me, I'm going. I'm going now."

Cork made his decision. "My Bronco's parked at LePere's cabin. Meet me there."

He left Lindstrom in the office. At the dining-room table, he lightly touched the shoulder of Agent Margaret Kay. She jerked awake and lifted her head from where it had been cradled on her folded arms.

"I'm going home," Cork told her. "Call me if . . ." He let it drop.

She nodded. Then she said, "I'm sorry."

Cork didn't offer her any solace. He walked away and quickly left through the back door. He could smell rain in the air, a wet, dusty scent. He felt the wind that swept in over Grace Cove, and when the lightning flashed, he could see the black, restless water. He hurried across the lawn. As he entered the woods between LePere's cabin and Lindstrom's home, he felt the first fat drops hit his face.

It was raining heavily by the time he'd stumbled out of the woods. The wind had become a powerful force, shoving the drops nearly horizontal. Cork hustled into his Bronco and started the engine. His wet clothes steamed the windshield, and as he wiped the glass clear with his hand, Lindstrom opened the passenger-side door and got in.

"Let's go get our families," the man said.

Cork shoved the Bronco into first gear, hit the accelerator, and headed it for the north shore of Lake Superior.

S TEVIE!" Jo yelled toward LePere's little house. "Turn the light off! He's coming back!"

It was only one light, and it shone west, away from where the narrow lane approached the cove. Still, in all that darkness, it seemed to blaze.

"The light, Stevie. He'll see the light! Turn it off!" She was shouting so hard it made her throat raw. God, couldn't he hear her?

The grumble of the engine and the rattle of the undercarriage were audible. If she shouted anymore, she was afraid Bridger might hear. But she had to risk it. Just as she opened her mouth to scream again, the light died. Jo watched for Stevie's little body to emerge from the dark of the house. He never came. The van parked in the yard. The door opened. The interior light blinked on. Jo saw Bridger slide out, then reach back. He pulled out what looked like a big canvas mailbag. He glanced her way, and Jo shrank back from the window. Bridger headed toward the house.

"Oh, Stevie," she said, quietly and desperately.

The light in the house came on. Through the window, Jo could see Bridger moving about inside.

"What's he doing?" LePere asked.

"I can't tell."

Grace was beside her. "Can you see Stevie?"

"No."

"Then he's hiding," Grace assured her. "Jo, he's a smart little boy and he's hiding."

The front door opened, and a blade of light from inside slashed across the yard. Bridger stood silhouetted in the doorway. Jo watched as he lifted his arm to check the gun he held in his hand. He cast a long, black shadow before him, and when he stepped forward, the shadow touched the fish house wall.

"He's coming," Jo cried in a whisper.

"Behind the door," LePere said. "Everybody behind the door." He hefted the splintered two-by-four he'd broken earlier trying to wedge apart the bars.

Jo huddled with Grace and Scott. LePere stood before the door with the board raised, ready to swing. Jo was breathing hard and fast, so loud she was afraid Bridger could hear. Lightning ran across the sky and lit the inside of the fish house with brief, startling flashes. Mixed with the thunder that followed was the crunch of Bridger's boots on the gravel as he came. There was a deadly quiet as he paused at the door. Jo heard the jingle of keys as he searched for the right one. She held her breath. And a cell phone rang.

"Yeah?" Bridger said from the other side of the door. "No, I just got here." He was silent, probably listening. "Look, I told you. It's all set."

Jo felt Grace tense and wrap her arms more tightly around Scott.

"All right, all right. I'll check. How long before you're here?"

LePere adjusted his stance and his grip on the board.

"Jesus, relax. Everything will be fine."

Bridger was quiet for a while. Jo figured the phone call was finished. She waited for the sound of the lock being released. It didn't come. Bridger simply walked away. Jo rushed to the window and stood on the crate.

"He's gone down to the boat dock," she reported. "He's getting on one of the boats."

"Where's your boy?" LePere asked.

As Jo peered at the house, she saw a small form edge through the front door and slip into the dark away from the porch. A moment later, Stevie was at the fish house.

"Which key?" he called softly through the door.

"It's the only silver one on the ring," LePere said.

"It's hard to see."

Jo could hear her little boy's voice choked with fear. "You're doing fine, Stevie," she told him, trying to keep her own voice calm. "Just fine."

The lock rattled. The door opened. Jo flung her arms around her son and thought it had never felt so good to hold him.

"We've got to go," LePere said. "To my truck."

Thunder rolled out of the clouds that spilled over the Sawtooth Mountains. The first drops of rain splatted against Jo's cheek as she ran with the others away from the fish house. A strong wind came with the storm, and as the lightning etched a stark black-and-white image of the cove, Jo saw the water churning. She also saw Bridger on the deck of one of the boats. She prayed he didn't see them.

LePere opened the door of his truck. "Damn. He took the key."

"Isn't there an extra somewhere?" Grace asked.

"In the house. But he may have taken that one, too. Let's just get out of here." LePere dug into the glove compartment and brought out a flashlight. "Come on. Up the road."

He led the way, Grace and Scott right behind him, Jo and Stevie bringing up the rear. Rain had begun to fall heavily and the wind drove it into their faces. They hurried along the narrow lane that skirted the cove. Jo held Stevie's hand. Her heart beat wildly, and she dared to let herself feel real hope. They were almost free.

LePere stopped abruptly.

"What is it?" Grace called above the wind and rain.

Jo didn't have to ask. She'd seen it, too. Another set of headlights winding through the poplars, coming down to the cove from the highway. She remembered Bridger's phone conversation. Whoever he was expecting had arrived. She leaned to LePere and shouted, "We can hide in the trees until they've passed, then go up to the highway and flag someone down."

He shook his head, flinging rain from the end of his nose. "No one's on the road at this hour. And it's the first place Bridger will look."

"Then we hide in the trees until morning."

"That's the second place he'll look, and there aren't enough trees to hide us until morning."

The headlights frosted the trees at the nearest curve. In only a moment, they would shine fully on the place where Jo and the others stood.

"This way," LePere hollered.

He started through the trees, leading the way toward the dark, hard cliffs of Purgatory Ridge.

THE STORM MOVED EAST toward Lake Superior, and Cork moved with it, following State Highway 1 as it twisted and curled around the southern end of the Sawtooth Mountains. The whole North Woods was receiving its first significant rainfall in many months. Dust—gathered deep along the shoulders of the road—turned to mud and washed across the pavement in a thin, slippery coating that made the drive treacherous. The wheels drifted around sharp curves as Cork pushed his old Bronco dangerously fast. In the flashes of lightning, he caught glimpses of Lindstrom beside him. Although the man was tight-jawed and held to the dashboard with a desperate grip, he said not a word to Cork about slowing down.

"You carrying your Colt? The one you had at the marina," Cork asked.

In answer, Lindstrom reached to his belt and brought out the firearm. He held it toward the windshield so that Cork could see it without taking his eyes off the road. "What about you?"

"In the glove compartment," Cork directed him. "My revolver."

Like Lindstrom's handgun, Cork's Smith & Wesson .38 police special was something handed down from father to son, something he trusted.

"I keep the cartridges separate. In my tackle box in back. Mind loading it for me?" Cork asked.

Lindstrom pulled the handgun from the glove compartment

325

and climbed over the seat. Cork heard him rattling in the tackle box. Lindstrom started to return to the front, but the Bronco swung hard around a curve and he fell against the back door.

"I'll just stay put back here," he said.

Cork heard him release the cylinder and begin to feed in the rounds.

They drove mostly in silence. Cork's mind was occupied with the business he'd trained it for in his two decades as a cop—putting the pieces of a puzzle in place. The more he considered, the more everything came together, so that the holes became fewer and were more obvious to him.

A few miles outside of Finland, he broke the quiet inside the Bronco. "When you talked with the kidnapper, Karl, why didn't you ever mention your son's diabetes?"

"Not my son. My wife's son. He refused to let me adopt him." He slapped the full cylinder into place. "What good would it have done, saying something about the boy's weakness?"

Weakness? Cork thought.

"A man like LePere wouldn't care," Lindstrom added.

"Apparently, he cared enough to risk everything breaking into the rez clinic for insulin. You know, that's something I can't quite figure. If he was so concerned about keeping Scott alive, why would he be so quick now to rush to murder? It's almost as if there are two minds at work here."

"A man like LePere, he could be schizoid for all we know. Hell, he lost his whole family to Lake Superior—father, mother, brother. Something like that's bound to snap anybody's mind."

His father, his mother, and his brother? Cork had been acquainted with John LePere for many years, and this was more specific information than he'd ever learned about the man. How was it that Lindstrom knew?

Cork fell back into a meditative silence for a few miles. When he glanced into the rearview mirror, he saw Lindstrom sighting down the barrel of the .38.

"Nice heft," Lindstrom said. "You pretty good with it?"

"I generally hit what I'm aiming at."

They moved ahead of the storm, just beyond the edge of the rain. They passed through an open area where the wind kicked dust across the road and shoved against the Bronco. Cork held the wheel steady.

"At the marina," he said over his shoulder, "when Earl questioned you about your military service, you told him you couldn't talk about what you did. Does that mean naval intelligence?"

"Naval intelligence," Lindstrom confirmed. "Why do you ask?"

"I was just thinking. You've been well trained in gathering information."

"And?"

"Nothing."

But it wasn't nothing. Because Cork was thinking about Lindstrom's building a home in a place where his only neighbor was a man who had every reason in the world to hate the Fitzgerald name. It seemed to indicate a terrible lapse in reconnoitering. On the other hand, maybe it didn't. Maybe it was evidence of something else entirely. Something cold and abominable.

"Nothing?" Lindstrom said quietly. "O'Connor, I've observed how your mind works. You don't ask a question for no reason."

Cork heard the click of the hammer on the .38 as it was drawn back and cocked. In the next instant, he felt the cool metal of the muzzle against the back of his head.

"You know what I think? I think you've just about got it all put together."

Cork pulled the Bronco to a stop in Illgen City at the junction with State Highway 61. *City* was a misnomer for the intersection. There were only a couple of visible structures, a hotel and a café, and neither showed any sign of life at that hour. The highways were deserted. The swipe of the wipers and the drum of the rain on the roof were the only sounds. Cork made no move to continue the drive.

"You and LePere?" he asked.

"LePere's in this, but not the way you think. Or the way he thinks." Lindstrom waited a moment. "You're dead already, O'Connor. I can do it here and now, or we can keep going. I'm figuring you might want to see your family one last time before you all die."

"They're alive?"

"About as much as you are."

Cork made the turn and kept on going. Whenever lightning crackled over the lake, he could see the angry crash of waves against the rocks along the shoreline. "She was going to divorce you, wasn't she?" he said. "That's why she wanted to talk to Jo professionally."

Lindstrom gave a slight laugh. "It only dawned on her recently. Me, I've seen it coming for a long time."

"And in a divorce, because of the prenup, you get nothing."

"I insisted on the prenup. It was such a selfless gesture that she insisted on making me her beneficiary—after the boy, of course. With both of them dead, I get everything. Over thirty million dollars, O'Connor. Now there's a motive. But, you know, nobody's even going to look my way. It was just a kidnapping gone terribly wrong. Eventually, all the signs would point to LePere, but he'd have vanished, dropped off the face of the earth along with my dear wife and her son. And now you and yours." Lindstrom gave Cork's head a little push with the barrel of the .38. "You figured LePere out too soon. Your mistake."

The muzzle stopped kissing the back of Cork's head. Cork heard Lindstrom tapping a number into his cell phone.

"Are the boats ready to go?" Lindstrom fell silent, listening. "Get them ready now." He paused, then spoke again with fire in his voice, "God damn it. Get down to those boats and check everything out. We don't have a lot of time, and I don't want any slipups." He shot out an impatient puff of air. "Ten, maybe fifteen minutes. Just have the boats ready when we pull up, got me?" He shoved the cell phone back into his pocket.

"You know," Cork said. "As a matter of standard procedure, they're going to check the record of all calls made to and from that phone tonight."

Lindstrom laughed. "Different phone, O'Connor. Different account. I've thought of everything. I've been planning this for a very long time."

They were passing through Beaver Bay, a gathering of a few businesses along the road. On occasion, Cork had eaten at the inn there. Good pie. But the inn was dark now, and empty, and offered him nothing.

"You built that house on Grace Cove purposely to goad LePere."

"Stroke of genius," Lindstrom said. Once again, he'd nestled the barrel of the police special against Cork's skull. "I stumbled across a magazine article from a few years ago. LePere's whole sad story. And bingo. The idea came to me in a flash. Built the house. Got LePere into position. And then you know what? Fate gave me a helping hand. Eco-Warrior. What a great smoke screen."

They were approaching Purgatory Ridge. In the flash of lightning, Cork saw huge waves surge against talus at the foot of the cliff and shatter there. A moment later, the Bronco entered a long, brightly lit tunnel through the ridge.

"When they find you gone, they'll ask questions," Cork said.

"I'll be back before anyone ever misses me. Slow down," Lindstrom said. "As I understand it, the turn's just ahead on the left."

Despite the heavy rain, Cork spotted the access road as soon as they were out of the tunnel. He pulled the Bronco off the highway and followed a narrow gravel lane through a wooded area. Where the road broke from the trees, it began a curve around a tiny cove. Up ahead, the headlights of the Bronco illuminated a small house perched near the water's edge.

"Park next to that pickup," Lindstrom instructed him. "Give me the keys," he said after they'd stopped. "Pass them to me slowly over your shoulder." He emphasized Cork's predicament with a little tap of the gun barrel. Cork did as he'd been asked.

Lindstrom got out first. He used the .38 to wave Cork out after him. As Cork stepped from the Bronco, a man he'd never seen before emerged from the night and the rain.

"The boats?" Lindstrom asked.

"Didn't I say I'd have them ready?" the man replied.

"It's when you're almost home that you relax your guard and make mistakes."

"From one of your fucking Annapolis textbooks?"

Lindstrom looked about. "Where are the others?"

"Locked in that old fish house." He pointed toward a building twenty or thirty yards from the house.

"Time for a tearful reunion, O'Connor. Let's go."

The stranger led the way. As he reached the door of the fish house, he stopped dead and said, "Fuck me."

"What's wrong?"

"It's unlocked." The man shoved the door open. "They're gone. Son of a bitch."

"How long?"

"Do I look like Kreskin? How the hell should I know?"

"You didn't check them when you came back from the ransom drop?"

"I was just about to when you called and insisted I get the fucking boats ready." He kicked the side of the fish house. "You're so damned anal."

"Wait." Lindstrom peered hard across the cove toward Purgatory Ridge. "What's that?"

Cork looked, too, and saw a long, slender beam of light moving along the face of the cliff, low and near the water.

"They're trying to make it to the far side of the ridge," the stranger said.

"All right. Take the van and go around to cut them off on the other side. I'll move up on them from behind."

"What about him?"

Lindstrom looked at Cork. "End of the line, O'Connor."

Although he knew it was probably useless, Cork broke away and ran toward the cove, shouting as loud as he could, "Jo, look out! They're coming!"

That was all he had time to say before Lindstrom pulled the trigger of the .38.

47

At a scenic turnout on Highway 61, a mile south of Purgatory Ridge, the Minnesota Geologic Society had long ago placed a marker bearing a metal plaque that explained the great rock formation. Over the years, John LePere had read the inscription many times.

Millions of years ago, the basalt rock that formed the north shore had been laid down by massive lava flows. Eons of weathering and glacial scouring had chiseled at the shoreline, eventually cutting it back almost to the foot of the Sawtooth range. However, rills of nearly impervious rhyolite overlay the basalt in several places. Long after the softer surrounding stone had been eroded away, those rhyolite rills continued to stand against the elements, often as solitary formations that seemed out of place. The top of Purgatory Ridge was two hundred seventy-seven feet above Lake Superior. The formation was nearly a quarter mile wide. Although composed of one of the most obdurate of minerals, the ridge had not escaped the ravages of time. Thousands of winters, thousands of cycles of freeze and thaw, hundreds of thousands of harsh, battering storms had left their mark on the ridge, the cumulative effect visible in the talus—great blocks of stone broken from the sheer walls—that lay in a formidable jumble along the base of the cliffs. Someday, the marker predicted, perhaps a million years hence, the ridge would no longer exist.

The geologists spoke about time as if it were an endless, incomprehensible quantity. To those who measured time in breaths and heartbeats, it wasn't hard to grasp at all. And John LePere, as he led the others over the talus at the base of Purgatory Ridge, was afraid time was running out.

When he guided the others toward the ridge, he'd thought he could find his way easily, could lead them swiftly and unseen over rock he'd known since childhood, along paths he and Billy had followed hundreds of times to the other side of the ridge. However, as a child he'd known enough to be well afraid when the waves rose up like raging giants and swept the cliffs clean of everything that was not rock, and he'd never dared to be there during a storm. As soon as he reached the base of the black cliffs, he knew he'd made a mistake. He would have to use the flashlight. If Bridger and his cohort were looking, they'd see the beam across the cove. He didn't like it, but by then, he had no other choice.

He moved ahead of the others a few yards, then turned back and lit the way for them to see. The Fitzgerald woman and her son were directly behind him. The boy Stevie and his mother brought up the rear. Those two held hands whenever possible. More often than not, however, they were forced to travel single file along narrow shelves and between huge rock fragments. Along the south side of the ridge that faced the cove, they made good progress. But as soon as they rounded the chest of the ridge, they were exposed fully to whatever the great lake threw at the shore. They slowed to a crawl. The crash of the waves became so loud, it was impossible to be heard. LePere directed them with hand gestures. Many times they had to grasp at a cold, wet face of rock for something to hold to as the lake threatened to sweep them away. LePere, who kept an eye to their backs, watching for any sign that Wesley Bridger was following, had seen a light dashing among the boulders far behind them—far enough, he thought, that if they kept moving, they would make it to the back side of the ridge safely ahead of Bridger.

They traversed the worst of the shoreline without incident and began to cross a broad plate of rock that sloped sharply toward the water. Although the waves couldn't reach them there, the driving rain made the rock slippery. Twice, LePere lost his footing, and it was only his powerful grip that kept him from sliding into the lake. He concentrated fully on his own crossing, then turned back to the others. They'd all stopped. LePere saw immediately why. The O'Connor boy was in the water. From her own precarious position, his mother tried to lean out to him, to grasp his hand as the swells lifted him and rolled him up the sloping plate. Without a moment of hesitation, LePere retraced his steps, handed the flashlight to Grace Fitzgerald, and went into the lake after Stevie.

The water was ice cold, but LePere barely noticed. He grabbed the boy, who was bobbing in the wake of a swell, and put his right arm firmly around Stevie's chest. When the next wave swept in, LePere felt the power of the lake lift them both as if they were nothing. He turned before he hit the rock, took the blow fully against his side and shoulder, sparing the boy. The lake tried to tear Stevie from his grasp, but LePere was damned if he'd lose the boy now. He threw his free arm out, groping for a firm hold. His hand grasped a ragged edge, and he clamped his fingers tight around it. He pulled himself up and pushed the boy ahead so that Jo O'Connor could reach him. As soon as Stevie left his arms, the next wave hit and scraped LePere across the rock, facedown. Two more waves manhandled him before he was able to pull himself from the water. He could feel a warm flow of blood down his face. He would have preferred to rest a moment, but even a moment was not something he wanted to waste. He waved them all to move ahead, and he followed.

Grace Fitzgerald now lit the way. When they reached the other side of the ridge, LePere could see the lights from resort cabins along the shoreline a half mile distant. He looked back. The light behind had gained on them significantly. He knew they wouldn't reach the cabins before Bridger caught up with them.

"Go ahead," he called to the others.

"What about you?" Jo O'Connor called back.

LePere pointed toward the approaching flashlight beam. "I'll take care of him. Go on. Just go."

The women went ahead with their sons. LePere found a boulder that would hide him, and he crouched to spring. As the flashlight beam slid past, he leaped and took the man down. They wrestled briefly on the rock before a gunshot stopped them both. LePere, who lay pressed on top of the man with the flashlight, heard Bridger's voice speaking at his back.

"Let him up, John."

LePere stood up. He saw that Bridger held a pistol trained on the women and the boys.

"He was waiting for us," Jo O'Connor said.

The man who'd followed them pushed up and used his flashlight a moment to search for his handgun. When he found it, he faced the others.

"Karl?" Grace Fitzgerald's voice was filled with bewilderment.

"Hello, Grace. Hey there, Scott. Good work, Wes," Lindstrom called to Bridger.

"You know this man?" the woman asked her husband.

"Know him? Hell, I hired him. Look, let's all go back to LePere's cozy little place and discuss this. Oh, and by the way, Jo, I've got a special surprise for you back there. And for you, too, Stevie. Would you like to see your daddy?"

"Cork's there?" Jo O'Connor asked.

"He was when I left. And I'm sure he hasn't gone anywhere." He waved them off the ridge with his gun. "Let's go. Time's wasting."

BRIDGER PUSHED OPEN the fish house door and turned on the light. He stepped aside, and Lindstrom ushered the others in.

When Jo saw Cork, she let out a cry. He sat on the floor, propped against the wall, his shirt drenched with blood. "Oh Jesus, no." She dropped to her knees beside him.

His eyes fluttered open, and when he saw her, a faint smile came to his lips. "You're alive."

They'd taped her wrists behind her again—taped all their wrists—so she couldn't reach out to him, couldn't help him in any way. She saw that he'd managed to unbutton his shirt and pull it aside. In his left hand was a folded, bloody handkerchief that he held pressed against his shoulder a few inches above his right nipple.

"How bad?" she asked.

"Just a hole," Cork whispered. "One little hole."

Stevie stood near his father, blinking as he tried to comprehend all the blood and his father's helplessness.

"Hey, buddy," Cork said. It was barely more than a mumble. He tried to lift his right arm toward his son, but the move made him groan, and he squeezed his eyes shut against the pain.

"I don't understand, Karl," Grace Fitzgerald said. She stood against the wall with Scott beside her.

"Sit down, all of you. Wes, see to the boats. Let me know when you're ready. And that gun you have. I'll take it."

"Why?" Bridger asked darkly.

"Because it's unregistered, and we're going to wipe it clean of prints and leave it in Mr. LePere's house. When they find it, they'll do ballistics and discover that it's the same gun that was fired in my home on Grace Cove. Further evidence of Mr. LePere's guilt." He held out his hand, and Bridger—a bit reluctantly, it seemed to Jo—yielded him the weapon.

After Bridger made his exit, Lindstrom leaned casually against one of the tables where LePere's father had cleaned fish. "You know, Grace, I loved you once, really loved you. I'd have died for you, you know that?" He stuffed the handgun Bridger had given him into the waist of his pants, but he kept the other pointed at his prisoners.

"I don't believe it," she replied.

He shrugged. "Fine. Whatever. I did kill for you once."

"What are you talking about?"

"Your beloved Edward. It wasn't the lake that got him. It was Bridger. At my direction."

Grace stared in disbelief. "You . . . killed Edward?"

"I thought that with him out of the way, I'd have a chance. But he still had you, even dead." Lindstrom waved it off, as if it were really nothing to him now. "The point is that when it became clear to me that you would never love me, it also became clear that someday you'd leave me. Now, that was a thing I couldn't abide. For many reasons."

"You . . . planned all this?"

"Meticulously, Grace."

"How'd you know Wes?" John LePere asked.

"He told you a story once, I believe, about a covert operation he was involved in as a SEAL that sank a Libyan tanker. That was my operation. Wes impressed me as a man with many skills and few scruples. I tracked him down when I decided to get rid of Edward."

Cork coughed and groaned. Jo longed to hold him, to give him some comfort, to ease his pain. She glanced at Stevie and saw that his eyes were glazed. He stared at her as if he didn't see her at all, as if he saw nothing anymore. She understood. How could so brief a life, so protected an existence, comprehend such horror as he'd been through?

Bridger opened the door and stepped in dripping rain. "All set. Here's the remote detonator." He handed the device to Lindstrom.

"We're going for a boat ride," Karl Lindstrom said to Jo and the others. "I'll tell you up-front that you won't be coming back. Now, I can kill you right here, or you can walk to the boats and have a few more precious minutes of life. I'd prefer not to have to carry you down to the dock, but the choice is yours." He glanced at his watch. "You'd better decide fast. I have to get back to Grace Cove before I'm missed."

He waited. LePere finally stood up. So did Grace and Scott. Stevie, who'd never sat down, stood blank-faced and rigid.

"You have to get up, Cork," Jo whispered desperately. "Please get up."

Cork slowly worked his way to his hands and knees, then pulled himself up by holding on to one of the tables. He stood, wavering, leaning heavily against Jo.

Karl Lindstrom said, "Give him a hand, Wes."

"He's all bloody."

"So buy yourself a new shirt tomorrow. You'll be able to afford it."

"Why don't you help him?"

"Somebody's got to hold the gun."

"Shit." Bridger worked his shoulder under Cork's arm and walked him to the door.

"Let's go," Lindstrom said, and he followed behind them.

They stumbled into the storm, walking a muddy path to the dock. Even with her arms bound behind her back, Jo managed to grab hold of the front of Stevie's shirt, and she pulled him along behind her. He followed like a zombie. Bridger had tied the stolen motor launch to the stern of the *Anne Marie* with a tow line. They all climbed aboard LePere's boat. Bridger hauled Cork over the gunwale and let him drop in the cockpit.

"That's as far as I take him," Bridger declared.

Lindstrom herded the others out of the rain into the deckhouse of the *Anne Marie,* but he left Cork where he'd fallen. "Just get him out of the way so we don't trip over him," he instructed Bridger.

Looking back, Jo saw Wesley Bridger roll Cork against the side of the cockpit, where he lay like a dead fish waiting to be gutted.

Lindstrom directed them to the other end of the deckhouse where a companionway to the left of the helm station led below. At the bottom of the short flight of steps, they entered the small, forward cabin that had a V berth shaped to the bow. Lindstrom shoved LePere to the floor. Jo and the others crammed themselves onto the berth. Bridger stepped down and joined his cohort.

"I'll take her out. You keep them out of mischief," Lindstrom said. He headed up to the wheel inside the deckhouse. Bridger closed the cabin door and stayed with the others belowdeck.

The *Anne Marie* pulled away from the dock. On the relatively calm water of Purgatory Cove, the boat rocked gently. As soon as Karl Lindstrom headed it out beyond the protection of the rocks, the bow began to buck wildly. Stevie sat beside Jo, stiff as a plastic doll. Grace and Scott were in the bunk on the other side of the V berth. LePere sat at on the floor with his back against a door marked STORAGE.

Bridger braced himself against the pitching of the boat and grinned at them. "Feels worse than it is. The waves are only three or four feet. Nothing, really. Relax and enjoy the ride."

"Where are you taking us?" Grace asked.

"Not far. A mile or so out, just beyond where the lake bottom drops away. We want you deep."

Jo thought about the remote detonator Bridger had handed to Lindstrom. She considered the motor launch in tow, and she understood. They meant to sink the *Anne Marie* and use the launch to return to Purgatory Cove.

Bridger seemed to discern her thought process. "We're not going to blow you up," he said. "We don't want to attract attention with a big explosion and we don't want any debris. No, I've rigged just enough of a charge to scuttle her. I figure it'll take fifteen minutes, maybe twenty. Then you and the boat and all the evidence will be gone. But you won't have to worry about that, because you'll already be dead."

Jo asked, "How much has he promised you?"

"What difference does it make to you? Thinking of trying a counter offer?" Bridger laughed.

"I was just thinking about something you said today."

"Yeah? And what was that?"

"The only way for two people to keep a secret is if one of them is dead. Your exact words, I believe."

"Lawyers," Bridger scoffed.

"Think about it. What more does Karl need from you? You gave him your gun and he has the detonator. Right now, all you are to him is a loose end. One of two people who share a secret."

"Shut up," Bridger said. But Jo could tell he was thinking.

The boat pitched hard to port, and Stevie nearly fell off the bunk. Jo threw her leg across him and eased him back. He didn't seem to be aware of it at all. He didn't even seem to be blinking. A part of Jo thought maybe that was best. If they were going to die, she'd rather her son were somewhere else in his consciousness, somewhere he couldn't see death coming.

"On the other hand," Jo went on, once again addressing Bridger, "what's he to you now but a loose end? You have two million dollars. How much more do you really need? The police *will* investigate him. They'll start sifting and sorting and even though everything points another way, they'll consider Karl Lindstrom seriously. The Fitzgerald fortune is such a magnificent motive. Has he really covered all his tracks? Think about it for a moment, Mr. Bridger. If they nail him and he wants to cut a deal, what does he have to offer them except you?"

She saw a look in his eyes, the kind she'd often seen in the jury box when she knew she'd put well into their minds the question of reasonable doubt. Bridger reached down and lifted his right pant leg. Strapped to his calf was a sheathed knife. He unsnapped the leather guard that secured the hilt.

"You all just sit tight," he said. He winked at Jo. "Could've used you in the SEALs." Once more he braced himself in the companionway and waited. When the motor cut out, he tensed.

Lindstrom pulled the cabin door open. He had the gun in his hand. He said to Bridger, "Topside, Wes. We need to confer."

"Confer," Bridger said. "Right."

Lindstrom stepped back on deck and Bridger followed warily. The door closed. The waves thumped the side of the boat, and the hull creaked and groaned. Jo slid quickly from the bunk. "Move away from there," she said to LePere.

He scooted from the storage compartment, and Jo tried desperately to open the door, hoping there would be something inside—a knife, anything—that might free them. Her taped hands were little help. She was still struggling when something slammed hard against the cabin door. A guttural cry of pain followed. Jo kept working at the latch as the sound of a fight in the deckhouse carried down to them. The crack of a pistol shot, followed almost immediately by another, brought the scuffle to an abrupt end.

They all stared at the cabin door.

When it opened, Karl Lindstrom stepped down. He looked drawn, and Jo saw a red stain on his right side above his belt line.

"He had a knife strapped to his leg," Jo said.

"Yesterday's news," Lindstrom replied.

"We were hoping he'd kill you."

"You were hoping we'd kill each other. Bad luck for you. Just a nick."

"How will you explain it in the morning? You cut yourself shaving?"

"I'll think of something," Lindstrom said. "I always have."

He held the gun in his right hand and the detonator in the other. Jo knew they'd reached the end. Would he shoot them first?

She didn't wonder long. Nor did it ultimately matter.

Lindstrom stumbled suddenly down the steps. A look of astonishment stretched all the features of his face. He opened his mouth, and Jo thought he might speak, but all that came out was a brief, hard grunt. He dropped the gun and reached backward as if trying to grasp something behind him. He dropped to his knees in the middle of the cabin, then fell forward, facedown. In three places, the back of his shirt was stained with widening patterns of blood.

Cork teetered at the top of the cabin stairway. In his hand, he gripped the knife Bridger had used in his fight with Lindstrom. The blade glistened with Lindstrom's blood from tip to hilt. The bow of the *Anne Marie* rose and dipped, pitching Cork down the steps into the cabin. He stumbled over Lindstrom's prone form, bounced off the berth, and fell at LePere's feet. He'd dropped the knife. Slowly, painfully, he reached out, took it again in his grasp, and lifted it toward LePere.

John LePere quickly turned himself around and ran the duct tape that bound his wrists along the sharp edge of the knife while Cork held it. He tore his hands free, took the blade from Cork, and cut the others loose.

Jo sat on the floor and cradled her husband's head in her lap. "Stay with me, Cork."

"Always," he whispered.

LePere said, "I'm going topside. I'll take us back in."

He hadn't a gone step when Grace Fitzgerald cried out, "No!" and reached toward Karl Lindstrom.

Jo saw why. She watched in horror what none of them was able to stop. Karl Lindstrom had turned his head toward his left hand, in which he still held the detonator. Before anyone could prevent him, he squeezed his fingers around the device. A muffled explosion followed, and the *Anne Marie* shivered as if she'd been kicked.

"You son of a bitch," Grace yelled.

"I always was a bad loser," Lindstrom murmured.

LePere danced around Lindstrom and hurried up to the deck. He came back a moment later, looking grim.

"He's blown a hole in the stern. We're taking on water."

"What about the other boat?" Jo said.

LePere shook his head. "The blast blew the tow line free. The other boat's gone. I can't even see it."

"Don't you have life vests?" Grace asked.

"In the deckhouse," LePere said. "Let's clear this cabin. I have to get into that storage compartment. I keep an inflatable raft there. Hurry. We don't have much time."

"Take Stevie up, Grace. I'll help Cork."

"You're not strong enough," LePere told her. "You get the raft. I'll take your husband." He lifted Cork in his arms and started up the steps behind the others.

Jo found the rolled, yellow rubber raft and two small oars where LePere had indicated. By the time she'd grabbed the items, water ran down the companionway and lay several inches deep in the cabin.

Lindstrom rolled to his back and said in a wet, bubbly voice, "Help me."

"Ask God, not me." Jo didn't even pause as she stepped over him and headed topside.

Without power or guidance, the boat had turned broadside to the wind, and it tilted dangerously as it rode up the waves and rolled into the troughs. Jo struggled through the deckhouse toward the stern doorway, the shifting angle of the boat throwing her off balance at every step. LePere shouted into the radio mike at the helm station, "Mayday. Mayday. Mayday. This is the *Anne Marie*. We have a damaged hull and are sinking fast." He repeated the message several times, giving the coordinates, then abandoned the radio and helped Jo with the raft and oars. They skirted Bridger, who lay facedown in the water that sloshed in the deckhouse, two blood stains merging across the back of his shirt.

Outside, the cockpit was awash with water calf deep. With both hands, Scott was holding tightly to the railing of the ladder that led up to the flying bridge. He wore an orange life vest that was too big for him. Beside Scott, Grace held herself to the ladder with one hand and held to Stevie with the other. Stevie, too, wore a big life vest. One more vest was draped across the ladder. Cork sat alone, propped against the side of the boat. Jo could see damage to the stern railing, and the list of the *Anne Marie* was becoming more obvious by the moment.

LePere cut the rope that held the raft in a roll, and he pulled the cord to open the air valve. The raft inflated quickly.

Jo saw immediately it was too small. "We won't fit," she screamed, beginning to lose control. She'd held herself together for so long, that she felt utterly exhausted, ready to give in to panic.

"The two of you." LePere pointed to Jo and Grace. "And the boys. You can fit."

"I'm not leaving Cork."

"He can't help you."

"*I'm not leaving him,*" Jo shouted at LePere. She looked toward her husband. He was flopping like a rag doll as the waves pitched the *Anne Marie* about. Even so, it was obvious that the shake of his head was intentional. He was telling Jo *no*.

She knelt beside him. "I can't go without you."

She had to lean very near to hear his answer.

"You have to," he said.

"How can I leave you, Cork?"

"We'll never leave each other." He nodded toward where Stevie stood, held steady by Grace Fitzgerald. "Get our son home safely. Do that for me. Promise."

Although rain ran in rivers down her face, it wasn't the rain that made her eyes blur. "Cork—"

"No time. Promise," he insisted.

She yielded. "I promise."

"I love you," he whispered against her cheek.

"I love you," she whispered back. She couldn't say good-bye, couldn't manage any more words at all. She kissed him, kissed him just that once, then she turned away.

LePere held the third vest out to Grace and Jo. "It's the last one I have. Who wears it?"

"You," Grace said to him.

"It won't do me any good. In this lake, I'd just freeze to death."

"Then could you put it on my husband?" Jo asked LePere. "I don't want to lose him forever."

She looked to Grace, who seemed to understand her purpose. Bodies without life vests did not float in Lake Superior. The lake didn't give up its dead. Grace nodded her assent.

"Into the raft," LePere shouted. Then, "Wait." He went into the deckhouse and came back with a small compass that he gave to Jo. "Hold a northwest heading, into the wind."

Jo put her arms briefly around the man. "Thank you."

"God be with you," he said and pushed her toward the raft.

The stern, riding low in the water, was the easiest place from which to launch. LePere held the raft as steady as he could while Jo and the others got in. The rough seas made it difficult, but finally Grace was settled in back with one of the oars and Jo in front with the other. The two boys huddled in the middle, Scott with his arms around Stevie. LePere shoved them off.

They headed into a wind that threw the lake at them. Jo dug at the water with all her strength. They rode several feet up a swell, then dropped into the trough behind it. The black water broke over them with numbing cold, and it was clear to Jo that they were not much better off in the little yellow raft than they'd been on the foundering *Anne Marie*. Holding the compass near her face, she checked direction. She allowed herself one look back. She could barely see the lights of the boat. The mouth of darkness was already open, ready to swallow Cork forever. She turned her mind and her will to keeping her final promise to her husband.

343

For a long time, they battled the lake, using the squat oars as paddles. Jo's arms had never hurt so much. Moving into the wind was tiring, but it was good in a way. They held their course more easily. Jo couldn't tell at all if they were making distance. She didn't speak to Grace, but she could feel the push of the other oar behind her as steady as her own. After three quarters of an hour, the wind slackened and the rain began to let up. In a few minutes, the storm passed. The lake grew calmer. As if a curtain had been pulled away, the moon and stars emerged, turning the water in front of them silver. At the end of the silver, Jo saw the black rise of land several hundred yards away, with lights scattered along the shoreline.

"We made it!" Grace shouted triumphantly at her back.

Not all of us, Jo thought, staring at the dark land ahead. *And not all of me.*

49

JOHN LePERE WAS ALMOST HOME. He stood at the stern of the foundering *Anne Marie* and stared down into the black water of a lake he'd known his whole life, whose vast existence suffused every aspect of his being but whose true spirit had eluded all his attempts at understanding. LePere finally let go of trying to understand and accepted the only thing he knew for sure. Below the raging surface, along the rocky bottom hundreds of feet down, the water was still and silent, and he would soon lie there, where he'd always been meant to come to rest.

After the yellow raft was swallowed by the night and the storm, LePere turned back and appraised the situation. Bridger lay dead in the deckhouse. In the forward cabin below, Lindstrom was dead—or dying. These things were as they should be. But there was one element that had no place in this final drama. Cork O'Connor should never have been a part of it. The man had done nothing to deserve the end that awaited him.

LePere slogged across the cockpit that was swamped with icy water. He sat next to O'Connor and helped brace him against the pitch of the boat. He offered the only bit of comfort he could. "They got away."

O'Connor lifted his head. "They'll make it?"

"They'll make it." LePere didn't just say this. He believed it, believed it because he'd seen firsthand what the two women and their boys were capable of. "They're strong, O'Connor. In all the important ways."

O'Connor had lowered his head again. John LePere didn't know if he'd heard, if it made any difference.

"Here." LePere took the life vest in both hands. "I'm going to put this on you."

O'Connor looked up and shook his head. LePere moved closer to hear his words. "You wear it. Wasted on me."

"I promised your wife," LePere told him. "It's a promise I'm going to keep."

O'Connor cried out in pain as LePere maneuvered him into the vest, but he didn't fight it. LePere didn't know if the man understood the true reason for his wife's request. Did it matter?

"There. That'll keep your head above water. Now if I could just keep you dry, you'd be fine until the Coast Guard comes."

He kept his words light, but when O'Connor raised his tired eyes, John LePere could see that he understood perfectly the truth of his predicament.

"I'm sorry," LePere said, because he felt responsible.

O'Connor shook his head slightly. Was it a pardon? John LePere wondered.

The two men sat together as the waves washed over the gunwales, filling the cockpit. LePere could feel the *Anne Marie* growing heavy and sluggish as she took on water. There was nothing now but to wait for the end. Lightning made the lake stand out in moments of stark black and white. LePere closed his eyes and remembered things that were alive with color. The blue of the summer sky over Superior and the deep aching blue of the lake below. The charcoal cliffs of Purgatory Ridge and the green tufts of grass that grew out of even the most solid rock. His father's eyes, golden as the sun when he looked down from the height of the ridge, pointing where the fish would run. His mother's cheeks, flushed with happiness as she stood beside her husband. And Billy. Billy most of all. Tanned from the summer sun, strong from swimming in a lake cold as ice, a tawny baseball mitt on his right hand, his eyes an earthy green-brown and shining.

Far out of place among all that memory, a thought came to John LePere—the dry suit he kept stowed in the compartment in the cabin of the *Anne Marie*.

His eyes snapped open. "Jesus," he said. "Of course."

He leaped up and fought his way through the deckhouse.

The *Anne Marie* was listing severely, her stern ready to disappear beneath the swells. As he reached the companionway down to the forward cabin, the lights flickered, but they didn't die. Lindstrom no longer lay on the floor. He'd managed to crawl partway up the steps to the deckhouse. He looked dead and LePere simply stepped over him. In the forward cabin, LePere threw open the storage compartment door. The diving suit lay folded on a shelf, wet from the deep water in the cabin. As LePere made his way back to the companionway, he saw that Lindstrom wasn't, in fact, dead. The man was watching him.

"They got away," LePere said with satisfaction. "Your wife and boy and O'Connor's family. They all got away. All this for nothing."

"A man's reach should exceed his grasp," Lindstrom mumbled. He looked at the dry suit.

"For O'Connor," LePere explained. "I think he's got a chance."

"No chance."

"We'll see."

LePere didn't waste any more time on Lindstrom. Up top, O'Connor had flopped over with the tilt of the boat. He was struggling to keep his head above water. LePere grasped him under his arms and began to pull him toward the bow, as far as possible from where the lake spilled over the stern.

"Listen to me, O'Connor," LePere shouted. "You have a chance. I'm going to put this dry suit on you. It will keep the lake off you. The Coast Guard will come, I promise. This will probably hurt. I'm sorry."

O'Connor stared at him and LePere didn't know if he understood at all. He undid the life vest and removed it. He took off O'Connor's shoes. Then he began the arduous task of pulling the tight vulcanized rubber over Cork O'Connor's body and zipping it in place. He could feel the bow rising, the boat slipping deeper as he worked. He tugged the hood over O'Connor's head, then began to work the life vest back on. At first, O'Connor had moaned in pain, but by the time the dry suit and vest were in place, he was limp and silent.

Christ, LePere thought, *I've killed him.*

At that same moment, the lights of the *Anne Marie* died.

In a flash of lightning, LePere saw O'Connor's eyes spring open, and he felt a hard tug on O'Connor's body, as if an invisible power were trying to pull him under the water that had followed them up the deck. LePere was confused. The water should have lifted O'Connor's life vest and O'Connor with it. Instead, he was being dragged down. In the unfathomable black of the stormy night, LePere felt along the man's body, down his legs, searching for what had snagged him. His hand touched a cold hand, touched icy fingers gripped hard around O'Connor's ankle. In the next explosion of lightning, he saw Karl Lindstrom climbing from the lake, using Cork O'Connor to save himself.

"No you don't, you son of a bitch," LePere cried. He pried loose the fingers, and he grasped Lindstrom in his own strong arms. He worked his way to the port side of the bow well away from O'Connor, then undid his belt and buckled himself to the brass railing of the *Anne Marie*. "When she goes," he shouted to Lindstrom, "you and me go with her." Lindstrom struggled weakly, but LePere held him fast.

In little more than a minute, the boat went under and began its own long journey to the bottom of the lake. LePere held his breath as he was dragged deep into the black water. Lindstrom fought briefly, then was still. LePere maintained his grip on the man's body a while longer, just to be certain, then let go.

Alone, John Sailor LePere continued down. As the boat swiftly descended, he felt his chest tighten, as if he were now in the grip of something enormous and overpowering, something that had always been waiting to embrace him. His lungs seemed ready to explode, and he became afraid, suddenly desperate not to release his hold on life. He reached down, fumbled with the buckle on his belt, but it was much too late. As the water pressure crushed his ribs, he opened his mouth to cry out. In that instant, Kitchigami filled him and took him into itself.

Cork was inside something thick, something that dulled his thinking, something he could not crawl out of. Even so, he knew what John LePere had done. He understood the sacrifice.

And he understood that now he was alone.

He felt the boat slip from under him. For a moment, the suck of it as it went under tried to pull him down, but the vest lifted him. His hands and his feet were cold. His face was cold. Sometimes when he tried to breathe, he swallowed water and coughed. The coughing hurt. He kept his eyes closed against the surge of the waves. That was easy. He had no strength to open them.

He sank into darkness often, and for long periods he was aware of nothing. Then he was suddenly staring up at a sky full of stars and a moon. The lake didn't feel angry anymore. He was tired. It was night. He wanted to sleep.

He dreamed. Or maybe he didn't. Maybe he went someplace where he could always have gone if he'd known the way; then he came back.

He opened his eyes and stared into the brightest light he'd ever seen, so bright it blinded him, yet he could not look away. Somewhere in the thick of his thinking, he remembered death came as a bright light, and he wondered, *Am I dead?*

A dark shape eclipsed the light. Cork saw that it was Jo's face. She was so beautiful with the light behind her like a halo. He wanted to tell her how much he loved her, but he could not speak. So he smiled. The smallest of smiles. All he could muster before he felt himself begin to yield to darkness, to the sweet pull of oblivion, thinking his wife's face was a good last vision, a good final gift to take with him into forever.

50

Jo O'Connor stood in ash that covered the ground like snow. Around her as far as she could see, the bare, blackened trunks of pine trees rose up and scraped against an empty sky.

The rain had helped firefighters control and eventually extinguish the multitude of blazes that, for weeks, had been burning large areas of the North Woods. The old-growth white pines known as Our Grandfathers, sacred to the Ojibwe Anishinaabeg of the Iron Lake Reservation, had not been spared. With every breath, Jo took in the smell of char, of senseless destruction. She felt, as she had so often lately, a deep sense of loss and grieving.

"What a tragedy," she said, then sighed.

Henry Meloux, who was among those who'd accompanied her to view the devastation, looked where she looked. His old face was soft and wrinkled. His brown eyes seemed amazingly calm. "Who can say what Kitchimanidoo is all about? We see little and understand less."

Grace Fitzgerald had walked ahead of them with Scott and Stevie. Stevie looked back often to make certain his mother was still there. At a fallen pine, he stopped and bent down. Scott stooped beside him, and they peered intently at something on the ground.

"Mommy." Stevie waved for Jo to come. "Look," he said. "A flower."

It was true. A small flower had thrust its yellow blossom up through the scorched earth and the ash.

"It's like magic," Stevie said.

"Not magic," Meloux told him. "The way of Grandmother Earth. Come with me, Makadewagosh. I'll show you other ways Grandmother Earth reveals her heart."

Stevie grinned proudly at the name the old man now called him by. Meloux had kept a promise he'd made several weeks before when the boy and his father visited Crow Point. He'd bestowed upon Stevie another name, an Anishinaabe name. He called him Makadewagosh, which meant "silver fox," for that was the name Meloux had dreamed. To Jo, who remembered her small son bathed in silver moonlight and slipping through the dark at Purgatory Cove to save them all, the name rang so true. Meloux led the two boys away a distance, pointing out things and talking softly as they walked.

"How is Stevie doing?" Grace asked.

"He wakes almost every night with nightmares. He wets the bed. He has trouble being separated from me. The psychologist says that in cases of post-traumatic stress, it often takes a long time to recover. But he's very optimistic about Stevie. How about Scott?"

Grace watched her son. Her face was gentle, touched with concern. "He seems to be doing all right. He talks about it pretty openly. I wonder if the loss of his father so early has made him stronger somehow. I guess only time will tell."

Jo heard the boys laugh at something Meloux said. She was more grateful to the old man than she could say. What she hadn't told Grace, hadn't even told the psychologist, was that Henry Meloux was also helping Stevie, using the ancient wisdom of the Grand Medicine Society to restore harmony to the spirit that was her son. It was Meloux who'd suggested visiting the devastation of Our Grandfathers. In the look on Stevie's face as he listened to the old man's words, Jo could see the flower amid the ash.

"Rose is signaling," Grace said.

Jo looked back. Her sister stood at the top of a slight rise, waving her hand. "He's giving them trouble," Jo said. "I knew he wouldn't stay in the car."

Jo left Grace. When Stevie saw her going, he abandoned Meloux and ran to his mother. They joined Rose at the top of the rise and looked down at the logging road that Lindstrom's company had built in anticipation of cutting the white pines. A dark blue Explorer was parked there, along with an old red Bronco. Jenny and Annie stood at the bottom of the rise. Between them, using their strength for support, was their father. His right arm was held in a sling, and under his shirt was a lumping of thick gauze and bandages.

At daybreak after that long, awful night at Purgatory Cove, Jo had been aboard the Coast Guard cutter when they pulled Cork from the lake and laid him on the deck. His face was white as hoarfrost. Behind his heavy lids, his eyes looked lifeless. She was certain he was dead. She leaned to him, for a moment blocking the morning sun. Then he smiled at her, so faintly she thought at first she'd only imagined it.

Stevie ran ahead of Jo. He wrapped his arms around his father's waist. Cork laughed and planted a kiss in his son's hair.

Jo started down the slope toward her husband. As she neared him, he looked up. The sun lit his face with a warm yellow light. A smile bloomed on his lips. And Jo found herself looking at yet another flower. The loveliest she had ever seen.